DON'T TALK TO STRANGERS

BETHANY CAMPBELL

BANTAM BOOKS

NEW YORK TORONTO LONDON SYDNEY AUCKLAND

DON'T TALK TO STRANGERS

ONE

⚡

And you want to travel with him,
You want to travel blind
And you think maybe you'll trust him
Because he touched your perfect body
With his mind.

"SUZANNE,"
LEONARD COHEN

HE WAS AN EXCEPTIONALLY HANDSOME YOUNG MAN, EVEN MORE handsome in person than in the photo he had sent her (and the photo had shown a face of such masculine beauty, her breath had caught in her chest, piercing her with a keen, knife-like pain).

Her plane had been over four hours late—as if fog, rain, and lightning had conspired to keep her apart from him. The lightning in particular had terrified her. It had played around the Memphis airport like special effects in a horror film.

Now, in Chicago, she hurried off the plane, nervous, frightened that he would have grown tired of waiting for someone like her. Her heavy duffel bag and big canvas purse had become awkward bundles, impossible for her to carry gracefully. No, he could not want somebody like her; it was too much to hope for.

Yet there he was at the gate, just as he'd promised. He was wearing the T-shirt she'd sent him, the one with the picture of Albert Einstein.

Her heartbeat leaped and accelerated, her throat went so tight she wondered if she could speak, and she was flooded by new fear. Would he be disappointed in her, would he think she hadn't been worth the wait, would he find her plain and ugly and dull?

Weeks ago she'd been full of qualms when she'd sent him her own picture. She'd warned him. *I'm not beautiful. I'm tall and I weigh too much, my chin is too big, and my hair is frizzy.*

All these things were true. She was five foot ten, and from childhood she had been heavy, carrying most of her weight in her torso, so that her lean arms and legs seemed as if they should belong to someone else. They were too thin, almost sticklike, in proportion to the rest of her.

From childhood she'd been wide in the hips, thick in the waist, and when she'd developed breasts they were so huge and sagging they shamed her. But men liked them. That part of her men liked, she knew.

She did have fine skin, however, flawless and creamy as a model's. Her eyes, too, were lovely, an unusual shade of clear greenish-blue, fringed with thick lashes.

Her skin and eyes were so striking that sometimes well-meaning people said to her, "You'd be such a pretty girl if you'd lose weight." They thought they were being kind.

Her brother, who never troubled to be kind, often said, "God, you've got a big ass."

Joachim never said such things. To this beautiful man,

this *perfect* man, she had confessed her insecurities about her body.

Joachim had told her, "It wasn't your looks that attracted me. It was your mind, your spirit, your soul." Joachim said that he saw past mere appearance to the real her, the inner her. They must meet in person, he said, at spring break. The time had come.

So here she was in O'Hare Airport, and as she looked across the crowd at Joachim, she felt more terrified than by the lightning in Memphis. Such a man couldn't love or want her. In real life, men like him didn't glance twice at girls such as herself.

But he came moving toward her, a smile curving his lips, holding his arms out to greet her with an embrace. She tried to shift her big purse out of the way and take a surer grip on her bulky duffel bag, to open her arms to him, too.

But he was on her, even though she accidentally hit him in the knees with her bag and her purse was caught between their bodies, jamming painfully against her breasts.

His arms wrapped around her, and his lips covered hers in a kiss that surprised her with its passion. His mouth was warm, firm, and questing, and it occurred to her, vaguely, that she'd believed men kissed like this only in the movies.

She dropped the duffel bag, let go of her purse (it remained wedged between their bodies), extricated her right arm and circled it around his neck. He held her so tightly she could hardly breathe. He was not much taller than she, and he probably weighed less, but he was surprisingly strong.

He ran his hand over her hair, which was badly frizzed, she knew, from the humidity back in Memphis. "Sweet," he murmured against her lips, "so sweet."

Her heart soared, she felt dazed by hope, and a giddy heat poured through her body, tingling beneath her bra and panties, in the parts of her she always kept hidden.

"Let's get out of here," Joachim said. "I want you to myself." She was even more dizzied to realize there was true hunger in his voice and that the hunger was for her.

He kissed her one more time, so fiercely she could feel her teeth cutting into her lip. Then he drew back and smiled at her, cupping her big chin in his hand. "How can you say you're not beautiful?" he asked, and her happiness seemed complete.

He picked up her duffel bag and looped his other arm around her waist possessively. "Any more baggage?" he asked.

She shook her head to tell him no, her eyes shining.

"Then let's get the car. It's in the lot. Come on."

She nodded as if she'd forgotten how to speak. She'd fumbled to catch her purse and still held it clutched to her chest. She could not stop drinking in the sight of him.

He was five feet eleven, slim, but with wide shoulders and well-muscled arms. He was dressed in jeans and dirty, tattered running shoes, and, of course, the Einstein shirt, one of the many gifts she'd sent him by mail.

He had straight black hair that he wore long, almost to his shoulders. His hair was, in fact, rather lank and in need of a wash. He hadn't shaven, either; his upper lip and square jaw were rough with several days of dark growth. The tender flesh of her face still burned from his stubble.

But she knew this unkemptness was a disguise he wore to hide his handsomeness, just as certain young film stars cultivated the "grunge" look.

Being good-looking, he'd told her with unhappiness, was a curse. He never knew whether women liked him for himself or merely for his looks. It had made him shy, suspicious.

"People want you for the wrong reasons," he'd said. "They don't care what you think or feel. They're totally shallow. They only want, want, want."

He admired Einstein extravagantly. "What a mind," he'd told her. "Was Einstein good-looking? No. Did it matter? No. What mattered was his intelligence."

She'd sent him the T-shirt after he'd said that. He told her it was one of the most thoughtful gifts he'd ever been given. *She* was thoughtful. She was intelligent, too, and he valued that in a woman far more than looks.

He led her into the gray vastness of the parking garage. He squeezed her waist more tightly and smiled at her again.

He had dark eyes and skin with a golden cast, and his coloring made his teeth seem startlingly white.

"So here we are," he said. "Finally together *irl*."

She smiled shyly. The term *irl* meant "in real life" and was part of the jargon of the "virtual community," as it was often referred to.

She and Joachim had met each other via their computers on the Internet, in a fantasy community called Omega MOON. People did not use their own identities in Omega MOON. They came and went as characters that they themselves invented.

Princesses, dragons, nymphs, and warlocks roamed Omega. So did Smurfs and talking teddy bears and vampires and knights and mermaids.

There were no flashy special effects in Omega's world; no lure of bright graphics, no music, no sounds of wind or singing birds or falling water. The community of Omega was entirely a creation of written words on a screen.

From all over the world, people communicated by typing messages on their computer keyboards. Yet the words could spring to life and the characters burn with vitality, wit, and passion.

Omega was an electronic Mardi Gras where inhibitions were flung aside, and people, masked, grew bold, even wild. Flirtation was rampant; irreverence flared and insults crackled, running as wild as brushfire.

People quarreled with a fury and eloquence seldom seen in real life. Allegiances formed, divisions yawned open, enemies warred. But sometimes by the chimerical light of Omega MOON, people fell in love, as she and Joachim had.

Her real name was Gretchen, which she disliked. Her brother called her Gretch—"Gretch the Wretch, Gretch the Wretch. Such a dog, she ought to fetch."

She had created an Omega character as unlike Gretchen as possible. Selena was not a lumpy, frumpy college student who hated her past, her present, and feared her future. Selena was nothing less than a goddess.

Specifically, she was a moon goddess. When Selena appeared anywhere, and another player wished to see her, he

entered the simple command to look at Selena. This message
would appear on his screen:

> You see Selena, goddess of the earthly moon. She is for-
> ever young, eternally fascinating, endlessly desirable.
> Her lush breasts are barely covered by a gauzy garment of
> cloudy starshine. A jeweled belt encircles her slender waist,
> and from it flutter veils that do not conceal the curves of her
> hips or the sleekness of her long, slim legs.
> Selena's wealth of platinum hair cascades down in rip-
> pling waves. If you meet her eyes of silvery blue, you know
> that she is capable of staring into your very soul.
> Selena is like the moon itself, mystical and infinitely
> changeable. Her touch is soft as moonlight, her smile as
> haunting.

This description, as Gretchen well knew, was shameless
and so self-flattering it was outrageous, but other characters
had descriptions just as shameless, just as outrageous. And
then again, some didn't.

Joachim did not. The first time the Moon Goddess Selena looked at Joachim, his description was unprepossessing:

> You see Joachim the Beggar. He is small, hunchbacked,
> pockmarked, filthy, scrofulous, and infested with fleas. Give
> him a penny or give him a kick; neither matters to him. He is
> past caring.

Obviously Joachim had been looking at her description,
too, for the first message he ever sent her was, "Are you
really that gorgeous?"

"No," she had typed back. "Not at all."

"Good," he'd responded. "I don't like gorgeous girls.
They're always conceited or manipulative. Or both."

"I've got nothing to be conceited about," she'd answered. "And I can't manipulate the cap off an aspirin bottle."

The message on her screen had said he laughed, which
had pleased her. "Are you really that ugly?" she'd asked.

"Not quite," he'd answered.

"Thank God," she'd said, and he'd laughed again. That was how it started. That was the beginning of it.

Now they reached his car, an inconspicuous-looking Mercury, blue and none too clean. "I know what you're thinking," he said, unlocking the passenger's side for her. "You're thinking this really looks like a beggar-mobile."

She shrugged and said, "You should see mine. I've got this Dodge that's older than God."

He gave her a teasing look. He always said he liked her self-deprecating humor. He tossed her duffel bag into the back of the car and got into the driver's seat.

She found that she was still awkwardly clutching her big purse to her chest, as if she could hide her enormous breasts from his gaze. And her hands were sweating, the palms hot and embarrassingly damp, even though the air was cool.

He gave her another look, this one not teasing but so steady and burning that it shook her to the pit of her stomach. "I'd kiss you again," he said. "But I wouldn't want to stop. I better wait until we're really alone."

Once again, no words came to her. All she could think was, *I'm really here. I'm with Joachim in real life.* She still called him Joachim, because he hated his real name, which was Stanley, and he called her Selena. She had come to think of herself as Selena, and that Gretchen was an unhappy incarnation she'd left behind.

"I'm taking you to my grandma's place, like I said," he said, starting the car. "We can have it to ourselves. Get to know each other."

Then he laughed and tossed her a look that was once again mischievous. "God, I'm stupid. I already know you. Sometimes I think I know you as well as I know me."

She smiled back, but the smile felt twitchy and nervous and dry-lipped. She hugged the purse more tightly. People said that MOON relationships did not tend to work in real life.

He seemed to read her thoughts. "You're scared. You can't quite believe it. Neither can I. I wasn't ready for another relationship. God knows I wasn't looking for one. But then—there you were. There we were."

He shook his head, as if marveling at the wonder of it. *There we were. And here we are.*

She felt awed, but guilty, too. For although Joachim was a perfect man, handsome, charming, intelligent, sensitive, sincere—there was one troubling flaw in their relationship. He was married.

He would not be married long, he'd assured her with feeling. He and his wife were separated; he had just left her.

Joachim told Selena that meeting her had been the deciding factor. He could not stay married to a woman he did not respect, for whom he'd come to feel nothing but contempt. He'd filed for divorce.

Joachim did not seem a bitter or vengeful man, but he had nothing good to say of his wife, not one thing. Why he'd married her was a bigger mystery than he could begin to understand, he said.

But his wife was always real to Selena, painfully real. It seemed as if the woman was a stubborn ghost, haunting them even in the moving car.

"She—she doesn't know we're doing this?" she asked.

"No," he said, his beautiful face grim. "She can't know. She'd fight me like a wildcat in court. She'd make life hell for us."

Selena nodded, but her face burned with shame. She understood about Joachim's wife, but she was unhappy about deceiving her, even though it was necessary.

Joachim took one hand from the wheel and put it over hers, lacing his fingers through hers.

"I know what you feel," he said solemnly. "I hate lying, too. But God, she lied to me so often. She told me she was pregnant when she wasn't. Like a fool, I married her. I was down, I was upset because my mom had just died, I wasn't thinking, I didn't know what I was doing. God."

She nodded again, wishing her hand wasn't so sweaty; his was so cool and dry and steady and strong. He had said all this before, but he seemed to know she needed to hear it again, from his lips, not from a typed message. He was extraordinarily perceptive. He always seemed to know what she needed to hear.

"Look," he said, tossing her an earnest glance, "I swear it's true. She's not a good person. I'm not even sure she's a *sane* person."

He squeezed her hand more tightly, as if hanging on for dear life. She thought she saw the glitter of a tear in his eye, but he blinked it back and swallowed hard.

She winced at his pain. Like her, he was the child of divorced parents and had been brought up by his mother. Like her, he'd lost his mother to cancer. Her mother had died two years ago. His had been dead for thirteen months.

Selena had cried and eaten, cried and eaten after her mother's death. She gained over thirty pounds in six months, which depressed her, so she'd eaten more. She'd drawn more and more inward, until she had only her studies left. Then she'd discovered Omega—and Joachim.

Joachim said he hadn't let himself cry when his mother died; society didn't approve of men crying. Instead he drank, and one morning he woke up with a girl with a devastatingly pretty face but her hair sheared off and dyed blue. She had five studs in each ear, a ring in her navel, and a black widow spider tattooed on her back.

She'd been an abused child, she said, and she'd clung to Joachim because he'd been the first man who'd ever been kind to her. He pitied her and, he confessed sadly to Selena, he'd pitied himself.

"I was depressed because of my mother," he said. "Lonely as hell. And Deidre was there, saying how much she needed me. Then she said there was going to be a baby and that she wanted a real family, and I thought, maybe there's a reason to go on."

He squeezed Selena's hand so hard that it hurt, but she endured it for his sake. "You don't have to say this," she told him, almost faint with sympathy. "I understand."

"I want to tell you in person," he said from between his white teeth. "God knows it's been hard on you, too."

"I haven't minded," she said and meant it. She was an honest person by nature, honest to a fault. But for him, she

had lied, connived, sneaked, and now, she supposed techni-
cally, she was about to cheat. If his divorce wasn't final, she
was an adulteress. But she didn't feel like one, because she
loved him so and because soon he would be free.

He threw her another of his burning gazes. "You're not a
home-wrecker. Deidre and I didn't have a home. It was more
like hell. I did feel like a beggar, a filthy, stupid beggar—until
I met you. God, I was afraid to tell you about her. Did you
hate me when I said I was married?"

"I could never hate you," she said. "And when you ex-
plained—"

"I was never married to her here," he said and thumped
his hand against his chest. Then he gripped the wheel again,
so tightly his knuckles turned white. "Not in my heart. With
you, it's so different. It's you I'm married to. Not her. Never
her."

When he talked like this, she thought she would die of
love for him. Not that they had often spoken in real life. She
could not call him at his home. His crazy wife might have
answered.

So Selena had waited, trembling and anxious, for the
rare times Joachim could steal a few moments to call her
from a pay phone. She could not write or send packages to
his house because of Deidre. So she sent them to an address
where a trusted friend of his would accept them and secretly
give them to Joachim.

She'd written more letters, sent more presents than he
did. But she had more time, more money than he. Her
mother had left her an inheritance that would see her
through college, graduate school, and beyond.

Joachim was poor; his mother had left hardly enough to
pay her funeral expenses. Joachim literally lived by his wits,
for after his marriage, his life had been so chaotic that he'd
lost his scholarship at the University of Michigan.

He tutored students in math and physics, and he played
guitar and sang in an Irish bar. He'd sent Selena a tape of
himself singing and playing. He had a beautiful voice, strong
and haunting, and his Celtic accent was flawless. His grand-

mother, he said, had come from Ireland in the 1930s and married a farmer in De Kalb, Illinois.

It was to this farmhouse outside De Kalb he was taking Selena. He had told his wife and friends in Michigan that he was going to De Kalb for an interview for a graduate assistantship at the Northern Illinois University, which was almost true. He had applied for such a position but knew his grades were not good enough.

But Joachim was brilliant, and if he wanted to go to Northern Illinois University, he would; Selena had sworn it to him. At first he didn't want to accept her offer, he was too proud. She had to cajole and persuade, and in truth she finally begged him until he agreed.

He might not have the money, but she did, and they both would go to graduate school at Northern. Gladly, gratefully, she would go wherever he wished.

> *Entreat me not to leave thee,*
> *or to return from following after thee:*
> *for whither thou goest, I will go;*
> *and where thou lodgest, I will lodge:*
> *thy people shall be my people . . .*

The grittiness and smog of Chicago fell behind them, and Joachim drove through the suburbs, still imprisoning her hand so tightly that it had grown numb. She wished he would loosen his grip, but he seemed so intense, so emotional, she didn't want to hurt his feelings.

"Is she—is she still doing drugs?" Selena asked.

His nostrils flared. "Of course. Being drunk was one thing. I was drunk a lot myself at first. I'm not proud of it, but it's true. But I'd never done drugs. I didn't recognize the signs. God, she's such a mess and she almost messed up my life forever. Thank *God* I found you."

"I can't believe it," she said dreamily. "Three whole days together."

His grimness lifted and he smiled, very gently and sweetly. "Yeah. Me, neither. But my grandma's farm—well, it's not fancy. It's going to be like camping out. You don't mind?"

She'd never camped in her life, but she would have slept in the desert on the bare sand if he had asked. "Of course, I don't mind. But we could stay at a hotel or motel. I could pay—"

"No," he said, frowning again. "Not until we're married. A man has to have some pride, and God knows Deidre didn't leave me much. You saved me, do you know that? You're my savior."

"No," she said, though he had told her that from the beginning.

"Yes," he insisted. "You don't know what I went through." And he poured his feelings out for her, in his earnest, intense voice, mile after mile, telling her in person the things he had reluctantly admitted, night after night on Omega.

The world of Omega MOON stretched on and on in the magic of cyberspace. It had hundreds of nooks and crannies where a young couple might meet and communicate. There were beaches, forests, grottos, and caves. There were gardens, meadows, waterfalls, riverbanks, and mountaintops.

Those characters clever at computer programming could actually extend Omega, building their own houses and rooms. Selena had never mastered this skill, but Joachim had, and a character could keep his room absolutely private.

They had carried on most of their courtship in the hut of Joachim the Beggar. At first it was a terrible, depressing place, but as she and Joachim grew closer, he changed it for her. The hut became a palace, because he'd said a goddess deserved a palace at the very least. Each night they met to talk there through their computers.

But nothing in these meetings seemed computerized or imaginary to her. Their conversations had been the most intimate and exciting and emotional Selena had ever had. They had revealed their naked hearts to each other in silent words on a screen.

Now he said, "Deidre's a junkie, that's all. I couldn't admit it, couldn't deal with it. Then I met you."

He raised her hand to his lips and kissed it. He didn't notice her fingers had turned cold and almost bluish in his grasp; indeed, she hardly noticed herself, she was so swept up in his spell.

"But she *is* getting help?" she asked.

"Some," he said, turning his gaze back to the highway. "She's going to a clinic. She's seeing a doctor."

"But she's really already living with someone else?"

"Two other guys now. Another one moved in. I pray for her. I honestly do. But I had to get out."

"It's tragic," she said, but felt more horror than sadness over Deidre. She had read of such reckless, tragic people in novels and scandal magazines, but she'd never had one touch her life. She shuddered slightly. Some people, she thought, must be doomed to self-destruction.

Vaguely she noticed that the suburbs had thinned out and disappeared. The land was verdant with early summer, but flat, the flattest she'd ever seen. It seemed as if she and Joachim were tiny insects on a huge, green-covered pool table, but the thought seemed too frivolous to utter in so serious a conversation.

A green and white highway sign said, "De Kalb 6 Miles." Shortly after they passed it, Joachim turned down a side road, then another side road, this one dirt. Freshly plowed fields stretched on either side, black earth, rich and raw.

"This is the road to your grandma's?" she asked. It seemed very far away from everything, all this green flatness and the solitary fields.

"Almost," Joachim said. "There's one more turnoff."

"Joachim?" she said in a hesitant little voice.

"Yes?"

"I pray for Deidre, too. I don't want to sound like a hypocrite. But I don't want anything bad to happen to her. I hope she gets better."

"I do, too," he said, his face solemn and unhappy. He made another turn, down a road even dustier, even narrower. Corn was sprouting in these fields, like dark green fingers thrusting up through the soil. The sky was cloudy, and no breeze seemed to touch the leaves or lift the dust.

The road turned a sharp corner, and Joachim drew the car to a halt before a small, tumbled-down farmhouse with empty windows and a fallen-in porch.

For a moment, Selena's heart sank in spite of the fullness of her love for Joachim. The house looked as if it had been deserted forever, for decades, instead of only three years, as Joachim had told her.

But he seemed happy to see it, and his smile was bright. "I know it doesn't look like much, but I love being here. We had some good times here, when the family was all together. I've got sleeping bags and everything in the trunk. God, but it's good to be back. And to share it with you."

He seemed so pleased that she would not have voiced her doubts for anything, although the house looked as if it might be full of rats and spiders. Even a tramp might hesitate to sleep in such a house.

"I'm going to pull up in back, so nobody sees the car," he said. "Then there's something I want to show you."

She blinked in surprise. There seemed nothing to see except weeds and brambles, and the surrounding fields of black earth and sprouting corn.

"A farming co-op bought the land," he said, swinging the car around behind the house. He parked behind a thicket of spindly, dying lilac bushes. "They'll pull the house down someday. I'll hate that."

She looked in growing dismay at the back of the house. Part of the roof was missing, caved in. The dark, glassless windows stared out like blind eyes, and a chimney beside the back door had fallen into rubble that was nearly covered with what looked like poison ivy.

"Come on," he said with almost boyish excitement. "Let's explore." He got out of the car, came to her side and opened the door.

It did not occur to her to set down her big purse. She carried it with her, clutched to her chest. He seized her by the hand and led her through the weeds toward the farthest corner of the yard.

The day was hot in spite of the clouds, and grasshoppers leaped away from them, big yellow and gray creatures with shiny black eyes. She hated insects and imagined them creeping into her jeans, but Joachim didn't seem to notice them. He led her to a small grove where several oaks grew, one shattered by lightning and overgrown with wild grapevine.

"Here," he said proudly.

She looked. All she saw were the oaks, even the best of which looked sickly, and a strange low, boxy structure made of cement blocks. It reminded her, absurdly, of the above-ground tombs she had once seen on a vacation in New Orleans.

"What?" she said, not understanding what pleased him so about the cement square.

"It's a cistern," he said and cocked his head, like a child who knows he has posed a clever riddle.

He squeezed her hand so hard that she could not help it—she cried out. She thought she heard a bone snap, and the sound and the pain sent a wave of sickness through her stomach.

"Ahh," he said. "Wuzza matter. Did I hurt you? So sorry."

He raised her hand as if to kiss it. Instead he bit it, sinking his bright white teeth between her knuckles until blood welled up, staining his teeth.

She stared at him in pain and stupefaction. He drew back his fist and hit her in the mouth so hard she would have fallen, but he caught her. She tasted blood in her mouth and saw the blood on his.

"Cunt," he said, bringing his face close to hers in a fierce snarl. "Big, fat stupid ugly cunt."

He pressed his fingers against her carotid artery, and he saw the terror in her eyes before he cut off the flow of blood to her brain—it took only seconds to do so. She sagged more heavily toward the weeds, unconscious. This time, he let her fall.

A grasshopper, startled, leaped to her cheek, crouched at the edge of her opened mouth, then leaped away. By that time, Joachim had his knife out and opened.

He was on her, cutting and cutting again. He kept talking to her, even though she could not hear. He said obscene things and mocking things.

He pulled up her pink T-shirt. He had sent her the shirt as a gift. It had a picture of a silver unicorn silhouetted against a cloud-swept blue moon.

"Salvation?" He almost spat as he cut into her round stomach. "There's no salvation, bitch."

He ripped the life from the body that had always shamed her so deeply. He violated that body in ways that gave him intense satisfaction.

When he was done, he pried open the wooden top of the cistern and put her inside, along with her unopened duffel bag and her stupid, oversized purse. He took the money from the purse, even though he didn't need it. He took her identification to destroy it later.

He'd lied about his poverty; he came from a family far more well-to-do than hers. His mother wasn't dead but alive and vacationing in the Bahamas. He had never been married; there was no such person as Deidre; he had made her up completely. He had never attended the University of Michigan. He could neither sing nor play the guitar.

Of course, his name was not Joachim, but neither was it Stanley. His grandmother had never owned this farmhouse, and he had never visited it when people lived in it. In his travels, his wanderings, he had found it, and known, with his hunter's instinct, that it could serve him perfectly and serve him more than once if he chose. Gretchen was the fifth woman he had killed. He was becoming expert at it.

He bathed in a small, muddy creek that ran behind the farmhouse and put on the clean shirt he'd brought with him. Then he got back into his car.

He drove off and left her body there in the resealed cistern, mutilated and disemboweled. He'd wrapped her last gift to him, the T-shirt, around her nearly severed head. The portrait of Einstein, the man of thought, was obliterated by blood.

TWO

⟡⟡⟡

A PRIVATE DETECTIVE'S OFFICE SHOULD LIE BEHIND A MYSTERIOUS door, its window blind with frosted glass. The doorway should be set in the poorly lit hallway of a decaying building, preferably in a sinister section of Los Angeles. That's what Carrie thought.

She wanted a 1940s atmosphere: venetian blinds slicing the dusty sunlight, a smart-ass secretary with a whiskey voice, and a detective who looked like Humphrey Bogart or Robert Mitchum or, at the very least, Jack Nicholson.

But this detective agency was on a main street of sleepy Fayetteville, Arkansas, in the bright white stucco building that had once housed the Jolly Baker's Shoppe.

The remodeled interior was styled in what Carrie thought of as Godless Office Modern. The linoleum was blandly beige, the furniture all angles and chrome, the walls white, the lighting stark. But she imagined a ghostly aroma of freshly baked bread still haunting the air, as if the spirit of the Jolly Baker hadn't completely relinquished the premises.

The secretary at the reception desk was plain and matronly enough to preside over the office of the strictest fundamentalist church. She wore a ruffled blouse, bifocals, and her blue-tinted hair was trained in waves so stern they might have been cast from metal.

"Mr. Ivanovich is with someone right now," the secretary said. "He'll be with you shortly."

It was noon, and Carrie was the only other person in the waiting room, so she sat on the hard tan sofa with its plastic upholstery and chrome arms and legs.

The secretary unwrapped a sandwich that smelled of tuna fish and pickles and began to nibble daintily at one triangular half. Idly Carrie picked up a *Time* magazine with a dark, moody cover. It showed a photo of two wounded young soldiers, half lost in shadows, their eyes bandaged.

"Vietnam," stark letters announced, "Twenty years later, it haunts us still."

Indeed it does, thought Carrie, with a pang. *But only some of us.*

She didn't want to touch the pages, didn't want to read about Vietnam, see the pictures. Almost superstitiously, she set the magazine aside. She took up one of the glossy pamphlets that said, "BURNSIDE INVESTIGATIVE AGENCY, ROBERT E. LEE BURNSIDE and Associates, ROBERT E. LEE BURNSIDE, Founder and President."

She forced herself not to smile at the formal portrait of Robert E. Lee Burnside, who looked portly, humorless, and righteously smug.

His poor associates, thought Carrie, reading the names of these lesser personages. Four associates were listed, and the name of the man she'd come to see, Hayden Ivanovich, was printed at the bottom, last and presumably least.

Hayden Ivanovich, however low on the pecking order he was, might have part-time work for Carrie. She didn't know what the job was, but she was curious enough and broke enough to check it out. Carrie's motto was "Wotthehell." It had served her well and brought her through much.

Carolynn Cornell Blue was forty-six, with blond bangs, freckles, and blue eyes that saw much, missed little. She was a lean, windswept tomboy of a woman, dressed for her job interview in the only skirt she owned, which was, of course, denim.

Her short-sleeved blouse was light blue and freshly, if haphazardly, ironed. She'd had to search half an hour to find her steam iron, discovering it at last in the bottom drawer of her file cabinet, next to a folder marked "Irony."

Carrie no longer wore a wedding ring. Her husband had died ten years ago, leaving her with two sons, fourteen and thirteen, to raise. She'd taught high school and, during summer holidays, worked at whatever job paid best, usually as a cocktail waitress. Once when both boys had taken summer jobs in a nearby city, she had driven a truck.

When Joel, her younger son, finished college last year, Carrie had thought, *All right, boys, it's my turn now.* She'd always wanted a master of fine arts degree in writing fiction. She'd chosen the University of Arkansas because she'd spent the happiest two years of her girlhood in Arkansas and could not resist returning.

She knew it was dangerous to go back looking for the lost glow of halcyon days, but she was not afraid to take chances. She'd taken them all her life and had learned she fared best when she followed her heart.

Once, long ago it seemed, she had been flirtatious, delighting in playing the games that men and women played. She knew she still radiated an offbeat sex appeal, but she no longer bothered to wield it. Twice since her husband's death, she had taken lovers, one for four years, the other for three.

She had parted amiably from both, but wasn't looking for a replacement. Relationships demanded so much attention; they claimed so much time; they needed such endless nurturing and maintenance. For the present, she didn't think of herself as between men, but *beyond* them.

Now that her sons were launched, this time was her time, and she wasn't interested in romance. Romance she'd had. She wanted completely new frontiers, frontiers larger than a double bed and more intriguing than a new man across from her at the breakfast table.

She heard a door open and looked up from the Burnside

pamphlet. A young woman had exited from the farthest office and fumbled to shut the door behind her.

The woman was tall, brunette, and extremely beautiful. Carrie wondered if she had seen her on campus before—a cheerleader? A beauty queen?

The girl—she was little more than twenty—was dressed to expensive perfection in a dark green silk pants suit. Gold glittered from her earlobes and wrists and at her throat. But her eyes were swollen, her expression stricken, and it was obvious that she had been crying uncontrollably.

Why? Carrie thought, with a frisson of alarm and curiosity. What had she learned inside that office that made her weep so bitterly?

The secretary looked up, saw the girl's distress, and glanced discreetly away. Delicately she lifted the second half of her sandwich and took a precise bite.

The girl pushed open the thick glass door of the waiting room as if desperate to flee and escaped into the hot June sunshine outside. She disappeared down the street, and Carrie stared after her in pity and wonder.

The secretary chewed her sandwich. The clock ticked. Then the office door opened a few inches, but Carrie couldn't see inside. A masculine voice with a southern accent said, "Give me a minute before you send in the next one, Alice."

"Yes, sir."

The door shut again. The secretary did not make eye contact with Carrie. She dawdled over her sandwich, giving it all of her concentration. At last she carefully bundled up the crusts in the wrapping cellophane, making little crackling noises.

She opened her purse, took out her compact, grimaced at herself in the mirror, inspected her teeth, then refreshed the powder on her nose. She clicked shut the compact, returned it to her purse, and clasped her hands together before her on the desk. She cleared her throat.

She nodded, reacknowledging Carrie's existence. "He'll see you now."

Carrie rose and went to the farthest office door, wondering if she was expected to knock. She raised her fist to rap smartly at the doorframe. But the receptionist said, almost pettishly, "No, no. Just walk in."

Carrie walked in. A tall man with straight brown hair, graying at the temples, stood behind the desk. He looked at her with an expression that was half frown, half displeased surprise.

He had a glass of water and a wet handkerchief with which he dabbed at his shirt front. He'd made a large damp spot on his chest, but he hadn't succeeded in wiping away the streak of red lipstick there. When he saw where Carrie's gaze had settled, he looked more resentful than guilty.

Carrie narrowed her eyes, wondering if he'd made advances to the girl. Sexual harassment was common in a college town, and it was something that infuriated her. She had never stood for it, and she never would.

The man looked Carrie up and down, his expression stony. It seemed as if he could read her mind and didn't give a damn what she thought, that the lipstick was none of her business.

Carrie considered this, and true, it was none of her business. Yet the weeping girl had registered on not only her sympathy, but her imagination. Just *what* had gone on in here?

Ivanovich made one more ineffectual wipe at the lipstick smear, then tossed the handkerchief aside. He kept his eyes fixed on Carrie. They were hazel eyes touched with dark green, and they didn't waver. He had straight thick eyebrows, a well-shaped jaw, an adequate nose, but his mouth was too wide for handsomeness, and it had a sarcastic slant that looked permanent.

He wore no jacket, and his white shirt was better pressed than her blouse. The shirt was open at the throat, and his tie had been cast on his desk. She saw why. The tie was of gray silk, and it, too, was smudged with lipstick.

Ivanovich saw her looking at the tie, picked it up, and stowed it in his top desk drawer, away from her curious gaze.

"You must be Carolynn Blue," he said with false pleasantness. "Dr. Holloway told me you were observant."

She thrust her hand out to him in greeting. "And you're Mr. Ivanovich. Holloway said you might have work for me."

He shook hands, firmly but briefly. He gestured at the chair opposite his. "Have a seat."

She sat, crossing her legs with almost military precision and making sure the unfamiliar skirt didn't hike up her legs. They were still good legs, but nothing like the girl's, she was sure.

Hayden Ivanovich sat, too, settling into a swivel chair that was oak, not metal. He showed no interest in her legs, but he studied her face as if determined to read more of her character than she wished to reveal.

He said, "I need a couple of women who can write, who can be—creative."

Why does a detective need writers? she wondered. *And why, specifically, women writers?*

Her expression must have indicated she was puzzled. He rubbed his jaw reflectively, opened a manila folder, stared at the top page.

"Holloway faxed me a copy of your application to the MFA program. He says you have a more varied background than most students."

"I'm older," she said. Ivanovich was a prospective employer, and by law she didn't have to tell him how old, but she didn't care. "Forty-six."

"Hmm," he said, looking faintly surprised. He darted a quick glance at her bare left hand, so quick that she almost missed it. His left hand, too, was bare, she noticed.

"I'm a widow," she said, although she didn't have to tell him that, either. "I've got two sons. Both out of college now. I decided it was time for me to go back—"

He raised his hand, a gesture that he didn't want to hear. "I'm interested in your work background. You were a police-woman once?"

She raised her chin slightly. "Once I was an officer. For almost two years."

There was a beat of silence between them. *Two years that were several millenniums ago*, she thought. When she'd started, she had been near the age of the pretty girl who had just left in tears.

"You were in law enforcement, too, weren't you?" she asked. "Before—this?" Instinct told her he'd been a lawman and he'd been tough.

He ignored her question. "Tell me about being an 'officer.'" He put an ironic spin on the word that she didn't like.

She decided he was overbearing and impressed by his own superiority, but she had her own way of handling such men. Let him underestimate her; the more he did, the bigger surprise he'd have coming. She gave him a wry little smile, intending to disarm him with her dimples.

"It was in Parkview, Nebraska," she said. "I was mostly a meter maid. I'd go up and down Main Street giving out parking tickets. Helped with traffic during the homecoming parade, the Fourth of July fireworks. That's about it."

"You went to the police academy?"

She gave a deprecating shrug. "Yes."

And in the written exam, I was first in my class, you condescending bastard.

"Did you ever use a gun?"

She smiled again, as if marveling over the oddity of her own past. A meter maid had little use for a gun, but she'd worn one; all the officers had.

And, once in a while, when the men needed inconspicuous backup in an undercover drug bust, she would be drafted. As soon as the drug money changed hands, she was supposed to whip out the gun. She'd pulled it more than once. She'd never had to shoot it.

"I never shot anyone," she said. "Or anything. Well, a rabid skunk once. I felt bad about it afterwards." She paused, showed him her dimples again. "I won't need a gun for this job, will I?"

"I was curious, that's all. Why'd you quit the force?"

Because it was the early 1970s, I was the only woman, and the police force of Parkview, Nebraska, was full of male chauvinist pigs, just like you.

"I was going back to college," she said. "Grad school. But I didn't quite make it until now."

"After that you taught? High school?"

Carrie nodded and looked brightly innocent. Teaching high school demanded nerves as steady as any police officer's, maybe steadier and steelier. If he didn't believe her, let him try it.

"All these other jobs? Cocktail waitress? Store clerk?" The sarcasm vibrated in his tone. "House painter?"

"Teachers don't get paid much. I had two boys to raise. I worked summers."

"Truck driver?" he said dubiously.

"It was a florist's delivery truck," Carrie said. "It wasn't an eighteen-wheeler, a big rig or anything."

"Anything else?" he asked, his green-brown eyes narrowed as if the better to measure her.

"Tutoring. Baby-sitting. Whatever came along."

She didn't add that she'd also written for the "true confession" magazines. The magazines paid her five cents a word, never gave her a byline, and nobody knew that she stayed up late at nights, writing the stories. Not even her sons. Certainly not Allen Holloway, head of the creative writing program. If he found out, he would be seized by a fatal attack of aesthetic revulsion.

Ivanovich looked at his file on her and again rubbed his jaw. "You live out by the lake?"

She did. She rented a one-bedroom fishing cabin from an elderly lawyer who no longer used it. The cabin was isolated, a bit ramshackle, and had a 'possum living under the tool shed. But it also had a million-dollar view of the lake, and she loved it more than any house in which she'd ever lived.

Ivanovich raised his eyes to meet hers again. "You live all alone out there?"

Her heart took an inexplicable skip. He wasn't handsome, she didn't like him, but he made her hormones wake up, stretch, and say, *How long have we been asleep?* She resented this. When the wake-up call came, she wanted to be the one in charge of ordering it.

"I live alone and like it," she said. "What's all this about? What kind of job is this? How much does it pay?"

"You have a phone? A computer? A modem?"

"A phone, yes. A computer, yes, if you're charitable about it. A modem is that gizmo that you hook up between a computer and a phone? So you can get access to the Internet and things? No."

He cast a discreet glance at her legs, then met her gaze again. "We can take care of that if you're interested. Can you navigate the Internet?"

Carrie's heart sank like a stone. She could use a word processing program for writing, that was all, and her computer was twelve years old. Her sons considered it prehistoric and called it "T. Rex."

"I know nothing about the Internet except it's there," she said carefully. "But I'm a quick learner."

Ivanovich's mouth kept its sarcastic slant. "Yeah. Holloway said you were. What you'd have to learn isn't hard. You could get it down in a day or less."

Relief danced giddily through her veins.

Ivanovich said, "Do you know what virtual reality communities are? Specifically the one called Omega MOON?"

Carrie lifted an eyebrow. Joel, her younger son, had played with the virtual communities, which went by strange acronyms like MUDs, MUSHes, MOONs, MOOs, and TinyMOOs. And she'd heard students talk.

"I know a little," she said. "Omega MOON's supposed to be the biggest and most sophisticated. People take on characters. It's like a giant masquerade."

He nodded, picked up a back issue of *Newsweek,* and handed it to her. "There's an article on Omega on page thirty-seven. Read it. That is, if you're interested. I need a couple of women to go on Omega as characters."

Carrie accepted the magazine, but gave Ivanovich a curious stare. "Go on Omega? As a character? Why?"

His expression became unreadable. He put his elbows on his desk, tented his fingers. "I've got a client," he said. "He was interested in a girl on Omega. She's disappeared."

"From Omega?" Carrie asked.

"Disappeared completely," he said, watching her face as if gauging her reaction. "Her name's Gretchen Small. A sophomore at Memphis State. She vanished during spring break. Seven weeks ago she booked a round-trip flight to Chicago. She went, but never used the return ticket. And after that, we know nothing."

The rest is silence, Carrie thought with an ominous little prickle deep in her bones. She said, "Her disappearance has something to do with Omega MOON?"

"She met another guy on Omega. Maybe the wrong guy. My client's worried. Her character's been erased from the MOON. He claims she never would have done that. And that she's not the first girl to disappear like this."

"Who was this man, this other man?"

"We don't know. That's why we need you."

The import of his words temporarily stunned her. She stared at him. "You want me to be *bait*?"

His expression didn't change. "It pays seven dollars an hour. You work as many hours as you want. Mostly at night. That's when the action is. You go on Omega, you chat up guys. Are you interested?"

She swallowed and held the magazine more tightly, her thoughts racing. She had only one class this summer, a seminar on Shakespeare, and, of course, she had to work on her master's project, a collection of short stories.

She was living on the pitifully thin salary of a graduate assistant's stipend. Her house in Nebraska hadn't yet sold, and she was desperately trying to keep from dipping into her savings.

If she could work thirty-five hours a week at seven dollars an hour, she could make nine hundred and eighty dollars a month—almost a thousand dollars—a fortune! The sum staggered her.

Her car's transmission groaned and clanked, sputtering threats to fail; her CD player had been broken for months and she fiercely missed her favorite music. She could buy the books she'd been yearning for, put money in the bank, send Joel a decent birthday present—

She said, "It's not dangerous, of course?"

"If I thought it was dangerous, I wouldn't ask you to do it." Ivanovich's aura of mild scorn had vanished. He spoke with such rough conviction that he startled her. She thought she saw something new come into his eyes, but she couldn't quite understand what it was, flickering there in the depths.

"Use your head, and you'll be safe," he said. "Nobody can find out who you are unless you tell them. Omega gives you total anonymity—if you want it. Use it."

She nodded. "And this man? That Gretchen Small might have gone off with? He had total anonymity, too?"

"Yes. The Internet's full of people damn near impossible to trace. The guy she'd taken up with called himself Joachim the Beggar. He disappeared at the same time she did. But he may be back, posing as another character. He could be anybody there, male or female."

Carrie frowned slightly. "He'd pose as a woman?"

"There's a lot of gender-bending. Nobody has to be what he says he is. If you go on, you'll be approached by both men and women. Some of these 'women' are men pretending to be lesbians."

"You mean people are going to—to try to—" She groped for a polite way to phrase it.

"Seduce you," Ivanovich said. "They'll offer sex then and there. You'll get used to it."

" 'Then and there'? What's that mean?"

Ivanovich lifted one shoulder in a cynical shrug. "It's called 'MOON sex' or 'netsex.' It's like phone sex, except they use words on the computer screen, not voices."

Carrie blinked hard. She'd heard of netsex, but not on the MOONs. "You mean people *type* dirty to each other?" she said with distaste.

"The joke is they type one-handed," Ivanovich said, but didn't elaborate.

He didn't have to. Carrie had a vision of a pimply, aroused college boy furiously typing erotic messages to a stranger while he rubbed himself.

"Computer sex?" she said with distaste. "You don't expect me to do that, for God's sake?"

"Gretchen Small probably had MOON sex with this

man. Play hard to get. Unless you think there's reason to do otherwise."

"You're serious? I'll be propositioned?"

His gaze met hers coolly. "Count on it."

She couldn't quite believe it and laughed. "Omega's full of college kids. I'm old enough to be their mother."

"They don't know that. Everything's illusion on the MOON. You're one more illusion."

Carrie nipped the corner of her lower lip thoughtfully.

Ivanovich watched her. "Holloway says you think fast, write fast, that you're more mature than the others. He thinks you can handle this."

Carrie shook her head. The thought of sitting at the computer night after night, lying to college boys, flirting and leading them on, filled her with profound distaste.

Ivanovich, his face harder than before, opened his desk drawer, took out a snapshot, and handed it to her.

She stared at the picture, which showed a plump girl with frizzy hair and a long chin, but beautiful eyes.

"This is Gretchen," Ivanovich said. "We have reason to think she may be dead. The man she went to meet may still be prowling Omega. Maybe other virtual communities as well."

Carrie gave him a sharp glance. "Dead? Why do you think so?"

"My client will tell you. Do you want the job or not?"

She studied the snapshot again. Except for the extraordinary eyes, Gretchen Small was not attractive in the least. But that wasn't what struck Carrie. What caught her sympathy was the insecurity in the girl's face, the vulnerability of her mouth, the hope and fear in her gaze.

Carrie had seen that expression on other young faces, and it always saddened her. The expression said, *I am lost, please love me. I would do anything to be loved.*

Carrie shook her head; young people that lonely could make terrible decisions. They could be misled, tricked, exploited, even destroyed.

She remembered one of her high school students from seven years ago. The same desperate, needy look had shown in Shannon Flannery's gray eyes—Shannon, a shy, sweet girl in Carrie's sophomore literature class, who seldom spoke and gave off an aura of being a permanent outsider.

One night at a teen dance, Shannon accepted a ride home with a stranger. Four days later her nude body was found caught in a raft of snags in the Missouri River. Petite, thin little Shannon who still had braces on her teeth and wrote poems about springtime and kittens and puppies. Sixteen years old. The killer had never been found.

The memory filled Carrie with bitterness and grief.

"I'll help you look for him," she said, her eyes still on the snapshot. "Who'll teach me how to get into Omega?"

"My client," Ivanovich said. "He'll give you an intensive session on Sunday. Both of you."

"Both? Who besides me?"

Ivanovich tented his fingers again. "Holloway recommended Brooke Tharpe."

The name surprised her. Brooke Tharpe was only twenty-three, one of the youngest women in the writing program, and certainly the most aloof. Brilliant but eccentric, she seldom said so much as hello and her gaze was the chilly sort that warned people to keep their distance. She was imperious and strangely absentminded, as if the details of daily life were beneath her.

Carrie said, "Frankly, I don't know if Brooke would accept something like this."

"She already has," Ivanovich said. "This morning."

Carrie was puzzled that Brooke would accept, but almost everything about the woman puzzled her. Brooke was strange and haughty, a squarely built girl with olive skin and black hair arranged in an old-fashioned crown of braids. She wore long dresses of batiked cotton that were made in places like Bali and Sumatra and Malabar. Her favorite word was *ignoramus,* as in "Hemingway's an ignoramus and I refuse to read him."

"Brooke and I would make an odd couple," Carrie said. "We're not alike at—"

Ivanovich cut her off. "It doesn't matter. Be at the Kimple Hall computer lab nine o'clock Sunday morning. Plan on a long day."

"The computer lab?" she asked. It was always tightly locked up on Sundays.

"My client's got clout." He said the words with something akin to contempt.

"Just who is this client?" Carrie asked.

"Edmon Welkin, Jr. You'll meet him Sunday."

Carrie blinked hard. One of northwest Arkansas's most profitable businesses was trucking, and its biggest trucking company was Welkin Brothers, Incorporated.

"One of the trucking Welkins?" she asked.

"An heir apparent," Ivanovich said. "Home from Dartmouth for the summer."

"My God," Carrie said. "I'll be working for a millionaire? And he's only paying seven bucks an hour?"

She thought she saw a glint of a smile in Ivanovich's green-brown eyes, but it didn't touch his lips.

"He's not a millionaire yet," he said. "His mama's indulging him. Mama's no spendthrift."

Carrie gave a little laugh, but Ivanovich's expression didn't change. *One of these days, tough guy, I'll get a smile out of you,* she vowed. It didn't occur to her to wonder why she would bother.

"All this is confidential," Ivanovich said. "Tell nobody."

"Even my family?"

"No. We want no security leaks. None."

He stood, a clear indication that she was being dismissed. She, too, stood, and laid the snapshot of Gretchen Small on his desktop. She gave it one last look, and again the girl's expression troubled her.

"I'll walk you to the front door," Ivanovich said.

Carrie thought of the other woman who had just left the office and wondered why he hadn't escorted her. Had he offered? Had the girl turned and simply fled from him?

"I can find my own way," she said. She paused, put one hand on her hip, and pointed at his chest. The water on his shirt was drying, but the red lipstick stain still stood out, clear and bright.

"You won't get that out with plain water," she told him. "Put liquid detergent on it, work it till it's sudsy, then rinse it. You may have to do it more than once."

He looked unpleasantly surprised by her audacity, and this gratified her. She said, "See you Sunday," turned, and left.

In the reception room, the faint scent of tuna fish still hung upon the air, and the secretary was frowning sternly at the screen of her word processor.

" 'Bye," Carrie said to her, and gave her a friendly wave.

"Good day," said the secretary, not looking up.

Carrie walked out into the warm sunshine, hoisted her purse to her shoulder, thrust her hands into the pockets of her denim skirt, and walked down Dixon Street to where her car was parked.

She was sorry that Ivanovich had sworn her to secrecy about this bizarre assignment. She imagined writing to her sons about this, her latest adventure. "Dear boys, Found work as Cyberminx. Love, Mom."

Hayden Ivanovich stared sourly at the door Carrie Blue had closed behind her. She was a cocky little thing, and she wielded those dimples like she had a license to kill. She was cute in a mutt-cute sort of way, and she knew it. Yet she carried herself in a touch-me-not way that seemed real, not a pose.

Who cares? Hayden thought cynically. Carrie Blue was too cool and confident for his tastes. But she was better than the other woman, Brooke Tharpe. God only knew why Holloway had endorsed her. The kindest terms Hayden could think of for Brooke were "snob" and "weirdo."

This whole Internet caper of Edmon Welkin's was eccentric, at best, and doomed to failure. Edmon Welkin himself was eccentric, and without the Welkin money behind him, he would also be surely doomed to failure. The kid didn't have a practical thought in his head. Don Quixote of the Ozarks.

Hayden had little doubt that something ill had befallen Gretchen Small. He didn't even doubt Edmon Welkin's theory that Gretchen had been surfing the Net and encountered the wrong man, some great white shark of a sicko.

What Hayden did doubt was that Edmon, even with the power of considerable family wealth, could do a damn thing about it. But the girl was on his mind and on his conscience, and the kid had to try.

Hayden understood because he had demons of his own, unappeasable ones. He tried not to think about them, just as he tried not to have feelings anymore. He was trying especially hard today, after saying goodbye to Anne. They'd pretended it wasn't goodbye, but both had known it was.

If things had gone differently, pretty green-eyed Anne would have been Mrs. Kyle Ivanovich, Hayden's daughter-in-law. But Hayden's son had been dead for two years, two weeks, three days.

Today Anne had driven over from Tulsa to tell Hayden that she'd found someone else; she was getting married at the end of August and she hoped he'd come to her wedding. But then she started crying about Kyle. "I'm sorry," she kept saying. "I'm sorry. I have to get on with my life."

He'd held her and told her she was right, that Kyle would want it this way. He supposed Kyle would. But he'd felt numb, empty.

Kyle had loved Anne, and now Kyle was nothing but ashes scattered in the river, the favorite river of his youth, the War Eagle. Hayden had gone to the War Eagle alone with his only child's ashes. He had watched their grayness vanish beneath the rushing water.

For the ten thousandth time, he told himself to forget the fucking past. He had other things to occupy his thoughts. As usual, they were sordid things. Once he had worked as an agent for the ATF, the Alcohol, Tobacco, and Firearms division of the Treasury Department. He'd specialized in major weapon violations. But he'd walked away from the agency the day Kyle was killed.

Now he spied on cheating husbands and two-timing boyfriends, ran surveillance on suspected defrauders of insurance companies, chased down witnesses and deadbeats.

He switched on the radio. He often used music as an

opiate. He put away Carrie Blue's folder and took out that of Regina Daily, a local woman who was concerned about her daughter's boyfriend. She had reason to worry.

The daughter, a bubbly sorority girl, was wildly in love, and Hayden was going to have to tell the Daily woman that the boyfriend was not only married but had Mafia connections.

If Mr. Mafia discovered Hayden was meddling in his love life, he might feel vengeful, might even come gunning. This didn't bother Hayden. Such things went with the turf, they always had, and he was hardened to them.

As if to affirm it, the radio played the "Mercenary Song." Steve Earle's rough voice sang of soldiers of fortune being bound for the border, ready to die for good pay.

Yeah, Hayden thought. Right.

THREE

—◦◦◦—

Carrie's cabin stood near the edge of a long, meandering lake full of coves and nooks. The shoreline was still wild and forested in some places; in others it had been tamed into farmland, fields, and pastures.

The rolling land could soar suddenly up into sheer cliffs of limestone, then drop back just as dramatically to ordinary hills and valleys. Carrie's house nestled in a forested stretch that was bordered on the north by meadows and on the south by a stony upthrust of cliffs.

A century and a half ago, the ground had been cleared and a farmhouse and outbuildings raised. But over the years, the homestead's young people left for towns and cities. The farm, at last deserted, fell into ruin. One night the empty house was struck by lightning and burned to the ground.

Wind carried sparks to the barn, and it, too, burned. Now the crumbling foundation of the house was almost hidden by vines and brambles, and no trace remained of the barn.

People desiring lake property lusted after the old farm site, but its owner refused to sell and swore he never would, nor would his sons. The owner's name was Chandler Sawyer, a retired attorney who lived in Fayetteville.

Sawyer was seventy-five years old, and his great-great-great-grandfather had cleared the land and built the farm. In his prime, Chandler Sawyer had been a passionate fisherman and hunter and a lover of canoes and boats.

At the farm site, he had saved one small, sturdy outbuilding from the advance of nature and built it into a weekend retreat. Over the years he'd enlarged it and improved it.

But now Sawyer's sons, lawyers themselves, were dispersed to Little Rock and Russellville and Arkadelphia, and his wife was dead. Arthritis had crippled him so that he could not comfortably leave his city house with its special lifts and bathroom railings and wheelchair ramps.

Rather than let the cabin fall into neglect, Sawyer reluctantly decided to rent it, and Carrie had become his tenant. She loved the house with all her heart.

This evening, before dark fell, she worked in the flower bed. She liked physical work; it cleaned out her mind, and the neglected garden demanded she use all her muscles.

Never before had Carrie had a flower garden and she delighted in wresting this one back from ruin. She supposed it must have belonged to Sawyer's late wife. It was outlined by a rectangle of flagstones that had been heaved askew by frost, and only one rose bush, running rampant, had survived the choking weeds.

As the sun set, she felt content and complete, like Eve happily watching over the Garden of Eden, unhampered by Adam, unmenaced by any serpent.

As sun set across the country and night descended, people at their computers began to join one another at Omega MOON.

Time zone by time zone they logged on, first from the East Coast, next from the plains and prairies, then the western mountain states, and finally—and most rowdily—from the Pacific Coast.

In Manhattan, Kansas, a college sophomore named Lynette Pollson sat alone in her dormitory room, tapping out the codes that would unlock the magic world of Omega:

Omega.Silicon.Val.Com 8888

Lynette was alone because her roommate was out, as usual, with her steady boyfriend. Lynette hadn't chosen this roommate for the summer, but at the last minute the girls had been assigned to live together. Lynette tried to make the best of it, but she and Tammy had nothing in common.

Every night Tammy came back late, smelling of beer and the musk of sex. She fell on the bed, too sated and tired to say anything except a mumbled " 'Night." She was wildly in love and it was all she cared about.

Unlike Tammy, Lynette had never had a boyfriend. She was a small girl, neatly built, with a tiny waist, nicely rounded hips, and small, pert breasts. But boys seldom paid attention to her body once they noticed her face.

When Lynette was eighteen months old, she had been riding in her infant's seat in her mother's compact car. The day had been rainy and the traffic on Interstate 70 heavy. A panel truck in front of them had blown a tire and spun halfway around, colliding head-on with the car.

The driver of the truck had died and so had Lynette's mother—killed instantly, people said. The hood of the truck crashed through the windshield, and almost every bone in Lynette's face had been broken.

She could not remember the accident or her mother or a time when she had looked into a mirror and seen a normal human face. She did not like to look at her baby pictures, taken before the accident, because they filled her with a sense of loss that made her feel helpless, and she hated feeling helpless.

Over the years, surgeons had reconstructed her face as best they could. Operation after operation: her life had been a series of them. Her nose and chin had been restored, the angle of her scarred mouth nearly straightened.

Every summer when school was out, other children

greeted vacation time with joy, but Lynette had feared and hated summers; to her they meant more surgery. And after operations, there was often secondary surgery to repair the scars the doctors had left.

"Run! Run! It's Frankenstein's monster!" boys used to shriek at her, then race away in comic exaggeration, as if fearing for their lives.

Lynette might have fared better if her father had been stronger, but the accident undid something in him. By day, he escaped into his work as an electrician and by night into alcohol. Lynette was raised mostly by her grandmother, and Lynette, too, escaped, into her books and studies.

She had enormous self-discipline. Her grades had always been A's, and she played piano with an almost ferocious technical command. She was at Kansas State University on a full scholarship, with a double major in history and literature.

Her grandmother had died when Lynette was seventeen, and her father had died of cirrhosis last winter. She did not want to go home to Kansas City, where too many memories lurked. So she stayed on at Kansas State University for summer school. She pretended to live a normal life although she knew that a normal life was probably impossible for her, now and forever.

From a distance, her face seemed nearly—but not quite—ordinary. But a closer view showed features that were disturbingly awry: asymmetrical lips, one eye smaller and set lower than the other, nostrils that did not align. She knew her face was not natural and mobile like other faces, that it appeared to be exactly what it was: the incomplete repair of an exceptionally bad accident.

Lynette fiercely refused to feel sorry for herself or to think of herself as a victim. With determination, she made the best of things, and she had a wry wit that had sustained her through much. Yet she was a loner and always had been—until this spring, when she'd discovered Omega MOON.

On Omega she was no longer bookish Lynette with her

rebuilt face. On Omega, she was known as Flair, and if one typed the command to see Flair, this description appeared:

> Flair has a ballerina's body, long-legged and slim. Her dark hair is pulled back in a smooth chignon that is circled by pink roses.
>
> Under wing-shaped eyebrows, Flair has large, dark eyes that would remind you of the eyes of a deer except they are not shy, but warm, inviting, and mischievous. Her complexion is flawless as the pale petal of a rose. Her high cheekbones could belong to a model, her slim nose is regal, her mouth ripe, full, and pink. She has a small, firm chin and a graceful neck. Silver hoops adorn her ears.
>
> Flair is dressed in silver-colored tights, a bodice and tutu of the same color, and matching ballet slippers. She is carrying a nosegay of pink roses.
>
> She smiles at you and wishes you would speak to her.

This description was not altogether a success. For one thing, it focused on the face too much, yet still didn't express what Lynette wanted. The face she tried so earnestly to describe was that of the young Audrey Hepburn, whom Lynette thought was the loveliest woman who had ever lived.

Audrey Hepburn as a ballerina was the most beautiful human creature Lynette could imagine. It did not matter that some of the male characters, on first encountering her, said things like, "What the fuck's a tutu?" Or "Nosegay? Does that mean you got a nose for gays? Are you a dike or what ha ha?"

But Lynette stuck to the description stubbornly, and she had made friends on Omega MOON, perhaps more than she'd ever made elsewhere in her life.

Their names were glamorous or heroic or comic or idiosyncratic. There was Blue Rider, TinTin, Merrycat, Nancy Whiskey, Redrum, Jester, Wholly Cow, Superhunk, Tireless, Love Machine, and Quicksilver.

She moved among them, laughing, joking, and flirting. Hardly a night went by without someone begging to make love to her. Yet, she kept her natural reserve; it was ingrained in her too deeply for her to cast it aside. She was friendly, but always remained a bit reticent, not allowing herself to get involved too deeply with anyone on Omega.

Then a new character had appeared. His name was James Dean. She'd liked his name and his description.

> You see James Dean. Rumpled blond hair, blue eyes that have seen and understand the world's pain. He wears jeans, a white t-shirt, and a red jacket. He is condemned to be a loner and has the air of a strange destiny about him.

She had started flirting with him innocently enough but had immediately sensed something different about him, a depth and sensitivity that the other men on Omega lacked.

Flair had created her own room, a prima ballerina's dressing room. It was airy and light, and bouquets were heaped on her dressing table and stood in every corner, their fragrance filling the air.

She and James Dean had been meeting in her dressing room every night for two weeks now. Though she knew it was insane, she was infatuated with him. She'd told him she wasn't beautiful; she'd told him about the accident and her face. He swore he didn't care.

He said he'd had a spectacularly beautiful fiancée, a model named Belinda. Belinda had also been spectacularly unfaithful; he did not trust beautiful girls; they were conceited and shallow and manipulative.

Tonight Lynette was going to meet him again. Her fingers were awkward with tension as she typed her character name and password: Flair Gypyl.

Words began to scroll rapidly down the screen.

> Welcome to Omega MOON. You enter through the Ivory Gate and find yourself on the King's Highway. It is twilight, and above you stars wink through a few delicate veils of cloud.
>
> On either side of you is the Enchanted Wood. The trees are black against the luminous blue of the sky, and their leaves rustle in the warm breeze. Somewhere a nightingale

sings. The scent of night-blooming flowers fills your nostrils, filling you with a giddy sense of intoxication.

The highway itself winds toward the Palace of Pleasure, whose imposing outline you can clearly see in the distance . . .

When Lynette first came to Omega, she'd spent hours exploring it, for its territory extended seemingly forever, containing surprises both lovely and frightening. She would stop at the various gathering places, the Palace Fountain, the Romance Ballroom, the Bathing Pool, Ye Silent Woman Pub. She would talk cheerfully to almost everyone she met.

But lately, she did not explore, she did not engage in idle talk. She knew the one place she wanted to go and the one person she wanted to see.

She typed the command @Go Dressing Room #2814CZ.

Instantly she was there, in her private room. Bright lights framed the big mirror of her dressing table, and when she glanced in it, she could see the reflection of her perfect face.

James Dean stood there, waiting for her. He took her in his arms and kissed her, long and passionately. "I've missed you," he said.

He held Lynette and kissed her and called her his "silver girl." She called him James because he told her in real life that was actually his name.

In truth, his name was Jon Rosmer, and he thought scornfully that James Dean was the most stupid, trite, unimaginative character he'd ever come up with; he'd been drunk when he'd invented him.

But Dean, the shopworn old rebel without a cause, had proven surprisingly effective. He'd scored almost immediately with the flirtatious but elusive ballerina. Little Flair seemed perfect, yes, very nearly perfect for Jon's needs. And, oddly, her disfigured face excited him in a way he didn't understand.

He knew what she was going to ask him tonight. He

took a long drink of beer, and sure enough, her question appeared on his screen.

"Did you get my picture?"

He sighed and put aside the beer. She'd sent her picture by e-pic, electronic photo mail, and to his surprise she didn't look as bad as he'd thought.

She wasn't drop-dead ugly, but she looked somehow unreal, patched together from random parts. Her face looked like a doll's that had been broken and imperfectly mended.

Her downloaded snapshot had shown a nice body joined to that off-center face with its too-tightly stretched skin. She had beautiful blond hair, long and smooth, and she wore blue jeans and a pale green sweater.

She had nice tits, the kind that made him start to get hard and hot when he looked at them long enough and thought the right thoughts. Little waist, and a nice ass from what he could see. A lot better than that pig Gretchen.

He typed his reply to her. "You look fine. I told you, appearances don't matter. People who judge only by looks make me sick."

He took another drink and waited for her answer to appear. There was always a time lag between messages; it was one of the most maddening aspects of the MOONs, MOOs, and MUDs. A man had to be patient, he had to want what he was after, want it a lot.

"You can't say it doesn't matter," she answered. "It's shaped my whole life."

He raised one dark eyebrow. He had rubbed her wrong, bad move. He answered carefully. "I don't mean your emotions don't matter. They do. But you shouldn't obsess about your face. It's yours, so I like it."

"You're so sweet it's unbelievable," she answered.

He thought, *Unbelievable is right, bitch.*

He wrote, "I went to grade school with this guy that was a dwarf. The rest of us shot up tall. He didn't. But people who knew him didn't care. I didn't. He was Alex, my friend. I stopped noticing his body."

Alex the dwarf was a lie, of course, the sort in which he specialized, designed to disarm and beguile.

He added, "I kissed you when you got here, didn't I? What does it matter if you haven't got movie star lips? I don't care."

"I'm sorry," she answered. "I don't mean to belabor the point. I shouldn't be that way."

That's better, he thought. She sounds humble, grateful, apologetic, like she damn well should.

He typed in his message and keyed it in to appear on the screen:

> James Dean kisses your sweet mouth. "I kiss it because it's yours and I want to."

He elaborated, wooing her, seducing her. He wrote that he took her face between his hands and studied it, smiling.

He kissed her nose. "I kiss this nose because it's yours."

He kissed her eyes, her chin. "I kiss these eyes because they're your eyes. I kiss this curve of your jaw, because I like it, and I like it because it belongs to you. I kiss you, the outer you, but mostly the inner you, the sweetness of my sweet Lynette."

He could almost feel her shuddering with stunned pleasure, all those miles across the darkness, in godforsaken Kansas.

He could have her soon if he wanted. He knew this instinctively, in the marrow of his bones. Soon he would type that he was touching her breasts—and what lovely breasts they were, so lovely they should be naked and kissed, and he would kiss them.

Slowly, sentence by sentence, he'd work his way all over her body, until she was wet and reckless and crazy, and she'd do whatever he asked. If he told her to suck his cock, she'd do it, she'd write that she was doing just that.

But he wouldn't ask that yet; she had a restrained streak, and he had to take things slow. He'd save that until she was hooked, when she would do anything for him.

"Kiss me back," he instructed her. "Put your hands under my shirt. Touch me. Tell me about it."

She told him she was slipping her hands beneath his shirt. She said she touched the hard, warm flesh of his chest.

"Your fingers are grazing my nipples," he said. "And I'm going to stroke yours. Gently. Making them hard."

A tremor of anticipation shook him. He thought of her soft little body beneath his hands and got ready to unzip his jeans.

"Touch yourself for me," he told her. "Touch your breasts, hold them, squeeze them. Feel me touch them, too. Feel me kissing them, sucking them."

But then, goddam, she drew back. She suddenly chilled up, she turned cold as stone. It not only surprised him, it angered him. He swore. Stupid ugly little cunt, she'd probably never had a real lay in her life.

"Lynette?" he demanded. "What's wrong? We can give each other so much pleasure."

"No," she told him. "Look, I've never done this. I'm not ready for it."

He said, "Don't be afraid. I love you. You love me. There's nothing wrong. We're consenting adults."

For a long moment she didn't answer, and he cursed, not knowing if the gap in communication was due to the electronic lag or her stupid reluctance.

At last she said, "I don't feel right about it, that's all. You've done this before, haven't you?"

"No," he lied. "Never. You're the first one I ever wanted. It's just a way of being intimate together. What's wrong? Are you ashamed to touch yourself? Don't be. If you can't love yourself, you can't love anybody."

He cajoled, he soothed, he reasoned, he twisted reason. She was regretful and polite—God, she was always so prissily polite—but she held her ground. No virtual sex. Not now, at least.

I'll get you yet, you tricky bitch, he thought. *I'll have you down on your knees begging for it.*

So he drew a deep breath and again typed I love you, and went through the tiresome business of comforting and cuddling and telling her more lies. She'd caught him badly off-guard. He'd thought she'd be easier than this, he'd been goddam certain of it.

Although her sudden shyness frustrated him, it also made him all the more determined to have her. He would get her, oh, yes. He would. But he was horny, she was wearing him out, and the drink was bringing on a fuzzy-mindedness that was dangerous.

After constant repetitions of "I love you," and "What we have is really pure, really beautiful," and all the usual crap, he managed to escape from her and logged off.

He could log on again immediately as a featureless "guest" of Omega, and she would be none the wiser.

There were other women on Omega who'd gladly give him virtual sex. Lady Lay, for instance, who was a total, hopeless slut. She was so degraded it was impossible to degrade her further, but she did not appeal to him in the least. She repelled him, she was a turnoff. Even the idea of killing her didn't excite him.

Lady Lay was not worth killing. Only nice girls were.

Lynette was too troubled to go back to the real world. She brooded about James. James was his real name, he'd told her, and he'd laughed that his name was really very similar to James Dean's. It was James Deason.

She'd always thought of netsex as a dirty little joke that other people might sink to, but never her. Now that James wanted it, it no longer seemed funny. Would she lose him if she kept saying no? It was an agonizing possibility, a choice she'd never expected.

She didn't want to be alone, so she teleported to Ye Silent Woman Pub, where she could count on company; people always gathered there. But tonight at the pub's big table there were only two other characters, and she knew one of them well, Quicksilver. *Everyone* knew Quicksilver.

Quicksilver seemed to spend every waking hour on Omega and called herself "your friendly messenger service." If you could relay a message by no other means, you could entrust it to Quicksilver, who was utterly dependable. She was also one of Omega's most irreverent and knowing citizens.

"Flair, sweetie!" Quicksilver said and gave her a virtual hug of welcome. "Haven't seen you lately. Been with James Dean?"

Flair typed a nod and a smile, but made no comment. She sat at the table, wishing she was alone with Quicksilver so she could ask her about virtual sex. Quicksilver practiced it, certainly. Lately she was always going off with a macho character named Blue Rider. In public, their talk was full of sexual innuendo and teasing, and Lynette could not even imagine the things they probably did together.

Yet Quicksilver said virtual sex was not for everyone; each case was different, she said, and some people shouldn't try it. Was Lynette one of those people? If she was, was that good or bad?

"Hail, beautiful lady," Sir Parsival said to Flair. "Greetings and salutations. Welcome to our midst. You are most welcome at our humble gathering."

Flair gave Parsival a smile, although secretly she thought him an odd duck. She didn't know him well and didn't want to. He tried to sound lofty and medieval, but he came across as merely pompous, and he could say nothing simply or briefly.

His description was pure Parsival, eight convoluted paragraphs about the Round Table, King Arthur, the quest for the Grail; his appearance, his armor, his weapons, his shield, his coat of arms, his steed, his steed's trappings and armor; and finally Parsival's ideals: honor, virtue, chivalry, respect, high thoughts, giving to the poor, and defending the defenseless.

Parsival was always wordy and often ridiculous, and people made fun of him, behind his back or to his face. Yet he seemed painfully sincere. Flair doubted if he'd ever had virtual sex because it would violate his ethics. (Would anyone *want* to have sex with Parsival—even virtual sex?)

But Parsival had been in love once, hopelessly gaga over Selena the Moon Goddess. She'd dropped him when she met an intense character named Joachim the Beggar. Then she'd vanished completely from Omega, and so had Joachim.

Parsival claimed Joachim had done something sinister to Selena in real life. Quicksilver had finally told him to stop obsessing about it. "Chill out," she'd said. "You sound like you got a loose bolt in your helmet."

Flair hoped he wouldn't start carrying on about his lost love tonight; she was in no mood for it.

Suddenly, a character named Cochise appeared. Another regular on Omega, he had the odd habit of materializing at a gathering for only a few minutes at a time. He would ask three or four brusque questions, then disappear back to his private room, a place he called simply "A Place."

"Has anyyone seen Lacewing?" Cochise asked. "Has anyybodyy hear from her? If yyou see her tell her I was lookin for her okayy? Tell her I was thinking about her."

"If anybody can deliver the message, I can," Quicksilver assured Cochise, but her virtual action showed her rolling her eyes in mock despair.

Cochise described himself as tall, dark, handsome, muscular, and bronzed of skin, a warrior afraid of nothing. But his typing, spelling, and punctuation drove Quicksilver to distraction, and the *y* on his keyboard always stuck.

Cochise was obviously in love with the elusive Lacewing, who came to Omega at odd and infrequent intervals. When she did appear, she often dallied with him at his Place, even though she seemed far more sophisticated than he.

"Okayy," Cochise said, then gave Quicksilver a hug. "Hi, Flair," he added, but he ignored Sir Parsival. Then he vanished back into the electrons.

Quicksilver shook her head. "Now he'll teleport himself over to the Bathing Pool, and ask if anybody *there's* seen Lacewing. The boy's got it bad."

Flair gave Quicksilver a mischievous wink. "He'd forget Lacewing if you'd give him a break. He likes you, you know."

"He's too young for me," said Quicksilver. "I'm no cradle-snatcher."

"But he sayeth in his description that he be of three and twenty years," Parsival countered. "And thou art but of only four and twenty years thyself. Of what difference doth one year maketh?"

Quicksilver rolled her eyes again. "He's *not* twenty-three. He's lying. If he's any older than seventeen, I'll eat my hat. Better yet, I'll eat yours, which is metal."

"T'is wrong to lie," Parsival said. "It may lead to harm, yay, even unto great evil itself."

"We all lie, you ninny," Quicksilver said, but gave him an affectionate smile. "You're not really a knight. I hope you *know* that."

"In my heart I am," Parsival replied with atypical economy.

Blue Rider suddenly appeared, smiling at everyone. He bowed to Quicksilver, kissed her passionately, and said, "Come away, gorgeous. I'm in no mood to share you."

Quicksilver laughed. "I hope that's not the only foreplay you planned."

"Baby," Blue Rider said, "I've got foreplay and five play and six play and all the numbers—up to sixty-nine."

"That," said Quicksilver, "is an offer I can't refuse."

She kissed both Flair and Sir Parsival goodbye and said, "See you tomorrow. Flair, don't be such a stranger. James Dean can't have you *all* the time."

Flair forced herself to smile, but the couple had already vanished from the pub, leaving her alone with Sir Parsival.

"I wish she wouldn't go off with him," Parsival said. "She's too good for him. I don't trust him."

Flair blinked in surprise. Parsival was talking like a human being—what miracle had God wrought?

"Nothing can happen to her," she said. "Not really."

"He could deceive her, hurt her," Parsival said. "Besides, I don't like to see her cheapen herself. She's a great girl. She should have a boyfriend in real life, not this pretend crap, please excuse my language. She should place a higher value on herself. Have some standards."

A hot wave of guilt washed over her. "Maybe netsex isn't so bad," she said. "They're adults. It's not as if they're hurting anybody. It's a way to show affection. And—oh, I don't know what to think. I really don't."

"You sound like you're trying to talk yourself into accepting it," he said, surprising her again. She didn't like Parsival, of all people, making surmises about her sex life, especially correct ones.

She changed the subject. "You're talking differently. Why?"

"Well, we're alone," he said. "I talk like that as a public persona. I stay in character, like in a play. But with just one person it seems kind of awkward."

"Oh," she said. "I see." But she didn't. All she could think of was how he said Quicksilver was cheapening herself.

"I guess we've never been alone together," he said.

"No. We haven't."

He paused, but not for long. "Blue Rider comes on too strong. All he ever talks about is sex. I don't trust that Cochise guy, either. Why does he just come out of his room once an hour, then go right back? I mean he never has any company except Lacewing. He sits up there paging girls and trying to get them to join him. If he wants to mingle, why doesn't he stay where the people are?"

Oh, good heavens, she thought impatiently. *Everything's a conspiracy to him. I can't stand any more of this.*

Parsival picked up his virtual mug of ale and took a virtual sip. He sighed. "I still think about my girlfriend all the time. Selena. Did you ever meet her?"

"Excuse me. I have to go," she told him. "See you another time. Goodnight." She typed the command @quit and waited, teeth set.

"She's an extremely sensitive girl," he said, clearly ready to talk all night long. "She's really special. For instance—"

The connection broke. Her link to Omega was severed, plunging her back into the real world. She left Parsival in the pub alone and talking only to himself.

She turned off her computer and threw herself on her bed, her eyes burning. She shouldn't let Parsival's words hurt her—all he ever did was talk too much, and he sounded like an old woman when he did.

But that was the problem. He made her think of her grandmother. Her grandmother used to lecture her about virtue, values, and standards, and never, ever cheapening herself. "Self-respect," she always said, "is worth more than gold."

Her grandmother Katherine had lived with them, and she pounded her stern morality into Lynette all through childhood and adolescence. Lynette hadn't minded. She'd loved Katherine deeply and looked on her as the one absolutely dependable person in her life. The last time Lynette had cried was when her grandmother died.

She wanted to cry again tonight, but she did not let herself. She buried her face in her pillow and clenched her fists and wondered what to do about James. If he were there, really in the room with her, she had no doubts she'd give him her virginity.

But to pretend to do so by computer repulsed and frightened her. To write each other messages so they could simultaneously masturbate? It didn't seem an expression of love, only an ugly parody of it.

And how could she know that he loved her in spite of her face, when he had never seen her? If he really loved her, wouldn't he wait until he could hold her in his arms and touch her with more than empty words?

In Arkansas, Carrie sat swaying gently back and forth on the porch swing on the screened-in deck that overlooked the lake. The night was dark, and the lake shimmered, reflecting stars and the moon-silvered clouds.

The frogs sang shrilly to one another, and the crickets conversed in shorter, more rhythmic, bursts.

Next to the swing stood a small table holding a kerosene lamp, and she read by its light. Moths batted softly at the screens, enchanted by the flame that burned so cheerfully within the smoky glass chimney.

The book was worn because she had bought it years ago, when she was a sophomore in college. She would finish re-reading the first act of *Romeo and Juliet,* then blow out the lamp and ready herself for bed. She was tired from working in the garden, for the earth was stony and the weeds, which seemed to spring up magically each night while she slept, were deep-rooted and stubborn.

The play was so familiar to her that its tragedy didn't depress her; she was moved more by its beauty than its sadness. As she came to the end of the first act, she shook her head. Poor little Juliet, in a quandary over loving the wrong man.

Love, she thought. *What troubles young people got into because of it. What messes and muddles and heartbreaks.*

She was glad to be beyond it all.

FOUR

⟨∾⟩

ON SUNDAY MORNING, CARRIE DROVE TO KIMPLE HALL. THE UNIversity campus was nearly deserted, its lawns stretching out lush and empty. The big shade trees nodded sleepily in the breeze and the scent of honeysuckle haunted the air. From the surrounding town came the chime of church bells.

The brick building looked empty and locked against the outside world, but when she tried the front door, it swung open easily. She walked down the vacant hall, her footsteps echoing eerily. The door to room 27 stood open as if silently beckoning. *Wotthehell*, she thought and entered.

She was five minutes early, but Hayden Ivanovich and a thin, blond young man were already there. They stood by the lecturer's desk, before a green chalkboard filled with precise handwriting.

Both men turned when Carrie entered, and she smiled her most beguiling smile. Ivanovich's eyes ran up and down her body once, as if taking her measure without emotion. He did not smile back.

"Hello," she said, undaunted, and kept her smile in place. The young man gazed warily at her, but she thrust out her hand to him. "I'm Carrie Blue. You must be Edmon Welkin."

"Pleased t-to meet you," Edmon Welkin said. His mouth twitched crookedly, as if he were trying to smile but could not manage. Yet for such a wispy-looking boy, his handshake was surprisingly strong.

He was only a few inches taller than Carrie, five foot eight at the most, with a slight build and shoulders narrower than her own. His straight, fair hair was precisely trimmed, his nose was childishly snub, his lips prim, and his chin too short for the rest of his face.

His eyes were pallid blue with almost blond-white lashes, but they held her gaze with an almost fanatic steadiness. Carrie sensed a vulnerability in him, an insecurity deeply at odds with the determination in his gaze.

"Pleased to meet you," she said, and meant it. She turned to Ivanovich. "And to see you again," she said, with less sincerity.

She offered him her hand, and he shook it brusquely, released it quickly. "Take a seat," Ivanovich said, nodding at the rows of computer terminals.

She nodded and sat down, placing her notebook beside the computer. Edmon turned back to the board, took up the chalk, and began inscribing computer codes in his meticulous hand. Hayden Ivanovich, his face unreadable, crossed his arms and stared out the window at a magnolia tree.

Bold footsteps sounded in the hallway, growing nearer, and then Brooke Tharpe appeared at the door, looking as if she would rather be elsewhere, her chin held defiantly high.

Her dark hair was arranged in a gleaming coronet of braids almost too perfect to be real. But her horn-rimmed glasses sat askew on her nose, and her stocky body looked lumpish in a caftan of mustard yellow.

Ivanovich surprised Carrie by greeting Brooke almost warmly. He introduced her to Edmon, which made her expression grow haughtier than before, and Edmon's gaze did not seem nearly as steadfast when trained on someone his own age.

Ivanovich told Brooke to take a seat, and she did, to Carrie's left. She'd acknowledged Carrie's presence with the coolest and stiffest of smiles.

Ivanovich cleared his throat and said, "Let's start. Edmon? The audience is yours."

Carrie was taken aback when Ivanovich sat down at the terminal on her other side. His eyes met Carrie's, and he nodded almost imperceptibly toward Edmon as if to say, *Listen carefully.*

Carrie stared at the boy, who stood behind the desk fingering his piece of chalk and looking profoundly uneasy. His posture was tense with nervousness that seemed to war with his resolve.

Edmon Welkin was nineteen years old and he hated and feared public speaking with all his heart. His palms and armpits grew slick with sweat, his knees turned watery, and his heart banged in his chest as if it would explode through his breastbone.

He tried to ignore this. He put down the chalk and gripped the edges of the desk podium. The blond woman, Carrie Blue, smiled to encourage him; that helped. The Tharpe girl stared down at her desktop, as if purposely snubbing him. Paradoxically, that, too, helped.

Hayden Ivanovich watched in that cool, quiet way he had, but his scrutiny was not what so disquieted Edmon. Edmon was one of those unfortunates who fear only fear itself, and his anxiety over his own anxiety sometimes paralyzed him.

But he wanted these two women to hear the story of Monica Toussant and Gretchen Small from him; he knew it best because he'd lived it. He drew his breath in sharply and prayed to control his stuttering.

Carrie Blue nodded, as if to say, *Yes, I'm listening. I'm interested in what you have to say.*

Edmon said, "About a year and a half ago, I discovered the virtual reality communities." He hated how affected his voice sounded, but the only way he could keep from stammering was to speak so carefully he sounded aloof and stagy.

He said, "I became a character on Omega MOON. I met a girl, Monica T-Toussant from the University of T-Texas. Her character was named Galore. The character was flamboyant, but Monica wasn't. Not in real life.

"We were becoming—close. Then another character came between us. His name on Omega was Zimon. I don't know what it is in real life."

He pressed his lips together for a moment, struggling for the shortest way to tell his story. His thoughts always tumbled through his mind too swiftly and repetitively, outracing his stumbling tongue.

Carrie Blue jotted notes in her spiral notebook and looked at him expectantly. Brooke Tharpe scribbled so prolifically God only knew what all she was taking down. She was so short and round in that yellow thing she wore that she reminded him, uncharitably, of a plastic mustard dispenser.

He suddenly found himself painfully mute, unable to form a sentence. He could only stare at Brooke's rapidly moving pen, wondering how she could be writing so much. Was she writing down how nervous and fearful and foolish he looked?

Hayden Ivanovich glanced idly at Brooke, as if she didn't matter, then turned his attention back to Edmon. "Tell us about Monica."

Edmon came back to himself. "She and this Zimon became an—an item. He didn't log on every night. More like three or four nights a week. But when he did, she was with him the whole t-time, t-talking in her room with the door locked."

With painful clarity he remembered that locked door. Once it had always been open to him, but after Zimon came, Edmon was shut out.

He had to be honest about this, about everything. "If he wasn't there, she'd t-talk t-to me. But not about him. About him, she was mysterious. Then last fall, she said she was going t-to Atlanta. She wouldn't say why. But I think it was t-to meet him. And nobody's seen her since."

Carrie Blue stopped writing and sat up straighter. She asked, "But you're not sure she went to meet this Zimon?"

Edmon squared his thin shoulders. "No. But his character disappeared from Omega right after she disappeared in real life."

Brooke Tharpe never looked up at him; she just went on writing, writing, writing. How in God's name could she keep *doing* that?

"And what about Monica's character?" Carrie asked.

Edmon swallowed hard. When an Omega character wasn't being used by its owner, it "slept." When Monica disappeared, she'd left her door unlocked as it had been in the happy days before Zimon. Edmon could enter and see her in her big canopy bed, like a woman under an enchantment. He'd type @look Galore.

> Galore believes with all her heart that life should be a Mardi Gras that is both sensual feast and an intellectual adventure! She loves fantasy and is a hopeless romantic—are you one, too?
>
> Galore is an eighteen-year-old student of life and love, with long blond hair, seductive blue-green eyes, and a mesmerizing smile.
>
> She wears a skintight catsuit of glittering blue-green that shows the curves of her lithe body and a feathered emerald mask.
>
> She seems to be sleeping.

Edmon swallowed hard. For weeks Monica's character slept, and he felt compelled to go to her, as if holding a vigil by her bedside.

Then, after she had been inactive for three months, Omega removed her. Her character vanished and her room disappeared, and if he typed @who Galore, this message appeared: There is no character by that name.

Carrie Blue studied Edmon, one eyebrow cocked

thoughtfully. "No one's seen Monica since she went to Atlanta?"

"No," Edmon said, working harder to control his voice.
"I tried to get in touch with her and couldn't. Finally I called
the University of T-Texas in Austin. But they were closed-
mouthed, like something was wrong. So I called the Austin
police. They said her mother had filed a missing person's
report. Monica'd paid for a round-t-trip flight to Atlanta.
She went. But she never came back."

Brooke Tharpe kept her head bowed, writing away. Carrie looked grim. She asked, "Did you tell the police about
this Zimon character?"

"I t-t-told them," Edmon said. "They weren't interested.
I had no proof he had anything t-to do with her disappearing. They thought I was just jealous."

Carrie frowned and glanced at Hayden. He slipped her
an unreadable sidelong look, then nodded at Edmon. "Tell
them about Gretchen Small."

Edmon gripped the edges of the podium so tightly his
fingertips stung. "I met Gretchen in December. At first we
didn't hit it off, but then we got t-to know each other. We
t-talked on the phone. We sent each other e-mail and letters.
We were going t-to meet during spring break."

He hesitated. Never, in the best of times, had he been
Monica's only suitor. He'd been infatuated with her, but he
felt more deeply about Gretchen. She had seemed to him to
be the special person he had always hoped to meet.

He said, "About six weeks before break, a new character
showed up. His name was Joachim the Beggar. It was the
same story, almost exactly. He t-t-t-t—" Edmon stopped,
tried to get his breath. He willed the slamming beat of his
heart to slow, but it only banged harder.

"He t-t-took-took-took-took—he stole her. He was
mysterious, and she wouldn't t-t-t-talk-talk—she wouldn't
speak about him. She changed her mind about meeting me
for spring break. She went t-to Chicago instead. I know it
was t-t-to-to see him. But she never came back."

He had lost control of his speech, and done so badly, he
realized, pressing his lips together again. His face was hot

with embarrassment. He could feel the sweat in his armpits and palms and knew he might as well be standing before these people naked.

"Gretchen's got no family," he said, gritting his teeth. "Except a brother in southern Florida. Nobody reported her gone. I couldn't stand it. Last week I went t-t-t-to Memphis. The police acted like I was insane."

"Tell them about her apartment," Hayden said, his voice quiet and even.

Edmon fumbled with his collar button. "She lived alone in a little rented house close t-t-t-to Memphis State. She was keeping it for the summer. I found the landlord, and I bribed him t-to open it up, said I was worried about her."

Carrie stared so earnestly at him that he felt she was trying to buoy him up by sheer willpower, give him strength. He was grateful, for he'd reached the hardest part of his story.

"Right away we knew something was wrong," he said, trying to keep his voice from choking. "She had one of those doors with a mail slot. There was mail all over the floor, weeks of it. Her plants were all dead or dying. The refrigerator was full of spoiled food."

He paused, his lower lip trembling with emotion. "She had a cat, an old cat. She loved that cat, she'd had it since she was a little girl. But we found it by her bedroom window. It had tried to claw its way through the screen. It had caked blood on its paws. It had starved t-t—t-to death. She *never* would have let that happen. Never."

His voice broke and he hated himself for his show of grief. "The landlord called the police. They contacted her brother. He came t-to Memphis. When he saw the place, he filed a missing person's report. But she's never been found. I'm afraid for her. I—love her."

There, he thought fatalistically, he'd said it aloud in front of real, live people: he loved Gretchen Small.

For no other reason would he have stood up like this before strangers, put his speech defect and stage fright on display, reveal his private life, show his most intimate emotions, except for Gretchen. For her, he would brave anything, even ridicule.

He set his jaw and said, "Are there any questions?"

A dozen questions surfaced in Carrie's mind, and she began to ask them, rapid-fire. Edmon answered, serious and logical. Yes, he thought the same man had lured off both girls, the cases were too similar for coincidence. Yes, he feared something sinister happened.

Carrie asked exactly what did he expect her and Brooke to do?

"Find out if he's back," he said without hesitation, "looking for another girl. He seems t-to like a certain type. She may seem confident at first, but deep down, she's shy, sensitive. She doesn't have a lot of friends. Or much of a family t-to look out for her."

She said, "Both these girls were involved with you first. Do you think this man knows you in real life? That he has some kind of grudge against you?"

Edmon shook his head. "I don't think I have enemies. I think he just likes the same sort of girl I do. And he probably figures any girl who'd like me would be easy t-to steal."

You poor kid, Carrie thought. He had the same look in his face as Gretchen Small, the somebody-please-love-me look. She said, "Both girls were secretive, they didn't want to discuss the new man. You think he has a cover story that makes him hard to trace? So he can lie about who he really is and where he's at?"

Edmon nodded. "Monica and Gretchen were both infatuated with somebody. But they wouldn't talk about him. I don't know why. And there's no trace of him."

"Maybe there is a trace," Carrie countered. "But the authorities are keeping it quiet. That happens."

Hayden spoke, one corner of his mouth turned down. "That's my department," he said. "Our agency has contacts in Austin and Memphis. Authorities searched both women's places. So far there's no lead to any likely suspect."

"But," Carrie persisted, "are your sources telling the whole truth?"

Hayden's expression didn't change. "I don't know. I can't demand all the answers. I get what I can."

Carrie paused, considering. "All right," she said. "Suppose I'm on Omega and I find some guy who wants me to meet him in real life. Say that he's charming, he's charismatic, but I have no proof he's who he says he is. This is the sort of man you're looking for?"

"Yes," said Edmon. "Precisely."

Carrie felt a prickle of concern. "So what happens if a man like this asks Brooke or me to meet him? What then? Do we actually go?"

Hayden shook his head. "That's my department again. We'll hire a woman to meet him. I'll be right behind her; she won't be in danger."

Carrie's brow furrowed. "But are we supposed to give him our real addresses and phone numbers?"

"No," Ivanovich said. "Or your names. We've got aliases for you and mail drops. We've arranged to get you each an extra phone line. There's no way he can find out who you are or where you're at."

A black leather attaché case sat on the floor beside him. He snapped it open, drew out a gray folder and a white one. He stood, stepped to Carrie's desk and laid the gray one beside her computer.

He said, "You're Melissa Blanchard, sophomore here at the U. of A. Communications major, twenty years old, going to summer school. You've got a post office box in Blanchard's name at the main post office. On the first page is your code name and your password to log on to the Internet. Edmon's routed you through commercial systems, the hardest to trace. You're completely covered. You're safe."

Wow, thought Carrie, opening the folder. *This morning I was plain old me. Now I have an alias, a private post office box, and a second phone. AND I'm twenty-something years younger. Whoop-tedoo.*

Hayden handed Brooke the white folder. "You're Sandra Faircloth. Trinity College, Fort Smith, Arkansas. You're nineteen years old, a literature major, home for the summer in

Tontitown, Arkansas. We've got you a Tontitown post office box."

Carrie stole a glance at Brooke. Brooke nodded, her eyes cast stubbornly down, her dark crown of hair gleaming under the fluorescent lights. She had not asked a single question since Edmon had started talking. She had not deigned to say one word.

They did not break for lunch; they worked straight through. Edmon taught them the basic lore of the MOON, the simplest commands to communicate speech and action, how to "see" objects and other people, and how to transport from place to place.

Carrie's brain swam with codes and terminology. Edmon was a competent teacher, but his stutter made him a terse one; he clearly didn't like repeating himself. Hayden Ivanovich was taking notes just as she was, and she was curious as to why.

"Let's log on to Omega," Edmon said finally. "I'll log on with you as a guest. Each of us will be a guest named for some sort of animal."

He took a seat at a terminal. Carrie studied her notes and gritted her teeth, but beside her, Brooke was already softly tapping at the keys, moving the computer mouse, tapping again.

Carrie made a dozen mistakes before she could reach access to Omega. On her right, Hayden seemed to struggle, too. "Damn!" he whispered with more passion than she'd have expected.

He typed something, almost fiercely. He waited a moment, then muttered, "Ha! I'm in."

Carrie glanced at him and he gave her a smug look, then turned back to his computer screen. She stifled a swear word of her own; it was humiliating to be the slowest student. She wasn't used to it.

She was poised on the threshold of Omega, and all she had to do was type the words, "connect guest."

But she had a stiff forefinger on her left hand, a souvenir from her glory days as a shortstop on the women's softball team; she was tense, and she typed connect fuest and then connect guets but finally connect guest—and there, miraculously, she was. Words scrolled down the screen, telling her she was connected to Omega MOON under the temporary identity "Lark Guest."

She entered the Ivory Gate and found herself standing on the shade-dappled road that led to the Palace of Pleasure. Birds sang in the forest, and a brown rabbit hopped into the shelter of a patch of ferns. On either side of her, paths crooked off into the woods, one broad, one narrow. She saw that she was not alone.

> Hedgehog Guest, Goose Guest, and Tiger Guest are here.
> Hedgehog Guest bows graciously to you. Hedgehog Guest says, "Welcome to Omega MOON. I'll guide you as best I can, but be careful. This world is unpredictable."
> Goose Guest waves dips down in a graceful courtsey. Goose Guest says, "It's lovely here, don't you think? I love the way the sunlight turns the clouds' edges to silver, and the breeze rustles the leaves of the trees. Did you see the rabbit? He's still in the shadows, watching us."

Carrie looked up from the computer screen with a start, as if she had just witnessed an act of black magic. "Edmon—are you the hedgehog? Is Brooke the Goose Guest?"

Edmon gave her a tight little smile. "Yes. But talk to us on Omega, not here."

Carrie squinted at her list of codes, typed in her message, and saw it appear on her screen.

> You bow politely to Hedgehog Guest and Goose Guest. You say, "Thank you kindly. It's nice to be here."

She felt a childish thrill. This world seemed so foreign, she might have indeed just set foot on the real moon.

> Hedgehog Guest says, "All right, we're all here. Let's explore."

They explored. At the end of three hours, Carrie was exhausted. She'd been to the Elysian Fields, the Bower of Oberon, Ye Silent Woman Pub, the Hustler's Billiard Parlor, the Bathing Pool, the Romance Ballroom, Le Club du France, the Mermaid Tavern, the Marabar Caves, and fourteen rooms in the Palace of Pleasure, each more dizzying than the last.

She met dozens of strangers, both guests and characters. Some were cordial, some aloof, some rude, some crude, and some brutal.

Edmon inadvertently insulted a character named Gaston, who staked him to a virtual anthill, where Edmon was trapped for twelve minutes while ants bit, stung, and ate him alive. He emerged, whole again, and was remarkably philosophic about his temporary demise.

Carrie herself gave a sassy answer to a character aptly called Short Fuse. He teleported her to a South American river where piranhas stripped her flesh from her bones. She was no worse for it, except in mood.

She transported herself back only to find that Short Fuse had sent Edmon to the Hell, but Edmon, resilient, returned and led them to the Everlasting Hot Tub Party.

Fourteen other people were in the Hot Tub, and Carrie was bewildered by the babble. Half a dozen conversations buzzed at once, like mingling swarms of drunken bees.

She was even more distracted by actions. People poked, stroked, dunked, and hugged her. The hot tub party, like most of Omega, seemed completely chaotic, a madhouse without laws or logic.

She was also plagued by unseen people who could somehow see her and who paged her from other parts of Omega.

Hayden, as the Tiger Guest, had disappeared, but she had no time to wonder what had become of him. A character named Damian Two paged her from the patio of the Romance Ballroom. "Hi. I'm a horny guy looking for fun. Are you male or female?"

"Female," Carrie paged back, and winced as two other characters in the Hot Tub began to call each other obscene names.

"Female, huh?" Damian Two paged back. "You want to go someplace and have MOON sex? I look like Mel Gibson, and I'm awesomely endowed. You won't be able to get enough of me."

"Go to hell," Carrie paged back in disgust.

Another character, Wild Thing, immediately paged her from the Dark Tower. "Are you male or female?" Wild Thing asked.

"Which are you?" Carrie asked warily.

"Male," Wild Thing answered.

"Sorry," Carrie paged. "I'm male, too."

"Fine with me," Wild Thing replied. "Have you got a pretty mouth? You want to meet in the Sex Chambers?"

"No," Carrie shot back. "Buzz off."

Three people in the Hot Tub were having a fight, and two others had started to kiss and fondle each other. Carrie looked rather widly around the tub for Edmon but couldn't find him. Brooke, too, had vanished, and Carrie had a frightening sense of being abandoned.

Then Damian Two teleported in to the Hot Tub from the patio of the Romance Ballroom. Immediately he closed in on Carrie. "Hiya, babes," he said and began to lick her.

"Stop that!" she ordered, infuriated, and wondered what would happen if she gave him a virtual punch in his virtual nose. Would she be staked to an anthill? Sent to Hell? Fed to the piranahs again? Wotthehell. She typed that she drew back her fist and struck him, but it had no effect.

Damian Two kept licking her. He seized her hand, put it on his crotch, and whispered, "I'm hard. Touch me."

Carrie was so appalled she forgot how to teleport out of the Hot Tub. Someone named Zeno had edged up to her, and he, too, began licking her and groping at her breasts.

Then, as if heaven-sent, Tiger Guest paged her from the Art Gallery. Ivanovich, she thought, thank God!

"How are you doing?" he paged.

Damian Two unzipped his jeans, exposing his erect penis. "Does that turn you on?" he whispered.

"I'm doing terrible," Carrie paged Hayden. "I'm being molested. Where's Edmon? How do I get out of here?"

Damian Two closed her fingers around his penis and held them there, moving her virtual hand up and down, and Zeno thrust his hot, wet tongue into her ear. "Hey, pussy," he said. "How about a blow job?"

Someone in the Hot Tub was singing an idiotic song about a purple dinosaur. Somebody was calling somebody else a dumb fuck.

Hayden paged, "Type '@join Tiger Guest.'"

Carrie tried to ignore the bedlam around her, the scrolling words that said she was being licked, sucked, stroked, caressed. She typed @join Tiger Guest.

She would have liked to have given Damian Two and Zeno each a virtual kick to the groin, but there was no need. Magically she escaped them and found herself in a new place.

> You are in the mezzanine of the Art Gallery, by the glass case containing the bust of Queen Nefertiti. With her perfect profile, Nefertiti seems to gaze down the half-lit hallway leading to the east, as if something of great portent waits there for you.
> Tiger Guest is here.

Carrie was breathing hard and her pulses thudded. The incident in the Hot Tub had shaken her more than she could have imagined.

"Are you okay?" Hayden asked.

She refused to lie. "No. I was pawed. It was disgusting."

"Take it easy," he said. "Nothing really happened. People were hitting keys, that's all. Nobody touched you."

She answered, "I don't care. Nobody ever treated me like that. I feel used, dirty."

"No," he said, "you're all right."

The he did something she had not expected.

Tiger Guest put his arms around you. "It's okay," he says. "Everything's fine."

His imaginary touch, so different from the others,

should not have comforted her, but it did. She felt safer, warmer, no longer alone, no longer menaced.

It was an illusion, she knew, nothing but words on a screen. But for a few magical seconds, it felt real and it felt good.

FIVE

———✤———

Edmon paged Hayden. "Brooke's trapped. She's got to break her connection to Omega. Are you ready to log off?"

Hayden was ready, all right. He burned to get back to the solid, weighty world where he could see and hear and taste and touch things. Everything happened too fast and easily on Omega. And too crazily.

He said to Carrie, "Want out of this cockamamy place?"

"Yes!" she answered. "A thousand times yes!"

He paged Edmon. "We're ready."

"Fine," Edmon answered. "Talk to you later."

"You remember how to get out?" Hayden asked Carrie.

He still had her in his virtual embrace, but she'd said nothing, made no show of resistance. Was she ignoring him, as she should? Or maybe—quite possibly—she hadn't even noticed. How was a man to know in a madhouse like this?

She said, "I think so. Just type '@quit.'"

"Right. Let's get the hell out of Oz. Ready?"

"Ready," she said.

"I could use a drink afterward," he said, surprising himself. "How about you?"

"Absolutely."

"Good. You go first."

He waited because he didn't want her left behind alone again. She vanished from the Art Gallery.

He thought, *Fuck you, Omega.* With a feeling of renegade satisfaction, he typed the command @quit.

> You find yourself transported West of the Moon. Behind you, in the distance, you hear music and laughter. You pass through the Gate of Horn and dissolve into the ordinary . . .
> |Telnet| link broken
> We are returning you to the host system.

Hayden found himself staring at an ordinary computer screen with the ordinary Internet menu. He felt as if he'd just awakened from a chaotic and sinister dream.

He turned his gaze from the screen and his eyes met Carrie's. He felt an unaccountable jolt in his solar plexus and, simultaneously, a feeling of self-disgust. He'd truly almost forgotten that she'd been sitting safely beside him the whole time, and that Edmon and Brooke were in the same room.

For a time he'd forgotten everything except what had been on the screen. He'd done things he wouldn't ordinarily do, including embracing Carrie Blue and asking her out for a drink. Damn, he thought, displeased—what had happened to him on Omega—witchcraft?

Perhaps Carrie felt the same. Her expression was startled, almost wary. With a pleasantly guilty twinge he recalled that, only moments ago, he'd pretended to hold her in his arms. He didn't know how she felt about that particular charade, but she was looking at him differently than before.

For once she didn't seem so damn jaunty and self-assured. He didn't feel so self-assured himself, but he had an advantage and decided to push it.

"Still want that drink?" he asked.

She gave him a ghost of her old smile, not much of a smile, really, but enough to make those damn dimples play.

"Yes," she said, "I do."

Brooke's fingers trembled so much that she could barely write. Her blood hummed and her heartbeat was wild with exhilaration. She wanted only to go home, to the sanctuary of her apartment, and savor what she'd just experienced.

But Edmon was at the podium again, lecturing in his prissy, theatrical voice, warning them about the dangers of Omega as if he were their nervous maiden aunt.

"What happened t-to Carrie was extreme," he said. "But it happens. The MOON has guardians, however. They're called wizards, but they live in the mist. Page them for help."

Wizards in the mist, Brooke thought, an electrifying thrill running up her spine. Suddenly she could see these wizards, clearly and in enormous detail, and they were far more real to her than Edmon was.

"Wizards are just computer programmers," Edmon said. "They've achieved t-trust on the MOON, and they've been elevated t-to positions of authority, that's all.

Brooke barely heard him. In her notebook, she was describing wizards, bearded and hunched with age. Out of the shadows they peered at her with ancient eyes hypnotic and as yellow as topaz.

"But you also saw," Edmon said, "another sort of problem. Some characters have the power t-to t-transport you against your will. If you offend someone, he might send you to Hell. No big problem, it happens t-to everyone. Just t-transport back."

Brooke wrote this down dutifully, then made notes about the Fourth Circle of Hell, where damned lovers were transformed into flames that chased each other, forever ravenous with desire and forever unsatisfied . . .

Edmon droned on. "But some characters have programmed punishments and t-traps of their own. I got staked to the anthill. Carrie got eaten by piranhas."

He fidgeted, tugging at his shirt collar. "Once something

like that starts happening t-to you, the only way to stop it is t-to switch off the computer.

"Somebody sent Brooke t-to Araby and put her in a t-time t-trap," he stammered. "Once you get in a t-time t-trap, there's no escape. You *have* t-to shut off the computer. If she hadn't, she'd still be caught there."

Brooke cringed. Being caught in the time trap was the only thing that happened on Omega that had disturbed her. The trap was described as a hollow cube with sides of glass. There was no door, and no matter how hard she beat on its walls, she could not escape. She could see outside, but everything seemed to be happening in maddeningly slow motion, strangely lifeless.

"Some people program sex acts," Edmon said, blushing slightly. "Virtual rapes. This is supposed t-to be forbidden, but it happens. So if someone starts running a rape program on you, switch off your machine; it's the only way t-to escape. Then log on and report it t-to a wizard."

"Electronic rape," Carrie Blue said in disgust. "My God. This is better living through science?"

"I'm sorry," Edmon said, and looked embarrassed, as if it were his fault.

Rape—shut off machine, Brooke wrote mechanically, but went back to describing the doomed lovers in Hell. Oh, if only Edmon would stop talking! His prim voice dulled the exquisite sharpness of what she'd felt on Omega.

At last, praise God, Edmon finished his warnings, and she was free to go. Hastily she gathered up her things, mumbled a perfunctory goodbye, and escaped to the parking lot ahead of the others.

But there her car betrayed her. The motor groaned and rasped, but refused to turn over, and she was trapped again, this time in real life.

Carrie Blue and the Ivanovich man came out of the building together, with Edmon following. Edmon's frame was so slight and the briefcase he carried so large that he looked like a child unsuccessfully playing grown-up.

The three converged on her with relentless helpfulness, and she died a series of tiny deaths by embarrassment. Her rusted Chevy Nova was a mystery to her, as were most things mechanical. She cursed the all-too-familiar feeling of helplessness that engulfed her, but she feigned an almost arrogant indifference to her predicament.

She stood, looking bored, as Hayden and Carrie jumpstarted the car, and its engine finally coughed feebly back to life. Edmon had stood by watching, as useless as Brooke, but too chivalrous to leave.

Brooke thanked them tersely and drove off, her car rattling so loudly that she felt like a dog with a tin can tied to its tail. Her face burned with humiliation.

Never in real life did she feel competent or at ease— except when she wrote. Only then did she feel in touch with something powerful and mysterious and meaningful.

But this last year even writing had threatened to fail her. Almost fanatically Brooke had worked on the prose epic of a barbarian princess, a story that had obsessed her since adolescence. The tale was mythic, full of drama and grandeur and heroism, all the things for which she hungered and that real life had never given her.

She'd written and rewritten the first hundred and fifty pages so often that she'd lost count. Where the story actually led, how it ended, was vague to Brooke. Revise as she might, this didn't change. The pages were crammed with lavish descriptions and detailed characterizations—but nothing ever *happened.*

This drove Dr. Holloway mad, and he, in turn, filled her with despair. Lately he had taken to sniping at Brooke with acid personal remarks.

The most unfair thing he'd said was that she wrote fantasy because she was frightened of life. Brooke was not frightened of life; she ignored it because she found it dull and wanting.

The longer she spent in her dream world, the more awkward she felt in the real one; it seemed both humdrum and hostile. She didn't belong there, she didn't fit in, she didn't know how to act, and she didn't bother to learn.

Real life felt small, grinding, and empty; it had never welcomed her nor she it. Real life was like the time trap. It happened too slowly, it crept in a petty pace from day to day, it was a tale told by an idiot, full of sound and fury, signifying nothing, and she could not connect with it.

But today she had discovered Omega, and it was more wonderful than she could say—an entire world made of writing. The memory of it brought excitement rushing back, and a sensual tingle ran through her veins, like pleasant, lively fire.

Here, she had thought when she entered the Ivory Gate. A sense of rightness, of destiny gripped her.

Here. Here. I belong here.

Plato's was a subterranean little bar and restaurant just off the Fayetteville town square. To enter its depths, patrons descended a flight of narrow cement stairs and passed through an ancient green door. The interior was so dim that shadows swallowed up the corners even on a sunny afternoon.

After a beer and a cheeseburger, both satisfyingly real, Carrie felt closer to normal. Hayden ordered them each a second beer, and she didn't protest. Yet he wasn't talkative, and she wasn't certain what he expected of her.

"So how old did Edmon and Brooke make you feel?" she asked brightly. "Hopping all over Omega like crickets?"

The corner of Hayden's mouth took on a satirical quirk. "They grew up with computers. It's second nature to them. Brooke may not know what a spark plug is, but she burned up the keyboard."

His half-smile died and he studied her in that disconcerting way he had. "Are you all right now?"

Reluctantly, Carrie thought of the Hot Tub. The memory of her assault should be fading, but it was still vivid and stinging, and so was her anger.

"Being eaten by piranhas is one thing. It's just a stupid joke," she said. "But being manhandled is different. That's—personal."

"It may happen again. Does that throw you?"

She jerked her chin up to a defiant angle. "I'm not afraid, if that's what you mean."

"I didn't say you were."

"I know it wasn't real," she said. "But at the time, it *seemed* almost real. Words are very—personal to me. I was caught off guard. I won't let it happen again."

She realized part of the shock of Omega had been that she could not defend herself. In real life she could do so and had. During her stints as a cocktail waitress she had fended off drunks, and at school she had handled rowdy male students, some of them large. She knew self-defense well and had taught it to her boys. She could confront an aggressive man, and unpleasantly surprise him. But on Omega, she'd been helpless, and she resented it.

"You'll go back?" Hayden asked, sounding almost bored.

"Of course," she said. "It's a job."

"Do you believe Edmon's story?"

His scrutiny made her uneasy, so she stared at her glass. She traced her finger carefully down its frosted side, leaving a trail. "I do. I usually know when someone's faking. When he said he loved her, he had tears in his eyes."

Hayden's mouth twisted. "Right. He's a geek, but a sincere geek."

Carrie looked up sharply. "Don't call him that. He's different, that's all. It's hard being different. When you're as young as he is, it hurts. It hurts a lot."

She stared again at the glass and traced another line parallel to the first, but she could feel Hayden's gaze on her. It gave her a prickling sensation along her spine, and suddenly she wished she hadn't come.

He reached over and drew a third line down her glass, between the other two. "You care about kids, even the oddballs. You must have been a good teacher."

His action surprised her; it implied an intimacy to which she wouldn't assent, and if he was trying to flatter her, she would have none of it. Unsmiling, she said, "I wasn't good enough. Too many students. Not enough time. Never enough time."

"So tell me," he said, "what brought you here, away from the joy of teaching?"

"I wanted more."

"What does 'more' mean?"

She shrugged. "For one thing, teaching in a college or a community college."

"A community college?" His tone was skeptical. "That's more?"

"Yes," she said with feeling. "Wherever I go, it *won't* be Bitter Water, Nebraska. I've always wanted to teach college. Always, my whole life. And I can write what I want."

He gave her a crooked smile, and for the life of her, she couldn't tell if it was friendly or condescending. "And what will you write?"

"I'm working on a book of stories about my grandmother. I want it to be worthy of her. She was special."

He cocked an eyebrow as if in challenge. "Special how?"

"She was strong; she was wise," she answered. "She did everything. She was born on a ranch in southern Arkansas, and her family moved to Oklahoma by covered wagon when she was twelve. She was a nurse in World War One, she survived the great influenza epidemic. She came back to the States and married a doctor right here, in Fayetteville. She taught nursing at the university. When my father deserted my mother and sister and me, she took us in. And she was one of the only two people in my life who ever—"

She stopped, not wanting to finish the sentence. She smiled, made a dismissive gesture, raised her glass and took a drink.

He watched her. "One of the only two people who did what?"

She set the glass back down and made her face blank. "Who ever took my dreams seriously," she said blithely. "She told me to follow them."

"She was one. Who was the other one?"

For a moment she remembered the other one with such intensity that it hurt. In her mind's eye she saw him, tall and handsome and laughing, his dark golden hair glinting in the sunlight.

"Somebody I knew," she said vaguely and stared at the bubbles winking in her glass.

"A man?" he asked.

She nodded, her lips clamped shut.

"Ah." His voice was almost mocking. "What happened to him?"

She got an odd, sickly feeling in her throat. "Vietnam happened to him," she said. "He died."

"Oh," he said.

He didn't say he was sorry, and Carrie didn't know whether to be relieved or offended. She glanced at him resentfully and saw that he had a harsh, almost frozen expression on his face, his mouth set at a bitter slant.

At that moment, somehow, she knew. He, too, had been in Vietnam.

"You were there," she said, "weren't you?"

"Yeah," he said tonelessly.

"How long?"

"Three and three-quarters years."

She tried to read his face and couldn't. "A tour was a year. Why the three-quarters? Were you wounded?"

He raised his beer and took a sip, then set the mug back down. "I was never wounded. Not even once."

You pried out my secret, Carrie thought. *I want yours.* She pressed on. "Then what happened to you?"

His expression had gone from hard to merely cynical. "P.O.W. Not quite two years."

"Oh," she said.

Like him, she didn't say that she was sorry, but she knew she didn't have to. They both were sorry, it was a given. "God," she said, letting her gaze fall to the table, "it was a dirty little war, wasn't it."

"Nobody exactly said 'Welcome home, soldier,' " he said. "Nobody was too proud of that one."

She nodded. They were silent a moment. It was as if by saying very little, they'd achieved a strange intimacy, more than either wanted.

She said, "Students today think it's a war from ancient history. They don't understand what it was like."

"I know," he said.

She took a deep breath. "So," she said, "I suppose it was quite terrible being a prisoner."

He gave a short, harsh laugh. "It was no picnic. I fared better than most. I was always lucky. I never came close to dying. Lost a lot of weight. Had a bad bout with malaria, that was the worst."

Carrie studied his face, which told her nothing. He didn't seem blasé about being a prisoner, but neither did he seem to carry the experience like a cross.

She said, "And after you came home?"

A one-cornered smile flickered on his lips, then quickly faded. "First, got drunk and stayed drunk for three months. Then sobered up, went back to college, got married, graduated, got a job."

"What sort of job?" she asked. "You were in law enforcement, I can tell. Which kind? City? County? State?"

"Federal," he said.

She was impressed in spite of herself. "Which branch?"

He gave her his half-smile. "What is this? An interrogation?"

"I'm curious, that's all," she said and showed her dimples. "Which branch?"

"The one that's least popular right now," he said levelly. "ATF."

Carrie blinked with surprise. The Bureau of Alcohol, Tobacco, and Firearms was beleaguered by attackers who accused it of a hundred different abuses. The agency had been rocked to its foundation by its botched raid on the Branch Davidian compound in Waco, Texas, two years ago. The raid on the armed cult had gone horribly awry, turning into a forty-five-minute gun battle that killed six Davidians and four agents.

First the Davidian leader, David Koresh, held off the ATF; then he held off an FBI siege that lasted over seven weeks, ending when the Davidian compound burst into flames, leaving Koresh and eighty of his followers dead.

Although two separate investigations had confirmed the Davidians had set the blaze themselves rather than surrender, some held that a murderous federal government was lying, that Koresh and his followers were martyred heroes, and the agents of the ATF were fascists, "jack-booted thugs" as brutal and unprincipled as Nazi storm troopers.

Last spring, to protest what the government had done at Waco, sympathizers had blown up the Federal Building in Oklahoma City, killing 169 more people. Waco, some claimed, had started a "second American Revolution." The ATF should be dismantled, claimed its enemies; the gun was God in America and ATF was Satan.

She said, "Why'd you choose ATF?"

He shrugged, almost idly. "After the war, I liked ideas like 'law and order.' I chose federal level because after the Hanoi Hilton, this country looked pretty damned good. I liked ATF. It was a crazy agency, but I'd have worked the job twenty-four hours a day if I could."

Carrie was puzzled. "Then why'd you leave?"

"It was time."

"Did it have anything to do with Waco?"

"In a way," he said, sounding bored again. "Let's talk about something else. If you were living in Arkansas with your grandmother, how'd you get clear up to Nebraska?"

"My mother remarried, we moved. That's all."

"Why'd you join the police?"

She smiled ruefully. "It seemed like a romantic, rebellious thing to do. I did *not* want to teach high school English, it was my worst nightmare. I was going to be a writer and I wanted adventures. Besides, I was going to make money for grad school. I was going to be a writer *and* a professor. I had everything all planned. I was going to Iowa State."

He gave her a measuring glance. "But you didn't."

"Life got in the way."

"Life does," he said.

"I don't have any regrets," she said defensively. "I have two wonderful sons that I think turned out pretty well. I wouldn't trade that for anything."

He gave her a look that said all women talked like that. She retaliated by going into full motherhood mode.

"Phil's the older one," she said. "He's an accountant in Lincoln. He's very mathematical."

He nodded with the indifferent air that told her he didn't wish to hear any more.

She persisted. "Joel's a year younger. He's in medical school. At Creighton University in Omaha. He's engaged to a lovely girl. They'll be married next spring. They've been going together since seventh grade. I have pictures. Would you like to see?"

She reached for her purse, but Hayden touched her wrist, a signal to stop. His mouth took on its sardonic smirk again. "Another time, maybe."

It was only the lightest of touches, but it seemed to linger on her skin. She was startled, but refused to show it. "I could tell you some of the cute things they said when they were little."

He picked up his glass. "I'd rather hear what you think of Omega. Outside of the Hot Tub incident."

"Omega. It's scary, it's pointless, it's disgusting," she said. "But fascinating. Maybe even seductive."

"Interesting word choice."

"I mean I've heard it can be addictive. You can get too caught up in it if you don't have both feet on the ground."

"But you do?"

Carrie was unnerved by his puzzling manner, so double-edged. He seemed both disdainful and flirtatious, as if he couldn't make up his mind how to treat her. He kept her off-balance and feeling subtly threatened.

She smiled and tried to change the focus from herself to him. "What about your personal life?" she asked. "You said you were married. You're not any longer?"

"Divorced." He took a drink of beer and set the mug carefully back on the ring it had made on the tabletop.

"Any children?" she asked, searching desperately for neutral ground.

She thought she saw an almost furtive emotion register on his face, then disappear. He gave her his half-smile. "Why do women always want to talk about kids? Let's give the personal stuff a rest."

All right, Carrie thought in frustration. *But if you don't want us to get to know each other, why did you ask me here?*

"We were discussing Omega," he said. "Do you believe Edmon can track down this stalker he thinks is there?"

"Absolutely not," Carrie said. "Do you?"

He laughed. "Not a chance."

Again she was puzzled. "Then why'd you take his case?"

"By default. I was the only one in the agency who'd touch it with a stick. Everybody else thinks it's harebrained. Frankly, I do, too."

Carrie was even more puzzled. "Why'd you log on to Omega with us? Are you going along with us as a protector or something?"

"I'm nobody's knight," he said. "Leave that to Edmon. I'm curious about modes of communicating on the Internet. Omega's a new one to me."

She drew her brows together. "Why are you curious?"

"The MOON, the MOOs—they seem like toys. The students go there to play. But it's a new communications technology, which means a new frontier for criminals. There's damned little law to stop them from exploiting it."

"Crime on Omega? What kind? Besides stalking?"

"Think about it," he said. "You can set up private rooms and have private conversations. Omega even has its own mail system. You can't get to it from the outside. Anybody can use it, drug dealers, weapon smugglers, terrorists, pedophiles, anybody. All these people do use the Internet, it's a fact. So I wonder who's using Omega."

Terrorists, weapons, that's still what interests you, she thought. *You think you've walked away from it all, but you haven't, have you.*

She glanced at her watch and was startled to see that it was past five o'clock. She always called her sons before five on Sundays when the rates were lower—always. But today, she had forgotten.

"Oh," she said, truly distressed. "I'm sorry, but—"

"But it's getting late," he said, finishing for her. "Yeah. For me, too. I'll drive you back to Kimple Hall so you can pick up your car."

"Fine," she said.

As they ascended the stairs out of Plato's, she gave him her most noncommittal smile. "By the way . . ."

"Yes?"

"Back on Omega, when I was upset," she said, "you put your arms around me. Was that your law enforcement training? The standard 'comfort the assaulted woman' strategy?"

"No," he said.

She gave him a questioning look.

"I wanted to see if it'd give me a buzz," he said with his half-smile.

She didn't know whether to be angry or to laugh. "Well?" she challenged. "Did it?"

"No," he said. "Did it do anything for you?"

"Of course not," she lied. "It was only words."

On this Sunday, Jon Rosmer had no need to log on to Omega as James Dean before six P.M. Lynette, his silver girl, his little broken-faced ballerina, would not be there until then. So instead Jon, bored and slightly drunk in his motel room, had logged on as one of his alter-egos.

Most people had only one character on Omega, but Jon had three and the means to get a dozen more. He liked to think he came to the MOON in many guises, like a god who continually changed his shape, confounding all who tried to know his essence.

His character Zeno was sadistic, aggressive, and did little but harass female guests. Yet today as he'd moved from woman to woman, he'd done so mechanically, with no hope of real satisfaction.

He'd talked dirty to them, picking mostly guests so they didn't have the know-how to escape him. He called them filthy names, he grabbed at them; he even ran his rape program on one who seemed particularly stupid.

But everything, even the rape, left him empty and dissatisfied. His head seemed filled by a pounding fog. His penis stayed limp as a worm, yet was tortured by a pins and needles sensation, like a numbed limb trying to come back to life.

Sometimes, rarely, he could almost achieve potency as

Zeno. He would scare a girl so badly or use her so roughly that the worm would twitch out of its sleep, stir, stiffen—then droop, powerless again.

But when he thought of Lynette, he tingled with a strange, edgy hope. Lynette was like a delicious plum that was slow to ripen. But when she did ripen and fall into his hands, she would satisfy his hunger far better than Gretchen. She could grant him a desperately needed measure of peace. What he did was dangerous, and he needed an island of peace.

It had been barely two months since he'd killed Gretchen Small. Once a killing had lasted him half a year, even more. He could relive it repeatedly in his mind, and his body relived it, too.

But Gretchen, somehow, hadn't lasted. Only a few days after her death, his blood had begun to beating in his ears again like a drum. *More, more, more,* it thudded. *Now, now, now.*

The only thing that soothed him was drink and pills, but he'd been sucking down beers all day and it hadn't helped.

More, more, more.

Now, now, now.

It did no good to kill hookers. Hookers were too easy; it was like shooting fish in a barrel. Anybody with a little cunning could slice one of them to bits and never be caught.

He knew because he had done it. He'd killed a prostitute in St. Paul and it had done nothing for him, not one damned thing. He'd *wanted* to be satisfied, God knows; he'd prayed to be satisfied because his life would have been a hundred times easier.

But hookers were worthless to him. He needed a woman who fawned and doted on him, a "nice" woman, a "decent" woman, pathetic in her devotion, needing him and loving him too much.

The first large animal Jon Rosmer killed—larger than a minnow or frog or bird or hamster—was his grandmother's cocker spaniel, Pansy.

Jon had been nine years old and living with the old

woman as long as he could remember. She had nothing kind
to say about his mother, whom he rarely saw. No pictures of
his mother were allowed in the house.

His grandmother treated him coldly, as if he were a
burden she could bear only because God had endowed her
with the superior virtue to do so. She seldom touched him,
which was fine; he strongly disliked being touched.

But her dog, Pansy, whom she adored, was always all
over him, wagging and jumping and licking and whining for
attention. He despised the dog and sometimes kicked at it
when his grandmother wasn't near. Then he sweet-talked it
so he could kick it again, another time.

The animal was simply too stupid to understand his
hatred. It followed him about, staring ardently at him with
its rheumy eyes, yearning to stick its hot tongue in his face
and pant its stinking breath on him.

One day when his grandmother entertained her bridge
club, she had made brownies and left a half-full box of
Baker's chocolate on the kitchen counter. Jon remembered
his teacher had warned the class that dogs shouldn't eat
Baker's chocolate, it would poison them.

While the women played bridge in the living room, Jon
softly called Pansy into the kitchen. He put the package of
chocolate on the floor, as if it had fallen there, its contents
spilling out. The dog, which was fat and greedy, tore the
squares out of their white paper coverings and gulped them
down.

Jon went back to what his grandmother called the "rec-
reation room" and dutifully practiced the piano so his
grandmother and all the bridge ladies could hear what a
good boy he was.

Later, after the bridge ladies had gone home, Pansy began to act crazy. She howled, she ran in circles, she snapped
at Jon's grandmother and bit her savagely. The sight of blood
welling out of the old woman's hand had filled Jon with a
sudden, sensual joy.

The dog knocked into furniture, sent a lamp crashing to
the floor, then a vase. Jon's grandmother, her hand wrapped

in a bloody dish towel, tried to shoo Pansy outside, and the dog caromed out the door, shrieking.

Pansy tore down the street, clearly out of her mind. She darted in front of a mail truck, and the mailman couldn't stop in time. He hit Pansy, and she lay in the street, bleeding and twitching.

Jon's grandmother burst into tears. The mailman, obviously shaken, brought the dog back to the porch, but there was nothing to be done; Pansy was dying, her brown eyes glazing over in a way Jon found fascinating.

The dog died, and his grandmother cried like a child. She could not yet face the horror of burying the dog, so the mailman moved it to the corner of the porch, still on the bloody welcome mat. A neighbor came and took Jon's grandmother inside, weeping and inconsolable.

Jon stayed by the dog's side until evening, refusing to move, keeping his own mesmerized vigil. The sight of the dead dog pleased and aroused him.

The sympathetic neighbor found the chocolate box and put together an explanation of the dog's death. Pansy, in her innocent gluttony, had eaten the Baker's chocolate, which poisoned her. No one suspected Jon.

Pansy's death fulfilled him so much that the memory of it warmed and excited him for more than a year. But like a videotape that is played too often, it simply wore out. He needed another animal, and after that, another still. The killing had become an addiction, and it gave him the secret of his identity.

Even as a child he had suspected he was not like other people, that there was something freakish inside him that he must keep hidden. This frightened him, but he could not change what he was.

He passed as an ordinary boy, quiet, bright, a better than average piano student, otherwise unremarkable. But his secret hunger was always there, like a dark, subterranean river swelling to flood stage.

Now, Jon sighed raggedly, rose, opened another beer, and sat slumped on the edge of the bed. He turned on the television and rewatched the pay-for-view porn movie. It only made him more restless and sad.

He wanted Lynette, he needed her, and he had to have her as soon as possible. But things must go in the right order and at the proper pace. First there would be netsex with her, and for a time that would satisfy him. Night after night, she would bring him to a climax, and he'd never have to touch her or be touched by her.

But a virtual affair quickly lost its novelty and its power. She would grow to seem too easy and coarse for him, and words would no longer be enough. But he would not be done with her. Not yet.

He would invite her to some neutral ground where nobody knew either of them. Then he would touch her in reality, taking a pleasure forbidden but so intense that it shook his marrow and left him trembling.

He was not a fool; he had other candidates on the string besides Lynette, and he was always on the alert, looking for fresh prospects. But it was Lynette who filled his thoughts. On this endless, beery, bleary June afternoon, she came close to obsessing him.

He imagined kissing her flawless virtual mouth, while across the miles, her real and imperfect mouth sighed with virgin desire. He imagined parting her long, ballerina's thighs and entering her virtual body, while her real body heated and moistened and tensed to his words. He imagined his own release, pouring out and easing the pressure in his loins and his veins and his skull.

At five minutes to six he rose unsteadily from the bed, opened another beer, and sat down at the room's cheap desk. He booted up the computer, logged on to Omega as James Dean, and teleported to Lynette's dressing room.

She was always punctual, arriving precisely at six on Sundays, but he liked to be early, to seem an eager, loving suitor.

He looked around her hokey room and rehearsed exactly what he would say. He would choreograph his every action, he would perform a goddam ballet of seduction. He was pleased to feel himself growing hard just *thinking* about taking her little electronic cherry.

At exactly six o'clock she materialized, and he wrote that he took her in his arms and kissed her long and passionately. He ran his hands up and down her virtual body.

He was about to whisper to her, "I've missed you, and I've thought of nothing else but you."

But he had no chance to tell her, for she quickly and unexpectedly drew away from him.

"James," she said, "this is very hard for me to say. But I've been thinking about our relationship. Things happen too fast on Omega. I think we should stop seeing each other for a while. If we really care for each other, if our emotions are real, things will work out."

He stared at his screen in disbelief. He was as stunned as if she'd struck him with a hammer. Was she crazy—or what? No woman had ever treated him this way before.

"You can't do this," he answered, desperate. "I love you. Only you. You're the only one I want, now or ever."

But she was adamant. She said they should go separate ways, at least until the end of the summer. Their relationship had evolved too quickly and was taking turns that made her uncomfortable.

He felt as if he were trapped in a nightmare. He tried to beg, to caress, to argue, to compromise, but she would have none of it.

"It's for the best," she said. "And it's not like we're saying goodbye forever. We'll still bump into each other. I just don't think we should be so exclusive yet."

But when she kissed him on the cheek and told him goodbye, he had the sickening sensation that it *was* forever.

And then she was gone, vanished from Omega.

He couldn't believe it. He logged off the computer and tried to call her long distance. Her line was busy. She must have anticipated that he'd try to call; she had unplugged the phone or was hiding somewhere on the Internet.

He was so enraged that he snatched up the telephone and hurled it into the mirror of the dresser. Broken glass flew through the air and fell in a rain of silver shards. He drove his fist repeatedly into the wall, making a hole in the cheap plasterboard.

Then, spent, he sank to the floor of the room, tears in his eyes, his breath ragged, his knuckles bruised and skinned raw.

He'd wanted her so much, he'd counted on her. He had to have someone soon. He *had* to. He sucked at his injured knuckles.

He'd talked himself into believing that Lynette could and would ease his terrible yearning, and he'd let himself want her more than he had ever wanted any woman. Damn her eyes, he still wanted her.

Patience, he told himself, sucking his own blood rhythmically, like a child nursing. Patience. He would have her, he swore it.

In the meantime, he would take whomever he could get.

After a moment he rose, walked across the broken glass to the desk, sat down at the computer and switched it on again.

He logged on to Omega and started hunting.

SIX

───❦───

A<small>T TEN O'CLOCK</small> M<small>ONDAY MORNING</small>, <small>THE PHONE COMPANY TRUCK</small> jolted down the road to Carrie's house. The workman mounted an outside box for a second line, installed a second jack next to her desk, and plugged in a shiny new white telephone with lots of buttons.

At four o'clock, another truck pulled up in her dusty drive, red letters on its side announcing <small>LEARNING LAMP COMPUTER SALES AND SERVICE</small>.

A young man with a ponytail and wispy beard set up the new computer, installed the modem, tested everything and pronounced it "workin' fine as frog hair."

When he left, Carrie found the sleek new computer filled her with an almost superstitious wariness. Even when she turned her back on it, she could sense it, as if an alien had moved into the house and crouched there, demanding more than its fair share of space.

She told herself it was only a machine and tried not to

think of it. She studied *Romeo and Juliet* until the shadows lengthened, and the hot afternoon began to cool.

While twilight fell, she worked in the garden. She devoted her energy to a relentless attack on crabgrass, dandelions, and the vampirishly immortal plantain.

But when the sun sank behind a mountain, she knew the time approached to log on to Omega. She felt reluctant and apprehensive without knowing why. No one could actually harm her in cyberspace; intellectually she understood this.

> Sticks and stones may break my bones,
> But words can never hurt me.

Still, at eight o'clock, when she sat down at the pristine computer, foreboding filled her. For the first time she realized the import of what she was doing—looking for a killer. What in God's name would she do if she found him?

"Wotthehell," she muttered and switched on the machine. Command by command, she made her way to the Internet, and from Internet to Omega.

She gave the command to enter, and was connected as "Cat Guest." With eerie swiftness, she passed through the Ivory Gate and found herself once again on the King's Highway.

True to his word, Edmon had logged on early. As Sir Parsival, he waited in his tent for the others to page him. Carrie and Brooke would be guests and could not know their identity ahead of time; it was up to him to establish the lines of communication.

His hands were moist, he felt skittish with nerves, and stupid as well. Who did he think he was, Sherlock Holmes? Dirty Harry? James Bond? He was a fool.

If the other characters on Omega knew what he was doing, they would despise him. Bringing spies and moles to Omega was despicable. Ivanovich was a detective, and if anyone ever discovered his presence (God forbid), it would seem as if Edmon had imported his own thuggish law force. He would be called a traitor, a saboteur, a crypto-fascist queer.

Without doubt the wizards would expel him from Omega, the most ignominious fate that could befall a character. He would be "toaded." The wizards would turn him into a virtual toad and cast him into eternal exile.

It didn't matter, he told himself, squaring his shoulders. All that counted was Gretchen. As foolish or overweening as he might seem, what he did was for her sake.

A new message flashed on his screen:

> You sense that Cat Guest is looking for you on the King's Highway.
> She pages, "Edmon? It's Carrie. Good grief, there's a crowd here! What's going on?"

He smiled and paged her back. "It's always crowded Mondays. A lot of people are logging on after the weekend. Join me. Have you set your description?"

"Yes, but I've got a couple I want to try," she answered. "I'll be right there."

A moment later, Cat Guest materialized in Parsival's Tent. "Welcome," Edmon said, and hugged her. On Omega, characters on even merely civil terms always hugged each other.

Carrie hugged him back and kissed him on the cheek. He almost blushed. Hardly anyone on the MOON had ever kissed him—except Gretchen. He thought of the first time she had kissed him hello, and the poignancy of the memory made him swallow hard.

"Is Brooke here?" Carrie asked.

"Yes. She's Swan Guest."

Carrie said, "Your place is almost bare. Why? I thought people made their rooms as elaborate as possible."

Edmon had nothing in his tent except a pair of sleeping pallets, a ewer of fresh water, and a fire where a kettle of plain gruel simmered. A pewter bowl and spoon sat by the ewer. That was all.

He said, "It's against the spirit of the Grail Quest to

travel in splendor. I have to practice humility. I keep the tent open all the time, so the poor and weary can find shelter."

She smiled at him. "You're very sweet, Edmon. You really are."

This time he did blush and felt a strange surge of happiness. Carrie was such a nice woman and pretty, too, with her bright hair and lively eyes. Suddenly he desperately wished he were forty, then, just as suddenly, felt a pang for being disloyal to Gretchen.

Flustered, he said, "Let me look at you. Did you have any trouble setting your sex or description?"

"No. I just followed your directions. You were very clear."

Flattered, he typed @look Cat Guest, and her description appeared on the screen.

> You see a petite brunette, whose black hair falls in waves nearly to her hips. Her white Stetson hat is pulled down to a rakish angle, and mischief dances in her long-lashed emerald green eyes.
>
> She wears a white ruffled gambler's blouse with lace at the breast and cuffs, tight jeans, and white cowboy boots.
>
> When she walks, you hear the silvery jingle of her boot bracelets. As she passes near, you catch the scent of her perfume; it is sweet and clean and natural, like a breeze from a June meadow.
>
> She likes horseback riding, rodeo, country and western music. She tosses her hair playfully and flashes you an inviting smile.

Edmon was glad Carrie couldn't see his face, because he knew his disappointment would show. "Very nice!" he typed.

"Do you really think so?" she asked.

He hesitated. The girl Carrie described sounded pretty but not sexy, and she seemed too outdoorsy, not the sort of person who would come to Omega.

He forced himself to type "I mean it—very nice. Really!"

"I thought this might be a little different. I based it on a student I had in Nebraska. She drove boys wild. Everywhere she went, she left a trail of broken hearts. Scarlett O'Hara in spurs."

Carrie seemed proud of her creation, and Edmon didn't want to hurt her feelings. How could he tell her that Omega was full of computer nerds who didn't dream of petite charmers, but of voluptuous women with enormous hooters? They didn't want spurs and Stetsons; they wanted garter belts, spike heels, and lots of cleavage.

"Brooke's gone to the Romance Ballroom," Edmon said. "Where do you want to go?"

"I thought I'd start in the drawing room at the Palace of Pleasure."

"Good. A lot of people go there," he told her. "If you get in trouble, page me or join me. Or Ivanovich."

"Ivanovich is here?"

"He says he's just checking the place out. But I think he's protective of you two. He's Panther Guest. He's in the Archive Room."

Carrie didn't reply for a moment. "If I need anyone, I'll call you," she said at last. "You know your way around better."

Edmon felt an unwarranted surge of pride, and thought again of how pretty she was, how her denim skirt swung like a little bell when she walked in her brisk way. He wondered if she would kiss him goodbye as she had done hello.

She said, "I'm on my way, then. Wish me luck."

"Good luck."

She hugged him, that was all. Then she was gone. When she vanished, a wave of emptiness swept through him, quickly followed by one of yearning.

A woman in her forties wasn't so old, Edmon thought. There were gorgeous movie stars who were fifty or more. But then he was shamed by such thoughts and cursed his fickle heart. He stared at the framed snapshot of Gretchen that sat on his desk. *I'll be true*, he thought.

Yet, in spite of his vow, a terrible desolation descended on him. In the darkest part of his mind he feared Gretchen was dead. He always worked to suppress the thought, but it surfaced now, and it frightened and appalled him.

Lynette went fearfully to Flair's airy dressing room and found it empty. Her heart constricted. As she'd asked, James hadn't come.

He'd left a private mail message for her: "If you change your mind, send word. I love you and only you, Lynette— Yours forever, James."

If this were real life, she might run her fingers over the paper of the note, stroking his writing, thinking of his hand and its touch.

But the note was only a few terse lines glowing on a screen. She could not gaze at his handwriting because there was none, and she couldn't recall the touch of his hand because he had never touched her. That was both the siren song and the curse of Omega; everything, no matter how beautiful or shabby or debauched, took place in the mind.

Except, of course, MOON sex, netsex, cybersex, virtual sex, whatever you chose to call it. Then your mind and body merged with someone else's—only across the miles, and still without touching. The touching you did for yourself.

This was not the way she imagined giving herself to the man she loved, sitting before a computer, breathless to be stroked by nothing except words and her own hand. The point of making love was that another person touched you with tenderness and passion. It seemed that she had waited a lifetime for that touch.

She typed the command to see if James was logged on Omega. Could she resist talking to him if he was? But the message that flashed on the screen said that he was absent. Where was he now, and what was he doing in real life?

Lynette rose from the computer and walked to the window of her dorm room. She gazed down at the sidewalk where a pair of lovers strolled in the twilight, their arms around each other. They stopped beneath a tree, melted more closely into each other, and kissed.

It looked so easy, this loving and touching. It was happening all over the campus, the town, the state, the country, the world. Why couldn't it happen to her? She turned from the window, unable to keep watching.

She had real roses in her room tonight, not just the imaginary bouquets of her dressing room. James had wired her a dozen blood-red roses with the simplest and most eloquent of notes: "I love you. James."

Their perfume hung on the air, haunting her with thoughts of him. Suddenly she felt wracked by such loneliness that she no longer wanted to wait, she wanted only James. She would send him a MOON mail message: "I love you. I'll do anything you want."

She went to the computer, sat down at the desk, typed the command to send mail.

But then, as she stared at the waiting screen, something deep within her shifted, and she knew she was incapable of sending a message of such naked need.

Instead she wrote, "Thank you so much for giving me this time. Love, Lynette."

After Jon sent Lynette his message, he felt wild with anger and craving. He logged off and drank two beers as he browsed the Internet. He read a few entries in the kinky sex categories, but they did nothing for him.

He went back to Omega anonymously, logging on as a guest. He was connected as "Lamb Guest," and the innocent connotation of the name amused him.

He teleported to Robinson Crusoe's Deserted Island, because hardly anyone ever visited it. The island consisted of nothing but sand, a few coconut trees, and Crusoe's empty hut. Omega was full of such little-used nooks.

Jon set his sex, male, and a description that had served him before as bait.

> You see a weary searcher who wants to believe that somewhere in this world there is meaning, goodness, and love.

A good hunter needed the right tools: first, the power to check Omega for all characters and guests logged on as female; second, the power to see these females across the distance from where he was. He typed the commands to gain these magical skills, and the MOON granted them.

He asked if Lynette was logged on. The answer came swiftly. She was at Ye Silent Woman Pub. She was probably crying on the shoulder of that bitch, Quicksilver. He gave the command to peek into the pub from a distance.

> You see Ye Silent Woman Pub. A fireplace of native stone dominates the west wall, and within it, flames dance. The room's walnut walls glow warmly in the shifting light.
>
> The east wall is taken up by a well-stocked bar, with tiers of shelves rising behind it. On the shelves are ranged bottles that gleam like translucent jewels; they contain the rarest and most potent of liquors.
>
> In the center of the room stands a great trestle table, hewn by hand from oak. Sturdy benches flank it, inviting you to sit.
>
> Quicksilver, Mouse Guest, Short Fuse, Flair, and Lacewing are here.

Lynette was sitting quietly, doing nothing. He knew he could page her if he wished, send her obscene invitations and torment her as cruelly as he liked; she would never know who he was, and the insults would make her think with longing of sweet, loving James Dean.

But he would save that particular satisfaction for later. It was Lacewing who caught his interest. She was usually closeted with that pathetic loser, Cochise, and was seldom seen about on her own. Was she available again?

He'd once thought she'd shown promise; he typed the @look command to refresh his memory.

> You see Lacewing, a woman of 24, who finds Omega both fascinating and frightening.
>
> Lacewing is tall and shapely. She has short, curly auburn hair and deep blue eyes that are full of questions.
>
> Lacewing wears a long gown of black lace. Although this dress has a high neck and long sleeves, it cannot hide the alluring curves of her body.

A hopeless romantic, she loves long conversations, walks
by the seashore, and music. She is wearing a mood ring with
a twilight blue stone, signifying that she is undecided.

Jon's hunting instincts prickled. Her description hinted
at a doubleness in her nature that sounded promising. She
wanted to be seductive, yet she was insecure about it.

He would try to pick her up, but first he would search
the rest of Omega for likely women. First he would check out
the guests because they were the most naive targets. Only ten
guests had set their genders as female, and methodically he
looked them over.

Only one guest was in the drawing room, Cat Guest, but
her description turned him off. She was too little, she
sounded too fucking perky, and she was into rodeo and
country western music, for Christ's sake.

He moved on to scope out the Everlasting Hot Tub
Party, but both female guests there sounded suspiciously like
men in drag. One claimed to have "38-D boobs and a gorgeous heart-shaped ass." Jon thought, *Fat chance, faggot.*

He turned his attention to the Romance Ballroom. Two
women guests were there, and he examined them. The first
sounded discouragingly brainless and wholesome. But when
he examined the second, Swan Guest, his heartbeat accelerated.

Jon smiled and temporarily forgot Lacewing. Swan
Guest's description was that of a princess and a goddess, an
almost certain guarantee that in real life she was a pig. More-
over, she was an imaginative pig. She probably found the real
world unsatisfactory, harsh, even hostile. Just the sort of girl
he wanted.

From his island, he would page and woo her. As for
Lynette, let the bitch twist in the wind for now. She would
fall into his hands sooner or later. In the meantime, he
would find someone who was more willing.

Ripeness, as the poet said, was all.

• • •

In the Romance Ballroom, Brooke was weary of being bombarded by invitations, most of them flirtatious, some of them obscene.

Her description, long and sensual, had worked all too well. As soon as she'd set it, Damian Two had paged, "You're gorgeous. I'd like to lick you all over like a Popsicle."

Thrust had paged, "Why don't you join me in Sex Chamber Six. I can give you twelve inches of ecstasy. (grin)"

In the Ballroom itself, Mole Guest had got on his knees before her and begun kissing her feet and sucking her toes.

Brooke did not consider herself highly sexed, and the single-mindedness of these would-be suitors wore her down. She did not like aggressive men, and most of her crushes had been on movie stars. Whenever she tried to envision her perfect mate, she always seemed to see Tom Hanks as Forrest Gump.

Forrest was tall, well-built, sincere, and reasonably handsome. He loved faithfully, he wasn't bossy or demanding, and while she wrote he would do all the housework without complaint.

In the meantime, although she was attracting a horde of concupiscent men, she wasn't sure how to talk to them. Either they propositioned her or made moronic chitchat. To add to her frustration, Edmon paged her every fifteen minutes, like a nervous chaperone. "Are you all right? Can I do anything?"

Her head had started to ache, and all she wanted to do was to leave the Romance Ballroom and explore Omega on her own, unplagued by amateurish Don Juans. Right on schedule, Edmon paged again. "How are things? What can I do for you?"

Brooke wanted to snap, "You can leave me alone, you prissy fink." But at that moment someone else paged her.

You sense that Lamb Guest is looking for you on Robinson Crusoe's Deserted Island. He pages, "Your description is beautiful. You must have the soul of a poet. Would you like to join me, and get acquainted? I could show you around Omega."

For once in this madhouse, someone was making her a tempting offer.

Carrie grew increasingly tired of Omega. Everywhere she went, conversation managed to be banal and wild at the same time, and she was sick of being paged by men who seemed as immature as eggs.

The only intelligent exchanges she'd had all evening had been with Edmon, who kept paging to see how she was. At first his concern was touching, but it was growing into a nuisance.

By midnight, she was on her third description of herself and bored sick. She'd gone from being a petite cowgirl to a Japanese-American cheerleader and was presently a tall blonde in a spangled gown with green sleeves and a low-cut neckline.

An idiot named Thrust was driving her mad with his pages. "Wow, your description makes me so crazy, I'd like to dress you in chocolate lingerie and suck it all off. Interested?"

Carrie was tired of these games. "I'm going to meet somebody," she told him. "Leave me alone."

"It's your loss, beautiful. Call me when you want the biggest and best."

When hell freezes over, you twit, thought Carrie.

She desperately needed a break, but she'd had enough of Edmon for one night. On impulse, she paged Hayden. "Can I join you? I need to talk to an adult, dammit."

He paged her back from the Archive Room. "Fine."

She entered the command to join Panther Guest, and within seconds was in the Archive Room.

You are in the Archive Room of Omega MOON.

A cavernous, poorly lit chamber, it houses the records, documents, charters, atlases, rational and practical mechanics, chronicles, and literature of Omega.

A layer of fine dust covers everything, and cobwebs cloak the corners of the high ceiling.

In the center of this great dim room stands a single old-fashioned library table, elaborately carved from oak. On the table is one sputtering candle in a holder made from a human skull. Beside the candle is an enormous, hand-illuminated book, INDEX TO THE ARCHIVES OF OMEGA MOON.

Panther Guest is here. He says, "Hi."

Carrie started to reply, but a virtual rat raced from a corner and ran across her foot. An owl swooped down from the dim rafters, and seized the rat, which screamed once, then went limp and silent. The owl flapped away, carrying the bleeding body back up into the darkness.

"Ugh," Carrie said in distaste. "This is nasty."

"I like it," replied Hayden. "My home away from home."

"It's certainly not inviting," she said.

"It's not meant to be," he said. "This is the deepest cellar of the Palace of Pleasure."

"How do you know?"

"I found a blueprint of the Palace. And maps of Omega. Interesting."

"What are you looking for?" she asked. "Terrorists? The Mafia? Drug dealers? Space aliens?"

When he answered, she could almost see his scornful half-smile. "Whatever. What can I do for you?"

"Stop playing with your spiders and magic books and just talk to me, all right?"

"I'm all yours. Let me take a look at you."

Nothing happened on the screen, and she knew that from his end he was giving her the once-over. It made her oddly self-conscious.

She was never comfortable with this man. When they had parted Sunday after their conversation in Plato's, their goodbyes had been stiff, almost formal. She would not go out with him again, and she knew he would not ask her to do so.

Yet out of curiosity, she took a furtive look at him, wondering if he'd bothered to describe himself. She typed the command to look at Panther Guest.

You see an average guy.

She cocked a dubious brow. He might be many things, but he was not average.

"Edmon told me you were a cowgirl," he said. "I see a supermodel in medieval drag. Is there some mistake?"

"Nobody seemed interested in a cowgirl," she said. "Virtual blondes have more virtual fun."

"Are you having fun?"

"No. Omega's crazy. Everything seems shallow and chaotic. Couples disappear together, but I have this eerie feeling that they're phantom people having phantom relationships. That none of it really matters. As courtship forms go, it's lousy."

"To you and me it's lousy," he said. "To them it's fine. It's how they do it these days."

"Did you apply for a character?" she asked.

"Yes. Did you?"

"Yes," she said. "I'm already sick of being a guest."

Edmon had told them it took the MOON a week to process applications for a character. In the meantime she and Brooke must do the best they could. Guests had no status, received no respect, and were fair game for anyone. She had no more rights than a medieval peasant and was afforded no more dignity than a cockroach.

She said, "This place makes me want to go off and live in the woods like Thoreau."

"You do live in the woods like Thoreau," Hayden pointed out.

She thought, *Not quite.* Walden Pond had not been wired, and Thoreau had to cope only with live bugs, not electronic ones. She glanced at the disk slot on her computer. She and Brooke were recording everything that appeared on their screens on floppy disks in case they needed to review information.

"These disks," she said, "are we supposed to turn them over to you when they're full?"

"No. Hang on to them. Just in case we need to go back and look for something."

"Have you been in this mausoleum all night?"

"The first two hours I explored."

"Did you find anything interesting?" she asked.

"Graffiti," he said.

She was puzzled. "Graffiti?"

"It's all over. Haven't you noticed?"

"I didn't pay much attention," she said.

"You can read it if you want."

"I never bothered. I thought the graffiti would be as down and dirty as everything else here."

"It is. But a few characters are politicized. There's somebody named Slate Wiper who writes hate notes about Waco and Oklahoma City. 'Death to tyrants,' 'Kill all cops,' that sort of stuff. And someone called Nitrate does the same."

"They're probably just kids, trying to shock," she said.

"Possibly. Neither one can spell."

She said, "So after your graffiti-fest, you came here to curl up with a good book?"

"Right. Are you having any luck out there?"

"If you call being propositioned, insulted, mauled, and fondled by a half a hundred horny college boys lucky, I'm luckier than I can stand. Doesn't anybody proposition *you*?"

"Nope. Women are in short supply here. You're a valuable commodity."

Carrie didn't like thinking of herself as a commodity and was about to say so. But he surprised her with an unexpected question. "How long have you been widowed?"

Why's he getting personal all of a sudden? she wondered. "Ten years," she replied, and to keep things even, asked, "how long have you been divorced?"

"Two years."

She looked at his words flickering on her screen. There was no tone of voice, no expression of any kind to give her a clue to his feelings. She asked, "When did you come to Fayetteville?"

"Two years ago."

"Why?"

"I grew up here."

"You have family here?" she asked, truly curious.

"Not anymore."

It was maddening, how little of himself he revealed. "Then why'd you come back?" she demanded.

"The mountains, the woods, the lakes," he said. "Mostly the rivers."

She said, "You're an outdoorsman?"

"Oop," he said, "sorry. Got a call on my hotline. Something's up. Can you wait a minute? Be right back."

"Of course," Carrie said.

She found it curious that he had asked about her widowhood. And she was surprised that he had been divorced only two years. He seemed such a permanent loner, she could not imagine him as a husband or a family man. And she wondered if it was a coincidence that his marriage failed at the same time he'd left the ATF.

She told herself not to speculate about him, but she found herself wondering where he lived, in what sort of room he was. He was attractive in his mysterious way, but he had the air of a man who didn't care for people and who did not want to care.

She waited almost five minutes before he came back to his computer. She almost used the time to transform herself from a platinum blonde into a more voluptuous redhead, but she suddenly realized she was too tired. She stayed as she was, all platinum, spangles, green sleeves, and fatigue.

Hayden finally came back to the computer. "Sorry," he said. "It's a client. An emergency. Got to go. Sorry. I'll talk to you later."

"Fine," Carrie said, wondering what sort of emergencies private detectives had.

"For what it's worth," he said, "your description's fine, but I like how you look in real life. I like your freckles. I like your dimples."

Panther Guest chastely touches you on your freckled, dimpled cheek with his forefinger. He smiles at you.

"Goodnight, toots," he said. "Take care."

Then, like a genie vanishing, he was gone.

Carrie stared at the screen, her heart beating hard and

fast. He had actually flirted with her for a moment, even gave her a virtual touch—not much of one, but a touch, nevertheless. What did *that* mean?

Her cheek burned as if he'd really laid his finger against it for a moment. She was mystified and not sure she liked the nervous energy he'd awakened in her.

> You sense Cochise is looking for you in A Place. He pages, "Hi, I see yyou and yyou're beautiful. Would yyou please come talk to me, I am lonely and reallyy need someone to talk to. I mean, reallyy, reallyy. Would yyou like to join me?"

Carrie didn't want to talk to another lonely and hot-blooded adolescent.

"I'm sorry," she paged back. "It's after midnight, and I'm tired. Maybe another time. 'Bye for now."

She typed the command to quit, and was relieved when Omega released her. She switched off the computer and rose from it. She was surprised how stiff she was and realized that she'd sat at the terminal for four straight hours.

She stretched, then walked to the deck and stood gazing out at the lake. Somehow the lake, moonlight and starlight tossing on its surface, no longer seemed quite substantial. Even the chorus of frogs and crickets seemed a bit like an auditory hallucination.

Her cheek still tingled, and she was troubled that Hayden's imaginary touch still seemed real, while the real and living night struck her as an illusion.

Omega played tricks on the mind, she told herself. She must be careful.

SEVEN

———✦✦✦———

TUESDAY MORNING, HAYDEN IVANOVICH SAT IN HIS OFFICE, DRINKING bitter coffee and reading his e-mail. His office had no window, and the air-conditioning system poured out a manufactured chill that carried the faint, bleachlike scent of ozone.

The fluorescent lights glared down coldly, glancing off his computer screen. He ran his hand over his eyes and wondered if, at last, he needed glasses.

Last night on Omega he had stared at the stark white letters throbbing on the black screen until past midnight. He'd asked both Carrie and Brooke to keep notes on each trip they took to Omega and to transmit them to him to coordinate.

Both had been prompt. Carrie's had come in by regular e-mail, but Brooke had sent such a monster document that he'd had to download it. Her account was long, rambling, and read like an enigmatic poem. It was encyclopedic in detail but almost completely devoid of hard fact. How in God's name had she written so much—and so little?

Unhappily he skimmed through her report. She'd spent an hour with Lamb Guest, then most of the rest of the night with a character named Alhambra, but she gave no concrete information about either of them.

Hayden lost patience, printed out her account, and vowed he'd force himself to read the rest after lunch. But he'd have to have a talk with the girl—names and places, kid, *facts*. Stop describing every grain of sand on the beach and check these men out.

He took another drink of his nasty coffee—Alice, the receptionist, made the vilest coffee in Arkansas. She ought to get a trophy for it, a big one, perhaps a life-size brass replica of an ulcerated stomach.

He typed the command to bring Carrie's e-mail transmission to the screen. As soon as he read the first few lines, he found himself smiling. Her account was as brisk, organized, and irreverent as she was.

Ivanovich, heaven help the working girl because being a cybervixen is not all beer and Skittles. If you don't believe me put on a dress and try it.

Here's an alphabetized list of whom I met, what they told me about themselves, what they seemed to want.

OMEGA NAME	FACTS
Antelope Guest	Real name: Richard
	Age: nineteen
	Location: Cleveland
	Occupation: student, engineering
	Desire: to meet women, sounds lonely, inexperienced
Blue Rider	Real name: refused to say
	Age: refused to say
	Location: refused to say
	Occupation: refused to say
	Desire: netsex

Damian Two	Real name: refused to say
	Age: refused to say
	Location: refused to say
	Occupation: student
	Desire: netsex

Hayden shook his head. Carrie Blue had it down cold, twenty-two names in all. Nine had propositioned her, including the determined Thrust, who'd made her two offers.

> At about 11:58, Thrust made my patience snap, so I joined you. At 12:08, I logged off, leaving you to your many volumes of quaint and curious lore.
>
> It was a hard day's night.
>
> Yours in cyberspace,
> Carrie Blue

He stared at her closing words and rubbed his upper lip thoughtfully. *Yours in cyberspace.*

The phrase was provocative; he wondered if she meant it that way. A man might almost take it as an invitation. It might be like a seductive look or smile that could mean, "Come hither. Pursue me."

"Invitation, my ass," he told himself cynically. He printed her account, then stood, feeling restless. He turned away from his desk and wished he could go out and bang a raquet ball around the court for two hours.

Last night on Omega, he hadn't been able to resist. He'd asked her a personal question, foolishly given her that parting phantom caress. Such things were easier on Omega than in life; obviously they were too damned easy.

Talking to her in cyberspace, he'd seen her vividly in his mind's eye. Forget the platinum-and-sequined description, it didn't interest him. He'd imagined her as herself, with her alert eyes and the smile he was never sure he read correctly. He'd awakened this morning with the same images haunting him.

Well, why not? he thought. Why shouldn't he join the

living again? Otherwise, he should feel right at home on Omega. For the last two years he'd been drifting through life like a phantom himself, ghost-ridden and estranged.

For the first time in two years, he hungered to have a specific woman in his arms. Something about her warmed him like a fire, and that was the image that came into his mind; he was a man in an endless dark and arctic waste, and suddenly he'd seen the light of a distant fire.

She was the sort of woman he'd like to take camping, he thought, along one of the rivers where these days he always went alone. There were few women he would want with him there. She was the first in a long time.

The thought of lying in a sleeping bag with her hit him with such a strong, pure, sexual sensation, it jolted like the kick of a live wire.

He could phone her, ask her out. *Why not?* Or wait until tonight, talk to her on Omega again, push the flirtation a little further, see how she'd respond. *Why not?*

His second phone line rang, startling him. He picked up the receiver. "Burnside Agency, Ivanovich here."

A young woman's voice with a New York accent said, "This is Mr. Hayden Ivanovich, formerly of ATF?"

Warning signals shot through his nervous system. "Yes?"

"Mr. Ivanovich, I'm Lola McColl, a research assistant for *Time* magazine. We're doing a special investigative article on the ATF, scheduled for the July 24th edition. You are the father of ATF agent Kyle Ivanovich, who was killed six weeks after Waco, during a raid in Tulsa?"

His heart contracted and went cold, a dead fist in his chest. "Yes. I'm his father."

"Mr. Ivanovich, you resigned from the ATF after your son's death. Is that correct?"

The cold deepened inside him like frost sinking in.

"That's correct."

"The ATF is a troubled organization, Mr. Ivanovich. Some are calling it 'America's most hated agency.' Could you give us a statement in response? You worked twenty-three years for the ATF, your son died for it. How do you feel when you hear that people want it abolished?"

He had taken a deep breath as she spoke and held it until his forehead throbbed.

"Mr. Ivanovich?"

Between clenched teeth, he said, "No comment."

Lola McColl's perky Yankee voice drilled against his skull like an insect's stinger. "Could you be more specific? People like you and your son are being called Nazis, storm troopers, hitmen, conspirators. Do you feel betrayed by your agency?"

Hayden was reaching that dangerous stony ground beyond mere anger. "No comment."

"A source has told us that your wife insisted your son be cremated because she was afraid someone might desecrate his grave. Is that true? Would you care to comment?"

He hung up on her.

He stood and stared at the blank white wall for a moment, waiting for his pulses to stop pounding. He tried not to think of his ex-wife, who had gone a little crazy when Kyle had died. He tried not to think of how he'd blamed himself for her pain. He willed himself back to an icy calm.

He printed out Carrie's report and put it aside. He shouldn't be thinking of getting involved with anyone. Since Kyle died and since he and Karen had divorced, he kept his heart furnished with indifference. There should be no room left for anything else.

But an unwanted restlessness stirred within him, and it would not be stilled.

That morning Carrie awoke feeling fuzzy-minded and restless. My God, she thought, I've got a virtual hangover.

Even after a night's sleep, she could not forget Omega, and her disembodied MOON flirtations haunted her. When she remembered her encounter with Hayden, it both bothered and intrigued her.

A series of phantom would-be lovers had pursued her. They'd tried to tempt her with everything from kisses to orgies. Why did one playful touch from Hayden linger more clearly?

"I don't have time for this," she scolded herself, trying

to shake away the memories. She always kept her days as organized as if she were a general in a crucial campaign.

During mornings, when she was fresh, she worked on her fiction. The stories about her grandmother would become her master's thesis and later, she hoped, a published book.

For the last three weeks she'd labored over a short but complex story about her grandmother killing a rattlesnake in the garden by striking it with a spade. Carrie knew the material was strong and full of genuine drama, but today when she reread her work, it disappointed her.

Her prose seemed flat, forced, listless. Somewhere between her vision and her words, the drama had bled away, leaving a stiff and stillborn corpse, and she did not know how to breathe life into it.

She'd find a way, she told herself. Today she was having an off day, and why not? Yesterday she'd worked almost sixteen hours. For five straight hours she'd slaved over the rattlesnake story, rewriting it completely.

She'd skipped lunch, driven into town, attended her Shakespeare class, and spent three hours in the library doing research. She came home, worked two hours in her garden, took a shower, ate a sandwich, and connected to Omega for four more straight hours of writing.

After she'd logged off, she'd taken a short break, then written a ten-page e-mail report for Hayden. Today she could look forward to exactly the same killer schedule. Of course, she felt off-stride. But she'd get used to the pace, she was tough.

Still, when she quit struggling with the story, shortly after noon, she was deeply dissatisfied with it. Again she refused to be disheartened. Like Scarlett O'Hara, she told herself that tomorrow was another day, that tomorrow she could handle whatever she had to.

After her Shakespeare class and her stint in the library, Carrie drove home practically itching for the release of physical work in the garden. When she went out to battle the weeds, she glanced at her watch. *I have to be back on Omega in less than three hours.*

The thought filled her with strange uneasiness.

It was six o'clock in the evening in Council Bluffs, Iowa. The rain drummed at the big plate-glass window of the Buffalo Bar & Grill. Jon Rosmer sat alone in a booth, looking forbiddingly sullen.

The blond girl who'd waited on him kept giving him flirtatious glances. So did the redhead behind the bar.

He should have bought his supper at McDonald's, taken it back to the motel to eat alone, as he always did. But the rain had depressed him, and for once he wanted a decent meal and ice-cold beer out of a frosted mug.

He never drank on the job and he seldom drank in public, but tonight he couldn't help himself. It was Lynette's fault. He couldn't get her out of his head.

The chubby blond waitress came prancing over to him, walking with a wiggle and tossing her head to make her twin ponytails swing. She smiled beguilingly.

Shit, he thought. She was starting to remind him of Amy, the first girl he'd killed, the one who'd started it all. This one had the same eager, hungry, adoring look in her eyes.

He imagined the waitress dead, her body torn open, her glazed eyes staring at the rainy sky. Frightened by his desires, he looked away from her and lit a cigarette.

"How's the beer?" she chirped. "Can I get you another?"

Christ, he wanted another, but he'd had two already. He had fierce self-control when he chose. He exerted it now. "No," he said.

He would have sold his soul for that third beer, but he would wait until he was safely back in his motel room.

"Are you from around here?" the waitress asked, "or just visiting?"

"Visiting," he said. He picked up the beer glass and took a long drink, hoping she'd go away.

But she stayed, lurking over him. "You here for business or pleasure?"

"Pleasure," he lied. He was working, or at least pretending to work. His stepfather was partner in a used-car franchise, with ninety-two dealerships in nineteen midwestern and southern states. Jon traveled from dealership to dealership, checking "operations." It was a farce, of course.

The waitress beamed. "How long you gonna be here?"

"I leave tonight." This, too, was a lie. His schedule had him stuck in this hellhole for another day. It was a fucking stupid, useless job. But it kept him on the move, and that was good, it kept him out of trouble.

"Aww," the blonde said with exaggerated sorrow. "Too bad. 'Cause if you were free, I could show you around. I know this town. I know all the fun places."

I bet you do, bitch. He took another drink of beer, ignoring her.

"If you ever get back here," she said, "you could call me. Here's my name and number."

She thrust an open matchbook at him, her name written on the inside cover. He took it carefully, not liking to touch it, and thrust it with distaste into the pocket of his shirt. Slowly he raised his eyes to meet hers, knowing how it would affect her.

Here's your payoff, baby. Here's your cheap thrill, he thought with contempt and saw it was true. When he locked his gaze with hers, excitement sparked in her eyes like madness. Again she reminded him of Amy. *Stupid slut.*

He had to get out of there. He rose abruptly, paid the bill at the register, and pushed his way out the door and back into the rain.

Some rinky-dink poet had said to be beautiful was to be isolated. People saw his face and wanted him, like he was an object, a thing to be acquired. It had been happening since he was sixteen.

But not when he'd been a child. Then he had been quiet and fat and small for his age. His own mother didn't want him. That was all right; he didn't want her, either.

His mother had always darted in and out of his life like a crazed hummingbird. She would cover him with kisses and hug him until he couldn't breathe, suffocating him with her perfume. She would declare how much she loved him and needed his love in return. Then she would leave him, going off with her latest man.

His father sent money, that was all. Jon's grandmother said bitterly that he should have sent more, he could afford it. His grandmother had little money, and she resented it. "I have champagne tastes and a beer pocketbook," she always said.

"We're nothing but the poor relations to *him*," she said of his father. His father had partial custody of Jon but never exercised it. He sent cards at Jon's birthday and at Christmas. They had checks in them, but no personal messages. He never phoned. He kept his distance.

His father viewed Jon as a youthful mistake, an unwanted baby that had necessitated a short, disastrous marriage. It had been the first of Jon's mother's four marriages.

"She thinks with her pants," his grandmother said contemptuously. "She's happiest flat on her back."

But his mother was beautiful, and as he grew older he came to resemble her. He entered high school as a fat, childish boy whose long eyelashes made him look almost effeminate. But the summer he was sixteen, he shot up, his baby fat vanished, and as if by magic he turned into an extremely handsome young man.

He had no friends, and he did not like girls. They made him feel nervous and awkward and filled him with a painful mixture of desire and revulsion. But girls noticed him. They began to phone him at home. "Sluts," his grandmother said. "All girls think about these days is sex. They got no shame."

It was inevitable that he tried sex; the most daring girl in school tried to initiate him. She tried repeatedly, but he could do nothing, and his failure was torturous. He imagined girls laughing at him in the school halls and he hated them. He grew more aloof and remote.

And then Amy Swindler found him.

The summer he was twenty-two years old, he was between colleges, living in his grandmother's tacky house in Charleston, Illinois. His grandmother was sick all the time, and his life was falling apart.

Standardized tests told him he was intelligent, extremely so, but he kept flunking out of colleges, he didn't know why, and he didn't know what he was going to do with his life. Always he had lied, and nowadays he lied compulsively, constantly; he could not stop himself. He'd kept killing animals, he could not stop that, either. He frightened himself.

Then Amy Swindler came to visit her grandparents, who lived next door to Jon's grandmother. She was a round-bodied, sweet-faced girl, eighteen years old, and she told him she fell in love with him the first time she saw him.

She was shy, yet hopelessly smitten. One day he was in the driveway, shirtless, washing his car, an old Chevy compact. She came out of her grandparents' house, wearing very short red shorts and a checked halter that showed off her surprisingly nice breasts.

She thrust a note into his hand and stood there nervously as he read it. It said, "I love you and I would do anything in the world you want."

He looked at her, stunned by her boldness. She was breathing hard, and she stared at him with the prideless devotion of a dog.

"I mean it," she said, clenching and unclenching her fists nervously. "I would do anything that you want. Anything."

He should have wadded up the note and thrown it at her. But something about her fascinated him. She was shameless and innocent at the same time.

"My grandparents are at a funeral," she said. "They'll be gone for a couple of hours. We could go inside."

He looked at her breasts. A film of sweat gleamed between them.

"I'm a virgin," she said. "I really am. I've never done anything like this before. But I think about you all the time. I can't think of anything else."

And he thought, *Why not?* The other girl he'd tried it with had been different, more experienced, expecting too much from him. This one looked like she'd die of happiness if all he did was kiss her.

His grandmother was asleep, narked out on her medication. The thought of her lying there, drugged and helpless, while he was boldly getting it on right next door excited him.

He said, "Turn the hose off for me."

She gave him a look of sheer, dumb gratitude and went to turn off the hose. That's what she was like. She would do anything he said, like a slave.

And that's how he finally lost his virginity, with Amy Swindler doing exactly everything he told her. She had to work hard and do things that should have humiliated her, but she did them. When it finally happened it was fast and brutal—he hurt her so much she cried.

But she didn't care.

They spent the next two weeks meeting in secret. The Swindlers didn't like his grandmother, and his grandmother didn't like them. Hell, his grandmother didn't like anybody.

If the things he asked Amy to do were odd or different or painful, she didn't mind. But at the end of August, she had to go home to Evansville, and he didn't try to stop her.

In truth, she was wearing on him, she was losing her charm, and his grandmother was growing suspicious. "I don't like the way that Swindler girl looks at you," she said. "She's got no good on her mind."

He went off to a junior college in Springfield, but Amy wouldn't leave him alone. She phoned him, she sent him passionate letters, she begged to see him.

He didn't want her coming to his campus, didn't want to be seen with her. She was turning into an embarrassment. But finally he agreed to meet her in Decatur, Illinois, a city between Springfield and Evansville where he knew no one. They met at a public park, and he took her for a drive through the forested riverside.

All he wanted was to end their relationship. But she sobbed and carried on and would not hear of it, and he ended up trying to make love to her for one last time.

But it didn't work, he couldn't do it, and she begged and cried until he hit her in frustration, and once he hit her, he couldn't stop. He beat her unconscious. He had a folding knife, and he pulled her out of the car and used it. Only then did he achieve satisfaction. But it was transcendent, over-powering to him.

Afterwards, he was horror-struck by his own vulnerability. *What if they catch me?* He dragged her body deep into the woods and rolled it down a ravine. He drove back to Springfield in a daze, terrified by what he had done, but strangely exhilarated.

After that he was too restless and anxious for college, he couldn't concentrate, all he wanted to do was drink and stay drunk. He was flunking everything, so one morning he simply packed his car and went back to his grandmother's house in Charleston.

She was sick and bitchy. "What's the matter with you?" she said. "You're never going to amount to anything."

A week later Amy's body was found. His grandmother came into his room while he slept, something she seldom did. He woke up with a start and saw her standing by his bed. She'd lost a lot of weight and looked almost wraithlike.

"Amy Swindler's been killed," she said, staring at him. And he knew that somehow she *knew.*

"I'm going to call your mother," she said. "You'll have to go to her, now. I'm too old and tired." She turned and left the room.

Panicking, he rose and went into the hall. He heard her on the phone. "I don't want Jon here anymore," she said. "I'm a sick woman. You have to take him now. I can't do it anymore."

He felt frightened and strangely bereft. But his grandmother never came out and actually said what she suspected, not to his mother, not to him. She turned to him after she hung up the phone and all she said was, "At least let me die in peace."

His mother didn't want him around, of course, and neither did his stepfather, Randall. Randall created this stupid joke of a job to keep him out of the way. A remittance man, wasn't that the British name for it? They paid you to stay away.

Well, his grandmother got her wish. She died in peace,

and he felt a curious cold sorrow, not for her, but for himself. He did not go to her funeral. He did not send flowers.

Instead, a week later, he killed a girl in Beloit, Wisconsin, a hitchhiker who reminded him of Amy. Killing her wasn't the same, though; it wasn't the same at all, and he had been so bitterly disappointed that afterwards he'd sat in his car and wept.

He'd sobbed until his nose had run, and he'd thought, *I want it to be the way it was with Amy, for her to want me so much she'd do anything for me. But that's dangerous. I can trap myself that way. They could put me away, kill me.*

But Omega had saved him. It opened the door to a magic land full of lonely women.

He'd killed three more girls since the hitchhiker, the last two from Omega. Omega girls were best, and Lynette was the best of them all, and he wanted her so much he ached. If he could not have her soon, he had to have someone.

He parked the car in the lot, and made his way through the pelting rain to the sanctuary of his motel room. The computer sat on the desk, waiting to take him to the hunting fields.

That night on Omega, Hayden had to deal with Brooke. He told her to join him in the Archive Room. She did, but she turned rebellious and icier than usual when criticized.

"I'm exploring my métier," she told him. "Please respect that. This may be the ultimate deconstructive experience. I must particularize before I abstract."

He realized he was gritting his teeth. "I need names, places, facts. And don't waste any more time running around with Alhambra. He's a fourteen-year-old kid."

"How do you know?" she demanded.

"Edmon. He says Alhambra always chases guests because everybody else knows how young he is. He's been on Omega since he was eleven."

"Then his technical expertise might exceed yours *and* Edmon's—mightn't it," Brooke retorted. "In which case I'm correct to explore parameters."

He didn't believe this, Hayden told himself; this condescending child was actually taunting him.

"Another thing," Brooke said. "Please tell Edmon to stop paging me all the time. He ruins my concentration. I can't keep changing states of consciousness like that."

"You get me facts, I'll keep Edmon from paging."

"I have my own approach to things," Brooke said. "You want a writer? Let me write. Don't be so paternalistic. There are other modes than yours."

"Miss Tharpe, there may be dangerous people on Omega. Stalkers, drug dealers, crazies, terrorists."

She didn't answer. She simply vanished. He supposed it was the electronic equivalent of flouncing out of the room.

"Good riddance," he muttered aloud. For a girl who said little in real life, she had a hell of a mouth on her when she got into cyberspace.

He'd have to talk to Holloway about her. If she was this uncooperative, he'd have no choice but to fire her and find somebody else. He also needed to talk to Edmon, convince him to intrude less. The kid was trying to be chivalrous, but he acted more like a high-strung mother hen than a knight.

But first, on an impulse he knew he should resist, he paged Carrie. Edmon had said that tonight Carrie was Robin Guest. Brooke, fittingly enough, was Mule Guest.

"Carrie," he paged, "it's Hayden. I'm going to ask Edmon not to monitor you and Brooke so closely. Okay?"

He waited for her answer, wondering how she'd tricked herself out tonight. Was she the statuesque platinum blonde again, flowing green sleeves, spangles and all?

Her reply, materializing out of the stratosphere, appeared on the screen. "Edmon's sweet, but he breathes down my neck. Tell him to go out and mingle and have some fun. If I need him, I'll call him."

He paused for a moment. "Any luck tonight?"

"Well, Damian Two offered me his body. I can't tell you what a thrill that was."

He imagined Damian Two as a homely, horny college kid who'd probably never had sex in his life except behind the locked bathroom door, alone with a copy of *Playboy*.

"Ignore him," he said, then paused. *I should not do this, dammit,* he told himself. *I should not.*

He did it anyway. He thought of her again as a small strong fire in a cold and immense darkness. He typed, "How about around midnight you join me in the Archive Room? I've got a problem. Maybe you can help."

His heartbeat speeded slightly. He stared at the screen feeling as much of a foolish schoolboy as Damian Two.

Her reply was carefully worded, noncommittal. "What's the problem, may I ask?"

The problem is I keep wanting to have the real you in a real room with the real me. He answered, "Brooke. She writes bad reports, she hates following orders, and her attitude stinks. Think you could talk any sense into her? Or is it possible?"

He rested his chin on his fist and waited. Would she say yes, maybe, or get lost?

"I can try," she said at last. "I don't know her well, nobody does—she's a loner, very self-sufficient. But we're in the same Shakespeare seminar. I'll give it a shot. I'll join you at midnight, okay?"

"Fine," he said.

"How's your client?" she asked.

"Fine. It was an abduction case. Divorced father ran off with the son. We got the tip late last night. The boy's home with his mother again."

She said, "I'm glad it turned out all right. Drat, I've got another page—'bye."

" 'Bye," he said.

But she didn't join him at a quarter till midnight, nor even when midnight struck and the virtual chimes rang twelve sepulchral times.

He paged her, "Carrie, it's Hayden. Where are you?"

You sense Robin Guest is looking for you in the Bower of Bliss. She pages, "Oh, damn, Hayden, I lost track of the time. Listen, I'm with this man, and he's very interesting. I don't want to leave him right now. Do you mind?"

He was surprised that his first response was to think, *Hell, yes, I mind.*

But she was only doing her job. He realized he didn't much like what he'd hired her to do.

"No problem," he paged back.

"We'll talk another time," she answered. "Maybe I could call you tomorrow?"

"Yeah, sure," he said. Then he added, "How long are you going to stay with this guy?"

"Not much longer," she said. "You can log off. I'm fine. 'Night, Hayden."

"Goodnight," he told her. But he didn't want to log off. He stayed, checking on her every fifteen minutes without her knowing it. All he had to do was type the command "@who Robin Guest," and he was told if she was still on Omega and where.

She stayed in the Bower of Bliss until 3:25 A.M. What kind of place was it, he wondered, with a name like that? And what was so interesting about this guy, to keep her with him until well after three in the morning?

He was relieved when he saw that she'd finally logged off. But he was disturbed as well.

"Carrie," he murmured, "what the hell am I letting you get into?"

EIGHT

━━━━◆◆◆━━━━

THE ALARM CLOCK BLARED AS IF WARNING CARRIE OF A TWELVE-alarm fire. She groaned and reached, struggling to shut it off. With bleary eyes, she squinted to see the time.

It was only five-thirty in the morning. Outside the sky was dark as a bad deed, and rain beat down monotonously. *Go back to sleep*, its damp voice seemed to chant. *Back to sleep. Back to sleep.*

Why had she set the alarm for so early? Why was she so exhausted? And her body was weirdly stiff, as if overnight her joints had fossilized.

Back to sleep, back to sleep, back to sleep, crooned the rain. She started to sink back into the soft embrace of the bed, the sheets whispering around her.

Then she remembered. Her eyes flew open, her already stiff body tensed. She'd been on Omega until almost half-past three this morning.

She'd been too tired to e-mail a report to Hayden, and she'd promised herself to get up early to do it.

Willpower was a terrible thing, Carrie thought, forcing herself to rise. It led you into every sort of disgusting moral duty. But if she didn't do the report now, she'd not only be late, but she'd cut into her own writing time. She should not, would not, could not do that.

She took a cold shower, dressed in cutoffs and a T-shirt, and made herself a cup of instant coffee hot and strong enough to jolt her out of a coma.

She sat down before the new computer. "I hate you," she said to it. "I hate you a lot." She switched it on and groggily made her way to its e-mail system.

Lord, she thought, how had she got herself into this? She took a drink of the coffee. It had a heavy, bitter taste and burned its way down her throat.

She was uncertain even how to begin. "Dear Hayden?" He wasn't her dear, and she didn't want him to be. She thought of the only poem she'd written in the last ten years:

Love and sex
Are too complex.

She settled for just plain "Hayden," although even that somehow implied an intimacy that worried her. What was it about him that made her so edgy and self-conscious?

"Hayden—" she wrote. "I'm sorry I didn't meet you last night. Didn't mean to keep you waiting. Excuse it, please.

"Here's an alphabetized list of who contacted me, what they told me about themselves, what they seemed to want. I put one man into his own category at the end. You'll see why."

Resolutely she made her way through the list: Aardvark Guest, Biggus Dickus, Crystal Meth, Damian Two, Dasher, Goldfish Guest, James Bondage, Jazzman, Onfredo, Redrum, Short Fuse, Thrust, Trout Guest, Velveeta, and Xanax. Some had been lecherous, most had been lonely. But one had been different from the others.

She paused, not knowing quite what to make of her own reaction to him. She had actually *liked* this other man. In truth, she'd found herself attracted to him, flirting in earnest, as if she really were twenty years old again.

At 11:05, she'd been in the Rose Garden when he'd paged her. His name was The Highwayman.

"This one," she wrote to Hayden, "isn't like the other boys."

OMEGA NAME	FACTS
The Highwayman	Real name: didn't say
	Age: about twenty-three, but could be older
	Location: Detroit
	Occupation: computer programmer
	Desire: friendship, flirtation

She paused, yawned, and rose to make herself another cup of strong coffee. The sun was up, but the sky was so clouded and the rain so heavy that she could not even see the lake.

Last night she'd talked almost four hours with The Highwayman—four hours!—but she'd lost track of time. He was polite, educated, witty, and he was charming, very charming.

The Bower of Bliss was a secluded spot he'd discovered on Omega, a forest of giant ferns and tropical flowers. The description was sensuous, full of color and fragrance; there were warm breezes and rustling leaves and bursts of birdsong.

The Bower of Bliss certainly beat Hayden's Archive Room by a country mile. She'd given the command to look at The Highwayman.

You see a tall man in a long, black cape. He wears knee-high black boots, black riding breeches, and a ruffled white shirt with full sleeves and lace at the cuffs. A sword with a silver hilt hangs in a scabbard at his side, and a pistol is tucked into his scarlet sash.

A black tricorn hat shadows his face, the upper part of

which is hidden by a black mask. You look more closely, but all you can see is that there is a gleam of satire in his gray eyes and a faintly mocking smile on his lips.

He bows and kisses your hand in greeting.

Hmm, she'd thought, *not bad.* "Why a Highwayman?" she asked.

"We're on the Information Superhighway," he'd answered. "Seemed appropriate." He shrugged and smiled.

She'd liked that.

So she'd talked with The Highwayman, joked with him,—even danced with him. He'd led her in a virtual dance, which was complex and somehow graceful, and for a moment she almost felt as if she really were in a man's arms, dancing to secret music that only the two of them heard.

Then he'd taken her by the hand and showed her the surrounding woods, the enchanted Forest of Arden. Having a man take your hand in cyberspace, Carrie thought, gave you an odd feeling. If he seemed like the right sort of man, you liked it. She'd liked it.

When she finally told him she had to say goodbye, he'd asked if he could kiss her, and she'd said yes.

The Highwayman takes you into his arms and lowers his lips to yours. He finds your mouth so sweet that he draws you closer, wrapping you in the folds of his cloak.

Now, in the cold light of morning, Carrie blushed, something she seldom did. She'd actually kissed him back. It was a shy kiss, with no frills, but she'd committed it.

You kiss The Highwayman.

He smiles and keeps your lovely body pressed against his. He whispers, "Will you meet me here again tomorrow night at eleven? Please. I want to see you again."

She'd agreed and given him her e-mail address when he asked for it; after all, she was supposed to encourage any likely suitor. Then, with relief, she'd left Omega.

Now she was troubled as she sipped the coffee and stared out at the rain. It had been easy for her to play her role with The Highwayman, too easy, and the flirting had been exciting. But she'd told him countless lies about herself, and for all she knew, he'd lied as much as she.

Their relationship had seemed real, but her part, at least, was as false as Judas. If he was sincere, she was leading a nice young man down a devious path.

In spite of herself, she felt excited and attracted by this man. But, she rebuked herself, that was idiotic; he was over twenty years younger than she. Omega, by its peculiar leger-demain, had made her feel ageless.

Hayden was a real man, solid and physical and, yes, sexy in his harsh way. He liked her, she could tell. Why was it easier to yield to flirtation with a stranger? Because the stranger wasn't real?

The Highwayman was nothing but a shifting configuration of words on a screen. In real life, he might be almost anything. Although it was a very long shot, he might even be a murderer.

Carrie swore under her breath and went back to the computer. She wrote:

> The Highwayman seems far more mature than other men I've met. He's smooth, and he plays a lot of verbal games. But he told me little about himself, and when I asked him his name in real life, he was elusive.
>
> This guy's a charmer, very likeable, even seductive, but he takes his time; he doesn't push. He's also got an air of mystery. He said he doesn't talk much about his real life because at this point he doesn't much like it. He manages to be dashing and vulnerable at the same time.
>
> I meet him again tonight. I wish the guy wasn't such a night owl. I'm going to be in the Yawn Prison all day.
>
> I've got to come into town for class this afternoon. Maybe I could stop at your office and talk about Brooke. About two o'clock?
>
> > Falling asleep even as I sign this,
> > Carrie

She hit the keys to send the message. "Do your stuff, electrons." She secretly suspected that the stuff electrons did was black magic. Perhaps that was all Omega was, that old black magic trying to get her in its spell.

She glanced at the clock and sighed. It was time to get to work on her fiction. But while she fought to concentrate, her mind kept wandering back to Omega and The Highwayman.

I don't want to think about any man, she thought. *What's Omega doing to me?*

Hayden felt as if he were coming out of a long, unpleasant trance. Last night on Omega, when Carrie stood him up to stay in the goddammed Bower of Bliss, the reality of Edmon's case hit him.

After the carnage and chaos of Waco and its aftermath, Edmon's problems had seemed like small potatoes, the worried fantasies of a nervous rich kid.

But the nervous rich kid had a point. Two girls might be dead. And Carrie was out there, dancing in their footsteps, playing God knew what sort of games.

He'd read her e-mail report, he'd seen the hour she'd transmitted it. Hadn't she gone to bed at all? He himself was edgy from lack of sleep, and his eyelids felt like hot sandpaper.

He'd read Brooke's report, which was markedly more factual and organized than the first; he was surprised, he'd expected her to persist in her rebellion. But he still wasn't sure he wanted to keep her as part of the team.

Despite his orders, she'd spent two hours with Alhambra. She said that his real name was Kevin Winger and he lived in Princeton, New Jersey. She also said, rather snippily, that Kevin insisted he was twenty-one years old, *not* fourteen.

After Kevin, she spent the next hour with a character called James Dean. His real name was James, she said, and he was a troubleshooter for a computer company, traveling from place to place as he was needed. He was currently in California and was "very literate and sensitive," she said, "and about twenty-five." He was recovering from breaking up with his fiancée, a beautiful but philandering model.

James Dean had to log off at eleven o'clock. After that, Brooke took pages from Aardvark Guest, Damian Two, and Mephisto. She got no information on Aardvark Guest or Damian Two. But Mephisto was a twenty-six-year-old electrical engineer student in Denver, and his name was David. He was extremely intelligent, she said, but he had to log off early.

Brooke herself had left Omega without explanation at eleven, even though she had promised to stay on every night until midnight. Hayden didn't like this. She was such a compulsive writer, he found it out of character for her to quit early. He'd expected her, not Carrie, to be the one drawn into overtime.

He glanced at his watch. It was a little before two. Twelve hours ago he'd been sulking in the Archive Room, keeping track of Carrie like some electronic peeping Tom. In a few minutes, she'd walk into his office in the flesh.

In the flesh. He thought of flesh, its desires, its desirability, its fragility. Carrie was fair-skinned and freckled, and he wondered exactly how much of her trim body was freckled— her shoulders, her thighs, her midriff?

Forget it, he told himself. *Back to the monastery. Sit in your cell. Eat some saltpeter. Throw more ashes on your head.*

He tried to study a stack of insurance surveillance photos. They were not as clear to his tired eyes as the picture of Carrie in his head.

At precisely two P.M., Alice's voice came over the intercom. "Ms. Blue here to see you."

"Send her in," he said gruffly, and straightened his tie. He tried to arrange his expression to look unconcerned, even bored.

Carrie waltzed in the door wearing wrinkled white slacks and a gray T-shirt with a picture of Krazy Kat. She looked far too perky for somebody who'd been up half the night. There were slight shadows under her eyes, that was all. She hadn't tried to hide them with makeup.

"Hi," she said, a shade too cheerfully.

"Hi," he said, a shade too coolly. "Have a seat."

She sat, crossing her legs at the ankles in that curiously prim way she had. She wore scuffed running shoes that were beat to hell. He wondered if she couldn't afford to replace them.

"You put in long hours last night," he said. "I hope the guy was worth it."

Did he imagine that a blush stained her cheeks?

She said, "The question is, do you think he's worth it? Does he sound like the kind of man we're looking for?"

Hayden searched her face. "Yeah. He sounds smooth. How smooth?"

She looked him in the eye. "As silk. I wished I really were twenty again."

Twenty, hell, he thought. He liked the laugh lines around her eyes, the character that experience had written on her face. Twenty was a baby, a pup, a tadpole.

He said, "Be careful. Edmon says on Omega relationships get intense, and they get that way fast."

"I can see that," she said.

"Don't get carried away."

"I won't. But I see how people do."

He made a meaningless notation on her report and underlined the words, <u>This guy's a charmer, very likeable, even seductive.</u> He underlined <u>seductive</u> twice.

"What would happen," he asked, "if Brooke met this guy? Could she keep her cool?"

Carrie's expression grew troubled. "I can't say. She seems almost contemptuous of relationships. Somebody said she was dating a waiter here, a boy just out of high school, but it fizzled out. I don't even know if that's true."

Hayden tried to choose his words carefully. "She did better work last night. She's fluent, she's imaginative, but it's almost too much of a good thing. She's intellectually arrogant, and she likes going her own way. I don't know why Holloway chose her."

"Give her a chance," Carrie said. "I think he picked her because she's like me, she needs the money. And he probably hopes it'll help her get more involved with people her own age. She's so self-contained and remote."

"Wait a minute," Hayden said. "He wants her more normal, so he sends her into this pack of weirdos? That's like trying to keep somebody dry by throwing them in a lake."

"Holloway says everything she imagines comes from myths and legends, not experience. He says when it comes to social relations, she's running on empty."

"He sent her my way as therapy, for Chrissake? Since when does he think he's God?"

"Since forever," Carrie said with a toss of her head. "It's an occupational hazard for teachers. I've had the urge myself sometimes."

He leaned back in his chair, rubbed his chin, and regarded her. "So why'd he pick you? Don't get me wrong. You write fine. But did he have some ulterior motive for sending you to Omega?"

She shrugged and stared off into a corner, her chin held high. "Holloway has this thing about my middle-class morality. That I've got too much of it."

Hayden allowed himself half a smile. Maybe her middle-class morality was one of the things he liked about her.

He said, "Moderation in all things."

"Fine," Carrie said. "Let him moderate himself. He also thinks I'm sexually repressed. Which I'm *not.*"

"Well, of course, I only have your word for that."

She gave him a sharp look, a schoolteacher's look of stern rebuke. On her it was nice. She said, "He likes the stories I do about my grandmother, but he always asks why there's no sex in them. It's because they have nothing to *do* with sex. He wants me to write more about women's sexuality. Maybe that's what he wants to read, but it's not what I want to write."

"He's actually told you this?" Hayden said. Academia never ceased to amaze him.

"Yes. And I told him what I thought. I've had my spats with him. Most of the women students have."

Hayden wondered if Holloway, who wore a wedding

ring, secretly had the hots for Carrie. He said, "How's he know there's lots of sex on the MOON?"

"He said his son used to play around on the MOOs and Omega. For all I know, Holloway cruises it himself. Nothing would surprise me at this point."

Hayden considered this. A married guy like Holloway living a wild second life, via his computer. Commit adultery in the comfort of your own home; avoid the damning evidence of an actual partner.

"Anyway," she said with a dismissive wave of her hand, "we're supposed to talk about Brooke. She wasn't in Shakespeare class today."

Hayden frowned. "Why?"

"I don't know. But she did do better on Omega last night?"

"She could do better still. She's wordy, she goes off on tangents, leaves things out. And she logged off early. I hope she didn't log on again, without us knowing it. There are dangerous people there. I can *feel* it."

"Your terrorists?" she asked, a little sadly.

"Maybe," he said. He thought of the graffiti. Slate Wiper had struck anew at the Rose Garden wall, writing, "REWARD! $$$ FOR DEAD FEDEREL AGENTS!" Nitrate had been there, too: "The FBI kills womean and children!"

But what troubled him more was that among the Archives he had found an instruction book on making ammonium nitrate bombs, exactly the sort that terrorists had used on the New York World Trade Center and the Oklahoma Federal Building.

Anyone could add books to the archives. Who, he wondered, had gone to the trouble to create a virtual how-to book on explosives? The ammonium nitrate recipe was all over the Internet, but he was unpleasantly surprised to find it in as obscure a place as the basement Archives.

He tried to focus on present concerns. "I'd like you to talk to Brooke. She's skating on thin ice."

"I'll try," Carrie said. "She really does need the money. I heard she lived on nothing but oatmeal for three weeks last winter."

He shook his head noncommittally; he didn't intend to feel sympathy for Brooke. She did her job or she was out, that was that.

"Is that all?" she asked.

He took a deep breath. *This is incredibly stupid,* he told himself. *Why am I doing this?*

He said, "I've got tickets for a folksinger at the Walton Arts Center Saturday night. Would you like to go? I can sweeten the deal by offering you supper. There's this rib house called Herman's. Not fancy, but world-class food. What do you say?"

A strange look crossed her face, like longing mixed with—what? He didn't know. He wondered again if she had freckles on her shoulders, maybe even between her breasts.

"Thanks, but no," she said. "I've got to work. All this time on Omega puts me on a tight schedule."

Faint heart never won fair lady, he told himself grimly. "You've got to take a break sometime," he said. "All work and no play . . ." *I'm a fucking fountain of clichés,* he thought.

She met his eyes with her steady blue gaze. "I'm flattered you'd ask. But I don't date these days. It's a decision I've made. But thanks again."

Hayden cocked his eyebrow and hoped he looked appropriately cynical. She'd shot him down in flames and hadn't so much as blinked at the smoke. "It's your loss. The ribs are good, even if the company isn't."

She showed her dimples. She said, "It probably is my loss. Thanks. I'll see you on Omega."

"Yeah," he said. "Sure." But he got the message. She'd put a chain-link fence twelve-feet high around herself, topped with coils of barbed wire. She'd hung out a big sign that said "Do Not Trespass."

As if eager to escape him, she was already on her feet.

He said, "I'll walk you to your car."

But she was already at the door. "Don't bother," she said, and showed her dimples again. But he thought there was something haunted in her eyes. She opened the door, and then she was gone, shutting it behind her.

He stared at that closed door. Then he tried looking at the insurance surveillance photos again.

He turned on the radio. A golden oldie was playing about what the world needed now was sweet, sweet love, love for everyone.

He switched it off.

Brooke's phone rang. This seldom happened, and when it did, the caller was usually a telephone solicitor trying to sell her storm windows, aluminum siding, or long-life light bulbs.

Her family never phoned her. She was estranged from them. They thought her godless, headstrong, wicked, and proud. She had offended them by going to college at all.

She picked up the receiver warily, and when she heard Carrie Blue's voice, she was surprised.

"Hi," Carrie said. "How's it going?"

Brooke secretly envied Carrie. The woman was intelligent and a decent writer, but it hadn't made her strange. She seemed completely at home in the world, unlike Brooke, who hid all too successfully behind her cold facade.

"It's going fine," Brooke said vaguely.

"Are you okay?" Carrie asked. "You weren't in class."

Brooke had skipped Shakespeare because she'd stayed on Omega until two o'clock in the morning, logged on through her university account.

"I was tired," she said. "And I'm catching a cold."

"I'll loan you my notes if you want," Carrie said.

Brooke was touched in spite of herself. People usually treated her as if she were a space alien and seldom made friendly gestures. "Thanks," she said.

"I'll give them to you tomorrow. Maybe after class we could have a cup of coffee or something. Talk about Omega. We should probably compare notes. I never have time to talk to you while I'm logged on."

"If I have time," Brooke said, unsure. Of course, she had time. Her social schedule was so empty that she had great stretches of time, wastelands of it.

"Did you imagine Omega would be so strange?" Carrie

asked. "It plays games with my mind. It's probably my age. Maybe it doesn't seem so weird to you."

Everything in the real world seems weird to me, Brooke thought. *Everything is passing strange.* "It's okay," she said tonelessly.

"Hayden—Ivanovich—worries about us," Carrie said. "Omega's like a crazy Mardi Gras. Everybody's wearing masks. It's hard to know what you're really dealing with."

"Umm," said Brooke.

"So," Carrie said cheerfully, "we need to stick together, not lose sight of our goal. And I particularly need your feedback, because I'm so much older. I feel a little out of it, you know?"

I've felt out of it my whole life, Brooke thought. "Umm, yeah. Well," she said.

"Ivanovich keeps giving me orders," Carrie said. "It's irritating. But he's just trying to do his job. He's concerned, that's all."

"I do things my own way," Brooke said.

"I understand that," Carrie said. "But we have to keep him happy. A job's a job. And aren't you going to hate to give up these great computers?"

Brooke said nothing. She hadn't thought about the fact that by estranging Ivanovich she could lose the computer. She was in love with it, and it was the only way she could get to Omega. Her own computer didn't have the capability. *Damn,* she thought. *Keep him happy is right.*

"Well, let's keep in touch," Carrie said. "I need to stay grounded. Omega's very seductive. I found myself actually liking one of the men I talked to. I—feel odd about that. We're dealing with strange stuff here."

Brooke said nothing. She, too, had met someone attractive. Not merely attractive, but wildly so, the most exciting man she could imagine. She was going to meet him again tonight. But she wasn't about to tell Ivanovich about the turn this relationship had taken. No way.

"I mean," Carrie said, "we have to stay focused. We're a team. And Ivanovich is the captain. Sort of."

"And Edmon's the owner," Brooke said. She didn't like the idea of being owned.

"Well, I suppose he is. But he's a nice young man. He means well."

He's a hopeless, stuttering nerd, and I've seen cats with stronger chins, Brooke thought, but she said nothing.

"I just thought it'd be nice to touch base with you," Carrie said rather lamely. "Don't be shy about calling me. Some of the things that happen on Omega—it's hard to discuss with a man."

"Yeah. Well," said Brooke.

"Damian Two and Thrust, for instance," Carrie said. "I'm not repeating what they say to Ivanovich."

Brooke gave a contemptuous laugh. "Oh, Damian Two," she said. "God!"

"That's what I mean," said Carrie. "And did a character named Velveeta page you last night and ask you to do something to him with handcuffs and a hamster?"

"Yes," Brooke said, giggling in spite of herself. "Only with me, he said gerbil."

"Variety's the spice of life." Carrie laughed, and Brooke giggled again.

When Carrie hung up, Brooke had a pleasant and unfamiliar feeling of warmth. Carrie was acting and talking to her like a friend. Three times in Brooke's life she'd had lovers, but she'd never had a real friend, and sometimes she felt the lack keenly. And Carrie, stable as she was, admitted to being secretly drawn to a man on Omega—and was even asking Brooke's advice!

But Brooke was not ready to confide her own secret. The man she'd met on Omega was marvelous, fascinating. More wonderful still, he liked her and actually seemed to *need* her. All day long, she'd thought of him.

He said he'd been waiting and hoping and praying for someone like her.

Someone just like her.

One week passed, then half of another. Carrie felt trapped in a haze of unreality. The rain seemed never to stop; it had fallen for nine days straight, and the lake was rising dangerously. It lapped almost at the edge of her neglected flower bed, where the flowers sagged, beaten down.

She'd received her Omega character, Greensleeves, a few days ago. Brooke was now Shalanna, and Hayden had become Average Joe. He kept his distance from her. He wandered Omega alone in search of new graffiti, and he studied in the Archive Room.

Each night she talked to The Highwayman, until two or three in the morning. She could *not* get a fix on the man, no matter how hard she tried.

Edmon said The Highwayman was a new character, and nobody, not even Quicksilver, knew anything about him. "Some characters don't mingle much," he said. "They come on, make one or two contacts, then stay with those people."

Carrie's work suffered. She was barely keeping up with the Shakespeare seminar. By mornings, she was too tired to work on her fiction and found concentration difficult.

She made it a point of having coffee with Brooke after Shakespeare and was actually starting to like her. She saw the girl was not as self-possessed as she seemed—far from it. But Brooke was closed-mouthed and hard to talk to, and the only subjects they had in common were school and Omega. Always Omega.

Slowly the MOON had begun to possess Carrie. And so had The Highwayman. He said his name was Paul, but he wouldn't give his surname. He said he was self-employed, he set his own hours, and he stayed up late because he preferred it that way.

He flirted with her outrageously and wanted to know all about her. She flirted back and lied and lied and lied. He hugged and kissed her when they met and when they parted. He had begun to hug and kiss and caress her a great deal.

Carrie was confused. It seemed she was coming to know this man well. She knew his favorite rock group, his all-time favorite movie, his favorite novel. She knew he loved Indian food, the spicier the better, and that he hated eggs in any form. She knew the names of all his childhood dogs.

He disliked rap music, but liked rhythm and blues. He

had a scar on his chin from a minor motorcycle accident he'd had eighteen months ago. "It makes me look like Harrison Ford," he said, and she liked to imagine that he did.

He was getting over a romance that had left him down but not out. "She was a nice woman," he said. "We just weren't right for each other. Simple as that."

Carrie knew everything about him, and she knew nothing. The Highwayman could be nineteen or he could be sixty; he could be married or single, black or white. He might be as dashing as his description and as charming as he seemed, or he might weigh four hundred pounds and have a collection of severed human heads in his refrigerator.

If he was new to Omega, he seemed to know his way around it exceptionally well. He understood things she didn't and had powers far beyond hers. He was strangely reluctant to share his knowledge with her.

"I like knowing more," he said. "It makes you seem kind of helpless. That's a turn-on."

"You're a chauvinist pig," she told him.

"Yeah, but I'm *your* chauvinist pig," he said. "Hopelessly devoted to you."

She was aware that he was doing his best to charm off her virtual pants. He was getting more touchy-feely all the time, and she was shocked that she could almost feel his virtual caresses. They repelled her, but against her will, sometimes they excited her.

The Highwayman was like a daemon lover, a phantom who came to her in the dead of night, not quite human and wielding more than human powers.

In the meantime, Hayden Ivanovich no longer seemed interested in her; his communiqués to her were brief and businesslike. This, too, made her feel strange.

She had avoided taking real chances with a real man. Instead she threw her energy into a false love affair with a suitor as insubstantial as a will-o'-the-wisp.

Hayden had told her he was more satisfied with Brooke. Her reports were better: terser, clearer, more factual. But she still could ramble off in distraction, she spent an irritating amount of time with Alhambra, and she kept logging off every night at exactly ten forty-five. She said she got too tired to keep going.

Carrie was tired in a different way. Omega filled her with a sense of emptiness and spiritual fatigue. Tonight, Saturday, she turned on the computer with her usual sense of why-am-I-doing-this?

An e-mail message from Hayden was waiting for her.

> Carrie: Brooke's been seeing a lot of Mephisto, but she never says much about him. See what you can find out, will you? —H.
>
> P.S. You're spending more time with Onfredo. Are there any possibilities there?

He sounded strictly professional. And in an equally brisk tone, she would write him that Onfredo seemed to be the one safe man on Omega, a minister's son struggling to get the courage to come out of the closet and act on his homosexuality. She felt freer and more comfortable with Onfredo than anyone on Omega, certainly more so than she did with Hayden.

I don't want you to want me, Hayden. I can't let myself want you back. I'm afraid to.

The thought startled her. She'd promised herself not to get involved with anyone until she was finished with her degree and was settled, that was all. She didn't actually *fear* involvement, did she?

She stared out at the rain and felt depressed. Her roof had developed a leak, and she kept a rusty bucket sitting in the kitchen to catch the drops. Her road was growing so rutted by the torrents of water that she feared soon she would not be able to reach the highway.

"Cheer up," she grumbled to herself as she logged on to Omega. "Things could be worse. I could still be stuck in Bitter Water, Nebraska."

But it occurred to her that she could also be out tonight with someone like Hayden and away from the accursed computer, which had taken over her life.

Except for The Highwayman and the irreverent Onfredo, Omega had grown boring. There was a horrible sameness to it. It was always chaotic and silly, and she wondered if any of the people who thronged there had real lives.

Tonight she logged on at exactly eight and transported to Ye Silent Woman Pub. Quicksilver was holding court while Blue Rider nuzzled her. Flair, the rather aloof little ballerina was there.

Lacewing came teleporting in. "Hi," she told Quicksilver. "Are there any messages for me?"

"Let me see," said Quicksilver, as Blue Rider kissed her shoulders. "Lacewing, Lacewing. Yes. Marcus will log on at eight-thirty. He'll meet you at the Garden Maze."

Lacewing hugged Quicksilver in gratitude. "You're a treasure," she said.

"Who's Marcus?" Blue Rider asked. He nibbled Quicksilver's ear.

Lacewing said, "He's a guest. He's applying for a character. And he's *wonderful.*"

"What happened to Cochise?" Flair asked. "He was mad for you."

"Oh, God, this is Omega," Lacewing said, settling down beside Flair. "He found somebody else. I'm glad. He's too immature for me. He's also weird once you get to know him. I mean, scary weird."

"Run away with me," Blue Rider said to Quicksilver, burying his face between her breasts. "Mmmmmmm," he said. "Delicious boobies. Let's go to a sex chamber. I'll chain you to the bed."

"Promises, promises," said Quicksilver, but together they vanished.

"Blue Rider's not faithful to her," Lacewing said to Flair. "He hits on all the women, all the time. He's like a satyr or something."

"Maybe she doesn't care," Flair said.

"I don't see you with James Dean lately," Lacewing said. "Did you break up?"

"Not really," said Flair. "I just wanted to slow down. Things happen so fast on Omega. Too fast."

Lacewing smiled at her. "Sometimes fast is nice. So do you still see him?"

"We talk on the phone. He sends me flowers. We leave each other mail messages."

The two women seemed to have forgotten Carrie was there. *Hmm,* she thought idly. *This is just like Bitter Water High School. Who's dating whom? Gossip, gossip, gossip. Buzz, buzz, buzz.*

"Maybe I shouldn't say this," Lacewing said, "but do you know James is on here every night with some female guest?"

"I know," said Flair. "That's all right. He should see other people. I don't mind."

"Maybe he's trying to make you jealous?"

"Maybe," said Flair. "I think I'll log off early tonight. Go study. Hardly anybody's here on Saturday nights. It's lonesome."

"Yeah, it's kinda dead."

"Goodnight," said Flair, and a few seconds later she vanished. Lacewing left, too, without so much as speaking to Carrie.

Carrie leaned her virtual elbows on the virtual table and looked around the pub. Its description hadn't changed an iota, of course, it never did. But this was the first time she'd ever seen it empty.

So some of these people, at least, actually did go out in the real world on Saturday night. They did have social lives aside from Omega. Who was left here tonight? Only losers and the hard-core MOON addicts? She felt sorry for Flair, who seemed sad.

Hayden paged her from the Archive Room. "All alone?"

He'd startled her, and she tensed. "I'll go to the Hot Tub," she paged back. "There's always action there."

"It gets wild. Be careful."

Carrie was growing hardened to Omega's wildness. Last night in Le Club du France she'd seen two male guests rape a third. It had been nasty, brutal, and highly explicit.

"I'm always careful," she paged. "What are you learning up there in the spiderwebs?"

"Humility. I'm no computer whiz."

She smiled. "Any more graffiti?"

"Yeah. In the Meditation Book in the Chapel of Robyc."

"What's it say?"

"Slate Wiper says, 'The revolution has begun,' that sort of stuff."

"I thought the Chapel was supposed to be the one holy spot on Omega," Carrie said.

"There is no holy spot on Omega," said Hayden.

The Highwayman appears. His eyes meet yours. Your pulses speed, your heart leaps. You know this man is both charming and dangerous.

Carrie blinked in surprise. "Oh," she said to The Highwayman. "You're early."

The Highwayman strides across the room and stares into your eyes. He puts one arm around your waist and draws you to him.

He says, "I couldn't wait."

He kisses you passionately.

You cannot resist. You are on fire sexually.

You are on fire with wanting him.

NINE

‹‹‹‹‹‹•››››››

THE HIGHWAYMAN WAS WILDLY AMOROUS TONIGHT. CARRIE WAS caught off guard.

>The Highwayman pulls your body more tightly against his. His lips capture yours, pillaging their sweetness. You yearn to surrender to his desire—and your own.

"Excuse me," Carrie typed, her mouth set grimly. "But you are not pillaging my lips. I am not clinging to you. I don't even know your name. I find you wildly attractive. But anonymous sex does not make me yearn to surrender."

>The Highwayman kisses the pulse throbbing in your throat. He whispers, "This is fantasy, love. Give yourself to fantasy."
>He unfastens your bodice and his lips press hotly against the delicious valley between your breasts.

Carrie grimaced. She answered, "Stop this, or I'm going to log off. You're not kissing my boobs, delicious as they may be. I won't have virtual sex with somebody whose name I don't know. I want to know you as a person. Who are you?"

"I am The Highwayman," he breathes as he uncovers your breasts. "I am the lover from your dreams."

He takes one of your taut nipples into his mouth, sucking it sensually, running his tongue around the tender edge.

"Holy foreplay," Carrie muttered to herself. "He's heading straight for the Batcave."

"I mean it," she told him sternly. "Unless you tell me your name, I'm logging off. If we make love, I want it to be as people, not as characters."

The Highwayman caresses both your breasts. His warm tongue glides down your body, toward your navel. "I am your fantasy," he whispers.

Carrie was repelled. She felt no ardor, and his desire for her seemed to press down on her like some sort of torturous weight. "Who are you?" she demanded. "Tell me, or I'll leave."

The Highwayman runs his hand up your thigh, making you tremble with desire. You are growing hot and wet, wild with need for his huge cock.

"Bye-bye," Carrie said and hit the computer's reset button, turning it off. It was not considered good form to leave Omega that way, but she'd had enough.

Her head ached, and she put her elbows on the desk and buried her face in her hands. Wasn't sex complicated enough without putting an electronic spin on it? She sat motionless, her eyes squeezed shut.

Her new phone, the white one full of buttons, rang and she tensed. Only a handful of people knew the number.

She answered it, her heart beating hard. "Melissa?"

asked a man's voice. "Is this Melissa?" His accent seemed midwestern.

"Yes?" she lied. "Who's this?"

"This is The Highwayman. I didn't mean to offend you, honest to God. I wanted to find a fantasy lover so I wouldn't get involved. But I am involved. I think I love you, Melissa. My name is Paul Johnson."

She wrote his name down in her notebook, her hand shaking. His voice was slurred and he sounded a bit drunk.

"Tell me about yourself, Paul," she said.

"It's a complicated story," he said. "But I need you, Melissa. I need you desperately."

Carrie sat listening, her teeth on edge, as The Highwayman poured out his heart to her. Or pretended to. Either way, she felt terrible, like someone who finds herself staring at the scene of a ghastly accident, sickened but unable to turn away.

An accident was what he tried to describe to her. "I don't remember any of it," he said. He sounded close to tears. "For some reason I swerved. There was never an explanation. I remember us starting out. I remember Heather hanging on to me, and me laughing at her for being scared."

"I'm so sorry," Carrie said, but in truth she did not know what she felt. Was his name really Paul Johnson? Was any of this true?

He said he was a twenty-three-year-old Canadian from rural Ontario. He'd bought a used motorcycle while he was at the University of Toronto. He'd driven it to see his fiancée, Heather, in London, Ontario. Despite her fear, he'd cajoled her into going for a ride. Then, he told Carrie, the accident ripped a chunk out of time.

He'd come back to consciousness in the intensive care ward, his spine broken. They didn't tell him right away that Heather was dead. Nor did they tell him yet that he might never walk again.

In painful detail he told her about his hospitalization, his therapy, the difficulties of life in a wheelchair. He said his left leg tingled, as if sensation might be coming back. He prayed it would.

He began to cry softly. He sounded truly upset and Carrie, miserable, leaned her elbow on her desk and covered her eyes again.

"I'd been at Toronto on a track scholarship," Paul said in a broken voice. "I was a track and field man."

"Oh, God, I'm sorry," Carrie said. *If this is the truth,* she thought, *I'm going to hate myself forever.*

"My specialty was the hundred-meter dash," he said. "I loved running. I loved the high it gave me."

She could think of nothing to say.

"I missed tying the province record by a fraction of a second," he said. "Two-tenths of a second less, and I'd have been in the record books. God. Two-tenths of a second." He made a small, strangled sobbing noise.

"Steady, now," Carrie said. "Pull yourself together."

"I'm sorry," he said. For a moment he was silent. Then, his voice steadier, he said, "After the accident, I pretty much went into a tailspin. Depression. Big time. My folks didn't know how to handle it."

"It's okay," Carrie said. "Don't apologize."

"My older sister, Terry, in Detroit, offered to take me into her house," he said, his voice steadier now, but bitter. "She was a trauma nurse. Now she stays home with her two kids. She's also a pushy, know-it-all bitch."

Carrie had spent years weighing students' stories, separating the true from the false. As skeptical as she tried to be, this man did not sound like a liar to her. He *knew* what he was describing. Her stomach contracted sickly.

"Melissa," he said, "this is like being naked and helpless in front of you. Intellectually, I *knew* I could have sex. But I didn't *care.* Until I found you."

Carrie's forehead hurt, and the beating of the rain against her window was driving her mad. She said, "I'm flattered. Really, I am."

"I don't have much to offer you," he said. "But I'm learning to make a living computer programming. And, honest to God, you've made me want to live again. I love you. Does that count for anything? Do you care for me at all?"

She kept her hand pressed over her eyes, covering them. "Of course, I care for you. You're smart and charming and"—she hesitated, took a deep breath—"outrageous and brave."

"Oh, fuck brave," he answered. "I'm not. But for the first time, I'm thinking about sex again. I think about it with you. All day long. I've dreamed about it. Okay, you want the truth? I had a wet dream about you last night. Oh, God, could you make it more than a dream? Do you know what that would mean to me?"

Carrie's head ached so hard it banged. She swore under her breath. To The Highwayman she said, "I don't know what to do. Give me time to think."

"You're angry because I lied to you," he said. "I'm sorry. The Highwayman is the man I wish I was. I didn't set out to deceive anyone."

Oh, God, oh, God, oh, God, thought Carrie.

"I'm not angry," she said, and swallowed. "That's not it at all."

"I shouldn't have told you," he said. "I'm—I'm kind of drunk. Everybody else went to the movies tonight. That's why I logged on early. I usually wait until they're all in bed. None of them knows about Omega, about any of this."

"Maybe you should tell," Carrie said, trying to steer the conversation in a safer direction.

"Christ, all my sister ever does is carp that I have to face reality. This would totally fry her brains. No way."

"Oh," she said inadequately.

"You sound as pretty as you look on the MOON," he said. "You've got a really pretty voice. Sexy."

Carrie knew she must stop this before it went further. "Look," she said, "this has turned serious so suddenly. I just need a little time. Please."

"Melissa, log back on Omega, please. Wanting you is about more than sex. I mean it's your personality and your mind and your sense of humor and everything that I fell in love with. I do love you. I mean that."

"I—I have to think," she said. "Let's meet at the usual time tomorrow, okay?"

"I love you, Melissa. Is it impossible for you to love me back? Just a little?"

She rubbed her burning eyes. "Nothing's impossible. But let's say goodnight now. Please."

"You promise you'll be there tomorrow?" he asked.

"I promise," she said. "Goodnight now, Paul."

"Goodnight, Melissa."

Carrie hung up, bent over her desk, and buried her face in her arms. She was emotionally spent and physically exhausted. She was supposed to work another three hours on Omega, but she couldn't face it.

Her own phone, the one without all the fancy buttons, rang. *Hayden,* she thought, tears of frustration stinging her eyes. Calling to check why she had logged off early.

She didn't want to talk about this yet to him, she didn't want to talk about it to anybody. She disconnected the ringing phone with one short, hostile pull of the cord. Then she disconnected the shiny new white telephone.

The house was silent except for the unending monotony of the rain. She went on the deck and sat on the porch. The night air was hot and humid, the lake barely visible through the shifting veils of rain.

The deck, the night, the rain didn't seem real to her. Nothing seemed real anymore.

After a restless night, Carrie rose to a gray morning. She went into her kitchen, made a cup of her industrial-strength coffee. Rain still beat at the windows, and she had to empty the bucket from the leaking roof.

She put it back into place and listened to the steady *plink, plink, plink* of water hitting metal.

From the window she could see that the lake had risen enough to cover the edge of her once carefully tended flower bed. Marigold blossoms bobbed forlornly on the water's surface like drowned, blond heads.

She plugged in the new phone line and sat down at the hateful computer, which seemed vain of its newness and smug about its capabilities.

"I'll be glad to send you back to Edmon, you cyber son-of-a-bitch," she muttered.

She shook her head at her own foolishness. She hadn't liked the messages the machine had brought her, so she blamed the messenger. Stupid, stupid, and all too human.

She booted up the computer and saw that she had two new pieces of e-mail messages. The first was from The Highwayman.

"Melissa, sweetheart—Please, please forgive me for holding back the truth for so long. I didn't go to Omega expecting to fall in love. But I couldn't help myself. I'm yours, even if you don't want me, I guess. I think of you all the time. You're in my mind constantly. Kisses, Your Highwayman."

I can't stand this, Carrie thought gloomily. *I feel completely morally compromised.*

The second message was from Hayden.

"Carrie: Are you okay? H."

She typed the command to reply to him, then wrote:

"Ivanovich—No, I'm not okay. I refuse to play this awful game any longer. It's interfering with my work, my sleep, and my peace of mind. I quit. Have somebody come get this @$*&!! computer.

"I mean it. I'm in no mood to argue. I'm behind in my seminar, my roof's leaking, and the lake is lapping at my door. Adieu forever, Carrie B."

She reread the message. It struck her as too raw, too revealing. She should revise it into something prim, sterile, and utterly emotionless.

She didn't care. She hit the keys to send it and unplugged the phone again.

At four o'clock that afternoon, Carrie drew large, angry *x*'s over the whole first half of the rattlesnake story. Her prose seemed as leaden as the sky, as mind-numbing as the ceaseless rain. She remembered this story clearly, why couldn't she tell it?

She heard a vehicle pulling up in her drive and her muscles tensed. She didn't want to see anyone, but now she had company. Who? She rose and went to the window.

A black jeep, splashed with mud, parked in the middle of her streaming drive. Hayden got out. He wore no hat, and the rain immediately drenched his brown hair and flowed down his face.

Carrie swore softly to herself, but went to the door and flung it open. "What do *you* want?" she asked, not caring if she sounded rude.

"Shelter," he muttered, brushing past her.

She shut the door and stared up at him. She'd forgotten how tall he was, and in her tiny living room, he seemed to fill more than his share of space.

She had never seen him dressed so casually. He wore faded jeans and a pale blue work shirt that was damp with rain.

"I don't know what you're doing here," she said. "I don't work for you anymore. I quit. I sent you an e-mail message."

"I got it," he said, wiping rain from his eyes with the heel of his hand.

"Then what are you doing here?" she asked.

"I came to tell you that you can't quit."

"I can, I did, and I do," she said. "Did you come clear out here to change my mind? You can't."

"I wanted to see if I could even get to this place. Your road's about washed out. You'll never make it out of here in a car, know that? You're pretty much marooned."

"That's my problem," she said.

"We'll deal with that later. I also came to see what it would take to fix your roof."

"My roof is not your problem, either," she answered. "I can take care of myself."

"You sounded upset," he said. "Something happened between you and The Highwayman. What?"

She flinched slightly. His hazel gaze was steady and held hers.

"I don't want to talk about it," she said. She couldn't

help it, tears welled in her eyes. She blinked them back, but she knew he'd seen.

"Carrie—what's wrong?" he said, taking a step nearer to her. "What did he do?"

She turned away from him and moved toward her little kitchen. The dented bucket sat in the middle of the floor. *Plink, plink, plink,* said the leaking rain.

"Carrie?" Hayden's voice had a note almost of warning.

She went to the stove, keeping her back to him. "I'll make you a cup of coffee," she said. "Then you have to go. Don't try to change my mind. I'm quitting, and that's that."

She turned on the burner beneath the kettle. "All I've got is instant," she said, reaching into the cupboard for a coffee mug. "And when you go, you might as well take the computer. I don't want it near me."

"Carrie?" he repeated, and moved to her side.

Her head swam drunkenly. He was too tall, too broad through the shoulders, and the kitchen was too small. He smelled of rain and aftershave lotion, and his wet hair fell over his forehead.

He took her by the upper arms. *Don't,* she thought. He brought his face nearer to hers, gripped her more tightly.

"Listen to me," he said in a low voice. "You can't quit. I need you. So does Edmon. The FBI was at his door this morning. To question him. They've found Gretchen Small. She's dead. Murdered. Nearly beheaded."

Shock rippled through her. She stared up at him numbly. "She was hardly more than a child," she said.

He said nothing. He nodded.

She remembered the girl's photograph, the young, plain, innocent face with its lovely green eyes that seemed to be begging for acceptance and love.

Hayden gripped her more tightly. "I know," he said.

She did not know how long she stood there, stunned, half-wanting to sink against him for comfort and be held. But when the teakettle began to whistle, she pulled away from him, self-conscious and confused.

He looked at her, frowning as if in concern. She glanced away. She took up the coffee mug and spooned the instant

powder into it. Her hand was shaking, and she hated herself
for her own weakness.

"What happened to you last night?" he asked. "Why
won't you say?"

"I told you, I don't want to talk about it," she said, and
steeled her nerves to steadiness as she poured the hot water.
"I have sugar, but no cream. I'm sorry."

"I drink it black," he said. "Carrie? You won't quit on
me, will you? I need you."

"Why did the FBI question Edmon?" she asked, handing
him the cup but not meeting his eyes. "He has an alibi."

"Because he'd gone to the authorities about her. There
was a record of it."

"If the FBI's investigating this, let *them* go to Omega,"
she said. She made herself a fresh cup of coffee, just to have
something to do, although she didn't need more caffeine
pumping through her system.

"Maybe they will," Hayden said. "But they may not believe Edmon about the MOON. He has a hunch, that's all."

She held the mug in both hands and took a sip. The
coffee tasted bitter as wormwood. She set it aside, and Hayden watched her, the expression in his eyes unreadable.

"Where did they find the girl?" she asked.

"In a cistern at an abandoned farmhouse. The owners
were going to level the place, make it a cornfield. She was
badly decomposed. But from the nicks on her spinal column,
it looks like somebody cut her throat to the bone."

"Oh, God." She fought off a shudder. The summer air
was warm, but she'd gone cold to her marrow.

"They can't suspect Edmon?"

"No. But he'd called attention to himself. Let's face it.
He's an odd kid. But they only questioned him. They didn't
arrest him. He couldn't have done it. He was at Dartmouth
taking exams."

"I think I'd like to sit down," she said. She made her
way past Hayden and into the living room, sat on the tattered brown sofa, plucking nervously at one of its loose
threads.

He followed her and sat next to her. "Are you okay?"

"Yes," she said, although she felt weak and sick to her stomach. "How did Edmon take the news?"

"Hard. But I think he's been afraid for a long time she was dead. He phoned me. He cried."

Carrie put her elbows on her knees and hid her face in her hands. Edmon in tears. The Highwayman in tears. And poor love-hungry Gretchen Small murdered. *The world is a bad place, a sad place, a terrible place.*

"Did you see Edmon?" she asked, hoping that he had.

"Yes. I came from there. He's concerned about you. He knew you logged off abruptly and didn't come back."

"You didn't tell him I quit?"

"I came to change your mind. This Highwayman of yours, Carrie, he sounds good. I want you to draw him out more. And to compare him with a man Brooke's met, Mephisto. I'm going to get Brooke's disks. I want you to compare the way they write. Will you?"

"I don't *want* to draw him out." She pressed her hands more tightly against her eyes. "I don't want to go back."

He set the mug on the coffee table. "Carrie, look at me."

She struggled to keep control of her voice. "No."

"Yes," he said. "Are you afraid to? Why?"

She let her hands drop to her lap, straightened, and gave him a resentful glance. But she couldn't hold his gaze, and so looked at the window instead, where the rain blurred the glass to a gray translucence.

"I know you were in the pub last night, alone," he said. "Then The Highwayman came in. You broke your connection, and he logged off immediately after. He never came back."

"How do you know all this?"

"I've learned a few tricks. I can see you from a distance. Where you are and who you're with. But not what you're doing."

"You learned to do that from reading the Archives?"

"Yes."

"You spy on me?"

"I monitor you and Brooke. Every fifteen minutes."

Carrie shrugged and said nothing.

"So what happened with The Highwayman?" he asked again.

"That's my business."

"It's my business, too. There's a girl in a morgue in Illinois. Doesn't that matter?"

Her cheeks went hot and she shot him a glance of rebuke. "Of course, it matters."

"So what about this Highwayman? What in God's name went on between you?"

Oh, hell, she thought wearily. If Hayden wanted the truth so much, she'd give it to him, right between the eyes. She no longer gave a damn about her pride, and it was Hayden who'd led her into this nasty farce.

"He was drunk. He wanted netsex. I said I wouldn't, not with someone who wouldn't tell me his name. So I broke the connection."

"I tried your private line," Hayden said. "It was busy. He phoned you?"

Carrie took a deep breath and told him what Paul Johnson had said. "I believe him. It makes me feel sick. This poor, disabled kid in love with a girl who doesn't exist. I want to hang myself."

Her chin trembled, and she thought, *I will not cry again. I will not let him see me cry. No one has seen me cry in ten years.*

Hayden's expression grew guarded. He might have been surprised or repelled, but all he said was, "Carrie, Monica Toussant and Gretchen Small believed somebody, too. What if it's not true? It's a damn good story. He loves you and only you can heal him."

Carrie resisted the desire to pick up the coffee mug and fling it at his head. "If he's lying he's contemptible. If he isn't, I'm contemptible. And if he's telling the truth, I couldn't stand it. The very thought makes me feel slimy."

He frowned. "He says his name's Paul Johnson? And he's not a citizen of the U.S.? How many guys do you suppose are named Paul Johnson in North America? He's got your phone number, but do you have his?"

"No," Carrie said. "So what?"

"He's living with a married sister, but you don't know her last name?"

She tilted her chin at a rebellious angle. "No."

"So how do you trace him, Carrie? How do you know he's for real? Do you have his address?"

"No," she said. "Stop trying to change my mind."

"I've got to. What if he's not some poor, disabled kid who thinks he's in love with you? What if he's an excellent liar who's stalking you?"

"What if he's not?" she challenged. "What if he's a twenty-three-year-old man who may never walk again? What then?"

"If we find out that's true, you let him down easy. It's not as if the two of you really know each other."

"He wants to have netsex with me, for God's sake. And I've encouraged him. I've let him hold me in his arms, hug me, kiss me."

He searched her face for a long moment. Her confused emotions grew more tumultuous. *Something's going to happen,* she thought. *And I haven't got the strength to stop it.*

He said, "He's never touched you."

He put his hand to her face, his fingertips grazing first her cheekbone, then her jawline. With thumb and forefinger he lightly cupped her chin. "This is touching."

Her heart thudded crazily. She told herself, *Don't let this happen.*

"And he hasn't really kissed you," he breathed.

He tipped her face to his and brought his mouth to bear on hers, gently at first, then more hungrily.

Oh, God, oh, God, oh, God, she thought, her heart leaping.

He's real. He's real.

Her mouth was exactly as soft as he'd imagined. But it was resistant, unresponsive, as if she were frightened of showing emotion.

She turned her face from his and drew away. "That sort of thing," she said, "will solve nothing."

"No," he said, his hands moving to her shoulders and

resting there. He could feel the tension in her body. "But we both might feel a little better."

"I don't equate sex with comfort."

"What do you equate it with?"

"Trouble," she said. "Way too much of it."

Okay, he told himself. *She's upset. This is not the best moment to attempt seduction. I don't even know how this happened.*

But he found himself rubbing his knuckles against the silky skin of her jaw. She let him, but she looked reluctant, undecided if she liked it or not.

The phone rang, and she gave a startled little jump and pulled away from his touch.

"Please go," she said, rising. "Take the computer. Tell Edmon I'm sorry."

The phone rang again.

"No," he said. "Talk to me first."

"We've already talked," she said.

The phone rang a third time, and she picked up the receiver. Her expression began to do complicated things.

"Hello? Joel? I was going to call you. How are you, honey?"

As she listened, she fingered the phone cord nervously. She put her hand over the mouthpiece, glared at Hayden, and whispered, "It's my son. At least go into another room and give me some privacy."

He nodded and rose. He headed for the door across from the kitchen and eased it open. It was obviously her bedroom. He entered it, shutting the door behind him. He could still hear her voice, brittle with nerves, but he couldn't make out her words and didn't try to.

Her room was small and boxy with faded wallpaper. Against the far wall, beneath the only window, was a double bed, neatly made, covered with a patchwork quilt. The only other furniture was a bedside table and a chest of drawers.

On the chest was a pair of framed photographs. He crossed the bare floor to examine them. In one, two small boys in jeans and striped T-shirts stood, their arms around each other's shoulders. The shorter boy, blond, smiling, looked exactly like Carrie, even down to the dimples. The taller boy was different, squarely built with straight dark hair and a dour expression.

Only one other snapshot was on the chest. He picked it up. Small, black and white, it showed an old woman in jeans and a little girl sitting bareback on a big white horse.

Carrie, he realized, and she could have been no more than six. Her fair hair was wildly tousled, and her wide smile revealed a tooth missing. The dimples were killer-class, even then, and gave him an odd pang.

And this old woman, lean, erect, with thick white hair, could only be that semi-legendary figure, her grandmother. She looked ordinary enough, a smiling old woman, and her appearance gave no clue to the lasting spell she'd cast on her granddaughter.

He set the photo back in place. There was no picture of anyone who might be the late husband, and he wondered what that meant.

He turned and looked at her closet. Its door was missing. He stepped to it and within it he could see her meager wardrobe. On a nail hung a sleeveless nightgown of blue and white checked cotton, faded from many washings. He touched it. The fabric was thin and cool beneath his fingertips. He imagined her in this flimsy gown and liked what he saw in his mind's eye. He imagined her with no clothes at all and liked it better.

On the wall by the bed a single wooden shelf was mounted. It held a mismatched collection of objects: a pair of sports trophies that said, "Bitter Water Women's Softball Champions," a woman's heart-shaped locket, two clay sculptures of dinosaurs, obviously made by children, a set of rattlesnake rattles, a chain with military dog tags, a wedding ring.

He stepped to her window, drew aside the curtain and watched the rain stream down. Her road was badly washed out, the water running in torrents down the ruts. This was a hell of a place for a woman to be alone.

He watched the rain a long time, listening to her muted voice from the living room. Then there was silence.

She opened the door and said, "Stop lurking in my bedroom."

"You wanted privacy," he said, turning to face her.

"I asked you to leave completely," she said, her chin up. Did he imagine it, or did she seem happier, less distraught?

He crossed his arms and leaned against the wall with its faded paper. "You have fewer possessions than any woman your age I've ever known," he said.

"I don't depend on things for happiness."

"Or people?"

"I have people that make me happy. My family, especially my sons. And pretty soon, I suppose I'll have some grandchildren."

He looked her up and down. He would never have grandchildren. He envied her.

And he wanted her. He supposed he had wanted her from the first time he'd talked to her.

The expression on her face was chagrined, as if she could read his mind. "I'm sorry," she whispered. "Please go now."

"I need you, Carrie."

She crossed her arms, looked confused and angry. "I'm tired of men needing me," she said. "Ever since I can remember, there's always—oh, forget it."

She'd made a verbal slip and it was revealing. He thought, *You were always the strong one, weren't you? You don't want to lean on anyone. Are you afraid he'll fail you?*

"I need you on Omega," he said. "Not in real life. But in real life I want you. There's a difference."

Her posture went tense. "Don't talk like that."

"Why?" he said. "Because it's true? Are you to used to the lies of Omega? This isn't Omega. And I'm not lying."

He moved to her and put his hands on her tense shoulders. "Nothing about this is pretend," he said.

He moved still nearer and slowly, almost involuntarily, she raised her face to his. His body quickened with desire. He bent to take her lips again. This time she did not draw away. The rain drummed and drummed like his blood.

• • •

Carrie lay beneath the sheets in Hayden's arms, her eyes closed, listening to the rain beat on the roof. His breathing was regular, but he wasn't asleep, for from time to time, he ran his hand up and down her arm, slowly, as if savoring the feel of her.

She shut her eyes more tightly and nestled against him. He was a tall man, hard-muscled and warm with life. To lie with her bare body so close to his was comforting, and she still glowed with pleasant tingling from his lovemaking.

She hadn't meant to go to bed with him. *The rain made me do it,* she thought tiredly. *Omega made me do it. The devil made me do it. It won't happen again. At least it won't happen very often again.*

Once again he caressed her arm. He kissed her shoulder. He was an affectionate lover, far more than she was used to. He drew her more closely into his embrace, sighed against her hair. She felt his breath on the tip of her ear, her throat.

They lay together in silence, the only sound the percussion of the rain. Once one of them spoke, she thought, the spell would be broken.

After he had kissed her here in the bedroom, neither of them had said a word. Things just happened. They happened naturally, almost inevitably and with no awkwardness. There had been no need for words. Unlike Omega. Oh, completely unlike Omega.

But now Hayden stirred and kissed her behind the ear, and she knew the charmed part of their interlude was ending. "Carrie?"

She kept her eyes closed. "What?"

"I need to get back. I've got to call a client. I want you to drive me home, keep the jeep. I've got a truck I can use. You'll never get in and out of this place with your car. The road's going to have to be regraded."

She drew away slightly, opened her eyes and looked into his. He rose on his elbow, bent over her, and kissed her on her lips, her chin, her cheek, her lips again.

"Okay?" he breathed. "I don't want to leave you, but I have to."

"I don't want your jeep," she said, turning away from

him. She stared at the chest of drawers where the pictures of her sons and grandmother were ranged like a formation of promises and duties.

He put his hand on her shoulder. "Why? Because you'd feel beholden?"

The word was quaint, but accurate, although she hated admitting it. It had taken her so many years to be free, decades really. She didn't want to owe anything to any man. Or to need a man again.

"That's it, isn't it?" he said, stroking her arm.

She nodded unhappily.

"How can you get to your seminar tomorrow?" he asked. "How will you get anywhere?"

She shrugged, as if it didn't matter.

"Carrie, borrow it," he said, his breath tickling her ear again. "No strings attached. If you want our relationship to go back strictly to business, it will. It's your choice."

"I said our business was over," she said softly, but she knew, in her heart, she was no longer sure she meant it.

"Edmon and I need you. If you won't do it for us, do it for Gretchen Small. She was young, she was innocent. She had dreams, too."

She said, "You don't really care about any of these people. I can tell. It's just a case to you."

"You're right. I don't care about them. But you do."

Carrie sighed in exhausted sorrow. He was right, of course, she did care. "Omega's creepy," she said. "And evil. I don't want to hurt Paul Johnson."

"What if he wants to hurt you? You've got to admit, he fits the profile."

She said nothing.

"I'll check him out," he promised. "If it's humanly possible, I'll find out if he's who he says he is. Just take it easy with him until then."

She felt his hand stroking up and down her arm.

He said, "You'll go back?"

She stared at the pictures across the room and thought of herself at Gretchen Small's age, her life not yet even half-lived. At that age, she had not yet met the love of her life. At that age, her sons were still unborn, and all her deepest joys and sorrows were still ahead. Gretchen would never know either such joys or sorrows. In violence they had been stolen from her.

"Carrie?" he asked softly.

She said, "I'll go back."

TEN

CARRIE AGREED, AT LAST, TO BORROW THE JEEP. HAYDEN TOLD HER to drive, to get used to the feel of it. Her road was almost washed away, so rutted that the jeep pitched about like a little craft fighting big seas. She gripped the wheel so tightly that he saw her knuckles whiten.

At last they reached the highway, a winding ribbon of asphalt. Although the windshield wipers slashed back and forth, visibility was limited. Hayden watched her, her back straight as a soldier's, her profile grim.

When she'd gotten dressed again, it was as if she'd put on some kind of emotional armor as well as clothes. She had been quiet ever since.

"You live a hell of a long way off the beaten track," he said. "Do you have a gun?"

She shook her head. "Not since my first son was born. I wouldn't have a gun in the same house with a child."

"I'll get you one," he said. "There are no children to worry about now."

"I don't need one," she said, keeping her eyes on the streaming windshield.

"After this much rain, it gets snaky," he said. "You'll have water moccasins swimming in your front yard. I guarantee it."

She said nothing. He told himself, *Don't push your luck. You barely got her to borrow the jeep.*

But he would get her a gun. Besides snakes, there were bears, coyotes, and packs of wild dogs. And there were humans, the most dangerous animals of the lot.

"You ever think about getting a dog?" he asked. "You could get one at the pound."

"I don't want to get anything I might get attached to," she said. "I don't know where I'll live next. I might not be able to keep it."

Touché, he thought. The windshield wipers seemed to echo the mockery. *Tou-ché. Tou-ché. Touché, touché, touché.* But he thought of getting her a dog anyway. A jeep, a gun, a dog. God, he was a romantic bastard.

"You hate anybody trying to take care of you, don't you?" he asked.

"I take care of myself," she said. But she gave him an odd little smile that took the edge off her words.

"Since when?" he asked.

"Since forever," she said. "Let's talk about something else. What's the FBI going to do about Gretchen Small?"

He shook his head. "If they take Edmon seriously, they'll try to get what records Omega has. But the Internet's a hotbed of free speech rights. Nobody's going to turn anything over to the feds, not without a court order. Even then, there'll be a fight."

"But Omega doesn't have a record of who Joachim the Beggar was," she said. "They only have his e-mail address."

"Right. And if he's stalking, he won't have that address registered under his real name. And he may have more than one character."

"He'd have to have more than one e-mail address, then."

"He could buy extra accounts from a big supplier like Delphi. Expensive, but simple."

She nodded and drove in silence a few miles. At the stop sign at the highway junction, she glanced at the odometer. "Nice jeep. You've hardly got any miles on it."

"It was my son's," he said. "I took over the payments."

Kyle had bought the jeep three months before he died, excited as a kid with a new toy. Kyle and he had planned to meet on the Fourth of July and canoe the War Eagle.

Instead Hayden had made the trip alone. He thought of the cliffs of the War Eagle and the lonesome wind sweeping the fragments of ash down to the churning water.

"I didn't know you had a son," she said. "Are there others?"

"No."

"Where is he?"

The rain pelted against the window, and the whole world was a dark and dying gray. He said, "He's dead."

She gave him a stricken look. "I'm sorry."

After a moment, she said, "How old was he?"

"Twenty-three," he said, and stared out the window. He clearly remembered the day the boy was born; it had been, quite simply, the happiest day of his life. He had thought, *This is why I'm here. This is why I survived Nam, survived prison. So this child could walk the earth.*

She swallowed and said, "I can't think of anything worse. Was it an accident? An illness?"

His stomach knotted as it always did when he thought about it. "He was in law enforcement. Like me. He was shot to death. In the line of duty." He put a mocking spin on the word *duty*.

The only sounds were the rain and the steady thump and sigh of the windshield wipers. Carrie stared at the road and at last said, "Will you tell me what happened?"

A muscle twitched in his cheek. "Two months after Waco," he said, "he was shot to death trying to serve a federal warrant on an illegal arms dealer in Tulsa."

Out of the corner of his eye, he saw her glance at him,

but he didn't meet her gaze. She said, "A federal warrant? He was in ATF, too?"

"Yeah," Hayden said, with a bitter twist to his mouth. "He wanted to be like his old man."

That, he thought, *was the cream of the jest.* He had gone through almost two tours of duty in Nam with nothing worse than infected leech bites. He'd survived being a prisoner of war by taking it a day at a time and imagining in minute detail being back in Arkansas, floating its rivers, the Buffalo River, the White, the Foursche, the Mulberry, the War Eagle.

He'd come home in one piece and married a pretty brunette with whom, it proved, he had little in common. The marriage was not successful, but it had been tolerable. Hayden, an only child, wanted four children. There had been only one, Kyle.

Karen had grown to hate Hayden's work. It became a constant source of contention, and she was appalled when Kyle went into the ATF. When he died, she could not forgive Hayden. Whenever they looked at each other, they could think of nothing but Kyle's death. It was best they parted.

Carrie said, "Is that why you quit ATF?"

"That's why," he said.

Hayden had loved the agency, but it had long been beset with problems. It had embarrassed itself at Ruby Ridge, it had humiliated itself at Waco, it was rent by dissent from within, and relentlessly attacked from without by its enemies. He would have forgiven it almost anything, but he could not forgive it for taking his son. Nor could he forgive himself for drawing Kyle into it.

He said, "His ashes are in the War Eagle River. We used to go there a lot. I don't go anymore." He didn't know why he told her. It seemed an admission of weakness, and she had no weakness in her.

"I understand," she said.

He nodded. They traveled without speaking for a while.

He turned, looked at her again. Her face was blank and serious, her chin up.

He said, "What's the strange shelf in your bedroom?"

"That's my mojo shelf," she said. "That's where I keep my magic things."

He almost smiled. "Baseball trophies?"

She, too, almost smiled. "In the first series, I hit a double in the bottom of the ninth. In the second, I hit a triple with the bases loaded. There had to be some mojo working."

"I suppose there did," he said.

"They're the only awards I ever got," she said. "Once I thought I'd have Pulitzer Prizes or something sitting on my shelf. For the great writer. Funny."

After that, she became quiet again, and by the time they reached Fayetteville, they'd both withdrawn into themselves, hardly speaking except about directions to his house. When they reached his driveway she stopped, but didn't cut the motor, the lights, the windshield wipers. She wanted to escape, he could tell.

His house looked particularly cheerless in the streaming rain. He didn't know why in hell he'd bought it.

"You're sure it's okay if I borrow the jeep?" she asked.

"It's fine," he said. "You can make it back all right?"

"I'm sure. Thanks."

They stared at each other for an awkward moment, and neither seemed to know what to say.

"In light of what's happened," he said, "should I shake your hand? Or kiss you? Or just say, 'Goodbye for now'?"

She looked away. "Just 'Goodbye for now,' I think."

He wanted to kiss her, but did not. "Then goodbye for now," he said. He started to open the door and get ready for the sprint to the house.

"Hayden?" she said.

He paused, looked at her again. "Yes?"

"Goodbye," she said, with a strange sadness in her voice.

He got out and dashed for the roofless porch, but he didn't go inside immediately. He stood watching as she backed out of the drive and headed down the street.

Things would not work between them, and they both knew it, and perhaps she even regretted it. He knew he did.

She was right; he didn't care about people and he didn't want to. She didn't depend on anyone and didn't want to.

It was not a promising combination. He unlocked his silent house and went inside.

Lynette's dormitory room was almost stiflingly fragrant with flowers: a vase of dark red roses, a second vase of white and pink ones, an embarrassingly large bouquet of mixed flowers in a copper bowl.

A brand-new teddy bear lay on her pillow, its chubby arms embracing the empty air. The bear had a scarlet bow around its neck, and fastened to the bow was a card that read, "I love only you. Will you talk to me Sunday night at eight? Passionately, James."

Lynette sat on the foot of her bed, legs crossed Indian style, trying to concentrate on the *Aeneid;* she had a test in World Literature tomorrow. She struggled to imagine the clash of spears at Troy, but the myth was overpowered by the scent of real roses.

Eight o'clock was only an hour away. She would talk to James on Omega for the first time in a week. The prospect filled her with a confusing mixture of desire and dread. What would she say?

She heard the scuttling sound of a key in a lock and winced. Tammy came in. Tammy's face was sweaty, her long hair limp, her T-shirt wrinkled and damp. "God, it's an oven outside," she complained.

"Where's Mike?" Lynette asked.

"Getting beer," Tammy said, heading for her dresser. She stopped in midstride and stared with disbelief at the bear on Lynette's pillow. She came to the bear, picked it up, and scrutinized it. "Good God, when did *this* come? It's expensive. All those flowers and this, too?"

"Yesterday," Lynette said, wishing Tammy wouldn't handle her things.

Tammy opened the card, read it and frowned. "He's *begging* you to talk. Will you?"

"I don't know," Lynette said, trying to sound uncon-cerned.

"You don't know? You're playing hard to get? Are you crazy? My God, he's too good to be true."

"That's the problem," Lynette said. "He is too good to be true."

Tammy rolled her eyes, as if to say, *Can you really afford to be picky, Lynette? You of all people? Don't delude yourself.*

Lynette bent over her book again. She didn't want to talk about it.

"Let yourself go for once," Tammy said, going to her dresser and rifling through a drawer. "I won't be here to cramp your style. I'm going back to Mike's for the night. I just need clean clothes and my bong. We broke his."

Lynette said nothing. Every night this week, Tammy had stayed at Mike's apartment, drinking and getting stoned. She said they had a manual of Hindu sexual positions and were working their way through it.

Tammy said she loved everything about sex, the feel, taste, touch, and smell of it. She and Mike liked to watch themselves in a big mirror that he'd bolted to the ceiling.

Lynette didn't want to imagine what that mirror saw. Tammy was overweight, and her skin and hair were oily. Mike was tall, emaciated, and his skin was the sick bluish white of skim milk. Lynette had never seen a heroin addict, but she imagined if she did, he would look exactly like Mike.

But Mike, Tammy said, was hung like a garden hose and the hose had play in it all night long. She gathered up her underwear and stuffed it into her backpack with the bong, a jar of Vaseline, two clean T-shirts, and a pair of cutoffs.

"These flowers make it smell like a funeral home in here," Tammy said. "But hey, it's the thought that counts."

Lynette said nothing.

Tammy thrust her arms through the straps of her backpack and headed for the door. She put her hand on the knob, then stopped and looked at Lynette. She cocked her head knowingly.

"You probably don't give a damn what I think," Tammy said. "But you better not fool around and lose this guy. What if he's the best you'll ever get? Think of that, why dontcha?"

Then she was gone, and Lynette was left alone with her

flowers and the bear, whose glass eyes stared up, blinkless, at the unmirrored ceiling.

Sex, Lynette thought unhappily; it was the hot, irrational axis on which the world spun, the tingling center around which everything whirled. It was what Tammy wanted. It was what Mike wanted. It was what James wanted.

Most of the people on Omega wanted it. What was wrong with *her*?

She rose and went to her bureau. On one side of its mirror stood the red roses, sent on Wednesday and now drying to an unpleasant, blackish color. On the other side were the pink and white flowers, sent on Friday and starting to wilt before they'd fully opened.

Why, she wondered, was he so lavish with his gifts? They seemed excessive to her, almost beyond reason.

She was not beautiful, not pretty, not even acceptably plain. She raised her hands and touched her asymmetrical cheekbones.

This is not, she told herself, the face that launched a thousand ships. How could it have even launched these dozens of flowers? The expensive teddy bear? The daily messages through e-mail and MOON mail?

James wrote every day, filling his notes with idealistic clichés like "Love is blind," and "Beauty is in the eye of the beholder," and "It's what's in your heart that counts."

But he wrote of carnal longings, too. He'd e-mailed her poems about seizing the day, making much of time, and gathering rosebuds.

This morning's message said:

Dearest Lynette—These lines seem to have been written just for you:

"Had we but world enough and time,
This coyness, lady, were no crime."

If there were world enough and time, Lynette, I would spend a century worshiping you from afar. But life is short, and I want you so much *now*, every minute, waking and dreaming.

It will be a month before I can break away from California and come see you in real life. *I know you are the one for me.* I'll be waiting for you on Omega tonight at eight. Will you show me mercy? I love you, James.

When she'd first read this message, it had excited and touched her. It still did, and yet something about it struck her as too eager and ardent, far too extravagant.

Then there was his picture. Yesterday he'd sent her his photo by e-pic, picture mail. The photo was fuzzy, but even so, she'd drawn in her breath in wonder.

He was so handsome. He was incredibly handsome. He was too handsome.

She'd always known he was supposed to be good-looking, but that he attached little value to his appearance and didn't like to be judged by it. But for him to be so absolutely beautiful, and to desire her so much, this troubled Lynette deeply. In an imperfect world, he seemed impossibly perfect.

Still, she was haunted not merely by doubts about James, but about herself. Was she frightened of a close relationship and priggish about sex? Was her disfigurement not merely of the body, but of the heart and soul as well?

Was there some sort of tragic lack in her that made her not only suspicious, but frigid? Did she not believe she could be desirable because she feared desire itself?

Love was blind, James kept saying. Surely Mike and Tammy were proof of that. What if Tammy was right, and James was the best Lynette would ever find her whole life long?

She was aloof by nature, careful about her emotions. She'd viewed netsex with distaste. But others saw it as natural, healthy, exquisitely exciting. Fantasy in sex was supposed to be normal and enhancing, wasn't it?

But what if all he wanted was a netsex partner, an electronic whore? What if he was simply playing a nasty game? She'd heard stories of people who talked others into netsex and recorded the sessions, then posted them on the Internet for the world to see. It was an evil and humiliating trick, but common enough.

No, no, she thought. Her suspicion, her fears and inhibitions were running wild again. James simply wanted to have a full-fledged love affair by computer. Maybe the affair could only work out that way, in fantasy.

Wasn't fantasy better than nothing?

Tammy's questions came back to stalk her, wolfish and grinning: *What if he's the best you ever get? Think about that, why dontcha?*

The hands of the clock were cocked almost at zero hour, five minutes to eight. Her computer sat on her desk, silent and waiting, an instrument full of choices and possibilities.

She closed her book and forgot about the burning of Troy.

Carrie drove home through the rain trying not to think about Hayden Ivanovich. He intrigued her, yet she sensed he was as much a loner as she was. He was a complex man who seemed full of unresolved emotions. She could not resolve them for him and mustn't try.

She'd sworn to have nothing more to do with men until she found out who she was as a woman. Men had complicated her life beyond reckoning and perhaps beyond remedy.

But now she'd gone to bed with Hayden. And she'd liked it, it had felt good. So what? So nothing, nothing, nothing. If he wanted sexual healing, she couldn't give it to him; she had been giving and giving and giving for over twenty years. She had come to this place to satisfy, at long last, her soul, not her body.

When she got home, she took a hot shower, called her son Phil, and then with great reluctance logged on to Omega. She found she had new e-mail. It was from The Highwayman.

"Sweet Thing—Will you be on Omega tonight? I've been thinking of you all day. In my thoughts I touch your beautiful body, I kiss your lovely face. My heart is haunted by you and is happy to be haunted. Love and Caresses, Your Highwayman."

She frowned in self-disgust. The Highwayman was dreaming of an illusion, a twenty-year-old named Melissa Blanchard who did not exist.

He sounds good, draw him out, Hayden had said. Her body still tingled from Hayden's lovemaking, and she wished the memory of his touch would fade.

Against her will she was attracted to Hayden, and she, who was frightened of very little, was frightened by this. Better than anyone, she knew what sex and love could be: a dangerous and inescapable trap.

"I love you," Jon Rosmer told the girl. "But I've got to go. If I can get back tonight, I will. If not, I'll see you tomorrow."

"Don't go," she said. She was hot to trot, this one, and desperate and possessive—after only little more than a week. On the MOON, love affairs could blossom swiftly, like flowers opening in a time-lapse film. Emotions accelerated at warp speed, with no normal restraints.

He kissed her goodbye, and she was all over him, giving him virtual French kisses, pressing her virtual breasts against him, whispering that she wanted to do it again, she'd do anything he'd ask if he'd just stay.

He didn't much like her because she'd fallen so fast she seemed cheap. But she was inexperienced, eager, and highly imaginative, and that combination started to make him hard, even now as he tried to escape her.

"God, I want you," he said. "But people are at my *door*, baby. So I've got to go. I love you, baby love."

"I mean it," she said. "I'd do anything you want."

Christ, the woman clung like an octopus. But he swore yes, yes, yes, he'd get back to her later, and finally he managed to break away from her.

He logged off, then logged on again as James Dean. He was five minutes late to meet Lynette, for which he cursed the octopus bitch, but it was Lynette's own damn fault for driving him to other women in the first place.

He still had his partial erection, compliments of the octopus, and it made him all the hungrier for his ballerina. He paged her. "Lynette? It's James. Will you talk to me, please? It's been hell without you."

Her answer came, "Join me."

A hot giddiness swarmed through him. The octopus bitch had been too easy; she could not satisfy him long, he knew. It was Lynette who would really rock him, his little broken-faced girl.

He transported to her dressing room, his blood pounding. He took her in his arms and kissed her. "I love you and I've missed you," he whispered. "It's like a part of myself was gone. Have you missed me?"

"Yes," was all she said.

"Did you get the teddy bear?"

"He came yesterday. He's darling, but you shouldn't spend all that money."

"I hoped you'd sleep with him in real life until you could sleep with me. Do you? Sleep with him?"

"No," she said. "But I sit him next to my bed so I see him when I wake up."

"Someday," he said, "I want to see you when I wake up."

She made no reply. *Don't rush her,* he thought, but he couldn't help himself. He'd left the sure thing, octopus girl, to come here, and he felt as if Lynette had set his nerve endings afire, and the worm of his penis twitched harder, trying to rise.

He said, "I dream of you at night. I dream we're making love. It's been a long time since I've felt this way about a woman. I can't tell you how long."

"I got your picture," she said. "You didn't tell me you were so handsome."

He'd sent her the photo by e-pic, hoping his looks would fuel her desire for him. It had always worked with the other women, but she was so damned hard to predict.

"I'm nothing special," he said. "It's a flattering picture, that's all."

"You look like a movie star," she said. "You could have been a model."

"Please," he said, "don't mention models. You know how I feel about models."

"I'm scared," she said. "What if you're just overcompensating by being interested in me?"

Shit, what's going on in her head now? he thought in frustration. *Is this some new excuse?*

"What do you mean? What scares you?"

"Your fiancée was beautiful, and I'm scared that you only feel safe with someone like me. It's not so much that you're attracted to me as you're reacting against her. She still controls your emotions."

His mythical fiancée, the faithless model? Jon was astonished and angry that Lynette could twist his own creation to work against him.

"That's not true," he protested. "I met lots of girls on Omega. I was attracted to you long before you told me how you looked."

God-*damn*, but she was playing hard to get. Why were women ever given brains? Jesus, he'd love to knock hers right out of her patched-up rag doll head.

"If I'd been beautiful, you wouldn't have trusted me," she said. "You just said so."

He muttered an obscenity, but answered, "It's your personality, your character, your mind I fell in love with. I'm only trying to say that beauty doesn't count for me. I've seen how meaningless it is."

"It's meaningless when you can't see me," she said. "But when we meet you might feel different."

"I won't feel different, I know it."

"James, I've been thinking hard about us. People say MOON romances don't work out in real life. I mean, everybody says it."

"Lynette, there are exceptions and you know it."

"Maybe so, but the odds are bad. I think before this goes any further, we should meet in real life."

"Sweetheart," he lied, "we can't. I have at least another month to spend in California."

"Where are you now?" she asked.

"Oakland," he said, although he was in western Iowa.

"As soon as I'm through, I go to Salinas. They're jerking me back and forth along the whole coast. I never know for sure where I'll be next."

He paused, took a long drink of beer. His erection was wilting, and rage drummed in his blood. "Lynette, the minute this California assignment is over, I'll come to you, I swear. Until then, this is the only way we can meet. This and talking on the phone."

"I could come out there," she said, taking him unpleasantly by surprise. "I've got the money. I could take a day or two off school, make it a long weekend."

He stared angrily at the screen. *I'm in charge, bitch,* he thought. *I'm the one who runs this show.*

"I haven't got long weekends," he said. "I put in a ten-hour day yesterday. I spent all this morning doing calculations. They could pull me out of here tomorrow and send me anywhere. How can we plan anything?"

He took another pull from his beer and watched the screen, hoping he'd blocked her ploy.

"James, I'm extremely attracted to you," she answered. "But Omega's not the real world. We've gotten too deeply into this relationship too fast. Sometimes I'm afraid that you don't *want* to meet me in real life."

"Are you accusing me of lying?" he demanded. "Is that what you think of me after all this time?"

"It hasn't been so long. We've known each other for about four weeks, that's all."

"My God, people meet each other and get married in four weeks," he said. "It happens. I was going to ask you in real life as soon as we met. Do you want me to ask now? Will you marry me? I mean it. I'm proposing to you."

"Marry you? James, I keep telling you, we've never met. We don't really know each other."

"I've poured out my heart, my life to you," he argued. "I've told you every secret I have. I thought you'd been open with me, too."

"I *am* being open," she said. "But nothing like this ever happened to me before. It seems too good to be true."

"I feel the same about you," he said. "Why are you so frightened of intimacy? Lynette, there's nothing wrong with netsex. It's just another aspect of sexuality. When we can't be together in person, at least we can be together in fantasy, and I would make it very, very good for you, I promise."

"I'm not comfortable with the idea. I'm sorry. If we met, if we touched in real life, it might be different."

"You don't love me. You enjoy torturing me."

"I'm not trying to torture you. But if we make love, I don't want to only *pretend* to give you my body. I want to save that for reality. It's important to me, James. For somebody like me, it's more important than you can imagine."

You freak, you bitch, you cunt, he thought. *I'd kill you this minute if I could.*

But he said, "I'll make everything more beautiful than you can imagine. Trust me, Lynette—please."

He gave her a passionate virtual kiss. "Please," he repeated. "You mean so much to me. Please."

Hayden paged Edmon from the Archives, but the boy said he didn't feel like talking. He wasn't at Parsival's Tent, as usual, but somewhere called the Bridge of Sighs.

Hayden typed the message, "It might be easier on you not to be here tonight."

"I don't have any place else to go," Edmon answered.

Hayden gritted his teeth. How pathetic, he thought, that Edmon's only refuge was this electronic wasteland.

"Look," he told the boy, "watch what you say to people here about Gretchen. It's best if you say nothing at all, understand?"

Edmon didn't answer.

"Listen to me," Hayden ordered. "Don't go broadcasting that she's dead. The less that people know about this, the better."

"People *should* know," Edmon answered. "They should be cautious. Lives could be at stake here."

Hayden sighed. "I understand. But consider this: if the

killer is here, the last thing you want is to tip your hand playing vigilante."

"A man has to trust his conscience," Edmon said. "Let's not talk. Please. I just want to be by myself."

"Yeah, fine," Hayden said, resigned. "Take care of yourself, kid. If you need me, page."

"I will," Edmon answered. "I'm sorry. I don't mean to be rude. I just want to keep a sort of vigil for her. And to think of what to do next."

Don't do anything stupid, Hayden thought. *Don't take your damned half-baked knight act too far.*

But he wouldn't page the kid again. He knew when somebody needed to be left alone with his devils.

Suddenly a message came from Carrie on the King's Highway. "Hi. This is just to let you know I've logged on."

His heart took a kind of sideways hop that made him feel as inexperienced as a teenager. He paged her back. "You got home all right? Jeep drove okay? No trouble with the gearshift?"

How suave of me, he thought in self-disgust. *Mr. Romance here, a regular silver-tongued devil.*

"No problem," she answered. "I should get to work. Is Brooke here yet? I haven't checked on her."

"Not yet." And Brooke didn't know yet about Gretchen Small. He'd tried to phone her this afternoon, but couldn't get through.

Carrie said, "I paged Edmon, but he said he just wanted to be alone for a while. I feel terrible for him, Hayden. He must be devastated."

"If he wants to be alone, why does he come to this damn place? It doesn't make sense."

"Maybe he thinks of it as his real home. A lot of these people do."

"They must not have much in the way of real lives." He immediately thought, *Look at your own life, hotshot. Look who's talking.*

"Some of them don't," she answered. "They take what they can get."

"Carrie?"

"Yes?"

"Did you hear from Highwayman?"

"I'm supposed to meet him at eleven."

"Just take it slow. I'll call London, Ontario, tomorrow to see if there was a motorcycle accident."

"I don't know whether I hope there was or wasn't."

"I know."

"I should get to work," she said. "Onfredo's paging."

"Right," he said. "Maybe we'll talk later tonight."

"Maybe," she said. " 'Bye."

Their conversation, nothing but silent messages on a screen, was over. No word had actually been uttered, yet it was as if her voice, ghostly, still resonated in the air of his room.

He wondered what was going through her mind now. She regretted going to bed with him, he knew; he wondered how much she regretted it and why. In his arms she had been warm, eager, and giving.

He shrugged cynically. So she'd needed a comfort fuck, that was all. There they'd been; he'd wanted her, and she was vulnerable, wanting somebody, and tricked for a short while into thinking she wanted him.

He remembered the satiny feel of her bare skin beneath his hands and against his body, and he thought with repugnance of his own empty bed. *Stop it*, he ordered himself. *Stop it. Get back to work.*

He rubbed his eyes, forced himself to start reading another Archives document, and wondered where in the hell Brooke was tonight.

Brooke had chosen not to log on as her character today, but as a guest, not telling Ivanovich. There was no law that said she had to work seven days a week like a slave in a sweatshop.

She'd gone to Omega early this afternoon, just for the fun of it, and played all day. Tonight she'd been lucky enough to have an unexpected rendezvous with the young man who was her lover, but their meeting had been all too short. Real life, like an unwelcome visitor, had interrupted and forced him to leave.

Now, still an anonymous guest, Brooke wandered Omega, exploring its seemingly endless riches. Alhambra had taught her well about this magic land; she'd learned much from him.

But she was chagrined to admit that Edmon was right; under Alhambra's facade of sophistication, he seemed very young, a glib child, vain and fond of posturing. He was also madly infatuated with her, which was beginning to bore her to tears. But he *did* know Omega.

Tonight, however, she would blithely go her way without him. She'd disguised herself with a new and different description; he might seek her, but he wouldn't find her. She transported herself to the Japanese Cherry Orchard, one of her favorite spots.

She sat beside the ornamental pool and thought not of Alhambra, who was probably searching for her at this very moment, but of her lover. He'd told her his name was Boyd Burdette, and she'd lied about him to Hayden Ivanovich from the start. Boyd was none of Ivanovich's business.

Boyd was so exciting he frightened her in a delicious sort of way. He made it seem possible that, with him, her real life could be transformed into something more fulfilling even than Omega.

She did not for a moment worry that Boyd could be Edmon's phantom stalker. Boyd was not like that, although Ivanovich might not believe her. No, Boyd was a romantic, almost tragic figure, and he swore he had been searching the whole MOON over for someone like her. He needed her in every way, body and soul, he said.

It had seemed easy and natural and beautiful to become Boyd's mistress. He was so intriguing that Brooke liked net-sex better than any regular sex she'd had.

She happily imagined that real sex with him would be exalted, transcendent, cosmic. And they would soon enjoy sex in real life, she knew this with joyous certainty.

She would go to Boyd, willingly, eagerly, because they gave each other's lives meaning. Only she and the love she gave him could save him. And all her life she had dreamed of being a heroine—and being loved beyond reason.

She no longer had merely to imagine a woman on the edge of fabulous adventure. Adventure had come to her, it stood stretching its arms open to her, beckoning and welcoming her to her destiny.

ELEVEN

E DMON HAD CAUTIONED CARRIE THAT SUNDAY NIGHT WAS SELDOM lively on Omega, and he was right. She transported herself to Ye Silent Woman Pub. Quicksilver was there holding court as usual, and with her were Lacewing, Redrum, Jester, and Love Machine.

Lacewing was complaining about Damian Two. "Ever since I broke up with Cochise," she said, "Damian Two keeps paging me. I've told him a hundred times I've found someone else."

Quicksilver gave Lacewing an arch look. "What about this wonderful someone else? Is he going to get a character?"

"Of course," said Lacewing. "Any day now. He's fabulous."

"Cochise certainly didn't waste any time finding someone new, either," Quicksilver said. "Soap opera, thy name is MOON."

Merrycat materialized, "My God, everybody, guess

what? Yukon Goldie just committed MOON-ocide. She's terminated her character. She's gone forever."

Quicksilver yawned. "It's been coming for months."

"Who's Yukon Goldie?" Lacewing asked.

"Here, she was a hopeless slut," Quicksilver said. "In real life, he's totally swishy, and he's got a new lover who doesn't approve of netsex. You know, the jealous type."

"Yeah," laughed Love Machine. "Damian Two had sex six times with Yukon Goldie before he knew it was another guy."

"Thruster did him seven," said Redrum. "God, was he mad when he found out."

Most of the characters laughed and several fell on the floor and rolled about. Carrie didn't think it was funny, but nothing about Omega seemed funny to her any longer.

"I want to know about suicide," Love Machine said. "What happens to you?"

"You go to the cliff at the edge of the world," Quicksilver said. "You have to surrender all your virtual possessions and give them to the Wizards. Then they turn you into a toad, and you jump into the chasm. There's a little flash of light, like a falling star. And then—poof! You're gone for good."

Jester gave a virtual shudder.

"Do many people do it?" asked Love Machine.

"It happens," Quicksilver said. "They have a bad relationship or they meet somebody in real life. Whatever. *C'est la vie virtuelle—et le mort.* I drink to the memory of Yukon Goldie."

Quicksilver raised her virtual wineglass in tribute. Other characters did the same.

"To Yukon Goldie," said Redrum.

"To Yukon Goldie," said Jester. "May he rest in Cyberpeace."

Carrie mentally echoed the toast like reciting a prayer. *To Yukon Goldie. May he rest in Cyberpeace.*

"Can you have sex with a dead person?" Redrum asked.

"Sorry, darling," said Quicksilver. "Only in the real world."

•   •   •

Edmon, as Sir Parsival, sat on a lightning-blasted tree stump near the east end of the Bridge of Sighs. On this shore, everything was bare and desolate, a land of perpetual twilight, where the shadows always lay long and crooked.

The River of Despair flowed beneath the Bridge's stone arch. Edmon knew that on the far shore was the waste called the Slough of Despond, but he could not see it; its landscape was veiled in a murky mist.

Beyond the Slough was the Edge of the World, where one went to commit virtual suicide. Someone had come here weeks ago and terminated Gretchen's character, and it had to have been her killer. Edmon could never believe she'd done it herself, never.

But that meant she'd trusted her killer enough to give him her password. On Omega, that was like entrusting someone with your immortal soul. Gretchen had trusted the wrong person, and now she was dead.

Now she was dead. Edmon gave a tortured little hiccup and bent his head, trying not to cry. He could not count the times he'd nearly dissolved into tears today. His mother kept banging on the door, demanding to know if he was all right. Of course, he wasn't all right, and that's why he didn't want her to see him.

He knew the FBI men had frightened her; good God, they had frightened *him*. When they'd announced who they were, he'd known immediately that Gretchen was dead.

They told him she'd been murdered, and it was as if they had laid a massive stone on his heart, and his heart, long numbed, died. For weeks he'd feared this news would come.

Then the agents had questioned him. Shocked, stuttering, unshed tears stinging his eyes, he'd repeated his story. The agents listened, watching him with the flat, unblinking gaze of men who think they are beholding an idiot.

They asked many questions—he could barely remember what the questions were—and at last they left. His mother kept repeating, "Should I call Malcolm? Should I call Malcolm?"

Malcolm was the family's chief lawyer, a hunched, wily

old spider of a man whose web of influence and contacts stretched far beyond the state. Edmon kept shaking his head *no, no*. He knew he was innocent, and it seemed self-serving and petty to worry about lawyers.

Instead he'd called Hayden Ivanovich, and that was, to his shame, the one time his tears had spilled over. Now he sat at his computer, struggling to stay dry-eyed. He wondered, bleakly, if he should terminate his character so at least he could symbolically join Gretchen in oblivion.

Nobody on Omega would miss him, he was sure. Well, maybe Carrie Blue would. Most people thought Sir Parsival was a joke, an ineffectual buffoon, a fool and a bore who talked too much and took himself too seriously.

But termination would be an empty gesture, more melodramatic than selfless. For Gretchen's sake, he'd sworn himself to a quest. He had lost her forever, but he could serve her still. He could do that much.

Tonight, here at his computer, he was holding his vigil for her, and he didn't intend to break it. He stared morosely at the computer screen, lost in his grief, unconscious of the passing of time.

Then, with a start, he saw he was not alone any longer.

Flair is here.

Edmon blinked in surprise. The ballerina was always so self-contained and self-possessed; what was she doing on the shore of the River of Despair?

"I'm sorry," she said. "I didn't know anyone was here."

Although Edmon's emotions felt dead, his sense of chivalry was still intact and alive. He regarded Flair with puzzled concern. Hardly anyone came to this place unless they were thinking of termination. "Are you all right?" he asked.

"I've had a terrible fight with my boyfriend," she said. "That is, if he really was my boyfriend. It's so hard to tell what's real and what's not on Omega that I'm sick and tired of it. I wish I'd never come here."

He was surprised at her frankness, for she had never

seemed like a person who poured out her feelings. She must, he thought, be terribly upset.

"Your boyfriend James Dean?" he asked. "I don't mean to be nosy. But if you need somebody to talk to . . ."

He let the sentence dangle, unfinished. He was hardly in the mood to console anyone, but neither was it his nature to leave a damsel in distress.

"I'm thinking of leaving Omega forever," she said. "Why put myself through all this?"

"Don't do anything rash," Edmon counseled her. "You're a respected member of the community. Omega would be poorer without you."

"Ha," she said. "Tell me something. You were in love with that girl here, Selena. Do you think you really loved her? Or was it just some fantasy you had?"

A pang of grief stabbed him. "I loved her, absolutely."

"How do you know? Did you ever meet her in real life?"

"I know because it's what I feel in my heart," Edmon answered. "I was never privileged to meet her, but I loved her. Love is an emotional, spiritual, and intellectual attraction. I knew her in her purest essence here."

"Some people," she replied, "would say love is also physical. Very physical. And should be, even here."

Oh, hell, thought Edmon. *Netsex rears its ugly head.*

"Love certainly has a physical aspect," he said primly, "but the higher aspects should take precedence. There's a time and a place for everything. That's my personal opinion, of course, and I don't mean to judge others."

"So," she asked, "you're too high-minded for netsex? Is that it?"

Edmon was unsure how to answer, because Gretchen's hugs and kisses had excited him sexually and filled him with keen yearning. But he had never pushed for more; he had dreaded that she'd think he was trying to exploit her.

He supposed he owed Flair an honest answer; she was being uncommonly open with him. "I'm not too high-minded," he said. "It was a question that never came up in our relationship, that's all. If she'd wanted to, I probably would have."

"But you didn't ask her?"

"No. Never." *Now she'll think I'm a wimp. And I am, of course. If I'd been more dashing with Gretchen, would I have won her?*

"Why didn't you?"

"Well," Edmon said uncomfortably, "I guess I was trying to respect her. My mother always told me that the woman in the relationship is allowed to set the limits, and a gentleman does not push beyond those limits."

She said nothing in reply, so he bumbled on. "Besides, cybersex is so weird. I always thought that the main pleasure of having sex with someone was that they were there. I'd prefer not to be alone when I lose my virginity."

"You're a virgin?" Flair asked.

He struggled to explain. "I'm not proud of it, but I'm not ashamed of it, either. I was taught I should save myself for my bride. Unfortunately this hasn't been nearly as difficult as I'd hoped."

"God," Flair said, "you're horribly old-fashioned. You're really like from another century or something." But she gave him a virtual smile. He was glad he could make her smile, even if she was making fun of him.

"To tell the truth, I've never been fond of this century," he said. "That's why I used to play Dungeons and Dragons and then the interactive dungeons, the MUDs. I like the medieval stuff. That's why I'm a knight here."

"I like you better when you don't talk like the knight," Flair said. "It's nicer when you're just yourself. When you're the knight, you're so wordy. Why?"

He swallowed hard, then answered her. "In real life I stutter. I try to say things as briefly as I can. Parsival can say everything he wants. Maybe it's a good thing in real life I don't talk much. I'm pretty boring."

"It's sort of refreshing to find somebody old-fashioned," she said. "I'm old-fashioned, too. Too much, my boyfriend says. If he ever really was my boyfriend."

"James Dean?" asked Edmon. "Why do you keep wondering if he really likes you? You're a likeable person."

"Well," she said, "in real life I'm not pretty. Not at all.

He knows that. But he keeps pressuring me for sex. He says he's serious about me, but I've never met him. All I know is what he's told me. He seems almost too perfect and too eager. What if he's lying to me about everything? What if he's married or something?"

Edmon considered this. He knew there were married men who cruised the MOON looking for a little hanky-panky in cyberspace. He personally suspected that Blue Rider, Quicksilver's lover, was one of them.

But his mind was full of Gretchen, and he feared far worse dangers on Omega than adultery. He said, "I can understand your concern. And I'm sure you're more attractive than you'll admit. But you should be careful. The girl I loved—her real name was Gretchen—I told you she met someone here, and I think she went to meet him, and she disappeared."

"Maybe I should just log off," she said. "I shouldn't take up your time like this."

She thinks I'm obsessed and silly, a paranoid dweeb. "No," he begged. "Please listen. That girl's been found dead. She really has. You *must* be careful about who you take up with here. You're absolutely right to be careful."

"What?" she said, as if she didn't believe him. "Dead?"

He ignored Ivanovich's advice not to discuss Gretchen's death. He began, earnestly, to tell Flair all he knew.

But her reaction surprised him. She interrupted him when he was explaining how Gretchen's body was found.

"I don't want to hear this," she said.

Edmon was wounded. "You don't believe me?"

"I said I don't want to hear it," she replied. "I'm leaving."

He tried to protest, but she logged off and left him alone by the Bridge of Despair.

Jon lay on the bed in his motel room, sobbing with frustration and rage. He'd been so angry with Lynette that he'd almost kicked his computer apart. Instead he'd opened a pint of bourbon and logged on to Omega again as Zeno.

He'd run his rape program on three different women

guests, but it had given him no satisfaction, he only wanted Lynette. And one of the guests, unfortunately, had wits enough to complain to a Wizard, and the Wizard warned him that if one more complaint was lodged against Zeno, Zeno would be toaded.

"Fuck you," Jon had snarled at the screen. He'd logged off, and realized the bourbon bottle was half empty and he was more than half drunk. He was to meet the octopus girl at his usual time, but he knew she would give him no release. Lynette burned in his blood like a viral fever.

So he'd stumbled to the bed and, his face in the pillow, could not keep from weeping. The liquor, which should have dulled and blurred everything for him, only sharpened his grief.

Most girls he lied to for the pleasure and power of lying. But with Lynette he had sometimes been astonished to find himself telling the truth.

With other women, he dissembled and pretended to have things in common. But with her, he shared strange, deep bonds that went beyond coincidence. She was like a soul mate, a mirror image of himself, his other, long-sought half.

Each of them was an only child. Each was motherless; Lynette's mother had died, his had abandoned him. Each had an inadequate father, hers because of drink and his because of indifference. Each had been raised primarily by a grandmother, hers good and affectionate, his cold and hateful. They had both played piano as children and both had been considered gifted—such things could not be chance!

Most fearful and marvelous to him was the eerie confluence of their minds and bodies. What set them apart from the rest of the world was what bound them to each other. Inwardly she was reticent and exquisitely, maddeningly moral. But outwardly she was scarred, abnormal, a freak.

Outwardly he had been burdened by good looks that made women want his body when he couldn't give it to them in normal ways. Inwardly he was the one who was a freak and a monster, the one no one could truly love.

The longer he knew her, the more she seemed the

woman created for him to find. She would complete him, and he would complete her. Yet the longer he knew her, the more elusive she became, and if she kept it up, she would drive him insane.

He *would* possess her, he told himself. He *would*. Perhaps by possessing her, he could cleanse himself and his inner deformity would die with her. His strange and dangerous appetites would leave his body as her breath left hers. In her death he would be reborn, and they both would find peace from suffering at last.

But in the meantime he had no peace, only a terrible, yammering hunger that filled his body and could be satisfied in only the most complex ways. He needed a woman tonight, a special woman, innocent and sweet and trusting and giving. Not the octopus bitch, who was already beginning to bore him, but someone fresh and exciting. If he could not find her, he would have to get the octopus bitch to come to him, for he had no choice but to kill her.

Otherwise, the war between his body and his desires would torture him until he could not think clearly, and if he could not think straight, he could not win back his sweet Lynette, his broken-faced girl, his other self, and he would be trapped forever in this ring of fire and longing.

He forced himself to sit up on the edge of the bed. He wiped his running nose on the back of his hand. He must go back to Omega and buy time with someone. Anyone.

Each night, by habit, Hayden scanned the index of the Archives, and tonight he was unsettled to find a new book had been added, THE PATRIOT'S ARSENAL, by X. He typed the commands to examine it and found it was a tract on "Improvised Incendiary and Explosives."

Damn! he thought, reading the table of contents. It was a regular devil's cookbook, with how-to's on fire jars, contact explosives, lead azide, Lewis bombs, ether bombs, culvert mines, and syringe fuses. There was a five-part section on car bombs: coil ignition, solenoid, magnetic, tilt-fused, thermal-fused, and calcium carbide.

The spelling and punctuation were faulty, but the information one hundred percent accurate, a handy-dandy bombing brief for terrorists. Maybe the thing was meant only as a sick joke, but it was still a precise and detailed blueprint for mayhem. Who'd created it or added it to the Archives? The same person responsible for the tract on ammonium nitrate?

Christ, Hayden thought, was the whole Internet riddled with this rot? This wasn't the work of kids; it was serious and potentially deadly information. In disgust, he left the Archives and went exploring. Maybe his anarchist vandals would leave him a clue.

Half an hour later he found a new source of graffiti in the virtual Graveyard. The west wall of the crematorium was filled with notes, insults, and slogans. And, true to form, his old friend Slate Wiper had been there.

Among the declarations of love and vulgar affronts, was a typical Slate Wiper war cry, "Fuck the syystem! Power to the Constitution! Slate Wiper the Doomster."

Slate Wiper's less literate friend had added a postscript, "Burn on Waco! Burn on Oklahoma!—Nitrate (The Time of Death Approaches!)"

Hayden's mouth twisted in contempt. Waco was burning on, all right, and there was a charred ruin in Oklahoma City to prove it. Yeah, Waco. Burn on.

He found nothing more of interest in the Graveyard. The tombstones had no names, no individuality. The place reminded him of a stage set, two-dimensional and illusional.

A mournful wind was programmed to make the tree limbs creak eerily from time to time; a toad was programmed to emit a melancholy croak at scheduled intervals. The land of the virtual dead was haunted only by its own predictability.

Carrie, Edmon, and Brooke were supposed to ask discreet questions about Slate Wiper and Nitrate, but only Edmon had come up with any answers. "People say they're just a couple of kids who log on at odd hours," Edmon had said. "They write graffiti and try to pick up girls."

So, Hayden thought ruefully, he was probably shadowing a couple of naughty seventh-graders. Their capabilities for terrorism would not extend beyond shooting at stray cats with BB guns. But X, the mysterious writer of explosives manuals, was another matter, one that troubled him.

He was ready to transport back to the Archive Room, when Carrie paged. "Hayden," she said, "can I join you? I just had an extremely unsettling experience—two, in fact."

He wondered what was wrong. "Sure," he paged back.

In a twinkling she was there. "My God," she said, "I just escaped from Onfredo."

"Onfredo?" Hayden said. "I thought he was your gay friend, your 'one safe male on Omega.' "

"I'm mortified. He just declared he loves me. Netsex with one so fair as I just might swing him over to the hetero side of the fence. He came on *strong*."

"Are you okay?"

"I'm fine, just angry at myself that I didn't see it coming. My God, I liked him better than any of them. He set me up, and I fell for it. I wonder how many times he's played this cute trick."

"You're sure it's a trick?"

"Positive. He wasn't like his old self at all. He seemed angry and strange. He didn't just ask for netsex, he campaigned for it—this boy's had practice."

Hayden wondered if her instincts were right. Maybe Onfredo had been setting her up all along. Did that mean that her other hunch was right, too, that The Highwayman was telling the truth? For her sake, Hayden hoped not.

He said, "You said two unsettling things happened. What's the other?"

"I'd been happy to join Onfredo because a character named Vladimer was after me. He lured me to his room, which turned out to be a bondage dungeon. He wanted me to chain him, whip him, and make him crawl naked on the floor to lick my feet."

To each his own, thought Hayden, but he profoundly disliked Carrie being exposed to these sorts of adventures. Perhaps he had been wrong not to let her quit when she'd wanted.

She said, "Why are you in this cemetery? Did you find

any more graffiti? Oops—sorry, I'm being paged. Oh, God, is it eleven already? It's Highwayman. I guess I'd better go. Wish me luck."

"Good luck," he said. But he wanted to grab her virtual body and keep it with his. The impulse surprised and frightened him. He was going as crazy as the rest of them, he thought, as all the other lonely, lustful males prowling the MOON.

The Highwayman had caught Carrie off guard. She'd had an unsettling night and hadn't had time to prepare emotionally, even though his message came, as usual, at precisely eleven o'clock.

> You sense The Highwayman is looking for you in the Bower of Bliss. He pages, "Melissa, I've thought of you every waking minute. Will you join me? Who's Average Joe and what are you doing with him?

She hated the possessiveness in The Highwayman's words, but she supposed she really had no business being with Hayden. She'd turned to him only because she'd been so upset and angry with herself over Onfredo.

She paged The Highwayman, "He's nobody. Just someone I met. I'll join you in a second."

She did not kiss or hug Hayden goodbye. She told him she had to go and hastily typed the command to join The Highwayman.

She was swept from the Graveyard to the Bower of Bliss.

> The Highwayman is here. He takes you in his arms, pulling you inside the folds of his cloak. He says, "Melissa, my love. My love, Melissa." Passionately his mouth swoops down to possess yours.

Mechanically, Carrie typed that she kissed him back and told him that she had missed him. Her head ached and her mouth tasted as if it had been washed out with ashes. She had greeted The Highwayman warmly, but she would have to spend the night fending him off.

Outside, in the darkness, the rain thudded against her window, as it seemed to have done for eternity.

"Kiss me there again," he said, and Brooke happily typed that she did so. Her description was explicit and elaborate.

"Oh God, that's good," he said.

She wrote a detailed description of how she snuggled against him, how she touched him, how her lips and fingers moved over his flesh.

"Do you really need me as much as you say?" she whispered.

"More. Much more," he answered and nuzzled at her breasts.

"And you really want me to come to you, to be with you in real life? You really want me and need me? With all your heart and soul?"

"Heart and soul," he said, and kissed her on the lips. "Will it happen? Will we be one?"

"Oh, yes," Brooke said, dizzy with fresh desire. "Oh, yes."

"Then come to me," he whispered against her throat. "Come to me and save me, please. Oh please. Come save me."

"I will, my love," she said. "I will."

TWELVE

———⟨∾⟩———

H AYDEN AWAKENED EARLY.
    The house was eerie with stillness, the only sound
the muffled percussion of the rain. He pulled on a pair of
jeans and padded shirtless and barefoot to the kitchen.

He made a cup of instant coffee and stared out the window. The sky was gray and the lawn sodden, with both grass
flattened and flowers beaten down. He thought of Carrie out
in the country in her isolated house with its ruined road and
the lake rising.

Taking his coffee, he went into his study and sat at the
computer. He hadn't planned on doing this, but the machine
seemed to draw him as if by a sinister magnetic force.

He told himself he could resist the pull if he wanted; he
only wanted to see if Carrie had sent her report before she'd
gone to bed. And Brooke. He hadn't heard from Brooke
since Saturday.

You have 2 new mail messages.

He typed the command read, and a message from Carrie rolled down the screen. His heartbeat gathered speed, and an involuntary smile twitched the corner of his mouth.

Hayden—It was a dark and stormy night, etcetera. Before meeting The Highwayman, I talked to nobody new except the following:

OMEGA NAME	FACTS
Armadillo Guest	Real name: Keith
	Age: twenty
	Location: Boston
	Occupation: student, physics, MIT
	Desire: looking for romance
Fanjo	Real name: Tony
	Age: forty-eight
	Location: Washington, D.C.
	Occupation: lawyer
	Desire: netsex, especially with teenage girls
Vladimer	Real name: unknown
	Age: unknown
	Location: unknown
	Occupation: unknown
	Desire: my feet!!!!

At eleven I met The Highwayman. He won't tell me his telephone number or address or his relatives' names. He said it would be "safer" for him to be the one to telephone me. He refuses to talk anymore about his accident.

He's sounding good, Hayden; he's laying some highly charged emotions on me, and I have no idea if a word he says is true. But he's very ardent, distinctly wants netsex, and I don't know how much longer I can stall him. He seems weirdly desperate.

I hate this. *Please* find out if this man is who he says is! —Carrie

P.S. I still feel like a fool about Onfredo.

His smile died as he read. She was right about The Highwayman, he sounded good. But Hayden was surprised to find jealousy twisting like a supple young snake in his chest. *Forget it,* he told himself. *I hired her to make men chase her.*

He typed the reply command and wrote "Carrie: Take it slow and easy with Highwayman. I'll check him out and be in touch. H."

He stared at his words critically. They had all the romance of a concrete block. To hell with it. He sent it anyway.

Then he turned to the second message, which was from Brooke. He frowned as he read.

To Mr. Hayden Ivanovich:

   I regret to inform you that I have to leave due to family illness. My grandmother has had a major stroke and is not expected to live. I am leaving immediately for Dubuque and will be in contact with you regarding my return. At this point, I cannot predict the length of time I will be required to stay.

                                    Sincerely, Brooke Tharpe

Damn, Hayden thought irritably; he thought he had her almost under control and now she'd upped and left. He wondered cynically if she was telling the truth and decided she was: her story was totally without imagination.

If Brooke was lying, he thought ruefully, she'd lie more originally. She wouldn't have a prosaic dying grandmother, like any other college student; she would have a brother who had been stung by electric eels in Borneo, a sister needing a kidney transplant because she'd been run over by a truck loaded with religious icons.

He'd wanted Brooke's disks of her conversations with her steadiest suitor, Mephisto. Like clockwork each night, Mephisto logged off just before The Highwayman logged on, and Hayden had a hunch they could be the same man. He'd wanted Carrie to examine Mephisto's writing and see if she could tell. Now he'd have to wait.

But when he reread Brooke's message, it disturbed him.

It took him a moment to realize what made him uncomfortable.

What she had written was so atypically *short*.

Lynette got back from class to find Tammy in their room, lying on her bed, her eyes red and swollen. She was reading a book or pretending to.

She turned her gaze almost sullenly to Lynette. "You got more flowers," she said and threw a poisonous glance at Lynette's desk.

Lynette looked at the bouquet and suppressed a small shudder. Another dozen blood-red roses sat beside her computer, their velvety buds just beginning to unfold. She crossed the room and took the card from the envelope.

"Lynette—I'm sorry I was sharp with you last night. I love you and want you so much that it makes me ache.

"Please don't give up on me. Please meet me on Omega at eight so we can talk again. I'm shopping for an engagement ring because I am totally sincere. Yours forever, James."

A ring? Lynette thought, her blood banging crazily in her temples. *And more flowers? This is crazy. He's starting to scare me.*

"What's the matter?" Tammy challenged. "You don't look happy. Aren't roses good enough for you? Or what?"

Lynette stepped away from the desk as if the vase were filled with poison. But somehow, she could not stop looking at them. What Sir Parsival had told her about the murdered girl had shaken her badly.

She set her books on her bed. "It's excessive," she said, gazing at the roses as if hypnotized. "It's too much. I'm starting to think something's wrong with this guy."

"Why?" Tammy asked. "Because he's nice? Because he's generous? Grab him and cherish him is my advice." She made a loud sound that was somewhere between a derisive snort and a muffled sob.

Lynette, startled, looked at Tammy. She lay stiff and propped against her pillow like some fierce statue. Only her lower lip moved, quivering.

"What's wrong?" Lynette asked, concerned.

"Mike and I broke up," Tammy said tightly. As soon as she uttered the words, she exploded into sobs. Her face crumpled, her eyes shut, and tears streamed down her cheeks.

She threw the book to the floor, sat on the edge of the bed, put her elbows on her knees and her face in her hands. She wept so hard that her back jerked as if someone were laying a whip to it.

Even though Lynette was not comfortable with scenes, she knew she must do something. She moved to Tammy and sat beside her. Gingerly, she put her arm around the girl's shoulder. "I'm sorry," she said. "Really sorry."

To her embarrassment, Tammy turned and seized her in a smothering embrace. She buried her face against Lynette's shoulder, her hot tears soaking through Lynette's blouse. "There, there," Lynette said, feeling inadequate.

Tammy clutched her so tightly that Lynette's ribs ached, but she held the other girl in an awkward hug. After three minutes, the ferocity of Tammy's grief wore itself out. Her sobs grew quieter and further between. At last she pushed away from Lynette and wiped her nose with the back of her hand.

"I thought he loved me," Tammy said and hiccuped. "This James that likes you? You've never even met him, but look at all the stuff he sends you. I gave Mike everything. But he never gave me so much as a goddam dandelion."

"Presents aren't everything," Lynette said, and put her hand on Tammy's shoulder.

Tammy bit her underlip and sniffled. "You know what Mike wanted? His carburetor went out and he's out of money—as usual. So he wanted to trade *me* to this greasy old mechanic for another carburetor. Like I'm a prostitute or something. I've never been so insulted in my life."

Lynette's eyes widened. "He wanted you to have sex with somebody for a carburetor?"

"Not even a new one," Tammy said with disgust. "A *used* one. And he got mad at me 'cause I *wouldn't*. He says, 'Oh, come on, it'll be a kick. And I gotta have a car.' And the mechanic wanted to do it, for God's sake. He's a married man. He's old enough to be my father. And he weighs about three hundred pounds."

Lynette squeezed Tammy's shoulder. "You didn't, though?"

"Of course I didn't," Tammy said angrily. "I don't do sex for money. I don't do sex for *things*. I do it for love. Or I thought that's what it was. God, he got mean when I said no. I never knew he could be so mean."

Again she bent and buried her face in her hands, and Lynette rubbed her back as if it were a baby's, in a soft, circular motion.

"What a cheeseball," Tammy said, her voice muffled. "He was always borrowing money. I mean I'm absolutely broke. I don't even know how I'll eat this weekend."

"Don't worry," Lynette said. "I can help you out."

"I always paid for the beer," Tammy said. "I always paid for the dope. I thought we had this *grand passion*. When I got mad, he said, 'Hey, it's only sex. You think you got stars in your twat or something? Chill out.' I hate him."

"You're better off without him," Lynette said earnestly. "Be glad you found out what he's like."

"I thought I loved him," Tammy said, breaking into tired sobs. "I thought I *knew* him. I didn't—how stupid. I hate myself."

"No," Lynette said. "Don't. Everybody makes mistakes."

Tammy sat up, but her shoulders were bowed and her face puffy and streaked with fresh tears. "And my grades are shot to hell. I'm not smart like you. The only reason I came to college was to find somebody to love, that's all."

Lynette felt an unexpected wave of sympathy. She had always thought she and Tammy were as opposite as the earth's poles. Perhaps they weren't.

She let her gaze drift back to the fresh roses on her desk, and Tammy's words echoed ominously: *I thought I loved him, I thought I knew him. I didn't, didn't, didn't.*

At noon, Jon had stopped to get his van's blinker light fixed in Quincy, Illinois, and bought a copy of the *Chicago Tribune* to kill the hour wait. Bored, hung over, he sat in a plastic chair in the Sears automotive office, his attention drifting from one story to the next.

He noticed a picture tucked innocuously in the inside pages of the state news. The fuzzy black and white photograph showed a face that looked frighteningly familiar, and in disbelief he thought, *Gretchen.*

He felt as stunned as if a lightning bolt had impaled him. Numbly he read the headline and subhead:

MURDERED WOMAN IDENTIFIED
Missing Memphis Student Found

Christ, he thought, feeling faint. Was it possible? He'd met her in this very state less than two months ago. Had they found her already? How? He read on, his heart galloping in his chest.

Last Friday, the story said, workers had discovered a woman's body concealed near a deserted farmhouse in De Kalb County. And over the weekend, she'd been identified by dental records as Gretchen Small.

Jon rose, his knees as weak as an old man's, made his way into a restroom and threw up. Christ, they'd found her so soon—so fucking soon. And identified her by her dental records. Why hadn't he cut off her fucking head? Put it in a bag with a stone and dropped it into the deepest river he could find?

The Sears store seemed suddenly tiny to him, and its walls crystal clear, unable to hide him. The place felt as small and transparent as a microscope slide, and he, like an exhibit, was mounted on it, for anyone to see and remember.

He'd walked through the O'Hare concourse in broad daylight with Gretchen hanging on his arm, so smitten and lovey-dovey that people had looked at them and smiled. *People had looked at them, and now her face was smeared all over a million papers.* He leaned over the toilet and vomited again.

His head swam and tears rose, burning his eyes. But he wiped his mouth and flushed the mess away. He straightened and went to the row of sinks with their bank of mirrors. *Get hold of your fucking self,* he ordered.

Six weeks ago he'd been unshaven and long-haired, his clothes purposely unkempt. Today his hair was neatly trimmed, his jaw cleanly shaven. His sports jacket was expensive, but he hadn't bothered to wear a tie.

He examined himself as coolly and critically as he could. He had a handsome face, memorably so, it was true. But it was a chameleon face, and he could change it by a mere change of style.

Forcing himself to be calm, he rinsed out his mouth, splashed water on his face. His hands no longer trembled as he took out his contacts and replaced them with his prescription sunglasses. The young man who stared back at him was not the scruffy, long-haired lover Gretchen Small had known. No, he looked as foursquare and conservative as a Secret Service man.

He would go into the men's department of Sears, buy a conservative black tie, and wear it. Nobody would see the man who had been with Gretchen Small because Jon no longer was that man. He refused to be.

When he stepped from the restroom, his step was confident again, but slightly stiff. He became an uptight young executive, pinched of nostril, his jaw set at a dignified angle.

In the men's department, the salesgirl smiled at him flirtatiously, but he didn't smile back. He went back to automotive, and a black man in a mechanic's jumpsuit told him his van was ready. Jon didn't look him in the face.

He paid his bill in cash, as he always did. He got in the van, glad that its windows were tinted so no one could see inside. His heart still beat like a crazed trip-hammer. He would be careful not to go back to O'Hare for a good, long, fucking time.

He was glad he'd arranged to meet the octopus outside Illinois. Before he met her, he would get his short hair cropped shorter still, maybe pierce his other ear, get one of those temporary tattoos or something.

It was eerie, he thought, driving toward the Quincy city limits, that the law's finding Gretchen didn't make him want another woman less, but more. It was as if the stakes of the game were rising, growing more critical, more exciting.

Not Lynette next time. Not Lynette yet. But soon. And until then, he would simply make do.

Carrie sat at the seminar table of her Shakespeare class, tired, bored, and nursing the now-familiar MOON hangover. Rain thudded dully at the room's windows, smearing the view to a blur of wet grayness.

Professor Irwin Cottle was a middle-aged man who seemed composed entirely of curves: round head, round body with a ball-like belly, rounded arms and legs—even his fingers were roly-poly. He looked soft as a baby, but the tones of his voice, which were also rounded, were a deep, resonating baritone. He was elocuting one of the speeches of Mercutio.

Carrie scanned the passage unhappily. Lately, even Shakespeare made her think of Omega. This, she thought ruefully, was not a consummation to be devoutly wished for.

> . . . *vain fantasy,*
> *Which is as thin of substance as the air*
> *And more inconstant than the wind* . . .

Vain fantasy, Carrie repeated silently, dreading that she must meet The Highwayman again tonight. Last night's conversation with him had been like a long, tense ballet.

The Highwayman had pleaded for her sympathy. She'd pretended to give it. He was passionate and flattering. She was coy and sweetly curious. He was evasive, she was elusive. He pursued her, she stalked him.

They kept at it for almost an hour and a half, a strange, flirtatious duel that she could not afford to lose, yet did not know how to win. She remembered their exchanges with frustration and distaste.

"Are you married?" he'd asked.

"Absolutely not." Then, she hesitated, as if feeling vulnerable, and asked him, "Are you?"

He gave a bitter virtual laugh. "No. I would have been. I can't talk about that. No."

"You could talk to me," she offered. "Please. Try."

"No," he said. "I imagine you as very beautiful. Would you send me your picture by e-pic?"

"Will you send me yours?" she countered.

They'd played a strange shuttlecock game, batting questions back and forth, avoiding answers until Carrie's head ached with tension. Before he'd hung up, he said, "I really care for you, Melissa. I thought I might not be able to go on living, but then I met you. Maybe that sounds melodramatic. But it's true."

Then he said, "Goodnight, love. Can you say the same thing to me? Say 'Goodnight, love'?"

She gritted her teeth and typed the words: "Goodnight, love." She logged off Omega, spent and drained, but her blood hummed as if she were wired on amphetamines. If The Highwayman was dangerous, or even only a mere seducer, she'd held her own in the contest.

But, she thought, her temples throbbing, what if he was honest? What if his suffering was real, but he believed he'd found release in love?

She could no longer say if she was on the side of good or evil. Reality had grown spongy, shifting and gray; nothing was fixed or permanent or solid, nothing clearly black or white.

Too shaken to go to bed, she'd stayed up late, writing her report to Hayden. *Hayden,* she thought dismally, *why in hell did I make love with Hayden? I don't need more complexity in my life, not a jot or tittle.*

When she finally dozed, her dreams had been troubled. This morning she overslept and had to mop the kitchen floor because the bucket had overflowed. The leak in the roof dripped more relentlessly now, like a wound opening wider.

She was running too far behind to give any time to her short stories, and she had no taste for them anyway. Her illusory romance with The Highwayman had become far more intense than any fiction she could invent.

"Carrie? I'm speaking to *you.*"

Professor Cottle's overripe voice hauled her back to the present. She stared at him, trying to disguise her startlement. He gave her a wry, superior smile that made her feel like Brooke, who was infamous for not hearing the questions she was asked.

Cottle said, "Please explicate Friar Lawrence's soliloquy in act two, scene four."

Carrie blushed and struggled to comply.

But even as she made her way through the speech about how closely linked virtue was to vice, she thought of Omega.

At 5:30 P.M., Jon was in Wingate, Missouri, driving toward the Franconia Inn. The afternoon sweltered.

He hated the Midwest in summer. The dry heat pressed down as heavily as hell's anvil. Beside him on the seat, he had two six-packs of cold beer, two pints of bourbon, and a paper bag from McDonald's. He shouldn't have bothered with the food. Its odor nauseated him.

Fear and excitement roiled his stomach. He was frightened because Gretchen had been discovered, but he kept assuring himself he was safe. He was smarter than the authorities; who with any brains would be a cop, for Chrissake? Lousy job, lousy pay, people hated you, and you could get your fucking brains blown out.

Still, he had to be careful, extremely so. The serial killer Ted Bundy's story was the Bible on that. As long as Bundy was careful, he'd been invulnerable, almost godlike. It was when he grew rash that he'd got caught. The moral was to stay calm. If you did so, you could kill as many women as you wished.

Soon the octopus girl would meet him. That would buy him some time and give him the relief he so desperately needed. In the meantime, he'd work to win Lynette.

He'd gotten angry at her last night, which had been stupid, but he couldn't help it. He wanted her with a growing hunger. So he was plying her with flowers again, and he would buy her a fucking ring. What girl could resist a ring?

She had said not to phone her, but he could not stop himself; twice this morning he had phoned her anonymously just to hear her voice say, "Hello? Hello?" He had an irresistible desire to do so again.

He reached the Franconia Inn, checked in, and unloaded his van. Once in his room, he switched the air conditioner on high, and flopped on the bed. He opened the first of the beers and drank it down in greedy swallows that gave him a pleasant buzz in his forehead. He opened a second beer. His food, forgotten, grew cold.

Tomorrow he would buy Lynette a diamond. He could get a decent diamond in a pawn shop. He'd lie and say it had belonged to his dead mother or some such shit.

The ring would need a nice box, something pricey-looking, but he could swing that, no sweat. He had plenty of money. He was wise as an owl and had plenty of money, and he wanted Lynette, his pussy-cat.

> The Owl and the Pussy-Cat went to sea
> In a beautiful pea-green boat:
> They took some honey, and plenty of money
> Wrapped up in a five-pound note.
> The Owl looked up to the stars above,
> And sang to a small guitar,
> "O lovely Pussy, O Pussy my love,
> What a beautiful Pussy you are . . . "

He had enough money to buy her a ring; he had money to burn, thanks to his father. Thanks to his father for being dead.

When his father died, Jon had gone to the funeral, oh yes, to see this man he'd never known. To see this family that had excluded him his whole life long.

He'd looked at his father in his coffin and felt nothing whatsoever. He met his two half sisters, pretty girls, nineteen and seventeen, and he'd thought how satisfying it would be to break their teeth with a crowbar, to stab them, to cut them open like pigs.

But he smiled at them, he was as polite as he could be to the whole family. They were a better class of people than his grandmother or his mother with her loud nouveau riche husband and his lousy used cars. Two of his aunts and several of his cousins went out of their way to be friendly to him. Perhaps they felt his father had wronged him by treating him so coldly.

His father must have felt guilty himself. The old prick had actually left Jon a bequest, a trust fund of fifteen hundred dollars a month. There was another funerary gift, accidental but exquisitely sweet. Just after his father's burial, at a gathering at an uncle's house, Jon learned about Omega.

Even mourners have to eat. The uncle's house had been full of food, an almost obscene amount of it. One of the cousins, a naive and dorky kid of fifteen, had started talking about the MUDs and MOOs and MOONs, and even took Jon up to his room and showed him how to log on to Omega.

Jon saw the possibilities immediately.

It cost money to get on Omega; you had to subscribe to an online service and get an e-mail address. But with an extra fifteen hundred dollars a month, he could afford a dozen Internet accounts under different names. He could rent mail drops in as many cities as he wished.

So he had become a phantom. He had purchased the power of invisibility and could buy all the identities he wished. He was currently three different characters on Omega, but nobody realized. Besides that, he could log on as a guest, completely anonymous, any time he wished, pretending to be anyone he wanted. He was no longer limited to being one person; he could be multitudes. He was invincible.

Carrie squared her shoulders in determination and logged on to the Internet.

The rain had slowed to a steady, melancholy drizzle, and dark clouds canceled the setting sun. The road to her house was part river, part ruin, and the lake had risen to half-cover her flower beds. The marigolds' golden blossoms bobbed in the water like shipwreck victims.

She loathed meeting The Highwayman again, but she forced herself to enter the Ivory Gate. No sooner was she on the King's Highway, than a dispatch greeted her.

You have 2 new mail messages.

Carrie sighed and typed the command to read her mail. Her first message scrolled down the screen:

Melissa, sweet Melissa,

I just wanted to tell you I've been thinking of you all day long. Last night on Omega I was treating you like a sex object, and it was wrong of me. I was insensitive and pushy (typical male, right?), and I hope you've really forgiven me.

You don't know how precious you are to me. What kind of spell have you cast on me? I came to Omega to be a heartless seducer, but you've seduced me and shown me I have an all-too-human heart.

With All Love, Your Devoted Highwayman (Paul)

Oh, Lord, oh, Lord. Either he was a world-class Casanova or she was a ruthless femme fatale. Or possibly both things were true, she could no longer keep track.

She typed the command to read her next piece of mail. The Highwayman's message flickered off into the black depths of cyberspace, replaced by a new one.

Carrie: Brooke had to leave town, I don't know for how long. See if you can make contact with Mephisto. Perhaps you can recognize his style.

I'll fix the leak in your roof for you when the weather breaks, if you want. Let me know. H.

She shook her head in despair. Hayden's tight-lipped concern touched her more than The Highwayman's effusions, and she found what Hayden didn't say was more provocative than what Paul said at length. Hayden would come again to her, but only if she wanted. Did she want? Well, did she?

I do and I don't. I don't and I do.

She sent his message to sleep among the electrons, and the next thing she knew, she was being paged. She winced.

You sense that Fanjo is searching for you in the Happy Yum-Yum Room. He pages, "Hello, Gorgeous. This is your friendly neighborhood sex maniac. Last night you weren't in the mood for love. Can I change your mind—grin, grin."

She remembered Fanjo, all right. He was the forty-eight-year-old lawyer from D.C. who had a taste for teenage girls. She'd dismissed him from her list of possibles because she couldn't imagine Gretchen Small being attracted to him.

"Sorry," she paged. "Better luck elsewhere. 'Bye."

But she couldn't shake him. He kept sending her lewd messages and obscene invitations until she could stand it no more. Men usually left her alone if she paired off with another man. She paged Hayden.

"Hayden, it's Carrie. Can I come there for a minute? I'm trying to shake somebody."

Seconds passed, and she held her breath until Hayden replied, "Join me." She typed the command and didn't exhale until the magic whisked her from the King's Highway and into the Archive Room.

"Welcome," Hayden said. "What's wrong?"

"It's that pedophile, Fanjo. Maybe he'll leave me alone if he sees I'm with somebody. Sorry to bother you."

"It's no bother," he said.

Carrie was suddenly as self-conscious as if she really was alone in a room with him. On Omega when friendly characters met, there were virtual hugs and sometimes even kisses, but never with Hayden. Although yesterday they had lain in each other's arms, neither of them made a virtual move toward the other.

Hayden said, "If you don't want pages from Fanjo, type '@gag Fanjo.' He won't be able to get through to you."

Gratefully she followed his instruction. She said, "Is that one of the tricks you learned in the Big Book of Archive Secrets?"

"Yeah," he said. "That's one. Listen, we've got a complication. The FBI's contacted Omega. Word's out about Gretchen Small, about the agency checking Omega. People are going to be suspicious, looking for feds. Don't walk into any traps."

She swallowed, nervous without knowing why. "The FBI? What happened?"

The virtual rat scuttled out of the shadows and ran over Carrie's foot. A few seconds ticked by, and, as always, the programmed owl swooped down on it, and the rat shrieked as talons pierced it. She winced.

Hayden said, "Edmon always logs on early. He went to the pub and heard it from Quicksilver, who heard it from one of the wizards. She's putting everyone on alert. The wizards are debating whether to put out a universal warning."

Carrie watched the screen helplessly as the owl flapped off, bearing the bloody rat. Her heart took an erratic skip, and she wondered how she had come to this pass, mixed up with love, death, virtual rodents, and the FBI.

"What exactly happened?" she asked.

"Agents contacted the god of the MOON, asking about records on Gretchen and Joachim the Beggar."

Carrie frowned. "Who's the god of the MOON?"

"The guy who created it, a computer whiz named Marv Yates. From Silicon Valley. And he's a jealous god. He won't say exactly what records he's got, he won't give them up without a court order, and he'll fight that."

"But why would he fight?" Carrie asked. "A girl's been killed. Why won't he cooperate?"

"Because the Internet's considered the last bastion of completely free speech in the United States. And he doesn't want the government invading anybody's privacy."

"That doesn't seem right," Carrie said.

"Yates alerted the wizards not to cooperate, and one wizard passed the news along to a few anointed prophets."

"Like Quicksilver?"

"Like Quicksilver."

"So now," she said, "people on Omega think they'll be invaded by federal spies?"

"They're preparing for the possibility."

Exasperation surged through her. Their job was difficult enough without galloping paranoia overrunning Omega.

The next thing she knew she might be snuggling up to an FBI undercover agent disguised as a virtual sheik.

"Did Brooke say anything to you about having a sick grandmother?" Hayden asked.

"She did, in fact," Carrie said. "Friday, after class. Is that where she had to go?"

"Yes."

"I'm sorry."

"Carrie?" Hayden said.

She tensed without knowing why. "Yes?"

"When the weather clears, do you want me to come out to your place? To take care of the roof, I mean?"

She sucked in her lower lip, and stared at the words flickering on the screen. "I don't know," she said at last. "And that's the truth. I'm sorry."

"It's all right," he said.

"I should go," she said.

"You're right. Try to meet Mephisto."

"I will."

Average Joe crosses the room. He takes you in his arms. He kisses you. He says, "Good luck."

Then he kisses you again.

THIRTEEN

—◦◦◦—

His kiss caught her by surprise; her own reaction surprised her more.

A pleasant heat coursed through her, livening her blood. His touch was not real, only words on a screen, but for a moment she had the vivid memory of his mouth upon her own. A loopy, irresponsible instinct made her want to kiss him back. She half-yielded to it.

> You put your arms around Average Joe's neck and give him a sad smile. You say, "You're extremely attractive. I wish I could get involved with you. But I can't. I'm sorry."

"Somebody waiting back in Nebraska?"

"No. Nothing like that."

There was no one waiting for her, she'd burned all her bridges. She'd wanted to leave Bitter Water, which the kindly man who had been her lover could not understand or quite forgive.

When she said she'd been accepted by the University of Arkansas, he did not believe she would go. He amazed her by asking her to marry him instead, and she had no choice but to tell him no as kindly as possible. She was distressed when tears welled in his eyes.

"Haven't you understood?" she asked. "I'm going back to school. I've always told you that."

He hadn't understood. She had never lied to him, but he had refused to believe her and now he felt misled, betrayed. He acted as if she'd disguised herself as a human woman but was in truth some creature utterly alien to him. "What you want is unnatural," he said. "A woman should want a home, stability, someone to depend on."

"I can depend on myself," she'd said, and with those words, the affair was over. They stayed friendly because neither of them was the sort to harbor a grudge, but since her move, they had stopped keeping in touch.

Hayden startled her back into the present. He said, "Your marriage wasn't happy, was it?"

Is it that obvious? she wondered. *Should I just tell him the whole thing so that he'll know? Oh, wotthehell, Carrie. It's not a state secret.*

She took a deep breath. "I 'had' to get married. You're old enough to recall that quaint custom, aren't you?"

"Yeah," he said. "I'm old enough."

She thought of Derreck Blue, her husband, who had been quiet, serious, and honorable. His emotions had run deep and silent, and he disliked talking about them. He'd loved his sons, but had insisted it was unmanly for him to kiss them, even as babies.

She swallowed and said, "It wasn't that he wasn't a good person. He was. It's just that we weren't really in love. We'd done it exactly once. We got caught. We tried to do the right thing."

"Doing the right thing. That's quaint, all right."

Oh, I shouldn't tell him this, Carrie thought, but she plunged on. "I was madly in love with his best friend. Mitch. Mitch was one year older than I was. We were supposed to get married when he came home from Vietnam. But he died.

He was killed by a sniper. Que Son Valley. He only had six weeks left to serve."

"That's whose dog tags are on your shelf?" Hayden asked.

"Yes. His."

Carrie remembered meeting Mitch with total recall and absolute clarity. She'd been a policewoman in Parkview, Nebraska, giving out parking tickets on a June Saturday morning. She'd just put one on the windshield of a centennial blue Ford Mustang parked in a tow zone.

Then the Mustang's owner had appeared: Mitchell O'Loughlin, a handsome young second lieutenant in full dress army uniform, with a fancily wrapped box under one arm. He was on his way to a wedding. They looked into each other's eyes, and that was that. Just like Romeo and Juliet.

"His funeral cut me apart," she said. "When they folded the flag from the casket and gave it to his mother—I never want to see anything like that again, ever. But I held up through it. And through the gathering at his mother's house afterward. So did Derreck. Derreck was his cousin and best friend. He was supposed to be best man at our wedding."

She paused, not wanting to remember. She tried never to think of this.

But she said, "We left together and drove to the river and parked just to talk. It was night by then. He had a bottle in his glove compartment. We had a few drinks to numb the pain. But I started to cry, he started to cry, and we held on to each other, and one thing led to another, and nine months later I was a mother."

Hayden said nothing. She wondered if he could imagine how ashamed of herself she had been. But other than the shame, she had felt only a great numbness. Her future died the day they buried Mitch. Her life turned into something she hadn't planned, never guessed.

"Mitch was killed in May," she said. "We were supposed to get married in August and go back to school. I got married in August, but to Derreck. I didn't go back to school. I moved to Bitter Water. It's where Derreck taught."

She said, "I don't want to sound like I think I'm a martyr. I'm not. If Mitch had to die and I had to choose again, I'd choose the life I had. I would want exactly the children I had. I would not change that for anything."

"I understand that," Hayden said.

"Neither Derreck or I liked Bitter Water. It was an ugly, gossipy little town right out of Sinclair Lewis, and we never fit in. We always meant to leave. But there was the baby, and then another baby, and then Derreck got leukemia. What he went through was terrible, just terrible. I had two boys to raise and debts on top of the debts, and we could never get away."

"Until now," he said.

"Until now," she said, and wondered if he could begin to comprehend what she was trying to say. Until Mitch died, she had always believed herself a free spirit in control of her destiny. But when he was buried, it was as if she deliberately buried her dreams with him.

She loved her sons passionately, and she'd grown to love Derreck in a companionable way. But that other kind of love, the kind that had nearly killed her, she did not want again. Nor would she ever put her fate or her happiness in the hands of any man. Never again.

"Between your husband and now," he said. "There had to be someone. Men wanted you. I know. Nothing worked?"

"Nothing worked," she said. "There was a man in Bitter Water before I left, but we wanted different things. I didn't mean to hurt him, but I did. So I vowed no more. Not until I do what I have to do."

There, thought Carrie in distaste, *I've taken out my poor, bleeding heart and shown it to him from every pathetic angle. Is this what Omega's reduced me to? I used to have more pride.*

"I see," he said, and she wondered if he did.

He said, "And when you're done here? What then?"

"I look for a job. The job market's tight. I'll go wherever the job is."

"And what if it's a place that turns out to be as bad as Bitter Water?"

"That's the chance I take."

"Taking chances doesn't scare you?"

"Taking chances scares me to death."

"Have you ever admitted that before?"

"No. Never."

"Why not?"

"No one ever asked."

What's happening here? she thought, feeling badly off balance. *Why are we talking this way? Why am I telling him all this?*

She was distracted by a page from St. Grobyc's Chapel. It was Onfredo.

"Greensleeves, I'm really sorry. I want to apologize for last night. I'd been drinking, and I wasn't myself. I feel rotten about it. Please join me if you can. I can explain."

Onfredo had broken the spell, and although she'd been angry with him, he made her almost weak-kneed with gratitude; he offered her escape from Hayden and from her own emotions. She paged Onfredo, "I'll be right there."

To Hayden she said, "You've been kind to listen, but I've stayed too long. I just got a page. I need to go. Goodbye."

Impulsively, she kissed his cheek. Then she typed the command to join Onfredo and let Omega whisk her away through the darkness.

When she left, a sense of emptiness resonated through Hayden. He was a real man in an imaginary room, missing a woman who hadn't actually been there.

What had just happened between them was mysterious and double-edged. Carrie seemed to have distanced herself from him permanently, yet, at the same time, to have drawn him closer.

Intending to shut him out, she'd opened her emotions to him as never before. Trying to build a new wall between them, she'd torn down an old one. She'd drawn a line to separate them at the same time she'd erased one.

On Omega you never knew what the hell was real and what wasn't, and the lines of demarcation kept shifting. He didn't know why he'd kissed her, although, of course, he hadn't kissed her at all.

She was probably kissing and hugging somebody hello

at this moment and thinking nothing of it. Later she'd kiss and hug The Highwayman. And God knew who else. He preferred not to think of it.

In the meantime, he had work to do. He wanted to find out who X was, the writer of pamphlets on explosions and fires and things that go boom in the night. He had no clues, so he was going to take a chance and try to feel out Quicksilver, who was always reputed to know more than anyone else on the MOON.

Hayden paged her. He supposed she might ignore him; she always had people dancing attendance on her, and why should she pay attention to him, a nobody?

He sent his message. "I'd like to talk to you in private some time. Would it be possible?"

She paged him back with astonishing speed. "Just how average are you, Average Joe? And what are you up to in the Archive Room? I've had my eye on you."

"I'm about average in averageness," Hayden paged. "But there are things I want to know about Omega that I can't find out. I need someone who understands this place. I hear you know it best."

"Are you only in love with my mind?" she asked. "Or is this your cute way of getting me all to yourself?"

"Both," Hayden replied, hoping it was the right answer.

Her reply was a long time in coming, as if she were thinking it over. At last she paged, "Meet me at midnight in the Gardens of Aphrodisia. Come alone. You interest me."

Christ, Hayden thought, gritting his teeth. The Gardens of Aphrodisia? Did she think he was making a play for her? He hated all this cybersex idiocy. He didn't want some incorporeal woman, the one he desired was maddeningly real.

But he answered, "I'll be there."

Edmon sat disconsolately by the Bridge of Sighs. Earlier, he'd gone to Ye Silent Woman Pub, but all the conversation had been about Gretchen and the FBI, and he could not bear it.

People were already blaming him for the FBI's visit to Marv Yates; he'd been too vocal too long about her disappearance. Soon they'd be screaming to toad him, and a toad was what he felt like, a miserable, slimy, powerless toad.

Perhaps the only good that would come of this mess was that Flair, the ballerina, would believe him about Gretchen's death. She'd probably thought he was a paranoid fool.

He checked to see where Carrie and Hayden were, but he didn't make contact with them. He was too dispirited. He would sit alone again, thinking of Gretchen.

> You sense that Flair is looking for you in the Dressing Room. She pages, "Parsival, I just heard about the FBI coming to see Marv Yates. Can I talk to you? Some disturbing stuff's been happening."

Edmon's heartbeat speeded up, and he felt a rush of concern for the girl. He typed, "Do you want to join me? Or should I join you?"

She answered, "Why don't you come here? It's more private. I'll lock the door."

Quickly he tapped out the command to join her, his fingers slightly unsteady. In a moment he was plucked from the Bridge of Sighs and found himself transported.

> You are in Flair's Dressing Room. The silver and pink room is spacious and airy, filled with light.
>
> An antique dressing table sits beneath an enormous mirror framed by makeup lights. The table is crowded with perfume, makeup, powder puffs, and vases of flowers.
>
> Flowers are everywhere—roses, orchids, camellias, tulips, and exotic lilies. Bouquets fill every corner, and their freshness and fragrance make you feel almost intoxicated.
>
> Flair is here. She hugs you and says, "Hello. Thanks for coming."

A surge of pleasure filled Edmon. A giddy sense of gallantry made him want to fall on his knees before her and kiss her hand, but girls mocked him when he made chivalric gestures. Other men did such things well, but he did not.

He gave her a hug that seemed both chaste and bold to

him. He said, "Hello," and suddenly found himself virtually tongue-tied. He could not utter another word.

"Parsival," she said, "I owe you an apology. Last night it wasn't that I didn't believe you. It was that what you said scared me. I heard the news. I'm so sorry that your friend is dead, I really am."

He swallowed hard. "It's still hard for me to believe."

"I wanted to talk to you. I'm frightened."

"Frightened?" Edmon's courtly impulses, as intoxicating as the fieriest liquor, coursed through his blood.

"James Dean won't take no for an answer," Flair said. "He sent more flowers today. And he says he's sending a diamond ring, an engagement ring. I don't *want* an engagement ring. I've never even met him. What sort of man would do such things? It's insane."

Edmon's mind spun. He himself was the sort of man who might think of doing such things; he was an impossible romantic and knew it. Still, there was such a thing as decorum. It was wrong to overwhelm a girl with display of any sort, and expensive jewelry was a compromising gift.

"Now someone keeps phoning every few hours," she said. "But nobody says anything. There's just breathing. I think it's him."

"You're right. It's disturbing," said Edmon.

"Another thing," Lynette said. "He sent me his picture by e-pic. He's extremely handsome. He could have any girl he wanted. Why does he want me? I'm disfigured. It makes no sense."

The matter-of-fact way she said, "I'm disfigured" startled him; she seemed to have no trace of self-pity. This impressed and somehow touched him.

He said, "You're probably too hard on yourself."

"Not in the least," she answered. "I know exactly what I look like. So does he, I've sent him my picture. He claims beauty doesn't interest him. He says his own looks are a curse, that nobody ever sees the real him."

"Except you?"

"Except me. I've looked on his naked soul, he says. And

it's my soul that he loves. But if all this love is so soulful and spiritual, why does he insist on netsex?"

Edmon wanted to say, *It's the curse of testosterone*, but did not. "He's wrong to pressure you," he said.

"Parsival, I don't know what to think. I really don't."

"My name is Edmon," he said. "I go to Dartmouth, but I'm home in Arkansas for the summer."

"My name is Lynette. I'm at Kansas State University, in summer school. And you know what? James knows where I am and how to find me. But I know nothing about him."

Edmon's heart took an apprehensive skip. "What do you mean?"

"He says he travels and he never knows where he'll be next. I don't know his phone number, he always calls me. I've got an address, but it's for a suite number. He says he's from Cleveland, but he could be from anywhere. He says his real name's James Deason, but I don't even know if *that's* true. In a way, he's like a phantom. You see?"

He saw, and a profound uneasiness began to creep through him. "Does he want you to come visit him?"

"Not yet. I offered. For some reason it seems important we have netsex before we meet. Maybe that's all he wants, a netsex partner, no real-life encounter at all. But if netsex is all he wants, he could find a more willing partner. Why me?"

Because you're a nice girl, Edmon thought. *Just like Gretchen was. And Monica Toussant. A nice, innocent girl who doesn't do things like that. That's why he wants you.*

"If you don't mind," he said carefully. "I think you should tell me all you can about this man."

Jon Rosmer was having a busy night, and he hadn't checked on Lynette for almost an hour. He was slightly drunk, and he had to concentrate carefully on his typing. He tapped out the command to search for Flair.

Character	Time Logged On	Location
Flair #b67426	49 minutes	The Dressing Room

So she'd come back, he thought with satisfaction. She couldn't stay away from this place anymore than he could.

Should he page her, whisper sweet nothings and flowery apologies in her ear? Or would he find himself getting too physical again?

His groin burned and throbbed. He needed relief, and he knew he would get it from the octopus bitch in person tomorrow. The anticipation made his skull ache, as if it had grown too tight for his thoughts.

He had other women on the string tonight, half a dozen of them. Let Lynette sit in her fucking dressing room and cherish her goddamn virginity all alone.

At least he supposed she was alone. He could not resist checking to see. He typed the command to see inside her dressing room. He saw the same old hokey description. But the last two sentences jolted him.

Flair is here. Sir Parsival is here.

Parsival? She was with Parsival?

Jon felt as if he'd been struck so hard in the stomach that something within him broke apart.

She was with that fuckhead Parsival? How long was this useless bastard going to haunt him? He used to think Parsival was a joke. Both Monica and Gretchen had known him and dumped him. They knew who he was in real life, too, and had laughed about him. His name was Edmon Welkin, and he was a stuttering little prick who lived in Fayetteville, Arkansas. "Poor pitiful Percy," Gretchen had called him.

But Parsival wouldn't let Gretchen go, he'd made a fool of himself by carrying on about her all over Omega. Jon had heard the new gossip. Everyone knew Parsival had brought the FBI right to the very throne of god, to Marv Yates. And what was he doing with *Lynette*, for Chrissake?

On impulse Jon typed the command to join Lynette. He'd barge into her room and tell her if she ever talked to Parsival again, he'd kill them both, he'd cut them wide open, as if he was gutting fish.

> You try to join Flair but are thrown back through space to where you started. Either you don't truly desire to go, or Flair rejects you.

"Bitch!" Jon spat, enraged. Not only was she with Parsival, but she'd locked herself up with him, making it impossible for anyone else to join her.

He started to page her, then caught himself. He didn't dare risk another display of anger. But blood pounded in his head, and if he could get to her at this moment, he would break her neck like a rotten twig.

As for Parsival, for the first time in Jon's life, he understood the urge to kill a man. And for the first time he understood the hatefulness of the word *rival*. He'd always thought of Parsival as a fool and an annoyance. But this annoyance, this fool, this miserable worm was turning into a cobra.

"Be careful, cobra-boy," Jon whispered to the screen. "You might meet a mongoose."

The Highwayman wanted sex, and he wanted it tonight.

He had been, by turn, seductive, sweet, pleading, cajoling, argumentative, assuring, and accusing. He used reason, he used emotion; in a dizzying display he used every mode of persuasion Carrie knew. And now he was threatening to end the relationship.

"I mean it, Melissa. If you don't love me, why should we go on? It tears me apart, wanting you this much. My life is hard enough. Let's just say goodbye."

Oh, God, Carrie thought. *I'm going to lose him.*

"Don't say that," she typed back fiercely. "I'm extremely fond of you. Just don't try to blackmail me into doing something I'm not ready for."

"Oh, FUCK blackmail," he retorted, "I should never have told you the truth. I should have died when Heather did. Maybe I should just kill myself. Shit. Goddam."

Carrie tensed painfully. She shouldn't play this game. Yet she was afraid—what if it wasn't a game and he truly felt suicidal? *Stay calm,* she told herself. *Calm.*

"Look," she said, "you're depressed, which is perfectly

normal. Are you taking anything for depression? Are you seeing somebody?"

"YES, dammit, this patronizing fucking shrink who keeps telling me to be patient. To be fucking patient! I thought you were the first good thing to happen to me in a year and a half. Wrong again. I wish I was dead. Let's say goodbye."

She rubbed her forehead in agitation. She didn't know if he was telling the truth or manipulating her like a puppet.

The Highwayman wraps his arms around you. He kisses you passionately. He says, "I love you, but everything hurts too much. Find a whole man."

She swore under her breath and gritted her teeth. He'd cornered her. She said, "Wait. I do care for you. Really."

"Prove it."

Oh, hell, thought Carrie. *"Prove it"—the oldest, stalest seduction line in the world.* She didn't know if her situation was farce or tragedy; she knew only that it was spinning out of control. "It's just I've never had netsex," she said. "I don't even know what to do."

"You just do what comes naturally."

If I'd done what comes naturally, I'd never come to this damned and blighted place, she thought.

"Calm down first," she said. "Let's just talk a while. All right? This arguing is hardly romantic."

"God," he said. "You don't know how you've stayed in my mind. It's like you've possessed me or something."

"Tell me about your day," she said. "And I'll tell you about mine."

She managed to get him to talk for several minutes, but soon he got physical again.

The Highwayman crushes you to his chest, and his lips descend on yours. His hot tongue explores the wet silk of

your mouth. His breath mingles with yours as he whispers,
"You're wonderful. Don't make me wait for you."

"No," Carrie said. "Please. Not yet."

The Highwayman's hand moves to your breast and strokes
it erotically. He says, "Touch your breast. Touch your right
breast."

Carrie kept her hands firmly on the keys. She made no
reply.

"Pretend your hand is mine," he said. "I'm touching
you, caressing you. I want to excite you, make you feel good.
I'm touching you. Can you feel me?"

"Yes," Carrie lied, but she felt, bewilderingly, as if some
ghostly hand did touch her.

"Now," he said, "you touch me. Unzip my jeans. Put
your hand on my cock." Carrie stared at the screen.

She thought of Paul Johnson in Detroit, sitting alone
before his computer in a wheelchair, his jeans unzipped. She
thought of a man who wasn't Paul Johnson, a liar, skillfully
maneuvering her, enjoying his power over her.

"I can't do it," she answered. "Not yet. I need time."

"Then tell me you love me. Say it."

"I love you in a way. I mean I'm fond of you, but we
don't really know each other."

"Say it. You don't have to mean it. Just say it. Say, 'I love
you.' "

Oh, God, she thought. *I hate this.*

"I love you," she said. For some reason she thought of
the marigolds drowning in the rain, their roots rotting.

"Say it again. Please say it again."

"I love you."

"Keep saying it. Say it again and again."

*I'm going to lose him, dammit. It can't be helped. What
will I tell Hayden?*

"I can't do this," she said in resignation. "I just can't."

But, strangely, this message did not flash on the screen

as it should. Instead, her former words to him kept reappearing.

You say, "I love you."
You say, "I love you."
You say, "I love you."

"Don't stop," he said. "Keep saying it. Please."

"I didn't say that," Carrie protested. "My computer's doing something odd."

But neither did that message appear on the screen, only the old one, still visually echoing itself.

You say, "I love you. I love you. I love you. I love you. I love you. I love you. I love you. I love you. I love you. I love you. I love you. I love you."

"What the hell?" Carrie muttered. Was the computer going berserk? She tried to tell Paul she wasn't typing these words, that the computer had a glitch and was stuck and stuttering.

But nothing she typed would go through.

"Don't stop," he said, his words briefly interrupting the torrent of *I love you*'s. "Don't stop. Oh, God. Oh, God. It's good."

Alarmed, she typed frantically, trying to explain, to make him understand. But nothing changed; the meaningless endearment multiplied, filling the screen.

"I love you. Ilove you. Iloveyou Iloveyou! Ioveyou Iloveyou Iloveyou Iloveyou Iloveyou IloveyouIloveyouIloveyouIloveyou iloveyouiloveyou ilove youloveyouloveyouloveyouloveyou

loveyouloveyouloveyouloveyoulove youloveyouloveyou
loveyou."

Carrie tried to page Hayden that something was wrong.
She could not. She tried to escape and join him. She could
not. Nothing happened except the *I love you*'s kept unfurling,
on and on, as if they would never end.

But then, suddenly, they did end. She stared at the
screen. Nothing happened. The words glowed and pulsed,
but no new ones appeared.

She typed his name almost fearfully. "Paul?"

For a moment there was no reply. Then he said, "Thank
you, baby. It was incredible. It really was."

She felt slightly sick. "What was incredible?"

"Making love to you," he said. "Letting me do all those
things. Being inside you while you said that."

Letting you do what things? she wanted to demand. *What
do you mean, being inside me?*

She was paralyzed with disgust and confusion. Had he
caused the message to keep repeating itself? Could he do
such a thing? She felt dirtied, betrayed, and used.

"I didn't mean for anything to happen," she said. "I
wasn't saying that." My God, what *had* happened? Had she
been trapped in some sort of sleazy electronic rape?

"It's all right," he consoled her. "The important thing is
that we did it. You've made me so happy, I've got tears in my
eyes. Thank you, Melissa. Thank you a thousand times."

Carrie could think of no reply. *What am I supposed to
say—you're welcome?* she thought bitterly. The rain
drummed at the windows with its hellish monotony.

The Highwayman took her into his arms, kissed her
gently. She was too numb to protest.

"I feel you're mine, love," he said. "Really mine."

I'm in hell, thought Carrie.

FOURTEEN

———◦◦◦———

A<small>T TWO MINUTES TO MIDNIGHT</small>, H<small>AYDEN TRANSPORTED TO THE</small> Gardens of Aphrodisia.

> You are naked in the Gardens of Aphrodisia. You have never felt so alive and sensually aware.
>
> At the heart of the garden is the Altar of Venus, where you will find unguents, oils, sex toys, and a copy of THE KAMA SUTRA. Open this erotic book and its pictures will come to life, dramatizing sex acts of every sort in bewitching detail.
>
> Everything is permitted here. Do what you will.

Disneyland this wasn't, Hayden thought. And naked he wasn't either, of course. He was clad in jeans, a white T-shirt, and Nike running shoes that he wore without socks.

But he felt eerily on edge here; it was a lascivious piece of turf. Quicksilver could have met him anywhere, why had she chosen this place? The seconds ticked into minutes and he waited. He occupied himself by running checks on Carrie and Edmon.

Edmon, surprisingly, was in some sort of dressing room with a girl called Flair. Hayden typed the command to see her and wondered idly why Edmon was with her. He didn't recall the kid mentioning her before.

Once again Carrie had logged off inexplicably early. She'd spent nearly an hour in the damned Bower of Bliss with The Highwayman, and Hayden wondered, none too cheerfully, what had happened.

> You sense that Quicksilver is looking for you in Quicksilver's Mansion By The Sea. She pages, "Hello, Average Joe. Are you eager to meet me? I see you're naked. Tell me what you look like naked."

Hayden swore under his breath and answered. "I look bare when I'm naked. That's beside the point."

"Maybe," she paged. "Maybe not. Are you married, Average Joe? I sense you are. Do you ever cheat on your wife? Will you lie beside her tonight thinking of the Gardens of Aphrodisia? And what you want to do with me?"

He muttered a swear word and paged her back. "I sleep alone. I'll think about the Archives."

"How dull. Why are you so interested in the Archives, Average Joe? You spend a great deal of time there. An intriguing amount."

"The Archives contain some mysterious things."

"Like the other copy of the Kama Sutra?" she asked. "There are two, you know. But the pictures don't move in the other one. The 'Peacock Position' is particularly nice, as is 'Sucking the Mango.' Did you look?"

"I'm not interested in netsex," he said. "I want information, that's all."

"I've been watching you," she said. "When you're not in the Archives, you wander about alone. The MOON is a social place, but you're solitary. You've found almost all the places on Omega where there's graffiti, and you revisit them every night. Looking for more? What are you seeking?"

Hayden's nerve ends prickled. She really had been watching him, and she knew so much it was eerie.

"Do you know where everyone on Omega is?" he asked. "Or are you only keeping track of me?"

"I can keep track of whoever I want," she said. "You called attention to yourself. Why study graffiti?"

He decided to take a chance. "I'm a sociology student. The real world doesn't intrude much into the graffiti up here. I see very little about politics, for instance. But I see somebody named Slate Wiper wants to burn down the government. And so does someone named Nitrate. They get around."

"Slate Wiper is a contemptible child," said Quicksilver. "And so is Nitrate."

"Still," he said, wondering how she'd respond, "it's a sobering thought. Anybody could use Omega as a secret channel of communications. Drugs could be dealt here. Weapons. Blackmail. Anything."

"Everything *has* been dealt on Omega, Average Joe. Everything. Trust me."

His heart did a quick-step. "You know this? You have certainty of this?"

"What do you want? Drug dealers? Terrorists? Pedophiles? Blackmailers? They're all here. Of course, they're here."

"You know this for a fact?" he asked. "You can name names?"

"Perhaps," she said. "Or perhaps I'm lying. Omega thrives on lies. Omega itself is a lie. You yourself are a lie, and so am I. To be human is to lie."

Goddam, he thought bitterly, *this woman loves playing games.* He said, "There are books on terrorism in the Archives. A new one just appeared. By X. Who's X? Why'd he put it there? Did he create the other one, too? Who is he?"

"Why does it matter?" she asked. "He's free to do what he likes. And so are you. Yet here we are, and you do nothing. You bore me, Average Joe. You're so dreadfully earnest. I'm going to meet Blue Rider. When he's around, something interesting is sure to come up. And up."

"Wait," Hayden said, trying to maintain contact. "Just tell me this—who is X? There's no character by that name. Is he a character going by another name?"

"Of course he is, Average Joe. But I said you bore me. So does X. You're both in love with the real world. You don't belong here. You're not our sort."

"If you won't help me, tell me who can."

"Why would anyone help you? You're too much of a loner, and loners, darling, are always up to trouble. Be careful. I'll be watching you."

"Wait," he said again.

"Dream of me," she said. "Make it a wet one. Ta-ta."

He ground his teeth in frustration and disgust. He tried to page her again, but his message was blocked. She'd closed the lines of communication.

Damn, he thought, had she been telling the truth about what was dealt on the MOON? Did she truly know who X was, or had she only been taunting him? And why was she watching him?

He was about to teleport back to the Archive Room when he got a page from Edmon:

You sense Sir Parsival is looking for you in the Dressing Room. He pages, "Hayden, I've found a girl who may be involved with the man we want. Will you talk to her?"

Hayden frowned and thought, *Jesus, kid, chill out. You'll blow our cover.* He paged back, "Have you told her about me?"

"I said there was another person who'd like to hear her story, that's all."

"Did you use my name?"

"Your real name or your character's name?"

"Either."

"No. But listen. She's been with this guy who calls himself James Dean, and he sounds obsessed with her. She's scared. I want you to hear what she's got to say."

James Dean? Hayden sighed wearily. Brooke had dallied with him, hadn't she? He had to check it out. It was past midnight, and he'd been up since dawn, but he shrugged in resignation. "All right. But don't tell her my name. I'll log off and log on again as a guest. I want to be careful."

"I think she's in real trouble," Edmon paged. "We need to help her. Why do you have to be so careful?"

"I'm logging off. Stay put."

Hayden typed the command to quit and watched the screen darken. He bowed his head, closed his eyes, and massaged the bridge of his nose for a moment.

He wondered if Quicksilver had noticed he'd left Omega. Or was she too busy with Blue Rider? Why had she feigned friendliness and invited him to the Gardens of Aphrodisia—curiosity? Or had she simply wanted the chance to warn him off as dramatically as possible.

Somehow he'd awakened her suspicion and perhaps even her enmity. He had no idea what the consequences might be.

Edmon sat before his computer, nervously sipping at a can of 7UP. Hayden had logged on again as Fox Guest and was questioning Lynette with a professionalism that Edmon thought was bloodless. He didn't like the turn the conversation was taking.

"Did the same florist deliver all the flowers?" Hayden asked.

"Mostly," Lynette said. "All but one came from Campus Flowers. It came from Berrigan Floral."

Hayden said, "I want you to call both shops the first thing in the morning. Find where the orders originated. This James says he's in California?"

"Yes," Lynette said. "Oakland. He doesn't know where he'll be sent next."

"First, see if the orders were actually placed from California. Ask for the numbers of the shop or shops he used. Get those numbers for us. I'll check it out."

"What if they won't tell me?" Lynette asked.

"Say either they tell you or they'll tell the police. They won't want the police called in."

"How do I get the numbers to you?" she asked.

"E-mail Edmon. Edmon, give her your e-mail address. Give her your real name and address and phone, too."

Dutifully Edmon did so. "Feel free to phone me any time," he told Lynette. "I'm at your service."

"And what about your friend?" she asked Edmon. "Fox Guest. Who is he?"

"The less you know about me right now the better," Hayden said. "I'm a friend, that's all."

"Why are you so secretive?" Lynette asked.

"I prefer to think of it as being discreet," said Hayden. "And I want you to be discreet about all this yourself. Understand?"

"I understand," she said. "But in the meantime, what am I supposed to *do* about James?"

"Lead him on," Hayden said. "Draw him out."

"Now wait a minute," Edmon protested. "You have no right to tell her that. This guy might be dangerous."

"Precisely. I want to know how dangerous."

"I don't like it," Lynette said. "He knows where I live. I don't want him showing up on my doorstep."

"If you feel uncomfortable, we'll move you where he can't find you," Hayden said.

"Now wait a minute," Edmon repeated. "Why should she trust *us*?"

"She can check you out easily enough. Your family's well-known in this town."

"I can't leave campus," Lynette said. "I'm taking classes. James even knows what classes I take and when."

"You should tape his phone conversations, too," Hayden said. "It could be useful."

"He's not supposed to call again," said Lynette. "And I don't know how to tape a phone conversation."

"You could call a private investigator," Edmon offered. "I'll gladly pay for it if you'll let me."

"Look, Edmon, I don't even *know* you," she protested. "I can't take money from you. This is getting too weird. You're as strange as James Dean is."

Edmon was hurt. "I'm sorry. I didn't mean to be pushy. I'm concerned about you, that's all."

"I'm concerned about me, too," she said. "I don't like all this intrigue. Let's forget the whole thing. It's late and I'm tired and I want to go to bed."

"I would never willingly offend you," Edmon apologized. "I would certainly never ask you to put yourself in danger."

"This conversation's over," she said. "You'd better go. Both of you."

"Will you be here tomorrow night?" Edmon begged. "Please say you will."

"Don't count on it. Goodnight."

Edmon's heart sank. "The lady doesn't want us here," he said to Hayden. "Please come to my tent. I'd like to talk to you."

"Goodnight, Miss," Hayden said.

"You could check me out through my pastor," Edmon told her. "I go to First Methodist in Fayetteville. Also ask the public library. I worked there as a shelver part-time, during high school. My father insisted we all work during high school. And not for the family company. He said we all needed a taste of real life."

"I said goodnight," Lynette said.

Edmon wanted to hug her goodbye, but he dared not. "Let's go," he said to Hayden. "Goodnight, Lynette. And I apologize for my friend. I don't agree with him at all."

He bowed to her. Then he teleported back to his tent. He sat down near the fire, feeling angry and miserable. Seconds later, Hayden joined him.

"You scared her and made her angry," Edmon accused. "What'd you mean—'Lead him on, draw him out'? What kind of irresponsible James Bond stuff is that?"

"Do you want to find out more about this guy?"

"Of course I do," Edmon retorted. "But I don't want Lynette putting herself in jeopardy. That would be wrong. She's a maiden in distress."

"She's something more valuable than that, kid. She's bait."

"Bait?" Edmon protested, appalled. "She's a human being, for God's sake."

"So's Carrie. You don't mind having her out there putting her ass on the line."

"Carrie's different," Edmon said defensively. "She knew what she was getting into when she signed on. She's older, she can take care of herself. She was even a policewoman. You told me so yourself."

"James Dean sounds good, Edmon. What if he's the one? You want him to slip away? If he loses Lynette, he'll go for somebody else just as innocent. Is that what you want?"

Edmon was half-sick with confusion. "She's a sensitive girl. Why'd you come on so strong? And what's with the mystery act? Why wouldn't you identify yourself? No wonder she shied off."

"Do you want people to know you've got hired spies on Omega? That you've got an investigator?"

"Well, no," Edmon admitted reluctantly.

"How well do you know this girl? Who's to say she won't talk? Quicksilver's already suspicious of me."

Edmon's mood swung to one of alarm. "Quicksilver? Suspicious? Why?"

"She's noticed how much time I've spent in the Archive Room. She doesn't like it."

"Quicksilver is not the type of person you want for an enemy," Edmon said. "Believe me."

"I understand that. In the meantime, we need to get your new girlfriend to cooperate."

"She's not my girlfriend," Edmon said sulkily. "And she'll probably never talk to me again. I don't blame her."

"He's coming on strong, and he makes her nervous. She'll be back in touch, all right."

"You don't know that."

"Where else can she turn? The cops won't help. She hasn't been threatened. They don't arrest guys for sending flowers."

"I just don't think you handled it well," Edmon said, and he meant it.

"You want to fire me? Get somebody more tactful? Go ahead, kid. I don't give a rat's ass."

Edmon sighed. "I don't want to fire you. I just wish you'd treated her a little more delicately, that's all."

"Yeah, yeah. I'll let you be Mr. Sensitive. Send her some MOON mail. Keep it short and sweet. Tell her you're there as a friend for her. Then the ball's in her court. Look, I'm tired. I'm logging off."

"Okay," Edmon said, but he could not shake off his depression. Hayden, as the Fox Guest, vanished, and Edmon already regretted his show of temper. But he genuinely liked Lynette. He didn't wish to lose her friendship nearly as soon as he'd won it.

He began composing a MOON mail note for her. He found it agonizing, trying to say just the right magic words that would bring her close to him again.

> Dear Lynette,
>   I want to be your friend. That is the truth.
>   Sincerely,
>   Edmon Welkin, Jr.

He reread his note and it seemed inadequate and childish, even simpleminded. But it was the truth, and he could say no more, no less to her. He sent the message.

The next afternoon Carrie parked on Dickson Street and walked up the hill to the Burnside Investigative Agency. The day was muggy and overcast with more rain predicted.

When she pushed open the door of the office, Alice, the receptionist, greeted her with a chilly stare. "You're late," she said.

"It couldn't be helped," Carrie said shortly. She owed Alice no explanations and felt like giving none. Her Shakespeare professor, Dr. Cottle, had asked her to stay after class. When the other students had left the room, he'd closed the door and given her a sad, stern look.

Something was wrong, he said. She was no longer participating in class discussions. She was late turning in her bibliography cards. Four times in the last week he'd had to repeat a question for her because she didn't seem to be listening.

This absentmindedness, he said, this inattention to detail, was what he had come to expect from Brooke Tharpe, but certainly not Carrie. Was there some problem she cared to discuss?

"It's personal," she answered, deeply embarrassed because all he'd said was true. "I'll have it worked out soon."

"I hope so," Cottle said archly. "If you can't give this course your full concentration, maybe you should drop it."

Maybe she *should* drop it, she thought fatalistically. She couldn't keep her mind on *Romeo and Juliet,* she couldn't keep her mind on anything lately. Except Omega. Omega haunted her all day long, a persistent dirty-minded ghost that she couldn't exorcise.

Alice gave her a condescending nod. "Mr. Ivanovich's waiting for you," she said. "Go in, please."

Carrie tried to smile, but found she couldn't. She went to the door and started to knock.

"Go right in," Alice ordered.

Carrie inched the door open. "Hayden?"

"Come in."

She entered his office. He stood and came to her. "Are you all right?"

She nodded, although she didn't feel all right in the least. She had the disconcerting urge to snuggle against his chest and rest there.

"I'm glad you could come," he said. "I have news. I wanted to tell you in person. Are you still upset?"

"Yes," she said, "I am."

"Sit down," he said, gesturing at the visitor's chair.

She sat, running a hand through her hair, which the humidity had turned into a tangle of unruly curls. She wore jeans and her old softball team T-shirt, and she knew she looked wan. When she'd put lipstick on this morning, it had looked like a blood-red slash across her face.

Hayden had phoned, asking her to stop by his office after class. She hoped he wouldn't ask about The Highwayman because she didn't really want to talk about him. Every time she thought of Paul Johnson, she was filled with suspicion, regret, foreboding, and scalding resentment.

But Hayden had insisted. Now he sat on the edge of his desk, his arms folded. The sleeves of his white shirt were rolled up in crisp, precise folds; his black tie was expertly knotted, *his* hair lay perfectly in place.

He is a handsome man, she thought with almost clinical detachment. And she had been to bed with him. Yes, she knew what his hair was like mussed, not only what his body looked like under that flawless white shirt, but how it felt and tasted.

Suddenly, she wanted very much to be in his arms again, because he seemed so solid, strong, and, above all, real. She wondered if her hunger for his realness showed in her face.

"Things might be starting to break," he said. "Something's happening with a friend of Edmon's, Lynette Pollson. She goes by the name Flair, the ballerina. Do you know her?"

"I've seen her at the Pub a few times," Carrie said. "That's all."

"She's being pursued hot and heavy. By a character named James Dean, the same one Brooke talked to once. Presents, flowers, he's even promised her a ring and won't take no for an answer. Edmon and I talked to her last night."

"Yes?" Her eyes held his. She felt as if they were having two conversations. One was in words, about Edmon and Lynette and James Dean. The other, unspoken, was about themselves.

"James Dean claims he's in California on business. But she checked with the florists who delivered the flowers. None of the orders originated from California. Two were placed from separate shops in Madison, Wisconsin. Two came from Iowa, and two from Illinois—one Rockford, one Moline."

Her heartbeat speeded. "So he's lying."

He nodded. "He's lying. And he gets around. I called every florist. He never used the same one twice. Their records show that whoever placed the orders paid cash. No credit cards, no paper trail for this guy. One clerk remembered him clearly. 'Very handsome guy,' she said. 'Dark and handsome.' He mumbled. Seemed shy."

"And you think he may be the same person as Joachim the Beggar?"

"It's possible. I want Lynette to pursue it. But she's scared."

"I don't blame her," said Carrie.

"She's afraid, but she's smart and she's ballsy. I think she might come through for us."

"Have you told the FBI?"

"The FBI wants Marv Yates's records. They're not interested in a girl getting too many flowers."

"You tried to interest them?"

"I left word, yes."

Carrie nodded but looked away, feeling slightly dizzy. She was having spells when real life seemed as phantomlike as a fading dream. "The Highwayman, he's still a suspect?"

"He's still a suspect. I'm trying to run a check on him. Are you sure he said the accident happened in London, Ontario?"

Carrie shook her head. "I'm not certain of anything at this point. I'd have to go back and check the disks."

"London's supposed to get back to me. But they'll take their time, I'm not one of them, and nobody owes me any favors. Stay after him. Can you do it?"

She shrugged, but the taste of ashes was back in her mouth again, acrid and sickening. "I suppose I have to."

"Carrie?"

"What?"

"You and he had netsex? That's what I inferred from your report."

She stared at an empty corner, not wanting to meet his eyes. "*He* had netsex. My computer was in some sort of limbo, that's all I was concerned about. I don't know if he programmed it to make it happen or not. At any rate, he had his fun."

She heard the bitterness in her own voice. "I kept saying I hadn't meant for things to—be consummated. He kept saying it didn't matter, we'd done it now, there was nothing to be shy about. I thought, what's done is done. The important thing is I didn't lose him."

"That's good," Hayden said. "You didn't get thrown."

She said, "He phoned afterwards, practically crying in gratitude. He said that it's the first shared sexual experience he's had since the accident. That I made him feel whole and normal again."

There was a beat of silence. "It's a great line. You've got to admit it."

"My God," she retorted in disgust, "what if it's *not* a line? What if it's true? What if there really was a computer glitch, but he thinks he's found love? All he's found is a malfunction and a lie. And I'm the one lying."

"He may be lying, too."

"I know that."

"Whoever he is, you didn't exactly hurt him. Don't be so hard on yourself. What are you? The last puritan in America? Some women would shrug this off."

"I can't help it. Sex shouldn't be casual. It should mean something."

"Should it?"

She met his gaze again. "Yes."

He gave her a slow half-smile, and her heart took an unexpected jump in her chest.

"What should it mean?" he asked.

"I don't know," she said, and was ashamed because her eyes immediately filled with tears. *Damn!* she thought. *Damn!*

His smile faded. He stood, took her by the shoulders, and drew her to her feet. He put his arms around her, gently pulling her close. She clung to him blindly, hiding her face against the comforting solidity of his chest.

Alice's voice came crackling through the intercom. "Mr. Ivanovich? Dr. Holloway is on the phone. He says it's urgent."

Hayden, jerked back to reality, resisted the urge to swear. Carrie tensed in his arms and pulled away. He let her go, but he couldn't take his eyes from her.

She'd fought her tears down, but she looked shaken and chagrined. *Christ,* he thought, *will she ever stop thinking it's a sin to lean on somebody else?*

"Hey," he muttered and reached for her hand. She let him take it, and he held it tightly. She tried to smile at him, but the smile failed.

He took up the phone. "Ivanovich here," he said.

Holloway's cultivated southern voice droned in his ear like a disturbed honeybee. "You wanted to get in touch with Brooke Tharpe. The secretary got her parents' number from the insurance files. They're in Dubuque, Iowa. But Brooke's not."

A nasty, nervous feeling prickled in the marrow of Hayden's spine. "She's not?"

"No. And there's no imminent funeral for a grand-mother because no grandmother's even sick," Holloway said. "Both her grandmothers are in the very pink of health. Brooke's parents have no idea where she's gone. Or why."

"*What?*"

"You heard me," Holloway said. "She lied. I don't know why, but she did. Nobody has a clue where she is."

Hayden gritted his teeth. "Okay. Give me the parents' number."

Holloway recited the number and Hayden scribbled it down, cursing inwardly. His vibes were not good about this, his vibes were terrible, they were rotten.

"Let me know," Holloway said. "Maybe she just snapped and quit the writing program. Walked out. It's hap-pened before. Please keep me informed."

"Right," Hayden said from between his teeth, and hung up.

Carrie's eyes were wide. "What's wrong?"

"Brooke lied to us. Her grandmother isn't terminally ill, she didn't go home, and her parents don't know where she is."

Carrie looked stricken, disbelieving. "She lied?"

"I'm going to call her folks," Hayden said. "To see if they'll give me permission to open her apartment. I'd wanted her disks so you could look at Mephisto's style. Now I want to see what the hell's going on."

He released Carrie's hand and picked up the telephone receiver. Carrie swallowed and said, "Should I leave?"

"No," he said, dialing. "If they let me look at her place, I want you to come. You may see something I'd miss."

She nodded and sank back into her chair.

The phone rang eight times before a woman picked it up. She spoke with a twang and said, "Hello?" as if she was suspecting only trouble would answer her.

"Mrs. Tharpe?"

"Yes?"

"The mother of Brooke Tharpe?"

"Why? Is this about her lyin' about her grandma? I don't know nothin' about that. I don't know why that girl tells such stories. We're good country people. We don't know how she got the way she is."

"Mrs. Tharpe," he said carefully, "my name's Ivanovich. I'm Brooke's employer. She was doing some work for me."

"What sort of work?" the woman demanded.

"Writing," Hayden said, keeping things vague.

"Writing," she answered in contempt. "Makin' up stories. That's all she's ever done. Writin' down things that's not true."

"Mrs. Tharpe, I'm concerned about Brooke's disappearance. She's been gone since Sunday, and nobody seems to have heard from her."

"We don't hear from her much under no circumstances," the woman said. "Not since she went off to college, and they filled up her head with craziness. It wasn't our idea she go off to that college. A woman don't need no college. It puts ideas in their heads."

"Ma'am, she may have been gone since Sunday. That's almost forty-eight hours. That's long enough to report her missing. You might notify the Fayetteville police."

"She has always gone off and done what she wants. I couldn't call up a policeman every time she did that. Nossir. Whatever she's up to this time, I just hope she don't bring shame on her family. That's all I hope."

Hayden rubbed his forehead wearily. "Mrs. Tharpe, your daughter has a computer on loan from my people. And some computer disks we need. I'd like your permission to go to her apartment and retrieve them."

She was silent. *Stubborn as her daughter*, Hayden thought and rubbed his forehead again. *Okay, lady, no more Mr. Nice Guy.*

"The computer's valuable, Mrs. Tharpe, and it's not her property. We need those disks. I'd hate to press charges. I'd hate to drag your family into court."

She hesitated. He could almost hear the wheels spinning, resentful and paranoid, in her mind. When she spoke, her voice was bitter. "Go look all you want. It's no nevermind to me."

"I'll need you to phone the manager of her apartment. Let me get the number out of the book."

"I can't afford long distance calls. We're not made of money. We're country people. We work for every cent we get."

"I'll give you the manager's number and my address, Mrs. Tharpe. You send the phone bill to me. I'll see you're reimbursed. I guarantee it."

Grudgingly she took the numbers. At last he hung up and looked at Carrie. "No harder than pulling teeth out of a grizzly bear," he said. "Come on. Let's go to Brooke's."

He took his suit jacket from the coat rack and slipped it on. He opened the door and ushered Carrie back into the lobby. "Alice, I'm going out. If anyone calls with any information about Brooke Tharpe, page me immediately. Understand?"

Alice gave a brisk nod that said of course she understood, did he think she was a simpleton?

He and Carrie got into the white pickup truck, and Carrie rode beside him in silence. When they reached the apartment house, Carrie gazed moodily at its bleak facade.

She said, "I never doubted for a moment that her grandmother was sick. It's such an ordinary story, so common at her age. I believed it."

"So ordinary it was brilliant," Hayden said.

Carrie shook her head. "She wouldn't run off with somebody she met on Omega. Surely she wouldn't. She knew the danger. She's *not* stupid."

"Yeah?" Hayden said. "Well, I don't think she exactly lives in the same universe as everybody else, either. Let's go."

They got out of the car and entered the building. The first door off the lobby bore a brass plate: "Lucille Arcadio, MANAGER." Beneath it was taped a cardboard sign that said, "No Solictors This Includes Religious."

He buzzed the manager's bell, and a lean, gray-haired woman in a flowered housecoat opened the door. She regarded them with a pale, unyielding gaze. "Yes?"

Hayden flashed his investigator's badge. "My name's Ivanovich. Brooke Tharpe's working for me, but she's left town. She's got my computer and some disks. I need them."

The woman cocked her head and regarded him without smiling. "Yeah? Her mother called here, sayin' to let you in. I guess I can. But I'll *watch* you. I don't want no funny business."

"Fine," Hayden said. The woman eyed him and Carrie suspiciously, but she stepped outside. She wore pink crocheted house slippers that matched the fading flowers of her housecoat, and she moved as soundlessly as a cat.

She led them up a dreary flight of stairs to the second floor and stopped before a door with the number *14* painted on it. The hallway smelled like mildew and burned cornbread.

"This Tharpe girl," Lucille Arcadio said, unlocking the door with a master key. "I didn't see her the last couple days. Her rent's due Friday."

Hayden nodded noncommittally. The lock clicked, and the woman swung the door open. He and Carrie stepped inside. The carpet was stained and worn, the blinds half-drawn. A double bed, covered only with rumpled sheets, took up one side of the room. An empty desk with a mismatched chair stood on the other.

The room had a palpable air of abandonment, as if Brooke had deserted it in haste. Lucille Arcadio muttered, "Jesus, Mary, and Joseph, what now?"

"This apartment," Hayden said, his eyes sweeping the barren room, "she rented it furnished?"

"Yes. She had hardly nothing of her own. Where's she gone? She can't just go off. She signed a lease."

"Hayden," Carrie said in a low voice, "it looks like she's taken everything."

She nodded toward a closet door that stood open. The closet was empty except for a few wire hangers on its floor.

The shelves of the lopsided bookcase were stripped naked except for a Fayetteville phone book. Next to the bookcase stood a battered bureau, half its drawers pulled out, and they, too, looked empty. Hayden took out his handerchief, walked to the bureau, pulled out its remaining drawers. They contained only a few ragged pieces of underwear and two mismatched socks.

The walls were bare except for one tattered poster held in place with transparent tape. The poster, badly faded, showed a warrior princess astride a winged white horse. The girl wore skimpy armor and brandished a silver sword.

Hayden moved to the bare desk, carefully opened its drawers one by one. They'd been cleaned out.

Mrs. Arcadio, muttering, strode into the bathroom.

"Don't touch anything," Hayden said, but she flung open the medicine cabinet. It held nothing except a crumpled tube of toothpaste without a cap and an empty aspirin bottle.

Mrs. Arcadio wrenched back the door of the linen closet. It, too, was empty. "She's crazy as a goat," she snapped, and marched from the bathroom, across the living room and into the kitchen. The kitchen had the same forsaken air.

The cupboard doors stood gaping open, only shadows within. On the counter sat a nearly empty box of cornflakes, a quarter-bottle of dishwashing soap, and a jar that looked as if it contained congealed grease.

"She's cleared out," Carrie said in a tremulous whisper.

Hayden nodded grimly. There was no sign of the girl. Or the computer. Or the disks.

In the pitted porcelain sink, he saw scraps of charred paper. She had burned something there, and a few larger fragments had fallen to the floor and drifted, neglected, to the corner. He picked up one.

The heat of the fire had scorched the paper brown, turned the ink a dark reddish color. The handwriting was feminine, tiny, its lines crammed so closely together they had an air of obsession.

> *lpha and Omega*
> *Lover Boyd Boyd Boyd*
> *yd Boyd Boyd Boyd Boyd My*
> *ever I am coming to yo*

Hayden felt like a man reading a death sentence.

Brooke's chest was aflood with euphoria. She'd lost track of the state borders and county lines she'd crossed. Now she was in the small state park between the towns of Hardener and Ree Village. Her blood thrummed with such force and swiftness that her hands were unsteady on the steering wheel.

The blacktop forked, and she went left as he had told her. Nervously she watched her car's odometer. Six-tenths of a mile, he had said. After she took the left fork, she would go six-tenths of a mile, and there was a scenic overlook, a height from which one could see a wide vista of hills, plains, and the river.

Just as the mileage showed she had almost gone the full six-tenths, the road took a long curve under a shadowy canopy of oak and maple trees. It was like driving suddenly into the dimness of a covered bridge.

But then the curve straightened, the trees magically thinned, and she saw it: the overlook, with its parking places and safety rails. The sky was a clear blue vault, flawless and tender, the land stretched out below like the scene from a painting, and the wide brown river glittered in the sunlight.

Only one vehicle, a battered gray car, was parked by the railing. Her heart hammered so much that it hurt her, and she couldn't breathe. She pulled up and switched off her engine. Even as she did so, she saw the door of the car open.

He's really here, she thought, half-faint with joy and the most intense excitement she'd ever known. *It's Boyd. It's Boyd.*

She struggled out of her seatbelt, fumbled with her door handle, then was outside in the hot, clear summer air. He was coming toward her, a smile curving his lips.

She moved so swiftly to meet him that she almost stumbled. But before shame at her own awkwardness could sweep her, he had her in his arms. He was so beautiful his face seemed to swim in her vision. He was the most beautiful young man she'd ever seen.

"Brooke," he said huskily. "My God. My God. You came. You've saved me."

Then he bent, and his perfect lips pressed against hers. Her eyes closed in ecstasy. The very earth seemed to shake beneath her feet. She was weak with love.

FIFTEEN

━━◦◦◦◦◦━━

CARRIE SAT CROSS-LEGGED AT THE EDGE OF THE ALLEY THAT RAN behind Brooke's apartment house, methodically going through a black plastic bag of trash.

Hayden knelt beside her, another bag of garbage lying open at his feet. The alley's dust had already filmed the sheen of his black shoes. His tie was askew, his once-immaculate shirt smeared across the chest with ash, his hair hanging over his forehead. His suit jacket hung on the corner of the apartment house's Dumpster.

He studied Brooke's checkbook, which had been scissored into uneven halves. The mutilated checkbook could mean only one thing, and he didn't like it.

"She must have cleared out her account," he said.

"On a Sunday?"

"Used a bank machine. Got all she could."

"She couldn't have had much," Carrie said, squinting at a Wal-Mart receipt.

Hayden said, "Three hundred and fifty-six dollars. And

eight cents. She can't get far on that. But she's got a credit card. There's an entry here for a payment to Exxon."

"She bought a map," Carrie said, showing him the receipt. "A road map. On Sunday."

She showed him the receipt. The cash register had neatly enumerated the purchases.

WAL-MART
ALWAYS THE LOW PRICE
ON THE BRANDS YOU TRUST
Fayetteville, Arkansas

RAND MCNALLY KIDS'		
US ROAD ATLAS	00003421	4.96
TROJAN RIBBED		
CONDOMS	00649227	6.96
M&M PEANUTS	00295836	3.96
HOT-KOLD HANDI		
THERMOS	00872998	6.96
FOLGERS INSTANT		
COFFEE	00298419	3.96
	SUBTOTAL	26.80
SALES TAX		1.91
	TOTAL	28.71
	CASH TEND	28.71
	CHANGE DUE	00.00

THANK YOU FOR
SHOPPING WAL-MART   6/23 11:44:23

Hayden stared stonily at the receipt, then at the ruined checkbook. "The last check she wrote," he said. "Jesus. A road map, coffee, peanuts—and condoms. Jesus."

Carrie wiped her hand on the thigh of her jeans. "She was getting ready for a trip. And a man."

Hayden's face grew harder and something haggard glinted in his eyes.

Carrie said, "Hayden, don't look so grim. This may be nothing sinister. Maybe she found an old boyfriend on

Omega. Somebody she knew. We don't know that much about her past."

He stirred through the contents of the trash bag. "A *kids'* map," he said. "She bought a kids' map. That says it all."

It did say it all, Carrie thought darkly. Everyone had thought Brooke so aloof, so critical and intellectual. But behind the ice-princess facade had been another lonely child hungry for love.

Carrie thrust her hand back into the bag and flinched at the slime from a rotting orange peel. She pulled out a textbook, *Barr's Composition. Uh-oh,* she thought.

The text was used in freshman English. She and Brooke had each taught two classes; it was how they earned their assistantship money. Brooke, like Carrie, was scheduled to teach again this fall.

Nesting between orange halves was a folder of papers, and Carrie pulled it out and opened it. The title page said, "The Heroine as Social Savior in *Twelfth Night,* A Seminar Paper for Shakespeare 6003."

Her stomach tightened in apprehension. "Oh, Hayden," she said and shook her head.

"What?"

"Her teaching text. And this. It's her seminar paper." In the bottom of the bag, Carrie spied a pack of file cards fastened with a rubber band. She drew them out. They were speckled with cooking grease.

"Her bibliography cards, too," she said, her voice stricken. "She's left here for good. Dropped out."

He handed her a stack of envelopes. "Bills," he said. "All unopened."

Carrie looked through them. The gas company, the water company, the telephone company, Exxon, Sears Automotive, State Farm Insurance.

He said, "She's not only dropped out, she's skipped out. She's not just leaving, she's running away, stiffing her creditors. Why?"

With an irregular little beat, Carrie's heart contracted.

Whatever Brooke was running to, it was more important to her than her credit rating. Or her career.

Hayden reached into the sack again, drew out a handful of charred paper, similar to the fragments in the kitchen sink. A few flakes wafted away, and others, finer, sifted threw his fingers and floated earthward.

Reluctantly, almost involuntarily, Carrie took the largest scrap from him. The scorched paper was so delicate that she could have crumbled it to powder simply by rubbing it. Over its browned surface, the fire-reddened ink formed a thick tracery of cramped handwriting.

> oyd Boyd Boyd Boyd Boyd
> Prince in Exile, My Everthi
> arkness Can Hold You No
> d Boyd Boyd Boyd Bo

"Hayden," Carrie said, "this Boyd can't be some person she just met on Omega and fell in love with—it can't. It's against all reason."

He crumpled the charred scraps in his fist, then opened his hand. The breeze toyed with the sooty remains, lifting the finer ash to drift away like dust.

"The Highwayman fell in love with you," he said.

"That's different," Carrie said, but even as she said it, she knew it wasn't true. Things happened swiftly on Omega; Edmon had warned them of that from the start.

Hayden opened his fingers and watched the ashes fall. "She's gone," he said simply. "Gone."

Lynette was a rational and methodical person, but today she felt as if she were under a spell, working compulsively. She could not stop checking things; the action obsessed her.

First, she'd phoned the local florists to see from where James had sent the flowers. When she'd learned he'd lied, it hadn't shocked her, hadn't frightened her, hadn't alarmed her. Instead she'd been filled with a dreadful acceptance. *Now what?* she'd thought. *Now what?*

She deliberated for over an hour before e-mailing the

news to Edmon Welkin. She had no reason to trust him, but it was his anonymous friend, Fox Guest, who had suggested she call the florists. Fox Guest might not be trustworthy, either, but he was smart.

Edmon must have been checking his e-mail regularly, for he'd sent a reply within the hour. His message was lengthy and made her wonder why he was making such a show of concern for her. What was his stake in this?

He'd written:

Dear Lynette,

Thank you for entrusting the information about the florists to me. I've passed it on to someone who will trace the matter further. Please stay in touch.

I know you have no reason to believe my sincerity in this business, but my main concern is your welfare. Again, here are some references you can contact if it would ease your mind.

Pastor Clyde Fenmore, First Methodist Church of Fayetteville, 7 W. Dickson, Fayetteville, Arkansas, 72701, (501) 555-3208

Bernard Blassingame, Chief of Police, 113 W. Mountain, Fayetteville, Arkansas, 72701, (501) 555-1111

Elizabeth Weschel, Director, Fayetteville Public Library, 217 E. Dickson, Fayetteville, Arkansas, 72701 (501) 555-4874

Please feel free to ask any or all of these people about my character.

My father is Edmon Eugene Welkin, Sr., of Welkin Brothers Transport, and my mother is Marietta Black Welkin.

Please do not hesitate to call on me if I may be of any assistance to you! I am at your service!

Sincerely yours,
Edmon Eugene Welkin, Jr.
(Social Security #432-9006-0000)
501 Rogers Blvd.
Fayetteville, Arkansas, 72701
(501) 555-3637

This answer seemed so sincere, so painfully naive, that it galvanized her to action. Edmon wanted to be checked out. Very well, she was checking him out with a vengeance. Since one o'clock, she'd been on the telephone.

Immediately her quest had taken a surreal turn. As soon as she reached Pastor Clyde Fenmore, she realized that he sounded exactly like the cartoon character Jiminy Cricket.

She would not have been surprised if he'd said, "Always let your conscience be your guide" or sung "When You Wish Upon a Star." But he confined himself, in his chirpy way, to talking about Edmon.

Fenmore had known the Welkin family for twenty-three years and said Edmon was a fine, upstanding young man and that he wished he had more young parishioners like him.

Lynette took notes as painstakingly as if she was in class. But all Fenmore's remarks were variations on a theme. Edmon was Mr. Wonderful.

The Fayetteville police chief, Bernard Blassingame, painted a slightly different portrait, flattering but tinged with a mixture of eccentricity and sadness. Blassingame was as gruff as Fenmore was chipper. He said the Welkins were a respected family, "exemplary citizens."

Blassingame had been Edmon's scoutmaster; he characterized Edmon as quiet, courteous, but painfully shy. Other children had teased him ruthlessly because of his stutter and because they thought he was a goody-goody. "But he's a genuinely nice kid, no meanness in him."

"Um," said Lynette, a noncommittal sound.

"Let me tell you about Edmon," Blassingame said, as if he sensed her doubt. "Once I had those boys fishing when they were on a Cub Scout camp-out. Edmon wouldn't put a worm on a hook. He wouldn't hurt a worm. I said, 'You don't fish, you don't eat.' He didn't eat. Later two boys got him, pushed his head in the latrine. To punish him, you know, for being a wimp. Half the kids wouldn't speak to him. Didn't make him no nevermind. He wasn't gonna hurt neither worm nor fish. And that was that."

She thanked Blassingame, rechecked her notes, then dialed the Fayetteville Public Library. The director, Elizabeth

Weschel, gushed about Edmon. "He's smart and sweet—so old-fashioned that he's downright *courtly*. There are only two things wrong with Edmon. Do you want to know what they are?"

"Certainly," Lynette said, her pencil posed over her notebook.

"All right," said Elizabeth Weschel. "First, he ought to have more confidence in himself. Second, he's too nice for his own good."

Lynette wrote this down, her mouth set at an ironic angle. Beside the words she drew a stick figure with wings and a halo. Practically a seraphim, this Edmon Welkin.

She thanked Mrs. Weschel and hung up. Okay, she told herself. Whoever Edmon Welkin, Jr., was, he seemed universally adored by the authority figures in his life, even if he was a dork on Omega. But was Sir Parsival really Edmon? Parsival might be the Mad Butcher of Cyberspace for all she knew, a psychopath using Edmon Welkin's good name.

"I hate Omega," she muttered under her breath. "It makes you a total paranoid."

She went to her bureau and started to brush her hair. She would put on her makeup to disguise her scars as best she could, then go downtown and hire a detective. It seemed melodramatic, but she was sick of ambiguity and wanted the truth.

She was blending her foundation when her intercom crackled into life. "Lynette? It's Kimberly at the desk. There's a package for you. The Fed Ex guy just left it. I signed for it."

She tensed. She was expecting no package. What was this, another present from James? She crossed the room and hit the reply button. "I'll be right there," she said.

Her pulses thudded in her temples as she made her way down the hall to the lobby. She felt giddy with apprehension.

"Yes?" she said to Kimberly.

"*Un cadeau pour vous*," said Kimberly, who was seldom above practicing her French. "*Voila.*"

She handed Lynette the red, white, and blue Fed Ex mailer. Lynette took it almost reluctantly. James's name was in the sender's information space, along with his company's name, Henly Computer Services, and an indecipherable address.

Numbly she carried the package back to her room. The box was big enough to contain a major city phone book, but it was suprisingly light. She opened it gingerly, as if it might be full of venomous spiders.

The inside was stuffed with coarse white paper, the sort people use for packing. Cushioned within the paper was a box wrapped in gold foil and tied with a golden ribbon. A card in a gilded envelope was fastened to the ribbon.

Her lower lip twitched unsteadily, and she bit it as she opened the card. "Dearest Lynette—Diamonds are forever. So is my love. Will you marry me? I dream of making you my own. This ring was my mother's. All my love, James."

Oh, God, a ring. He's really done it, she thought. All the air seemed to have been crushed from her lungs, and she couldn't get it back, couldn't draw a breath.

With trembling fingers she unwrapped the box, letting the expensive paper fall to the floor. Within the box was a smaller velvet ring box of sky blue. She opened it.

Inside twinkled a ring with a single diamond in a gaudy setting. She took a sharp, ragged little breath. A claustrophobic panic seized her, and her heart thudded like that of a trapped animal. Her only desire was escape.

He's crazy, she thought. *I've got a crazy man after me.*

Jon Rosmer drove from the St. Louis airport toward Cape Girardeux, Missouri. He had a car from one of his stepfather's lots, and he'd replaced its dealer's license plate with a stolen one. He kept a collection of stolen plates and fake ID's in his van.

He steered with his left hand, and with his right he possessively gripped the fingers of the octopus bitch, whose name was Kristin.

She was surprisingly petite and pretty, an elfin-faced blonde with a pointed little chin, slender nose, and tip-tilted eyes. But he didn't like her. She was built like a boy, flat-chested and hipless, and she talked too much.

She was gossipy and sarcastic, like she thought she was

funny. She was nervous, too, which set him on edge. She damn well ought to be nervous, the bitch: she was married and had a kid.

That put him off, her being a wife, a mother. She was used goods, and he couldn't get excited about her in the right way. Instead he kept thinking obsessively of Lynette; it was Lynette he wanted beside him, his beautiful, broken-faced girl.

But he had stupid, mouthy Kristin, who wouldn't shut up. She was frightened about cheating on her husband, but at the same time proud of it. Her husband's name was Douglas, the baby's name was Dougie Jr., and her mother-in-law was baby-sitting. Kristin laughed that her mother-in-law was actually *grateful* to baby-sit, that she felt privileged.

Kristin had lied that she was going to St. Louis to meet a cousin visiting from Denmark. Douglas was so dumb he believed this story, and that was one of the reasons she was being unfaithful to him; Douglas was just plain dense.

She'd married too young, blah, blah, blah. They had nothing in common, blah, blah, blah. He was so dull and conservative, especially about sex, that he'd practically driven her to look for adventure on Omega. Blah, blah, blah.

"So he's working the night shift every night," Kristin chattered, "and sleeping all day. He promised he'd go back to college, but I know he never will. He keeps his Internet connection so he can play his Dungeons and Dragons games."

Jon nodded in false sympathy and squeezed her hand. The more Kristin babbled and mocked, the more poignantly he yearned for Lynette.

Lynette would receive the ring today. Would she be pleased? Excited? He would call her tonight, when his mind was clearer and his body purged of its aches and fires. He would say all the right things. This time he would not falter or fail.

"One of his D&D friends showed us Omega," Kristin said. "But it didn't interest Douglas because nobody gets killed, so how do you win? But I went on, and I *liked* it."

She looked at him winsomely. Her little elf-face had surprisingly full lips, and she had a habit of thrusting them out in mock petulance, to be cute. Every time she did it, he wanted to slap her so hard her head would knock against the window and her pouty lips would split like too-ripe fruit.

"I wasn't looking to get involved with anyone," she said with her pretend pout. "I picked Cochise because he didn't offer any real temptation. He was just a boy, and I flirted, that was all. But he got so serious—and so weird. I mean *really* weird. He scared me. And then you came along."

"And then I came along," Jon said with a smile he didn't feel. She had been Lacewing, bored and eager to be led into the forbidden. He'd been Lamb guest when they met. He'd never bothered being anything other than a guest throughout their affair. She wasn't worth wasting a character on, she was only a stopgap measure.

She said, "The first time I talked to you, I knew you were different. Most of the others are so immature."

"I knew you were different, too," he said. This was true. She hadn't been a cyberslut, but he'd known she could be; his instincts were unerring. He'd courted other girls at the same time he'd courted Kristin, but he knew from the start Kristin was his if he was willing to settle for her.

She gave one of her nervous giggles. "I've done things with you on Omega my husband couldn't even imagine. All day long I tingle all over, remembering. I had to see you in real life. To touch you."

"I had to see you, too," he said.

She ran her free hand up his arm, under the sleeve of his short-sleeved white shirt, caressing his bicep. "Why don't you pull off on a side road? Stop and we can do it in the car. Why wait?"

Jesus, he thought, she really was a hot little slut, she was disgusting, she deserved to die. "Not in the car," he said. "There's not enough room. I told you—I know this great inn by Cape Girardeux. Water bed, a private deck closed in by trees, a hot tub. It's like a honeymoon suite."

She pretended to pout again. "It sounds like you've taken girls there before. I'm jealous."

"Nobody but you. I found it on a business trip. I dreamed of taking somebody special there. Now I am."

There was, of course, no such inn in Cape Girardeux. The water bed, the private deck, the hot tub, all were fictions like everything else he'd told her. The country they drove through was hilly and wooded, the edge of the Mark Twain National Forest, and he was heading toward its deepest and most deserted part.

"When's your divorce final?" she asked.

"In two months," he lied. "God, she's cold. I came to Omega hoping to find somebody who wanted to explore what sex could be. And love. Love and sex are completely separate to her—she thinks sex is dirty. Thank God I found you."

He squeezed her hand, a signal for her to say, "And thank God I found *you*."

Instead she said, "Ouch! Not so hard. Are you afraid I'll get away or something?"

"Sorry. Yeah. I'm afraid you'll vanish—like a dream." He raised her hand to his lips and kissed it with elaborate tenderness.

"That's what I like about you," she said. "You know how to treat a woman."

"I think I do," he said with a smile.

She settled back against the seat, studying his profile. She liked the way he looked, he could tell.

She said, "Cochise was such a kid. He came across as very adult and macho at first, but he's not. He's kind of crazy. Seriously disturbed. I'm glad he found somebody else. It got him off my back. Let *her* worry about him."

Jon nodded and thought of Lynette, so pure and cool and tantalizing. She was difficult to attain and therefore supremely desirable. Kristin was cheap, she was human garbage.

"Cochise's real name is Boyd," she said. "He started telling me he was in some kind of trouble, like he wanted me to come get him. I mean, it became this huge melodrama. This incredibly wild story. I started thinking, this dude could be dangerous."

Jon didn't give a damn about Cochise, and he wished Kristin would shut the fuck up.

But she didn't shut up. She gave her breathy, irritating giggle. "He says he's part of a paramilitary group. He's with his father and brothers and an uncle, and they're stockpiling explosives and stuff, but he wants out. Like, this is supposed to turn me on?"

"He's lying," Jon said. "Trying to impress you."

"Anyway, he found this girl from Arkansas," Kristin said. "I told him, 'I'm happy for you.' But he still wants to tell me the story of his life. He wants to look on me as his *confidante*. I listen. I stay on his good side. I mean I'm not going to cross this fruitcake. God."

"Arkansas?" Jon said. The name awoke a cold frisson in him, like ice flowing into his bloodstream. Edmon Welkin, his enemy, was from Arkansas. Both Gretchen and Monica had told him so. And Edmon, damn his eyes, had gone all over Omega, making a fuss when Gretchen disappeared.

"Well," Kristin laughed, "that's about his speed, right? Some hillbilly from Arkansas? But then the story gets even wilder. This girl is coming to save him from the evil militia. But she's part of some big plot, too. She's working with a detective and another woman, and they're all working for what's-his-face. Mr. Yak-yak. Sir Parsival."

"What?" Jon said. He stared at her so hard that he almost ran the car off the road.

"Hey, *watch* it," she said.

From between his teeth he said, "The girl from Arkansas—she's working for Parsival?"

"That's what Cochise said. Boyd said, yeah. They're looking for this MOON stalker."

He couldn't help himself. He let go of her hand as if it was poisoned, drew back his fist and hit her in the face. Her head snapped back, cracking against the window, and she screamed like a crazy woman. Blood started to pour from both her nostrils, an incongruously cheerful red.

"Why'd you do that?" she screamed. "Why'd you do that?"

"Shut up," he ordered. His mind spun crazily. He shouldn't have hit her. They were on the highway, for Christsake, and he was still miles from his destination.

"Let me out of this car!" she shrieked, and he had to hit her again.

"Shut the fuck up," he snarled, "just shut up."

This time she crumpled against the seat, her expression stunned, and she seemed to shrink physically. She looked no bigger than a child. Like a child she put her hands up to cover her face, and blood stained her trembling fingers.

He'd dazed her, but he didn't want to knock her unconscious. He needed to get her out of sight. He took the first side road he came to. Beside him Kristin wept into her bloody hands.

His knuckles hurt, and he felt ripped apart by dread and betrayal. Parsival, that idiot Edmon, that cocksucker had a *detective* on Omega? And Edmon had been talking to Lynette, *his* Lynette? Edmon had women working Omega, trying to draw him out? Christ, he'd talked to them, to both of them, he *knew* it.

He took another side road, this one dirt. It looked like an abandoned logging road and would have to do. The trees stood like a wall on either side, and parallel to the road ran a deep ravine full of pin oak, dogwood, and cedar. He followed the road until it petered out and the forest closed in around them.

He got out of the car, strode to Kristin's side, and wrenched her door open. She cowered and flinched, but he jerked her seat belt free and hauled her out of the car. Christ, she'd bled all over the front seat. It looked as if he'd beheaded somebody there.

"Don't hurt me, don't hurt me," she babbled. "I've got a little boy. He needs me—"

He slammed her against the trunk of a walnut tree, and her knees buckled. "Don't hurt me, don't hurt me," she begged. "I've got a baby. He's not even two years old."

She would have slid to the ground, but he pinned her shoulders in place. "What do you want?" she whimpered. "I'll do anything you want. Just don't hit me again."

His fingers dug into her shoulders. "Tell me about Parsival," he ordered. "And the detective. Tell me."

She tried to twist away, but couldn't. Tears and blood

streaked her face. "Parsival hired this girl. Her n-name is Brooke. She fell in love with Boyd. She's g-going to him. That's all I know."

He shook her so hard that her head wobbled like a broken doll's. "What about the detective? Who's the detective? He's on Omega, too?"

"Yes, yes, yes. I don't know anything else."

He slapped her as hard as he could. "Who is he?"

"I don't know, I don't know," she wept. "The detective doesn't know about Boyd. Boyd says if the law comes into it, there'll be trouble. The girl's going to him alone."

"The law?" he said, putting one hand on her throat and squeezing. "How's some private detective the law?"

"He was in the FBI or something. I can't breathe."

"FBI?"

"Yes. But he doesn't know about Boyd and the girl. I can't breathe. Please—"

"Why's Parsival hanging around the ballerina? Flair?" he demanded. "What's she told him?"

Kristin shook her head and coughed. He loosened his grip on her neck and brought his face close to hers. "What's she told him?" he repeated.

She shook her head. "I don't know. I swear I don't know," she rasped.

"Parsival's got more than one woman working for him?"

"Yes. Yes. I think."

"The other one. Who is she?"

"I don't know her name. I swear. I just know there's another one."

Jon felt exhausted and treacherously close to blacking out. Christ, Edmon of all people. Tracking him with his hired hounds. Christ, Christ. He should never go near Omega again. Exile. Fucking exile.

He licked his lips, which were dry as ash. He squeezed Kristin's throat again. "He still talks to you, Boyd does?"

"Yes," she said. "He says he wants someone to know. For her protection. If I talk to him again I can find out anything you want. I'll find out everything."

Jesus, she was bargaining for her life, and what could he do? Her sylphlike little face was ruined, her bloody lips shook, and her eyes were wild with terror, but with cunning, too.

"If you don't hurt me, I'll find out anything you want," she said. "I'll find it all out. You'll know everything."

His blood banged in his temples, and his skull felt heavy, stuffed with too much pressure. All he wanted to do was to kill her. He could feel the weight of the knife in his hip pocket and yearned to have it in his hand. He wanted to thrust it into her scrawny body and cut her open.

But he had to keep her alive, even if just until tonight, and he felt saddled by the unspeakable burden of it. He could not let her be seen. He would have to take her to a motel room with a computer port, and he would have to smuggle her inside and force her to absolute obedience.

The whole time she would scheme to betray him, to trip him up somehow. He could see it in her eyes. She knew that he would kill her. It was just a question of now or later.

He couldn't kill her yet and he couldn't kill her here. Everything was fucked up. And it was Edmon's fault. Edmon had caused all this to happen.

He stared into Kristin's desperate eyes and felt true hatred for her. She did not awake an iota of sexual desire in him. His groin felt as dead as if his genitals were made of clay.

"Please," she said. "Don't kill me. I can help you. I can help you get other women if you want. I'll do anything."

"Yes," he said from between his teeth. "You will."

He put his fingers over her carotid artery and pressed hard. It took only seconds for her eyes to roll backward and her knees to sag. He let her fall in a heap at his feet.

He stripped her blouse and bra from her body and ripped the blouse into strips. He bound her ankles together so tightly that he knew her circulation would be cut off. He didn't care; so much the better.

He tied her hands securely but not with such cruel tightness. She would have to be able to type, after all. He knotted a bloody strip of cloth over her eyes, and wadded a larger piece into her mouth to gag her, then wrapped a second strip around her head to hold the gag in place.

He picked her up and carried her to the open trunk. She was as light in his arms as a little girl, and her half-naked body had an unpleasant childishness about it. Her breasts were tiny. She'd worn the bra only because it was padded. It was knotted now around her wrists.

He laid her body in the trunk and slammed the trunk door shut. But when he drove out of the forest he felt as if he had ninety pounds of pure, lethal radium in his trunk, glowing like an atomic flash and poisoning him with its invisible rays.

Tammy had spent all afternoon in a bar drinking Jell-O shooters and had come back to the room and thrown up extravagantly in the sink. She lay on her bed, clutching her skull and mumbling that she wanted to die.

Lynette sat at her desk. Futilely she tried to make sense of the Doctrine of Manifest Destiny. She had a history test in the morning, but for the first time in her life, she did not give a damn about excelling.

The velvet ring box sat in her desk drawer, but it seemed to send out evil vibrations that distracted and frightened her. She did not intend to log on to Omega tonight. She wished she were in Madagascar or Antarctica or Fiji, somewhere where James could not find her or send her presents.

She had thrown out all the flowers. She would send back the ring if only she knew where to send it. She'd plugged the phone back in and, thank God, no strange phone calls had come all day long.

Tammy groaned from her bed. Lynette fidgeted and wished she could escape the room, take a long walk. But night was falling, and she had an irrational fear of going out alone. *He* might be there.

This fear was absurd, and she knew it. But she'd caught James in yet another lie. The Fed Ex box containing the ring hadn't been sent from California, but from St. Louis—fewer than two hundred miles from the Kansas border.

Didn't he think she'd notice? Did he think she was stupid? Or did he have such confidence in his charm and the lure of a ring he thought she'd ignore such trifling detail?

She hadn't yet sent word about the Kansas City address to Edmon. She didn't know how deeply she wanted to get involved with Edmon, but she believed she could trust him.

The Norton Detective Agency downtown had run a quick check on Edmon Welkin, Jr. Everything he'd told her—his name, address, phone number, social security number, his parentage—was true. Edmon was ready to be her knight in shining armor. Did she want such a knight?

She rose to make herself another cup of instant coffee. Tammy was lying on the bed, her arm over her eyes, her lips moving silently as if in prayer. The phone rang.

"If it's Mike, tell him I hate him," Tammy said, and rolled over to face the wall.

Lynette's pulses felt too rapid and thready. She picked up the receiver. "Hello?" she said.

No one answered.

"Hello?" she repeated. "Who is this?"

"It's me, honey," said James's voice. "How are you?"

Her heart jolted in her rib cage. She sank back into her desk chair. "I'm fine," she said tonelessly. *Where is he?* she thought.

She said, "Are you still in California?"

"Yeah, sweetheart. Oakland, still. I've been thinking about you. Did you get the ring?"

She closed her eyes and wished her heart wouldn't bang so hard; she felt almost ill. "I got it. Yes."

"Are you wearing it?"

She took a deep breath. "No. I can't, James. I'm sorry, but it's too soon for such a serious step."

"Please don't say that." His voice was soft and silky.

"I can't help it. I want to send it back to you. Where should I send it? Will you be in Oakland a few more days? I could send it to your hotel."

"Lynette, don't send it back. Think it over, that's all I ask. Maybe I seem too eager to you. But it's only because you mean so much to me. You're very special."

Was it her imagination, or did his voice seem unnatural, eerily mellow and calm? She said nothing.

He said, "Will you be on Omega tonight?"

"I don't think so," she said. "Something's come up."

"You sound tense," he said. "What's the matter? Is your roommate there?"

"Yes," she said, "she is. And she's not feeling well. She's having a kind of a crisis, in fact. It's not really a good time for me to talk."

"Would you rather I called back later?"

"Yes," she said, "that would be good. Tomorrow maybe."

He laughed. "I don't know if I can wait that long."

"It's not so very long," she said, a frightened catch in her voice.

"You do care for me a little, don't you?" he asked. "I haven't scared you off, have I? I'll take it slow and easy if that's how you want it."

"Of course, I care for you," she said brightly. "Yes, slow and easy. That's exactly what I've been saying."

"I could come see you if that's what you really want," he said. "I could take a few days off. We could meet somewhere. I'll come to you as soon as I can. Would that make you happy?"

"It would make me very happy," she lied. *I want out of here*, she thought desperately. *I've got to get out of here.*

"Then we'll do it," he said. "I promise you. You're my special girl, Lynette. Nobody but you."

From her bed, Tammy groaned like a woman in her death throes.

Jon Rosmer sat on the bed and opened another beer. At his feet lay Kristin, tied and gagged with the bloody rags. He'd scrubbed the blood from her face with wet paper towels, but she still looked like shit. Her nose was broken and one eye was swollen half-shut. Her body shuddered and sometimes spasmed convulsively.

As soon as it had grown dark, he'd checked into a cheap

motel on the major highway that ran through Park Hills, Missouri. There were almost no other guests.

He'd stripped a blanket from the bed and taken it to the car. He'd opened the trunk, thrown the blanket over Kristin, and carried her inside like a bundle of dirty clothes.

Now he put his foot in the middle of her naked back. She was so thin that her ribs showed and each vertebra of her back stood out, a distinct little bump. He wondered why any man would marry such a small, bony thing.

"On the phone," he said, nudging her spine with the toe of his boot, "that was Lynette I was talking to. My true love. I was going to cut her fucking head off, she made me so mad. Maybe I still will. What the hell. Who gives a shit?"

Kristin whimpered into her gag. It was a small, choked sound, like a kitten being hurt.

"Did you see what happened when I talked to her? I started to get a hard-on. You don't do that to me. Too bad. I might let you live if you could do that. You want to try?"

He pushed her with his foot. "You want to try?" he repeated. "You want to try to get me excited, bitch?"

She nodded, although her eyes filled with tears. She was so terrified she'd do anything to please him. He enjoyed that.

"Yeah," he said. "Let's try." He unbuckled his belt.

But he could not perform. It was no good without killing her, he should have known better.

It was Lynette he wanted.

SIXTEEN

CARRIE REACHED HOME JUST AS THE RAIN BEGAN AGAIN. AS SHE unlocked her front door, she heard her phone ringing and hurried to answer it. "Hello?" she said, slightly breathless.

"Carrie, this is Edmon." He sounded agitated. "Did Hayden tell you about the girl in Kansas—Lynette? She's got t-trouble."

More trouble we don't need, Carrie thought. "What is it?" she said.

"She just phoned. She's frightened. This James Dean sent her an engagement ring even though they've never met. He says he's in California, but he Fed Exed the box from St. Louis. He phoned her, and his voice sounded strange, like he was drugged or drunk or something. And now he's saying he's coming to see her as soon as he can."

Carrie's stomach tightened. "He's in St. Louis? That's too close for comfort."

"You're t-telling me," Edmon said. "He's only a four-hour drive from her. She doesn't know what t-to do, where t-to go. I said she could home here. I'd put her up in a hotel under a different name. But she says she doesn't feel right about it. I tried to ask Hayden what t-to do, but his line's t-tied up."

Nerves tense, Carrie pushed her hand through her bangs. She knew Hayden's line was busy. He'd reported Brooke to the police as missing, and now he was calling his FBI contacts, hoping to involve them in the case.

She frowned, trying to concentrate on Lynette. Lynette, pursued by one man she'd never met, wasn't going to spring into the arms of another for protection. But turning to a woman for help would be different.

"Listen," she said, "maybe she doesn't want to be indebted to a strange man. But she shouldn't be alone."

Carrie took a deep breath, thought for a few fleeting seconds, then made her decision. "Tell her to come stay with me. I was a policewoman. Dr. Holloway at the English Department will vouch for me. How's that?"

Carrie regretted the words almost as soon as she said them. Her house was not a hotel, and she was not a guard. But Brooke was missing, God knew where, and Carrie couldn't bear to see another girl at risk.

Edmon said, "You'd do that? Really?"

What am I getting myself into? Carrie thought. But she said, "Really. Just tell her this isn't the Ritz. I don't know how comfortable she'll be."

"Carrie, this is great of you," Edmon said, sounding so humble she winced. "She's really scared, and she needs somebody. Another woman would probably make her feel a lot more secure."

"Yes, yes, sisterhood is powerful," Carrie said wryly. "We can celebrate our femininity and worship the mother goddess together. Do you want to call her or should I?"

"I will. She's waiting for me to tell her what Hayden says. Should I check this with him?"

Carrie gritted her teeth. Hayden would probably not approve of this. She decided to play a bit fast and loose with the truth. "Don't bother. I can speak for him," she said. "He'd agree a hundred percent. After all, we were both in law enforcement, weren't we?"

There was considerable difference between an ATF agent and a meter maid, but she didn't give Edmon time to think about it. "Hayden's tied up in an emergency," she said grimly. "Brooke's disappeared. We think she's gone off with somebody from Omega."

"Gone off?" Edmon said, sounding stunned. "Brooke?"

"Yes, Brooke," Carrie said. "That's why we'd better protect your friend. I don't want another girl in danger."

Edmon's voice was stricken. "If anything's happened t-to Brooke, I'll never forgive myself."

You're not the only one, she thought unhappily. Hayden in particular would never forgive himself. She was almost as worried about him as about Brooke.

"I pray that Brooke's not in trouble," she said. "Hayden's doing all he can to find her. But in the meantime Lynette needs help. And we'd better move fast."

"You're t-totally right. Lynette needs sanctuary."

"Sanctuary," Carrie repeated, shaking her head. The word sounded medieval, high-minded, holy. It did not seem to apply to her little house with its leaking roof.

In the distance, the thunder rolled. She said, "Warn her that if the rain keeps up, we may be stranded out here. My road's bad, and if the lake rises any higher, we'll have trout in the living room."

"Carrie, you're a saint," Edmon said. "I'll leave a message for Hayden to tell him what we're doing."

"Don't," she said smoothly. "I'll tell him myself. I'm meeting him at Plato's in two hours."

She had, in fact, insisted Hayden have supper with her because he was so obsessed about finding Brooke that she knew he wouldn't eat otherwise. *Damn, damn,* she thought, *where* was *Brooke? How could she have done such a stupid thing?*

"Call Lynette," she said. "Do it now. Make arrangements for us to meet her. If she starts now, she can get here before ten o'clock."

"Tell me about Brooke," Edmon said. "Please. I feel sick about this."

"I do, too. But we'll talk about it later. Call your friend—now. Give her my number and have her call me."

Oh, hell, she thought in despair. Why was she doing this? Now she was baby-sitting a stalked college student, a girl she'd never met. Her life was no longer her own.

She should drop her stupid seminar, she was doing badly in it. The whole summer was shot to hell. Omega had kicked sanity out the door and taken over her life, right down to dropping house guests into her lap.

But how could she not volunteer to help?

Edmon said, "Carrie, you're a t-t-true friend."

She felt more like a true fool. This would take some explaining to Hayden.

Wotthehell, she thought fatalistically. And worried, for the thousandth time, about Brooke.

Brooke lay in the lumpy bed in unit 1 of the American Horse Motel just outside Yankton, South Dakota.

Her head was nestled against Boyd's smooth, tanned chest, and his arm was draped over her naked body. The air conditioner hummed and clanked in the window, and she and Boyd were covered only by a crumpled sheet. He snored lightly in her ear.

I'm in love, she thought, running her fingertips over the warm curve of his collarbone. He was eighteen years old, and the most beautiful man she had ever seen, tall and blue-eyed, with long blond hair like a pirate or an angel.

His body reminded her of Michelangelo's statue of David. She could have spent hours just gazing at him and touching him. His perfection was marred only by a missing front tooth, but that, she thought, could be fixed once they stopped running. If they ever *could* stop running.

When Boyd had gone AWOL from his father's farm compound, he'd stolen eighty-six dollars cash, a Model 17 Glock pistol, and sixty rounds of ammunition. He was now a traitor, and he knew too much. His father would hunt them down like dogs, Boyd said. He would shoot them on sight.

We're in love, and we may be doomed, Brooke thought. The drama of this thrilled her, because she and Boyd seemed thrust into some superior and more intense level of being, like characters in a play.

Yet their situation frightened her. Boyd meant more to her than words and books ever had done; he made the most ordinary moments of life seem precious. She didn't really want to die young, no matter how romantically.

Like the warrior princess she had always wanted to be, she had traveled across strange lands to save Boyd Burdette, her prince in thrall. But life was sloppier and scarier than fiction, and at best Brooke had been a bumbling savior.

First, right off at the state park, she and Boyd had been seen embracing by two teenage girls who drove by in a pickup truck. Boyd, shaken, said they were the daughters of a neighboring rancher, and they were certain to tell what they had seen, tell it all over town in fact.

Brooke was terrified that the girls would double back so they could take down her license number. She told Boyd that they must leave immediately, but she was so nervous she drove badly, and before she was even out of the county, she got a traffic ticket.

She'd seen a Sheriff's Department car in her rearview mirror and had been badly rattled. She'd sped up and turned off the highway without giving a signal. The deputy followed, siren keening, and pulled her over, and now he had a record of her name and license number and car.

In the first town they came to, Boyd stole another license plate, and he'd come heart-stoppingly close to getting caught doing it.

Then, just when they crossed into South Dakota, Brooke's car broke down, less than a hundred miles from their starting place. She and Boyd hiked four miles to a combination convenience store and gas station, and from there they called a mechanic.

The mechanic said the car's universal joint had gone out, and because the car was so old it was nearly obsolete, he might need up to a week to find the replacement part.

He'd given them a lift in his tow truck and dropped

them off at this fleabag motel, where they were now living on crackers and peanut butter. Brooke knew the repair bills would wipe out their meager funds—maybe they couldn't afford to get the car back at all, and then what would they do?

Boyd said the police wouldn't be looking for them; his father wouldn't want him falling into the police's hands because he might talk. More likely, his father was trailing them himself, a far more frightening prospect.

Boyd said his father was a resourceful and vengeful tracker. Even now he was probably on his CB radio asking if anybody had seen two people in a rusted-out, blue '77 Chevy Nova.

It was Brooke's job to get them out of this mess. Boyd was handsome and ardent and he treated her as worshipfully as if she were a goddess. But he was so unworldly he was touchingly childlike. "I got a strong back," he told her. "But you got to do the thinking."

Brooke had thought as hard as she could, but no answers came to her. She would sell or pawn the computer only as a last resort. But she and Boyd seemed to have reached the last resort in record time, and even sacrificing the computer might not bring them enough money.

Brooke hated the idea, but she was going to have to ask for help, and the best person she could think of to ask was Edmon. Edmon, after all, had tons of money, he was filthy rich, and he had hired her to fight evil. That's what she was doing, wasn't it?

She must phone Edmon and beg him to wire money. If she couldn't get through to him, she would try Hayden Ivanovich. Ivanovich was tougher and smarter and more dangerous, but if she had to she would take her chances with him.

If she couldn't reach them, she and Boyd would have to pawn the computer. They might have to pawn the gun, too, although it would break Boyd's heart. Boyd had no schooling beyond the eighth grade, but one thing in the world he understood thoroughly was firearms. If he gave up the pistol, he would surrender what slender power he had over his own fate. He would put himself completely in Brooke's control.

She kissed him on his right nipple. He had a beautiful chest, golden and unspoiled by ugly hair. He stirred sleepily and pulled her closer. "Hello, miracle," he murmured. "Miracle" was what he always called her, and whenever he said it, her heart reeled with happiness.

"Boyd," she said, slipping her arms around his neck. "I've been thinking. I'm going to call Edmon and have him wire us money. But maybe we'll have to sell the computer. And maybe the gun, too."

She felt his naked body tense. She kissed his neck again and again until she felt him relax. His voice was soft when he spoke and full of love. "That's what you think?"

"Yes," she whispered and licked the hollow of his throat.

He swallowed hard. "Whatever you say, miracle."

They clung together. His hands started to move over her body, gentle and adoring.

We're in love, she thought with giddy fatalism. *We're in love and it's worth dying for.*

"Bastard," Hayden muttered to himself sourly, but he hung up the phone quietly, he didn't slam it. Richard Elwood, his FBI contact in missing persons, wasn't interested in Brooke Tharpe.

"She's of age to leave town if she wants," Elwood had said with a bored grunt.

Hayden argued that Gretchen Small was dead, Monica Toussaint was still missing, and now Brooke Tharpe was gone; each had gone to meet a lover from Omega MOON. This was about a serial killer, not a mere runaway. But Elwood was immovable as a mountain. "I got real cases to work on," he said. "Don't waste my time."

Now Hayden sighed harshly and got ready to dial another number. He knew a retired agent named Cecil Groom who owed him more than one favor; maybe Groom could pull some strings. Hayden glanced at his watch. It was four-thirty, and he had an hour and a half until he met Carrie.

Carrie, he thought with a pang. Brooke's disappearance

had made him twice as anxious about Carrie, mixed up with the crazy Highwayman and living all the hell by herself in that isolated house.

He'd meant to give her a gun this afternoon, but the news about Brooke had knocked the thought out of his head. He opened his desk drawer and stared at the old LSU book bag that had once belonged to Kyle. The bag contained an automatic pistol and a dozen ammunition clips. He didn't know why he'd used Kyle's book bag, it was the sort of gesture he'd been compelled to make without understanding it.

He thought of Kyle and he thought of Carrie and shut the drawer again. Tonight, after supper, he'd make her take the gun. She wouldn't like it, but he'd insist. God only knew what had happened to Brooke; the possibilities sickened him with anger and dread. All his instincts told him to protect Carrie, even if she didn't think she needed protecting.

He reached for the phone to dial Cecil Groom, but it rang. He sighed in disgust and answered it. "Burnside Agency. Ivanovich here."

An operator said, "I have a collect call from Brooke Tharpe. Will you accept the charges?"

Brooke. Relief surged through him so strongly that for a moment, he was light-headed. But rage, as strong as the relief, also swept him. What did this dizzy, word-drunk girl think she was pulling, for God's sake?

"I accept," he snapped. "Brooke?" he asked. "Where the hell are you?"

"We're in a motel. I'm not going to tell you where. We need money. I tried to get Edmon, but his phone's busy."

Hayden frowned. "Who's 'we'?"

"Boyd. My lover. I met him on Omega," she said.

My lover. I met him on Omega. He winced at the sheer stupidity of it. He'd never noticed before how childish her voice sounded. He might have been talking to a girl of twelve.

But whoever she was with, he must not be the man who'd murdered Gretchen Small. Serial killers didn't let their victims make phone calls to private investigators. "Who's

Boyd?" Hayden demanded. "How do you know you can trust him?"

"I trust him because he needs me," she said righteously. "He's a pure and innocent soul. He's from farther west. His father's a survivalist and very militant. He wanted Boyd to drive a truck bomb into Cheyenne to blow up the federal building. So I saved him, but now the car's broken down, and we need money."

Hayden's free hand made an involuntary, spastic leap and knocked his empty coffee mug from his desk. He barely noticed. *Jesus Christ,* he thought, *the crazies. I was looking for them, but she found them. Her, of all people.*

"Brooke," he said, "for God's sake call the police, the FBI—right now."

"No," she said stubbornly. "They'll go to the ranch, and Boyd's father'll blow them up and himself, too. Boyd says it's true. Boyd doesn't want the law. Just send us some money so we can get far away."

"Wait a minute, wait a minute" Hayden said. "Boyd's father, what's his name?"

"I won't tell you, you'll tell the law, and then there'll be trouble. Boyd's got younger brothers there. And a stepmother. He doesn't want anything to happen to them."

Hayden swore under his breath. "Brooke, listen to me. This man, this father of his, is dangerous. He wants to blow up a federal building? Do you know what happened in Oklahoma City? Do you know how many people died?"

"Well, I'm telling you, aren't I? So you can warn Cheyenne, can't you? Besides, with Boyd gone, he's got to change his plans, doesn't he?"

Hayden hit the edge of his desk with the flat of his fist. "Maybe he'll change his plans and blow up something goddam sooner. Don't play games. Tell me who he is and where to find him."

"I can't. Boyd doesn't want agents going after his family. His father won't be taken alive. Boyd says it'll be just like Waco."

Just like Waco. Shit. Hayden tried to stay calm, to pry

information out of her. "Why does he want to bomb the federal building?"

"He says this is the second American Revolution. He says the people have to overthrow the murderous government."

Overthrow the murderous government by murdering, he thought, feeling a wave of nausea. He thought of Kyle. He thought of ashes settling onto the War Eagle's turbulent surface and sinking into its depths.

He tried to concentrate on Brooke and only Brooke. The little fool was literally sitting on a powder keg and playing with matches. "Why was Boyd on Omega?" he demanded. "Does his father use it as a line of communication? Are other people mixed up in this?"

"There's another," Brooke said vaguely. "I've told you too much already. Look, we have to get out of here. We have to think of a way to keep Boyd's brothers and stepmother safe. Then I can tell you more."

"Brooke, are Boyd's people mixed up in the Oklahoma bombing? Tell me, for your own safety. And Boyd's."

"Boyd says no. They had nothing to do with Oklahoma."

"Are you sure? Then why are they targeting another federal building?"

"Because it got attention. His father admired that. He was going to bomb a dam, but he thinks a federal building's a lot more symbolic and patriotic."

"Tell me where to find him, Brooke. If you don't, you're obstructing justice and so is Boyd. You can go to prison. Do you understand?"

"I don't want a lecture," she said. "I want money. You can wire it by Western Union. There's a Western Union office in Rapid City. On 25th and Lakota, at the WisePrice Grocery store. Have you got a pencil? WisePrice Grocery store in Rapid City. I need maybe two thousand dollars. Immediately."

Good God, he thought, how dumb was she? She'd just given away where she was, and he could have agents waiting for her the moment she stepped inside WisePrice.

Do it, he thought. *Do it. Trap her and let the chips fall where they may.* But her warnings about the boy's family nagged at him.

"I can't get two thousand just like that," he said, stalling.

"Get it from Edmon, *he's* got it," she said.

"It may take time," Hayden said. "I don't think he has much money on his own. He'll have to ask his family."

"Just get it," Brooke said stubbornly. "I've got to get Boyd someplace safe."

"And just where do you think is safe?"

"I can't tell you. Send the money."

He thought, *Okay, honey. You're out of your league, and I'm about to show you how far. It's time to play rough.*

"Your car's already broken down," he said. It was a statement, not a question. "You're desperate or you wouldn't be calling. And you're in Rapid City or close."

"Just send the money," she said, but there was a quaver in her voice, as if he'd brought her to the brink of tears.

"Listen to me carefully," he said. "If Boyd's father sets off a bomb and somebody dies, even one person, you're accessories to murder. You could get the death penalty, both of you."

"We haven't done anything," Brooke countered, but she sounded frightened. "Boyd doesn't want anything to do with his father. He just wants to get away."

Hayden shut his eyes and prayed to a God he no longer believed in. He made his voice cold and calm. "He can't get away from him, Brooke. You can't either. You love this guy? You want him sentenced to die? Are you going to let that happen to him? Is he going to let it happen to you?"

"He'll never talk to authorities," she said, but he heard the quaver of false bravado. "He's made a sacred vow. He won't betray his family. The police can't break him, and they can't break me."

Shit, thought Hayden and gritted his teeth. "If you don't talk, you'll never be free—ever. His old man owns you both. Boyd's got to choose, Brooke. His father or you. It's a tragic choice. But he's got to make it."

"He can't choose," Brooke said stubbornly. "I told you. His father won't give up. He'll fight to the bloody end. He'll take as many people with him as he can. And that includes Boyd's stepmother and brothers."

"The authorities can take him without hurting anybody," Hayden said, "if they have the proper intelligence. You know what went wrong at Waco, Brooke? Poor information. But Boyd knows the layout of his father's place. He knows how much firepower's there and where it's at. He knows the strengths in the system and the weaknesses. He knows everybody's habits. Does he want to save this woman and his brothers? He'd better talk."

Brooke was crying now. "I told you. He made a sacred vow. He won't ever turn his family over to the law. And neither will I."

"I'm not the law," Hayden said. "I'm just a P.I., a citizen, same as you and Boyd. And I can help you. Maybe nobody else can."

"I knew I should never have talked to you," Brooke accused. "You're trying to scare me. You're trying to mix me up."

"No," he said earnestly. "I'm trying to save you. You want to believe the two of you are better than his father, don't you? You want to believe you're on the side of right. Don't you?"

"We *are* on the side of right," she said. "We won't betray his family."

"Brooke, you see Boyd as a hero, don't you?"

"He *is* a hero."

"Whoever said being a hero was easy? Who said you get to be a hero without sacrifice? If he stays quiet and somebody dies, he's got blood on his hands. So do you. Is that heroic?"

"Stop it," Brooke said with passion. "You're trying to trap us."

"Wrong, Brooke. You've trapped yourself. I can hang up this phone, call the South Dakota police and have an all points bulletin out on you in ten minutes. You'll never leave the state. You're helpless without me."

"We just want *out*," Brooke wailed. "We just want to be together."

"I can help you," Hayden said, "if you'll let me. Will you?"

Have I gone too far? he wondered. *Probably. Hell, it's too late now.*

"How can you help?" she demanded. "You're on the other side."

"I'm on your side. I don't want the two of you screwing up your lives."

"If you set the police on us," she threatened, "we'll never talk—never. We'll—we'll shoot ourselves first. We've got a gun."

He passed a hand over his eyes thinking, *She's crazy enough to do it. Promise her anything.*

"I'll come to you," he said. "All Boyd has to do is talk to me. He can give me the information. In return"—he took a deep breath—"in return, I can give you peace. You'll have done your duty. Nobody can prosecute you."

She was silent except for a childlike sniffle.

"Nobody can prosecute you," he repeated. "And if Boyd talks to me, in exchange I'll get you out of the trap. I can even get you out of the country. The Virgin Islands? You like the sound of that? I can get you on a plane for St. John's. It's a U.S. possession, you won't need a passport. You want two thousand? I'll get it for you."

She said nothing, but he sensed she was wavering.

He said, "With proper intelligence, a raid can be planned in which nobody's hurt. And that's the only way that it'll work, if Boyd cooperates. It's a terrible choice, Brooke, but the only one. Are you brave enough to make it? Do you love each other enough to make it?"

She was silent for a long moment. Then, in a little voice, she said, "Why should we trust you?"

Good question, he thought, but he felt he had a good answer.

"Because I'm the only hope you've got," he said.

•   •   •

Carrie waited uneasily in a shadowy booth at Plato's. Hayden had promised to be there at six sharp, but it was twenty minutes after and he hadn't come, hadn't called. It wasn't like him to be late, and Carrie fretted, wondering if something was wrong.

She told the waiter for the third time, that no, she didn't want coffee, a drink, a glass of wine, anything. She sipped nervously at her ice water.

A subtle guilt haunted her, and she didn't relish telling Hayden that she and Edmon had both talked to Lynette Pollson and the girl was coming to stay at the lake. Lynette should be on the Interstate right now, heading toward Arkansas.

Carrie knew she had the right to invite whomever she chose to her house and she didn't have to account for her actions to Hayden. Yet, he was in charge of the search for Gretchen Small's killer, and she had taken affairs into her own hands.

Hayden was deeply worried about Brooke, and he would worry about her, too, and Lynette as well. He constantly harped that her house was dangerously secluded.

She glanced at her watch, twisted her fingers together and stared again at the front door. Lynette's persistent suitor was probably just a garden-variety stalker, she told herself, unbalanced, unnerving, but certainly not a serial killer. Lynette had sworn to tell no one where she was going; she and Carrie should be perfectly safe together. Brooke was the one Carrie was worried about.

The door opened and when Hayden entered, Carrie's heart first leaped, then sank. His expression was so grim that she tensed in apprehension. She met his eyes and was swept by a terrible foreboding; something was wrong, badly wrong.

He came to the table, pulled out a chair and sat. His mouth had a strange, bitter twist, and he looked deep into Carrie's eyes.

He said, "I've heard from Brooke. She's out of the state. She's picked up some kid who's on the run from his father. There's potential for big trouble there. I'm going after them."

For a moment, Carrie brightened. "She's all right?"

But the rest of his message sank in and sent a coldness through her bones. "She's in trouble? What sort?"

"She's all right," he assured her. "But I have to go to her. Can you hold down the fort?"

Carrie nodded. "Of course."

He said, "And stay off Omega tonight. Take some time off. Unplug your phone. Let The Highwayman be lonesome for one night. That's an order."

Carrie hardly heard him. "What sort of trouble is Brooke in? Please—tell me."

He didn't answer. Instead he stood and took her by the hand. "I'm sorry I kept you waiting. I can't stay. I have to leave now. Come outside with me."

It was an order, not an invitation, but Carrie didn't bristle at his gruffness. The look on his face frightened her, and she wondered why he wouldn't say what had happened to Brooke.

Nervously, she rose to her feet. He said, "Come on." He headed for the door and she hurried to keep up with him. Outside the evening was still light, and a fine sprinkle of rain fell. Carrie hardly felt it.

"Is this why you're late?" she asked, as they climbed the stairs to the sidewalk. "You were talking to Brooke?"

"Talking and talking and talking," he said from between his teeth. "To her, then to this boy she's with, then to her again. And if I'd had to talk any faster, I'd have skid marks on my tongue. Then I had arrangements to make."

"Where is she?" she demanded as he headed for his parked truck. "What's going on?"

"I can't tell you everything," he said. "I don't want you implicated."

"Implicated? My God, Hayden, what is this?"

"This boy she's picked up with, he's into something dangerous."

"Dangerous how?"

He reached his truck, opened the door and pulled out a worn LSU book bag. He thrust it into her hands. "This is a gun," he said. "Keep it with you."

"A gun? Hayden, I don't want a gun. It's been years since I used one."

"Take it," he said. "I want you to have it. I wish I'd never let you get dragged into this. I could wring Edmon's neck."

"Edmon didn't mean any harm," Carrie said. She stared up at him and without thinking seized his sleeve. "Hayden, why is this person with Brooke dangerous? You think he'll hurt her? Is this connected to Gretchen Small?"

"No," he said shortly. "The guy's mixed up in something paramilitary, anti-government; it's not good."

Alarm swept her. Her hand tightened on his arm. "Paramilitary? You mean like militias and—and Oklahoma City—and—"

Her voice failed her. No one knew yet if the Oklahoma bombing was part of a larger conspiracy and if it was, how far that conspiracy might extend. What in God's name was Hayden plunging into?

"I can't tell you more," he said. "Alice has got a letter in the office. If she doesn't hear from me by a certain time tomorrow, she turns it over to the FBI."

Her hand tightened on his arm almost convulsively. "The FBI? Why aren't you calling them in now? Hayden, are you going into this all alone? Don't. If it's dangerous—"

"There are people at risk," he said. "Because of that, Brooke's friend doesn't want to talk. I've got to make him. There may be a way to resolve this quietly, safely. Let's hope so."

Carrie was suddenly terrified by what he might do. "Hayden, don't try some crazy vigilante thing—please."

"My flight leaves in forty minutes," he said. "I have to get to the airport. You're sure you'll be all right?"

"Yes, of course," she said impatiently. "But at least tell me where you're going."

"It's better I don't." He touched her face. "Take care of yourself," he said. "Don't get into trouble, and don't let Edmon get wind of this. You're the only one I'm trusting with this information."

"Hayden, don't go," she begged.

"I have to," he said. He took her face between his hands and kissed her.

She clung to him as if she could keep him there with her if only she held him tightly enough, kissed him with enough abandon.

But she couldn't hold him back. He pulled away. "Wish me luck," he said.

She could say nothing. It occurred to her, numbly, that she should tell him about Lynette Pollson, but all words died in her throat. She could only stare at him as he got into the truck, shut the door, turned on the ignition.

Tears stung her eyes. Clutching the book bag to her chest, she stood in the soft drizzle of the rain and watched as he drove away.

He shouldn't be doing this, she thought. *This is too personal to him. He'll get reckless. He'll take chances. I know he will.*

Kristin was nothing but trouble. Jon had to watch her constantly because he knew he couldn't trust her.

He'd read about serial killers who kept their victims alive for days before they murdered them, but he didn't see how they stood it. Even the great Bundy was rumored to have done it—perhaps even to have kept *two* girls prisoner at once—but Jon had no stomach for it.

He yearned to kill Kristin and get it over with, but he couldn't, not yet and not here. Her filthy blood would get all over everything.

He'd removed her gag once to let her take a drink of water. He would not make that mistake again. She cried, she complained, she begged, she bargained. She wept that she was hungry, that she was in excruciating pain; she said he was going to give her gangrene in her feet. She sniveled about her kid and promised Jon anything he wanted; she said she'd even help him catch other girls and kill them.

She made him sick, but he needed her, he must find who Edmon had after him, who his hunters were. That Edmon had actually done such a thing infuriated him and obsessed him.

He let Kristin lie in the corner on the floor and blubber into her gag until six-thirty. He drank four cans of beer. He wasn't hungry. He watched a porn film on pay TV, but it was not good, it did nothing for him.

The afternoon sun was still shining brightly around the edges of the closed drapes when he connected the computer and logged on to the Internet. Then he rose, took out his knife, and bent over Kristin. Her eyes went crazed with terror. Roughly he sawed apart the rags that tied her wrists.

He hauled her to her feet and practically threw her into the chair before the computer. "Log on to Omega," he ordered. "Find your boyfriend. I want to know about this fucking detective. Do what I say, or I'll cut your throat."

He'd accidentally nicked her hand when he cut her loose. Drops of blood welled slowly from the base of her thumb, staining the keyboard. She nodded in a stupefied way. Her fingers moved slowly over the keys, awkwardly. She made mistakes, and didn't get logged on until her third try.

Then she was connected, and Lacewing was on the King's Highway.

"Go to your own place," he said, and again she obeyed in her slow, stunned way. She typed the command that took her to her private MOON "room," a hokey Swiss chalet with a bearskin rug. He felt a slight twinge of nostalgia remembering the times she'd given him netsex on that silly virtual rug. He hadn't known then that she was built like a damned boy.

"See if your friend's here," he hissed in her ear. And on impulse he bit her earlobe, hard enough to make her twist in pain.

"Do it," he commanded.

She whimpered, but she typed the command to ask if Cochise was logged in.

The screen answered her: he had not been there for more than twenty-four hours.

"Cocksucker," Jon whispered, staring at Cochise's name. He pushed Kristin's hands from the keyboard and typed the same command for information on Lynette and Edmon, that filthy fucker Edmon. He was compelled, driven to know if they were on Omega.

They were not. They had disconnected within minutes of each other, just past midnight. Goddam, he thought, where were they? Where was she? How did Edmon fucking dare to come between Jon and Lynette? How did he fucking dare to set spies on Jon, as if he were setting dogs on a rat?

Jon would find out who the bastards were, and he would do them as much damage as humanly possible. He did not yet know how, only that he would. He would find Edmon and cut his balls off and stuff them down his throat, he swore he would do it.

Kristin cast him a frightened look with her teary, bloodshot eyes. He knew what she was asking him: *Now what?*

He tickled her just below the ear with the point of his knife. "And now we wait for Cochise," he said. "Pray he logs on. Or I'll be unhappy with you. So pray, Kristin."

He picked up her injured hand and licked the blood from her thumb.

SEVENTEEN

────◦∾◦────

B ROOKE SAT PROPPED UP IN BED, SCRIBBLING MADLY. SHE WANTED
to describe every moment, every feeling, every nuance of
her time with Boyd. She wanted each detail preserved in the
precious amber of words.

Beside her, Boyd lay propped on his elbow, watching
television. Shirtless and barefoot, he wore only faded boxer
shorts. She felt as if she were lounging in bed with a young
god in his underwear.

Boyd had hardly ever seen television. Earlier in the day
he'd watched it as raptly as a child. But now he was watching
the news, and his expression was sad, almost haunted. The
announcer was talking about Oklahoma City, and it had to
make Boyd think of his father.

She put down her pen and stroked his blond hair. He
looked up at her with eyes so blue they sent shivers through
her heart.

"What's the matter, Apollo?" she asked softly. "Are you
grieving for your family?"

He nodded. She cupped his chin in her hand.

"I thought very hard about it," she said, gazing into his remarkable eyes. "What Ivanovich said is right. If your daddy kills somebody, the blood's on our hands, too. You don't want that, do you?"

"No," he whispered and touched the cloth of her caftan.

"Sweetheart, talking to Ivanovich isn't like talking to the law. He can help us. He's got connections."

"I don't want my family burned up like at Waco or shot down like at Ruby Ridge," Boyd said. Tears rose in his eyes.

She kissed him gently. "This is my fault, not yours," she said. "I didn't think far enough ahead. I only thought of us. I didn't think of the moral ramifications."

"The what?" he said with a helpless frown.

"I only thought about you and me. Not what might happen to other people. What you're doing is right, sweetheart. You trust me, don't you?"

He kissed the cloth over her thigh. "I got to trust you. You're all I got. It's like I knowed you all my life."

"We've known each other forever," she said. "We've been soul mates for eternity."

"I know. But I still feel like a traitor to my own." He clasped her thighs and buried his face against them.

"Oh, Apollo," she said, and again stroked his beautiful golden hair.

"You know what's right," he said, his voice muffled.

"I'm trying to learn, love." In truth, Brooke thought that she was leading Boyd into a sort of moral twilight zone by talking to Ivanovich, but she could see no other choice. Ivanovich had scared her nearly silly with his talk about murder, prison, death row, and lethal injections.

But he'd also sworn he'd use information about Boyd's father to defuse the situation as peacefully as possible—and he would help them escape.

Brooke was frightened, but a pleasant realization had dawned, warming and exciting her. She and Boyd were in a *very* dramatic plight, full of moral conflicts and life-and-death choices. It was like a mythic adventure, one that with a stylistic flourish here and there, would make an admirable plot for Amarinthia, the heroine of her stalled book.

Here, with Boyd, Brooke's book had finally taken shape in her imagination. Boyd was the captive prince, an heir to an evil Lord of Destruction, a beautiful boy condemned to serve the powers of darkness.

Amarinthia's task would be to liberate this prince and convert him to the powers of peace and creation. The story seemed to Brooke to have Homeric sweep, and a hero and heroine larger than life. (As for Ivanovich, she could convert him into a helpful troll or something.)

Boyd was truly her soul mate, he was bringing her to complete creative fruition. She bent and kissed him. "Sweetheart, let's turn off the television. I think it's depressing you."

He was silent a moment, his face still pressed against her thighs. Then he turned over, his head in her lap, and gazed up at her. "Miracle?"

"Yes?"

"Will we take the computer to the island?"

"I suppose Ivanovich will want it back," she said sadly. "It's Edmon's, really."

"Oh." Boyd looked so wounded that her chest contracted.

She knew what saddened him. He would miss Omega. He was so innocent and unsophisticated that Omega had been his only link to the greater world.

"I understand," she whispered. "I'll miss it, too. But we probably can't even connect to it from the Virgin Islands. We'll go back to it someday."

He swallowed and said, "You think I could log on? Just to see it one last time?"

She could not deny him such a simple pleasure. He had almost nothing to his name, not even a change of clothing. Beneath the mattress, wrapped in a paper bag, lay his last remaining possessions from his old life, the pistol and its ammunition.

"Of course," she said. With a sigh he sat up. He kissed her on the lips. Then he rose and went to the desk to plug the computer into the phone jack. Still wearing only his shorts, he sat down and switched on the machine.

"I'd like to find Lacewing and tell her we're okay."

She gazed at him fondly. She was not jealous of Lacewing, not in the least. Let him play, she thought. It would make him happy and leave her free to write. She bent her head and once more lost herself in the rich maze of her words.

Boyd logged on to the Internet and typed in his destination, Omega, his emotions painfully mixed. Would this be the last time he'd come to the MOON? The few people he'd ever known outside his rural world were here. Would he ever meet them again?

He connected and found himself on the King's Highway. Startled, he saw that a message awaited him.

> You have two new pieces of mail.

He felt a creeping sense of dread. Who would be writing him? He typed the command to read his mail, and the first piece appeared upon the screen.

> Well Boyyd yyou cocksucker if yyou read this it is one of the last peices of MOON mail yyou will ever get because Dad-dyy has got all yyour passwords and he is going to kill yyoure character and if he ever catches up with yyou he will make damn sure yyou are dead for real. God dam yyour eyes, yyou no good stupid pussyy coward. yyou're ex=brother Nolan.

Boyd flinched and his jaw hardened. He felt shamed and sick with loss, but anger, too, sparked within him. He typed the reply command and wrote:

> Nolan, I have always love you but a man's got a right to his own life. I have found a wonderful brillant girl and she is the world to me. I got no hate in my heart for none of you. Maybe that is to bad since hate is all you understand. Boyd.

With a fatalistic sense, he hit the key to send the message. He knew it might be his last communication to his family. He had made his choice and what he'd told Brooke was true; she was all he had.

He did not tell her of his brother's message. He was not sure he could do so yet without his voice breaking, and he had shown her too much weakness; he must learn to be as strong as she.

Mechanically he typed the command to read his second piece of mail, wondering if it was another hate letter. When he saw the missive was from Lacewing, relief and gratitude flooded him.

> Dearest Boyd, I've been thinking about you a lot and worrying how you are. Are you with your special someone now? Can I help you in any way? I hope we can talk. Please, please, please get in touch. Love, Kristin (your Lacewing)

Lacewing, he thought, with a rush of affection and gratitude. Reading her message was like finding a fresh, cooling spring in the midst of a desert. She did not hate him, *she* did not reject him.

She had been his first love, and now she was his only friend. He typed "@who Lacewing" to see if she was logged on, not daring to hope that she was.

With joy, he saw that she was indeed here, had been here for over three hours, and was in her Swiss Chateau. His heart beating hard, he paged her, "Kristin, its Boyd. Can you talk?"

He waited, holding his breath. Almost a full minute passed. Then she answered. "Boyd! I'm so glad to hear from you! Please join me."

He gave the command to join her, and almost instantly a new description flickered into view.

> You are in Lacewing's Chateau overlooking the Swiss Alps. A huge picture window looks out on the gorgeous panorama of the stately mountains. The walls are paneled in warm, gleaming wood, and a fire snaps and crackles in the fireplace.

There is a beautiful rug of bearskin before the fireplace. There is a rich leather couch, matching chairs, and a bar. The room makes you feel warm, safe, and cozy.

Lacewing is here.

Boyd, who was sentimental, was delighted to be rejoined with her. He gave her a virtual hug. After a moment, she hugged him back. For some reason the lag had grown; her response was agonizingly slow.

"Kristin," he said. "I am real glad to see you."

"I've been worried about you," she said. "How are you? Where are you? Are you with your girlfriend?"

He knew he must be discreet; his father had always taught him to be secretive, and Brooke had told him to be careful, but he trusted Kristin. She was his last link to the old world.

"We are together," he said. "I left home. We are on the run. We are going to leave the US soon."

Kristin's reply was slow in coming, as if she were half a world away. "Where will you go? How will you get there?"

He answered, "I am sorry but I shouldnt say where we will go. I probly will not be able to talk to you again. One of Brookes friends will help us, he is coming soon."

Again it seemed to take Kristin a torturously long time to respond. "Brooke's friend? Parsival? Or one of those other people she works with? Who?"

He hesitated, then replied, "One of the others. The guy."

"The detective?"

Boyd said, "Wow, its taking a long time for you to get thru. Is something wrong with your computer or what?"

Twenty seconds passed. "I burned my hand on the stove tonight. It makes it hard to type. Is the detective coming to help you?"

"Yes, he is the one."

"Where are you?" she asked. "Won't you even tell me that? We're friends, I won't tell anyone, I swear."

Boyd hesitated. He supposed he could tell that much. They would soon be leaving forever, and it would be comforting to share their ordeal with a sympathetic friend.

He thrust his tongue into the space where his front tooth was missing, a nervous habit. He answered, "We are on the west side of Rapid City. Brooke's car broke down. We hitch hike to a Gas and Go store and called a tow truck. He dropped us off at a motel."

"Rapid City, South Dakota?"

"That is right."

"When is her friend coming?"

"Late tonight but soon as he can."

"How will I ever know if you're all right? Is there someone I can ask?"

"You are the only person I know very good."

"What about Brooke's other friend, the woman? I could ask her. Please, please, Boyd. I'm really, really worried about you because you mean so much to me. I care about you a lot. Please tell me her name."

Boyd swallowed. He would have to ask Brooke if this was all right. She'd said the other woman on Omega was a good friend, perhaps her only friend. He turned to her. "Miracle?"

She was bent over her notebook, writing at a mad pace.

"Yes, love?" she said absently.

"Your friend that's working with you on Omega. What's her name? You know, her name is like a color or something?" He knew she would not tell him if it was something he shouldn't say to Lacewing.

Brooke's pen kept moving and she didn't look up. "Carrie Blue."

Boyd had thought the name was like Greendress or something and was puzzled. But Brooke was the smart one, and he didn't question her. He turned back to the computer and typed, "Her name is Carry Blue like the color."

"Her Omega name or her real name?"

"I don't know. I thought her MOON name was different but had a color in it too."

"Is she from Fayetteville, like Parsival?"

"Yes her and Brooke was in school together." He tapped his bare foot nervously against the pitted linoleum of the floor.

Kristin said, "What is the detective's name?"

"I cant spell it I cant even pronounse it. Are you alone tonight? I thought you would be with your new boyfriend are you still in love?"

Almost a full minute passed before her answer appeared on the screen. "He and I broke up. I was stupid to let you go. But I will always be your loving friend. Is there any way I can help you? Do you need money or anything?"

He was touched. "No we do not need money, Brookes friend will bring it."

"Will Parsival come with this man?"

"No I do not think so."

"Why is Parsival hanging around with the girl called Flair? Do you know? What does he want with her? Is he trying to turn her against her boyfriend?"

"I dont know nothing about that."

Lacewing said, "I am so worried about you. Your brothers are on Omega aren't they? Do you want me to send them a message?"

He fidgeted and tapped his foot again. "My family dont wish to hear from me."

She took so long in replying that he worried if something had happened to her. But at last she said, "I'm so sorry. What are your brothers' names on Omega? Slate Wiper and Nitrate?"

"That is their names but they dont want to talk to me and my father wants to kill me."

He swallowed hard and stole a glance at Brooke. She sat on the bed, propped up on the pillows. She was lost in her writing, her pen moving at its amazing speed. The light reflected on the lenses of her glasses. He was almost sick with love for her, and they were giving up everything for each other.

He turned back to the computer screen, feeling strangely helpless.

"Brooke's friends," Lacewing said. "They're all in Arkansas? They all live in the same city?"

"Yes," he said. "This might be the last time I ever talk to you. I will alway think of you tho."

"I will think of you, too. I was a little bit in love with you, you know. I should have hung on to you. Now Brooke is the lucky girl."

A choking sensation rose in his throat. She loved him after all, now that it was too late?

He said, "I hope you find somebody and you will be as much in love as Brooke and me. I really mean that and you will always have a spesial place in my heart."

He did not want to tell her goodbye. He had already left so much of his life behind; it was like he was being reborn, painfully, into someone new, a stranger even to himself.

She said, "You will always have a special place in my heart, too. I hope you find happiness. I will always remember you. I have to go now."

He swallowed again, but the lump in his throat wouldn't go away. "I hope you find your true love someday. I hope you find the guy you deserve."

> Lacewing puts her arms around you. She gives you a big hug. She kisses you lovingly on the cheek. She says, "Goodbye, dear Boyd."
> She vanishes.

Boyd felt abandoned, bereft. If he must leave Omega forever, he felt compelled to do it now; it hurt too much to linger. He typed the command to quit.

He shut off the machine and rose, crossed the room, knelt on the floor at Brooke's side. "Miracle," he said. "I just said goodbye to Lacewing. She was the last friend I got. I feel kind of all emptied out. I need you. You think you could stop writing for a little while?"

She smiled warmly, set aside her notebook and pen, then opened her arms wide to him. He clambered into bed and began to make desperate love to her.

So a fucking detective was after him? Jon would like to kill the bastard. The thought of being stalked like an animal enraged him.

He hauled Kristin to her feet. Her ankles were still

bound, and she tottered, falling against him. Her eyes were crazy with terror and she clung to him so that she wouldn't fall, her fingers digging into his shoulders.

In disgust he pried her off him and shoved her away. She collapsed on the bed, clawing at her gag. She snatched it off, pulled out the rags that he'd stuffed into her mouth. She sobbed and gasped.

"Why are you mad?" she pleaded in a thick voice. "I did everything you said. I did what you wanted."

"Shut up, bitch," he said. He seized her hands to tie her wrists back together.

She tried to fight him, scratching at him. "I did what you wanted!" she cried. "I did what you wanted!"

He hit her so hard that her eyes rolled backward in her head, and she fell back limply against the mattress. He put his knee on her chest to hold her in place, and he knotted the torn cloth around her wrists so tightly that it sank into her flesh like a cut. She closed her eyes and wept, tears running down her face, her flat chest heaving up and down.

He stuffed the rags back into her mouth, jamming them so deeply into her throat that she retched, and her body pitched beneath him in protest. He bore his weight down on her so relentlessly he felt a rib snap beneath his knee.

She made a great show of choking. He didn't believe her, she was a conniving bitch, always making a fuss. He tied the torn cloth around her face to gag her doubly, and she thrashed like a fish out of water.

He got up, turned his back on her and went to the desk. She made disgusting sounds, revolting sounds, but he ignored her. She was still logged on as Lacewing, and he again typed the command to look for Lynette and that bastard Edmon. It was a compulsive act, he could not stop himself.

He'd made Kristin check for Lynette and Edmon repeatedly. They possessed him like a pair of demons, they sent venom racing through his veins that made him feel both drunk and deadly ill.

But they were not to be found, they were eluding him.

Were they together on another MOON or MOO, talking about him? Was Edmon poisoning her mind against him?

Jon felt bile rising at the back of his throat, as if he were going to vomit from tension.

He hadn't been able to eat all day; he'd consumed nothing except beer and pills. Kristin's conversation with that fool, Boyd, had enraged and frightened him. Edmon actually *did* have spies on Omega, the stinking prick. He even had an honest-to-god detective, a fucker trained to shoot people for Chrissake.

It made Jon sick, it made him want to puke. He could not believe that Edmon, of all people, could set a trap for him, or that Edmon, of all people, could steal away Lynette. He wished he could kill Edmon, cut his stupid throat.

Jon knew he should never go back to Omega, never talk to Lynette again. Yet he could not stop desiring her. She lived in his head like a witch whose spell he could not break. He was in her power, under her domination, but now he might not ever have her. Never.

All he had left of Omega was Kristin, whom he loathed. Behind him, on the bed, she was still practicing her theatrics. His head ached, and his body burned for deliverance, but Kristin couldn't give it to him until he killed her, and he couldn't kill her here, it was too dangerous. She would be his last Omega girl. And it was Edmon's doing.

Fury besieged him. If he couldn't kill Edmon, he would sure as hell blow away his bought tin soldier. The computer screen glowed silently.

He yanked back the chair and sat down. With shaking fingers, he wrote the command to send MOON mail.

@send mail to: Slate Wiper

The machinations of Omega worked silently for twenty seconds. Jon held his breath and thought of Edmon and Edmon's spies and Edmon's puppets and Edmon's hired guns.

The screen signaled that the mail system was ready to accept his message. Jon angrily wrote:

Hello, Slate Wiper

Your fuckhead brother and his bitch are in a motel on the west side of Rapid City, South Dakota. Their car broke down and they hitchhiked to a Gas and Go store and called a tow truck. The tow truck dropped them off at a motel. Shouldn't be too hard to trace, huh?

But you better hurry. The bitch has a detective coming tonight. Your traitor brother's going to spill his guts. He's going to turn you in.

They're going to destroy you. You'd better stop them.

Good luck, a friend.

With satisfaction, he struck the key to send the message. Then he wrote an identical message to Nitrate and sent it as well. He hoped Boyd's crazy family would track him down and shoot him to bloody spatters, along with Edmon's tin soldier and spying bitch.

Behind him, Kristin made a sound deep in her throat, like a kitten being strangled.

Hayden sat in the Denver airport, nursing a beer and musing pessimistically on the whereabouts of his gun.

He was no longer licensed to carry the gun aboard a plane, it was against the law. His only legal alternative was to pack it in his duffel bag and check the bag in as luggage. And airlines these days specialized in losing luggage.

Flying from Fayetteville to Rapid City was a tortuous and illogical process. He went north by first going five hundred miles south to Dallas. In Dallas he ran like hell to make an American Airlines flight to Denver. Now in Denver, his commuter flight to Rapid City had been delayed indefinitely due to "mechanical failure."

Three different flights meant three different chances for the airlines to separate him from his luggage. He was probably going to arrive in Rapid City after midnight, while his gun was making a side trip to Saskatchewan. He'd be as unarmed as a Girl Scout.

Brooke's boyfriend had a weapon; she'd said so. If the kid was aggressive or scared, there could be trouble.

He took another sip of beer, but found no pleasure in it. Boyd's father was dangerous and had to be stopped, it was that simple. What wasn't simple would be getting the kid to talk. But the kid *had* to. He was the only means of taking the old man down with minimum bloodshed.

Hell, Hayden thought in disgust, did Brooke realize what she'd gotten herself into? She saw herself as a rebel heroine, like Princess Leia in *Star Wars*, but she was more like one of the goddam Three Stooges. And he was about to put his life in her hands. Or she was about to put her life in his. He wouldn't know until he'd walked in the door.

He knew, too, that Boyd's father could be tracking the pair. Brooke was not wily, she would not have taken a foxy path and didn't know how to conceal her trail.

He finished his beer and pushed away from the bar. He was restless and cynical, and he wondered if he were going after Brooke half in hopes that his luck *would* run out. He thought of Kyle, whose luck had. He thought of ashes in the wind, pale and coarse, ashes settling into the water, disappearing.

Suddenly, he wanted to call Carrie. When he'd left, she'd looked alarmed and had asked him not to go. She had hung on to him tightly when he kissed her. He wished to believe this meant something. He shook his head and refused to dwell on it.

He went to the big picture window overlooking the tarmac and stared out into the blackness. The night was cloudy here, and he could see no stars, no moon, no light in heaven at all.

Jon logged off, half-sick with anger and despair. He sat for a long time with his elbows on the desk, his head in his hands, his temples banging with the beat of his own blood.

I hope his crazy fucking father finds them and kills them all, he thought. *Kills them all. Kills them all.*

Damn Edmon, damn his frigging detective, damn his huntresses.

Kill them all, kill them all, kill them all.

Edmon and his little army were trying to tear Jon apart

from Lynette forever. *Lynette*, he thought, and wanted her with such primitive need, it was like having a dinosaur screaming within his head.

But all he had was Kristin. Her flat-chested little body repelled him, it would be like raping a boy. But she would have to do. He would drive her back to the forest, to the spot he'd intended. He'd pretend she was Lynette and he would do to her all the things he dreamed of doing to Lynette. He got a partial erection thinking of it.

He could no longer bear the tension of waiting. He pushed himself away from the computer and went to her. She lay very still on the bed, sleeping—or pretending to sleep. He knelt on the bed beside her.

"Guess what?" he whispered. "We're going for a ride. And then I'm going to let you go. How will you like that? You can go home to your husband and baby."

She said nothing, she did not move at all. There was something eerie in her motionlessness. He saw that her eyes were not closed, but half-opened, one lid drooping strangely. Her face was discolored—almost bluish—and a trickle of blood had run from beneath the gag and glistened on her chin.

He felt his rage and sexual hunger vanish beneath a wave of dismay. "Kristin?" he said, and waited for her eyes to flutter all the way open. "Kristin?"

But she did not move. Her childlike body lay in absolute silence. She did not stir. She did not breathe. She did not blink.

She was dead. The gag was bloodstained. He ripped it off and more blood spilled from her mouth. It dribbled down the side of her face and fell in on the bedspread.

He dug the rags out of her mouth; they were soaked with crimson. He thought, Oh, Jesus, no, no, she's strangled on her own blood.

No, no, no, no, no.

He pressed on her chest, trying to make her breathe. More blood spilled on the bedspread. In a panic he pressed his mouth to hers, trying to force air back into her body. He tasted her cooling blood, and her lips were lifeless beneath his.

He drew back in revulsion. "Why did you die?" he demanded. "Why did you die, you stupid bitch?"

He slapped her so hard that her head bounced against the mattress and blood spattered. His dismay turned back to fury and to frustration. What had she done to him? How could he kill her if she was already dead?

The first time he'd struck her in the forest he had opened up a cut on his hand; he'd nicked a finger on one of her front teeth. Now his subsequent blows opened the cut even wider. Her face was stained with her blood and his own.

"Oh, God," he said helplessly. "Oh, God." He took her in his arms, he held her tightly, he tried to pretend that she was Lynette, and he was about to have sex with her at last. He pressed his pelvis against hers, but it was no good.

She lay slumped across the bed like a sack of potatoes. His penis seemed to shrivel and his balls wither and rise into his body, trying to hide from this horror.

He rolled away from her and lay on his side, gazing sightlessly at the closed drapes. He wanted to weep in frustrated need and the tears burned at his eyes, but he was too stunned to shed them.

He hadn't wanted to kill her yet; he'd wanted to play it out, the way he always did. Kristin was every sort of whore, but now she was a whore who could never satisfy. First she'd been too eager for sex, and then she'd been too eager for death. She hadn't waited until he, too, was ready.

She'd cheated him and ruined everything. He put his knuckle to his mouth to ease the pain, tasting the hot salt of his own blood. He swallowed it and sucked more, wishing it were Lynette's. *Lynette.*

He rose from the dirtied bed and went to the window.

Parting the drapes, he could look up past the power lines and into the sky at the moon, which was silver, pocked, and nearly full.

What am I? he'd thought, his eyes stinging with angry tears, *a goddam werewolf, or what?*

He was impotent and full of despair and rage. He thought of carrying Kristin's body outside and loading it in the trunk again, of driving her deep within the forest until he came to the culvert where he had chosen to hide her.

But he didn't move; he seemed drained of strength. All he wanted to do was stand and stare helplessly at the moon. He began to shake so badly that he forced himself to go to the desk, uncap the bourbon bottle.

He took a deep, burning drink. He sat in the chair and stared at Kristin's body. He would drink until the shakes went away. And then he would go out and hide her, although he had no heart for it. He finished the half-pint of bourbon, and although the shaking stopped, he was still acutely conscious and full of pain.

But the liquor loosened his inhibitions. He put his face in his hands and wept in despair. For weeks, he'd yearned to break through to the forbidden again, to feel himself touched by its exquisite fire. He'd put himself in danger by bringing this girl here, and now she was dead, but what had he got out of it?

Nothing, nothing, nothing except to feel more helpless and hopeless. He went to the window again and looked out at the night. He was half-drunk and full of self-pity.

He raised his gaze to the moon and thought, *If I'm a werewolf, you rule me. If you rule me, help me. Help me, please.*

The moon, of course, was silent.

He'd drunk two more beers. He'd covered Kristin's body with an extra blanket he'd found on the closet shelf, but he could not bring himself to move her yet.

The bed was a mess, the sheets and spread bloody clear down to the mattress, the mattress itself stained; he didn't know what to do about all this blood, he'd never left such a palpable trail before.

He opened another beer and thought about Lynette instead. She hadn't appeared on Omega all night long; did she mean to leave him for good? He wanted her so much that it was like a blade twisting in his stomach. Only her steady coolness could ease the fire and turmoil within him. Only her brokenness could make him whole.

He could phone her, hear her voice, at least. He could do that much. He deserved that much. Feeling ill and desperate, he dialed her number and let it ring. Just to hear her voice but not to say anything in reply, that would be enough.

The phone rang repeatedly, but she didn't answer. He glanced at his watch. It was almost midnight, and she seldom stayed out late. Where the hell was she?

Then someone picked up the receiver, and he heard a woman's voice, but not hers. "Hello? What?" the woman said, sleepily.

"Who's this?" he demanded.

"Tammy."

Oh, hell, he thought, *Tammy—the infamous roommate, and she sounded like she'd just woke up or was hung over or both.*

"I want to talk to Lynette," he said. "Put on Lynette."

Tammy groaned. "She's not here."

"When's she getting back?" he demanded.

"Maybe she's not coming back," Tammy said, almost truculently. "She's gone away. She didn't say for how long. She said she didn't know."

He felt stunned, as if someone had struck him from behind, a hard, numbing blow on the head. "Gone? What do you mean?" he said in disbelief. His stomach heaved sickly, and he tasted the bile in the back of his mouth again.

"I mean gone—get it?" Tammy answered. "Now goodbye, you woke me up."

His mind raced furiously. "Wait—don't hang up. This is Kevin," he lied. "I'm in her history class. She borrowed my notes and I've got to have them back. It's urgent. I have to talk to her—she can't do this to me."

"Listen, is this James? 'Cause if it is, she doesn't want to talk to you."

"This isn't James," he said, a cold frenzy creeping through him. "This is Kevin O'Dell and she's got my goddam history notes. How'm I supposed to study? How can I get hold of her?"

"I don't *know*. She's gone. She didn't say where."

Fuck, Jon thought hopelessly. He felt like he was plunging down an endless well. "I've got to find her. I need those notes. I have to have them."

"I told you," Tammy said emphatically, "I don't know where she is."

But he knew and it sickened him; she'd gone to Edmon. "This is an emergency," he pleaded. "You've got to help me—please. Please."

He dreaded the answer. But Tammy's reply startled him and gave him a faint, swooping sense of hope. "She's with a woman named Carrie, that's all I know," Tammy said. "I heard her talking on the phone."

"Carrie what? What's her last name?"

"I *don't know,* you pinhead," she said. "Can't you understand English?"

She hung up on him.

"You cock-sucking bitch," he muttered, and started to dial the number again. But for a moment his mind cleared and he remembered what Boyd had said of Brooke's spying friend on Omega. "Her name is Carry Blue like the color."

And she worked for Edmon in Fayetteville. Jon had been in Fayetteville. It was a small city, hardly more than a town. How many people named Blue could there be in its phone book? And if he found the mysterious Carrie Blue, he might find Lynette.

He looked at the bundle on the bed that was Kristin's body. He did not care about caution anymore.

He was going to find Lynette, and he would not lose her again.

Carrie and Edmon had met Lynette at the Fayetteville police station, where a sergeant named Shroedinger had vouched for Edmon. The meeting was awkward; Edmon was overcome by shyness, and Lynette kept apologizing for causing such trouble. It was difficult to say which of them was more embarrassed.

Yet the girl impressed Carrie. She seemed levelheaded, not the sort to overdramatize her plight. She was obviously intelligent and had a wry, self-mocking wit. There was a sweetness and strength in her scarred, uneven little face that brought out Carrie's protective instincts.

Now the two women had left the lights burning in the cabin and walked along the lake's sodden edge. It was late, but there had been a lull in the rain, and Lynette was stiff after her long drive. Both women were restless and neither was sleepy.

The moon was high in the sky, and its reflection danced on the lake's faceted surface. The clouds had thinned. The frogs called noisily to one another, the crickets whirred. Lightning bugs silently flashed their golden lights.

"It's peaceful here," Lynette said.

"Yes," Carrie said. "I've liked it."

"It's kind of you to share it."

"I'm glad for the company," Carrie said, and she had to admit she meant it. She was haunted by thoughts of Hayden and the fear he was putting himself in danger.

Lynette seemed to tap into her train of thought.

"The girl who's gone," Lynette said, "Brooke?"

"Yes?"

"You were afraid that she'd gone off with whoever killed Gretchen Small?"

Carrie nodded. "Yes, but that's not it. She's gotten into some other kind of trouble. I don't know exactly what."

Lynette stared up at the moon. "I wonder if James has other women on Omega besides me."

Carrie looked at her sharply. Moonlight silvered the girl's uneven features. "Do you think so?"

"He could," Lynette said. "I never stayed on Omega much past ten o'clock. I had an early class. He could have logged on as a guest, talked to other girls, I never would have known."

"We've thought that the man we're looking for could have more than one character on Omega."

"That's possible, too," Lynette said. She gazed out over the moonlit water. "It seems very weird, you know, that I cared for him once. Or thought I did."

"I know," said Carrie. "Omega's a deceptive place."

Lynette cleared her throat. "Edmon seems nice. On Omega I thought he was a dork, but he's really very—gallant, I guess you could say."

Carrie smiled. "That's exactly what I'd say. Edmon is nice and he's gallant. He can be a fussbudget, but his heart is pure gold."

Lynette said, "I still feel odd about this. Even if James is sort of insane, I can't spend my life hiding from him. I mean, I'm not going to change schools or anything just because of him. I'll have to go back eventually."

"Give him a while to cool off," Carrie said. "Who knows? He may find someone else."

"At least he can't find me here," Lynette said. "There's no possible way he can trace me. I didn't tell anyone where I was going."

"That's right," Carrie said with an assured nod. "There's no way he can find you here."

"No," Lynette agreed. "None."

In the house, the phone began to ring.

EIGHTEEN

PERHAPS, THOUGHT CARRIE WITH A SURGE OF HOPE, IT WAS HAYDEN calling. Maybe he would say everything was all right, it was fine, he was on his way home.

She ran to the house, banged open the front door, and snatched up the receiver, her heart beating hard. "Hello?" she said breathlessly.

A man's voice, slightly slurred, said, "Is this the Blue residence?"

Her soaring hope died. Who was this, calling at almost midnight? "Yes?"

He chuckled softly. "Can I speak to C. Blue?"

She didn't like this. She felt her face stiffen. "This is Carrie Blue."

"No. I want C. Blue. It might be Camille. I can't quite read the writing."

"I'm the only C. Blue here," she said.

"You're the C. Blue on North First Street?"

"No. I don't live on North First Street."

"Well, I'm looking for the C. Blue on North First."

"Then you've got the wrong number."

He sounded disappointed. "This is area code 501? Fayetteville, Arkansas?"

"This is Fayetteville," she said. "But you've got the wrong number."

"No, wait, help me. Maybe you're the one I want. Where are you?"

Carrie said, "Look, what do you want? It's late."

Lynette came in the door. Her eyes met Carrie's, her expression wary.

The man said, "I was told to call C. Blue in Fayetteville. About a computer for sale."

"You've got the wrong number," Carrie said. "Goodbye." She hung up.

Lynette looked at her questioningly.

"Wrong number," Carrie said. "He sounded drunk."

The phone rang again, and in spite of herself, Carrie gave a little jump. She picked up the receiver gingerly. "Hello?"

But no one answered. The line was silent, but not dead. *Damn,* she thought. "Hello? Who is this?"

No answer.

Carrie pulled open her desk drawer. "Hello?" she repeated with false sweetness. "Who's calling? Has the cat got your tongue?"

No answer.

Her hand closed around a silver police whistle. She brought it to her lips and blew as hard as she could. The whistle shrilled like a banshee, and she winced. Then she slammed down the receiver.

Lynette's eyes were wide and her shoulders hunched as if warding off a blow.

"Sorry," Carrie said. "But I don't think he'll call back." She put the whistle back in the drawer and shut it.

Lynette said, "James called up sounding drunk. And sometimes he called up and didn't say anything. I know it was him."

Carrie went to the front door and locked it. "Don't

worry about James. He'd better not show up around here. I've got a gun."

"You do?"

"Of course," Carrie said with more confidence than she felt. She should take the gun out in the woods and practice with it, shoot at tin cans or bottles.

She would do that tomorrow.

Jon swore, rubbing his ear. She was a bitch, this Carrie Blue. She'd pay for that. All he needed now was her address.

He called Fayetteville information again. "I'm looking for a Carrie Blue. I think she lives on North First Street."

"There's no one named Blue on North First. There's a C. Blue on Old Spring Road."

"Wait," Jon said, "that sounds kind of familiar. What address did you say?"

"Number 101, Old Spring Road. Hold for the phone number please."

He wrote down the address, smiled to himself and hung up. He had her number now, in every way. He would find her, and Lynette would be with her. He had never killed two women at once; the thought stirred a cruel excitement in him.

He wanted to make sure Edmon wasn't with the women. He called Fayetteville information a third time and said he wanted Edmon Welkin's number. He dialed it, and at the other end, the phone rang four times.

"Hello?" said a sleepy voice.

"Edmon Welkin?"

"Yes?"

"Edmon Welkin at 1819 North First Street?"

Edmon yawned. "No. Rogers Boulevard."

"This is Domino's Pizza. Did you just order a large pepperoni with double cheese?"

"No," Edmon said with a groan. "Somebody must be playing a joke."

"Must be. Sorry to disturb you. Goodnight."

" 'Night," muttered Edmon and hung up.

Jon smiled and hung up. He drained the last of his beer.

He got out his road map; he could take the interstate past Springfield, Missouri, then drive the blue highways down to Arkansas and be in Fayetteville in less than four hours.

He would find Carrie's house and he would surprise her there. Her and Lynette? Yes, he felt an almost godlike certainty about it. Lynette would be there. The moon that he had prayed to was guiding him.

Then he would use the women to lure Edmon to him; he did not yet know how, only that it would happen. He felt a calm and powerful sense of infallibility.

Edmon and Carrie Blue would die for trying to steal Lynette from him. He would take Lynette down the interstate and then off into the heart of a national forest; Arkansas was full of forests, and there in the green and secret deeps, he would enjoy her again and again.

If they came after him then, if they caught him, it didn't matter. He would have attained all he wanted, the death of his enemies and the possession of his desired.

What he was doing was reckless and he knew it. He understood now why Bundy had grown reckless at the end; it was the ecstasy of letting go, the irresistible rightness of going beyond control, the feeling of final consummation.

He loaded his car. There was nothing to do about the bloodied mattress, and he did not want to take the time to dispose of Kristin's body. It was rash to leave her there, but with a cosmic indifference, he would do it.

When the room was cleared of all his possessions, he left her lying, covered, in the center of the bed as if she were an offering on an altar.

He shut the door and the lock clicked. He hung the "Do Not Disturb" sign on the doorknob, then got into his car and pulled out of the parking lot onto the highway. He left the motel behind him, and wished he'd had the dynamite to blow it to hell. He was in the mood for destruction.

Maybe another motel, in far-off Rapid City, was being blown apart tonight, along with everybody in it. He hoped all of fucking South Dakota would blow sky-high, and bloody little bits of Edmon's friends would rain down on the ruins for seven days and seven nights.

• • •

It was one o'clock in the morning, and Hayden was one of only three passengers who left the plane and crossed the tarmac to the Rapid City, South Dakota, airport building. He carried his suitcoat thrown over his shoulder and the case holding his portable computer slung from the other.

The inside of the airport had a deserted, somnolent air, and his fellow passengers headed in silence toward the empty and unmoving baggage carousel. It was time to pray to the gods of luggage that his duffel bag with the gun had made the same journey he had.

Across from the luggage carousel was an Avis rental car counter, still open, with a sleepy-faced clerk doing a crossword puzzle and looking as if she hoped nobody would bother her with the damn-fool idea of renting a car.

Hayden headed for the pay phones, dropped in his coins, and dialed the phone number he'd memorized. Brooke answered on the second ring, her voice childish and scared. "Yes?"

"It's Ivanovich," he said. "I'm at the airport. Are you all right?"

"Yes."

"Has anybody been in touch with you? Have you talked to anybody besides me?"

"No."

Jesus, he thought, *she sounds like a very small kid trapped in a very deep well.* "I'm coming to you," he said. "I'm renting a car. I've got your plane tickets in my pocket and two thousand dollars cash. I'll leave one ticket and half the money in a locker here. When Boyd talks to me and tells me everything I want, I'll tell you where the key to the locker is. You're out of here, free and clear. The deal's still on?"

The little voice came out of the well's depths. "The deal's still on."

"No funny stuff, Brooke," he warned her. "I know Boyd has a gun. Don't let him get in any more trouble than he's in already."

"We don't want any more trouble. We just want *out.*"

"I'll get to you as soon as I can—all right?"

"All right."

"Don't open the door to anybody but me. Understand?"

"I understand."

"Good. I'll see you."

He hung up. He felt uneasy, a creepy sensation between his shoulder blades. He walked to the Avis counter, his footsteps echoing. The clerk looked at him with a sulky expression, as if wondering what ill wind had blown him here to intrude upon her privacy.

He rented a Dodge Colt, because it was the only dark car available. The clerk gave him a funny look when he insisted on a dark car. "I'm going to a funeral," he said, and hoped he wasn't telling the truth.

She sulked through the paperwork and gave him a map of the city. She showed him where Deadwood Avenue met Interstate 90, although she seemed to begrudge the information.

At last she handed him the keys. "The lot's that way," she said, nodding toward a pair of glass doors that led outside. "Space Ten-B." She turned back to her crossword puzzle.

He took the keys and turned toward the luggage carousel. His plane's two other passengers stood there, staring dully at it, as if they were zombies, extras from *The Night of the Living Dead.*

Outside he heard a truck pulling up, and the baggage carousel groaned into life. It began to move. Somebody's luggage had made it—God knew whose.

He wasn't hopeful. The first zombie picked up his suit bag and lumbered off into the night. Moments later, the second zombie retrieved a suit bag and a black sample case, then trundled away to wherever zombies went in Rapid City.

Hayden waited. The carousel kept up its creaking cycle, and suddenly, against all odds, his duffel bag appeared. He scooped it up and headed for the men's room. The airport was nearly empty so he didn't expect company.

He laid his coat on the sink, unzipped the bag, took out the gun and holster. He checked the gun, strapped on the shoulder holster, and put his coat on over it. He zipped the bag shut, picked it up, and left the restroom, heading for the double glass doors.

As soon as he opened them, the heat of the South Dakota night hit him; it was like entering a dark, giant oven. The air smelled of cornfields and jet fuel, and he was jolted by a sudden, electric awareness of his surroundings.

All of his senses were heightened, as he was having a mystical experience that seemed on the edge of going wrong. He crossed a deserted street and entered a silent parking lot in which he was the only moving thing. He was hyperconscious of all that was around him.

He knew, with a sinking feeling in his belly, what was happening to him. He was having his own version of a flashback to Vietnam. Maybe it was the oppressive heat and humidity of the night. Maybe it was more.

When a shadow moved even slightly, he saw it move. When a cricket chirped, he knew from what direction and what distance, and he could have aimed an M-16 and torn up the dirt within a foot of it.

He knew this preternatural alertness was a gift beyond price, but it was also its own curse. Although his pulses drummed, he unlocked the car calmly, he got in as coolly as if he had ice in his bloodstream.

He put the key in the ignition and turned it. His heart beat like a trip-hammer in his chest, and it seemed to him to keep hammering out the same terrible syllable: *Nam. Nam. Nam.*

Carrie had the recurring dream she hated most. Her husband had just died, and his open coffin lay in the living room because she could not afford a cemetery plot.

She could not close the coffin no matter how she strained; the lid seemed frozen, it would not budge. The undertaker would not come to fix it because she had no money.

Derreck lay in the casket, his face wasted, a true death's-head with no resemblance to the solid young man who'd fathered her children. His hands, thin and fragile, lay crossed on the chest of his inexpensive suit.

The boys were small again, and they cried. Not only were they frightened by this corpse that would not leave the house, they were hungry, and she had nothing to feed them. The refrigerator was empty, the cupboards held nothing. There were no clothes in any of the closets, and when she looked up, the roof of the house had inexplicably been torn away. The sky loured above them, barren gray.

She thought, *We have no food, no clothing, no shelter, and we can't bury our dead.*

But she put her arms around the boys and pulled them close. "I'm going to take care of this," she told them. She made her voice sound strong and cheerful, as if she feared nothing. "We're going to be fine. I promise."

But then, as always, the dream changed, and she found herself standing alone in the deserted cemetery. Somehow now Derreck was buried, and there was even a stone to mark his grave. But the stone seemed too small, and she was ashamed she could not have given him better.

"I'm sorry you had to be buried here," she said to Derreck, grieved because she knew how little love he had for the town. "I didn't know what else to do."

Nothing answered her except the sweep of the everlasting prairie wind. The land beyond the cemetery was flat and drear with winter; the sky was darkening. "I can't stay in this town," she said. "We never meant to stay. You understand that, I know. I have to leave."

But then a terrible thing happened. Knotted tree roots suddenly thrust writhing out of the earth. Their earth-caked tips seemed to test the air like pointed snouts, twitching first this way, then that, as if hunting for the scent of prey.

Horrified, too frightened to run, she watched this almost sentient uncoiling and swaying. A twisting thicket of roots surrounded her, and she could smell the dank odor of freshly disturbed earth. The roots seemed to sense what they wanted, and what they wanted was her.

With viperlike swiftness they whipped around her legs, snaring her. A long, dirty root shot up and wrapped tightly around her waist, trying to pull her down.

Next to Derreck's grave, the soil wrenched itself apart

like the halves of a wound, leaving a deep raw gash the size of her body. The roots wrestled and dragged her toward this opening, as if the earth wanted to swallow her live.

She woke with a start, her heart banging in her chest. She sat up in bed and put her face in her hands. *I took care of my boys,* she told herself fiercely. *I fed and clothed and sheltered and educated them, my promises are kept.*

And she was not buried in Bitter Water, she had escaped, at last. She was alive and well and doing what she had vowed to do and what she loved. She was in her funny little house in Arkansas, her degree half-finished, her book half-done.

But tonight her home felt strange to her, and she realized why: the house was no longer her private stronghold, she had company. In the living room, the diminutive girl with the uneven face slept on the sofa bed because she had nowhere else to go.

Carrie wanted to rise and pace, to stand on the deck and watch the moonlight on the shifting surface of the water. The lake seemed to call her, drawing her from her bed, and she could not resist.

She knew she should not take a chance on disturbing Lynette, but the dream had made her restless. She rose and on bare feet silently made her way through the kitchen and out the door to the deck.

The lake glittered in the moon's silvery radiance, it moved and swayed like a living thing breathing softly in its sleep. She stood staring out at its shifting brilliance.

Her gaze fell on what was left of her flower bed. The rain had stopped, but the garden was ruined, the marigolds drowned, the begonias rotted at the roots. Weeds alone had survived, and they flourished, nodding in the moonlight.

It can't be helped, she thought. *What's done is done.*

She raised her eyes to the moon, and wondered where Hayden was, what he was doing, if he was safe. She whispered, "I miss you, Hayden. Come home to me."

She startled herself. She hadn't meant to say such a thing. She hadn't meant to feel such a thing.

"Wotthehell," she murmured and slowly she smiled at the moon.

Hayden drove past the American Horse Motel, slowly enough to give it a quick check, not so slowly as to call attention to himself. The motel stood by itself, no other building near. It was old, a one-story L-shaped structure. It was dark, except for a dim light in the office and a bright one in unit 1, where Brooke and Boyd waited. Only four cars were parked in the lot.

He had a weird feeling, an extremely weird feeling, and he couldn't shake it. A peculiar plan formed in his mind. He drove around the block and stopped at an all-night grocery store with an outside pay phone. Again he dialed Brooke's number. She answered quickly.

"This is Ivanovich. I'm only a couple of minutes away. Describe your room to me. Is there a door inside that's locked and doesn't lead anywhere?"

For a moment she didn't answer. He could feel her, a block away, gazing around the cheap room. "Yes," she said at last. "There's a locked door right by the front door, on the left. I thought it was a closet, but it won't open."

Good, he thought. Motel and hotel rooms frequently had doors that led to other rooms in case a renter wanted a suite for a reception, a party, a family reunion, a business venture, an orgy, whatever.

He said, "Is anybody checked in next door to you?"

"I don't think so," she said.

"I'll take that room," he said. "I'll open the door between us. First, I'll give you a password. Carrie's character name. You know what it is. Tell me."

She hesitated. "Greensleeves," she said.

"Right," he said. He hung up and went back to his car. His heart was still beating too hard, and he knew he was being paranoid; he couldn't help it. Forces stronger than reason told him to move in unexpected ways.

He drove back to the American Horse Motel. He checked in, acting surprised that he didn't already have a reservation. He told the sleepy-eyed manager that he worked for the Wanamaker Siding Company and he wanted unit number 2; he was always booked into unit number 2, it was part of his routine, what in hell could have happened that his office hadn't arranged it?

He went back to his car, looked around the nearly deserted parking lot, took up his duffel bag and his portable computer, unlocked the door of unit 2, and turned on the light. The room was small with outdated furnishings, and the walls needed painting. He flung his duffel bag on the bed and plugged the computer into the phone jack by the dresser.

He logged on to the Internet, gave the command to send mail, typed in Robert E. Lee Burnside's e-mail address, and went to a clean screen. Robert E. Lee had been with the FBI, he would know what to do with the information.

Hayden went back to the switch and shut off the light. Only the computer screen glowed in the darkness. He opened the cheap drapes of the front windows just enough to see out. The lot was unchanged. Nothing moved.

He knocked on the door separating the rooms. "Brooke?" he said. "Greensleeves. It's me, Ivanovich."

There was silence on the other side of the door. Then Brooke's voice said, "Yes?" She no longer sounded twelve years old. She sounded six.

"Okay," he said. "I've got your ticket and half your money in my pocket. You'll get the key to the locker when Boyd tells me what I want to know. There's no way you'll get it otherwise. Understand?"

"Yes," she said.

"Kill all your lights except your bathroom light. Then I'm going to open this door. All right?"

"All right," she said weakly.

He waited, watching between the drapes until the lights from her room dimmed. He took a credit card from his wallet and a pocketknife and started to work on the door. There were people who didn't believe a lock could be opened with a credit card. They were wrong.

It took him almost four minutes, and when he finally

swung the door open, Brooke stood there, looking both helpless and defiant, her arms crossed militantly.

Behind her, on the bed, sat a kid with long blond hair. The kid was well-built and handsome in a bovine sort of way. Even in the shadows Hayden could see he had a bewildered air.

"Why the darkness?" Brooke asked. "Why all this cloak-and-dagger stuff? Did you bring the money? Give it here."

He looked down at her. She wore a frumpy caftan and her hair was bound up in her old-fashioned crown of braids. He could not see her eyes because of the thickness of her glasses, and she made him think of a ridiculous child trying to play tough.

He needed her cooperation, but he didn't want her to believe she negotiated from any position of strength.

"I came to save your ass," he said as coldly as possible. "You'll get your money when I get what I want. Now tell your boyfriend to get over here and talk."

Brooke's nostrils flared and she jerked her chin upward. "And then?" she demanded. The courage in her voice was false; he sensed it and knew it was to his advantage.

"Whatever Boyd says, you type it," he said, "on my computer. I'm going to transmit it by e-mail. Not to the law. Just to someone I trust."

"Give us the ticket and the money first."

His eyes locked on hers, and he wondered how someone so foolish had tricked people into believing she was bright. "You want out of here?" he said. "First you talk to me."

In the semidarkness, she held his gaze for a long moment, but he was stronger and he knew it. She gave a toss of her head to signal the boy to rise and leave the bed.

"I don't much like this," the kid said, shambling toward Hayden.

"I never expected you to like it," Hayden said. "But you love this girl. Save her."

The kid confessed his name, Boyd Birch Burdette. He told Hayden what firepower his father had, and it was the stuff of nightmares. Almost two thousand pounds of fertilizer explosive and another half-ton on the way from a brother in North Dakota.

The old man had dynamite, too, not much, but enough to be dangerous. He had blasting caps, fuel oil, and he was trying to learn to make his own C-4 plastic explosive. He had automatic, semiautomatic weapons, sawed-off shotguns, and a homemade grenade launcher.

The weapons were kept primarily in an "armory" that had originally been a pig barn, and the perimeter of the farm was booby-trapped. The old man understood trip wires and pressure devices, he'd built his own crude claymore mines, and somehow he'd gotten access to a lot of ether, which he had set to destruct the pig barn in case of a raid.

It was a logistic hell, and Hayden kept making notes in his head: Have fire department at scene, have paramedics, have bomb disposal personnel, have chemists. We're heading into Armageddon again, boys. Always again.

In the dim light, the kid made a map of the farm, pinpointing the house, which was a secondary arsenal, the pig barn armory, the mines and charges and ground spikes and trip flares. Brooke looked at the map as if the farm was as exotic as Atlantis. *Welcome to the real world,* Hayden thought. *Where things go boom. Where people kill and die.*

"Tell me how your day goes," Hayden told the kid. "Everything. From the time you get up. What everybody does. And when. And where."

"The first thing is the cows and chickens," Boyd said. "We get up about five-thirty. And me and Nolan and Thurston go out to tend the stock."

"Nolan and Thurston are your brothers?"

Boyd nodded. "Half brothers."

"How old are they?"

"Fourteen and eleven."

"What do they think of your father?"

"Nolan kind of imitates him, and Thurston's scared of him but he tries not to let on."

"Okay. Go on. What else happens?"

"Inez, she makes the breakfast. And Daddy, he goes on patrol, he checks the perimeters."

"He's armed when he does this?" Hayden said.

"He's usually got a Smith and Wesson and a CAR-15."

"Has he ever actually fired on anyone or anything?"

"Coyotes mostly. Stray dogs. He might have killed a bum once. He buried something by the pond, but he never told us what and he told us not to ask."

Brooke's eyes widened and she stopped typing.

"Don't quit," Hayden told her. He turned back to Boyd. "Where?"

Boyd drew a small oval on the map and put an X beside it. "There, by the pond," he said. "Daddy hates bums."

Hayden underlined the X and wrote, "Something buried." "Where's your real mother, kid?"

"She couldn't stand my daddy. She run off."

"What about Inez, your stepmother? How's she feel about your father?"

"She's scared of him. He got her from the Philippines. One of those 'Get foreign ladies to write to you' ads in the magazines. He said he'd never have another American woman. He never lets her go off the farm. She don't speak much English."

"What are you doing on Omega? Who were you supposed to be communicating with and why?"

"My uncle. He found it. He said it was a double-secret easy way to communicate. He don't trust the telephone."

"Who puts the terrorist tracts in the Archives?"

"My uncle," Boyd mumbled. "To fuel the revolution."

"Why were you logged on so often?"

"So we'd know soon as a new message come."

"What were the messages about?"

Boyd swallowed. "Mostly about getting more fertilizer and about picking the target and setting a date."

"What date were they thinking of?"

"The Fourth of July," Boyd said.

Hayden's heart turned stone-like in his chest. The Fourth of July was seven days away.

• • •

Half an hour later Hayden heard a vehicle pull into the parking lot, and all his senses went on alert. It was late for anyone to check in, almost three in the morning.

He moved to the window and stared out. A battered panel truck had pulled in next to the manager's office. The truck gave him a bad feeling, a very bad feeling.

"Come here," he ordered Boyd. "Do you know that vehicle?"

Boyd moved beside him. The driver was not visible, but a hand flicked a cigarette out the window. A fiery dot arced through the darkness and rolled away.

Boyd swallowed hard. "That's my daddy," he said. "That's the truck he wanted me to drive to Cheyenne. It's his bomb truck."

Brooke made a small, strangled noise. Boyd looked at her, and he had a helpless, fatalistic expression. "I love you, miracle," he said.

"I love you, too," she said.

Hayden watched as a wiry man of about fifty-five got out of the truck. He was dressed neatly, in dark slacks and a pale shirt. He wore a tie and he walked with a slight limp. He went to the motel's office door.

"How did he know you're here?" Hayden said. "How could he trace you?"

"I don't know," Boyd said. "I don't know."

"Your father," Hayden said. "He's got fake badges, ID's—right?"

"Yessir," Boyd said, with another swallow.

Hayden knew what the Burdette man would do. He'd wake up the motel manager, flash a phony badge and talk fast, saying he was looking for two kids on the run. And the manager wouldn't question the badge or the story; he would tell the old man what he wanted to know.

He watched as Boyd's father rang the bell and waited.

"I reckon I should shoot him," Boyd said in a tight voice. " 'Cause he's come to kill us."

Hayden's mind had gone to a strange, cool level, and he believed he knew exactly what to do. He had a dream situation here; he had a chance to do what was never done in

Waco, get Burdette outside his stronghold. Cut off the head of the snake. "Nobody's shooting. Nobody's killing," he said.

"Go in your room," he said. "Call the police. Tell them there's been a car wreck."

"There's no car wreck," Brooke said, staring at him slack-jawed.

"There will be," he said, throwing on his jacket.

He hit the keys to send Boyd's information to Robert E. Lee. Then, pulling his tie askew and rumpling his hair, he headed out the door. He lurched across the broad sidewalk to his car. For effect, he turned and walked backward a few steps and yelled, "You're a no-good, two-bit whore, Denise."

The Burdette man watched suspiciously as Hayden unlocked his car door and got inside. At that moment the fat manager, belting his bathrobe, answered the door.

Hayden didn't take time to fasten his seatbelt, he started the car and threw it into reverse. Both the manager and the lean man on the doorstep stared as he backed up, too fast, his tires squealing.

The old man might be packing a load of explosives in the truck, but Hayden knew that an impact wouldn't trigger it; Burdette would have an electronic detonator so the blast could be set off from a safe distance.

Hayden threw the car into forward and swerved into the panel truck with a crash that shook his teeth. He hit his horn with his fist and leaned on it, as if its wiring had short-circuited.

He backed up, horn still blaring, put the car back into drive, and slammed against the truck a second time. He backed off a third time, changed gears, and smashed into the wall of the motel just to make sure the manager would call the police, no matter what the man said.

Hayden flung open his door and staggered to the two men who stood frozen and staring at him as if he were mad. Wildness flashed in Burdette's eyes, and he reached toward his ankle, scrambling perhaps for a gun. Hayden seized him, hauled him upright, and slammed him against the wall.

"I'm Mr. Ivanovich," he said. "I hate bombs."

He drew back his fist and drove it into Burdette's face,

hard enough to send his head cracking back against the brick wall. Hayden caught him so he didn't fall to the cement. With his other hand he fished in his pocket and pulled out his wallet.

He flashed his badge at the manager, who looked frightened and dazed. "Dial 911," he said. "Tell them there's a serious weapons violation here. Tell them to search the truck. This man's a terrorist, and I'm making a citizen's arrest."

The manager simply gaped at him. "Do it!" Hayden screamed in his face. "Tell them it's a fucking weapons violation. This man is dangerous!"

The manager scurried to the desk and picked up the phone. *Good,* Hayden thought. If the manager fed the weapons information to the police, they had probable cause to search the truck. He hoped to God the truck did contain explosives or at least illegal weaponry, or he was going to be facing a hell of an assault charge.

Hayden lowered the unconscious man to the ground, took off his own belt and strapped the man's hands to the bumper of the panel truck. He heard sirens in the far distance, coming closer. He pushed up the man's pants leg and took a Browning automatic from its holster. He rose and turned back toward unit 2.

Boyd and Brooke wouldn't be going to the Virgin Islands after all. It was for the best.

He hobbled to the room. Somewhere, in one of the crashes, he'd hurt his knee. He opened the door and limped in.

"Did you call the police?"

Brooke nodded, looking dumbstruck.

He went to Boyd, who held an unaimed Glock automatic as if he needed to shoot something, but didn't know what.

Hayden stopped in front of him and scowled at the gun. "Drop it," he said. The kid stared dully at him.

"Drop it!" Hayden repeated through clenched teeth. The boy flinched and slowly released the automatic.

Hayden glared at him and grabbed him by the shirt-front. "How'd he find you?" he snarled. "It wasn't dumb luck. He zeroed right in on you. Somebody knew where you were. You told somebody. Who?"

"Nobody," Boyd protested. "Nobody knew but you."

Hayden shook the kid and shoved him against the wall. "The cops are coming. You could have got away, but you blew it. Somebody had to tell him how to find you. You talked to *somebody*. Tell me. Or I'll by Jesus make sure you rot in jail and her, too."

It was a bluff, but he didn't give a damn. The kid was scared and stupid, and he must have talked to somebody; it was the only reasonable explanation. He shook him again.

"L-lacewing," Boyd stuttered. "I talked to Lacewing on Omega. I told her what happened to us. But she wouldn't—"

"She did. Who is she? What's her real name?"

"Kristin. Kristin Stanek. From Minneapolis."

"What else did you tell her, you little weasel? Did you tell her about me? About Edmon? Did you?"

"Only a little," Boyd said, practically weeping. "Don't let Brooke get in trouble. Please. I did it all. The fault's all mine. She didn't do nothing."

He shoved the boy against the wall again. "Did you tell her about Carrie?"

The sirens were loud now, they filled the air with their throbbing keen. Boyd said nothing. His eyes flashed with fear and confusion.

Hayden pulled him toward him, then smashed him back against the wall so hard that Brooke screamed. "Did you tell her about Carrie, you son of a bitch?"

"Some," Boyd said, tears spilling onto his cheeks. "Not much, honest."

"Did you tell her Carrie's name?"

"Kind of," Boyd said.

"Did you say where she lived?"

"Sort of," Boyd half-whimpered, and Hayden was seized with a sincere desire to kill him.

"Stop picking on him," Brooke cried. "You promised us you'd get us out of here."

"He got us trapped," Hayden said in disgust.

"Will they arrest us?" Boyd asked, wiping his nose with the back of his hand and looking at Hayden fearfully.

"Shut up," Hayden snarled. He ripped the computer hookup from the phone jack and reconnected the phone. Urgently he dialed Carrie's number. She did not answer on the first ring, or the second, or the third.

The sirens had grown deafeningly loud. Then they went silent. The silence seemed far louder than the noise and meant the police had arrived. He heard running footsteps.

Carrie's phone rang a fourth time.

There was hammering at the door, and screaming to open up. It was the police.

"Open the door," Hayden said to Brooke. She moved to the door with jerky little steps like a puppet on strings. Carrie's phone rang a fifth and then a sixth time.

Boyd stood staring at the door in sheer, mindless terror. Tears glistened in his eyes as Brooke fumbled with the lock. She swung open the door. Two Rapid City police officers stood there, guns drawn. Boyd gave a choked sob.

The phone rang a seventh time, and Carrie answered, her voice both anxious and sleepy. "Hello?"

"Carrie, it's Hayden. Listen carefully. Somebody on Omega knows—"

"Hands up," ordered the taller officer. "Everybody. You, too, asshole, drop the phone. You got explaining to do. Drop it!"

Brooke began to scream. She fell to the floor and covered her head with her arms. There was a confusion of men's voices outside, new sirens shrilled, and a dog was howling.

"Carrie, somebody on Omega knows who you are and where," Hayden said. "Maybe Edmon, too. I want you to get out of there now. Go to Robert E. Lee, go now. Tell him—"

"I said, 'Drop it,' " the tall officer snarled, aiming his gun barrel straight between Hayden's eyes. Brooke shrieked more wildly.

"Get out," Hayden repeated to Carrie. "Now."

Reluctantly he put the phone back in its cradle. He looked at Boyd, who cowered against the wall as if paralyzed. Tears streaked his face.

Slowly, Hayden raised his hands. He knew how the game was played from here on out. "Put your hands up, kid," he ordered Boyd.

Weak-kneed, crying harder, the boy obeyed.

Hayden's heart was stony. The kid was lucky. He didn't have to run anymore. It was over. With luck, his family was safe.

But Carrie, Hayden thought. *How badly had the fool compromised Carrie?*

NINETEEN

———◦∕∾∕◦———

SHAKEN, CARRIE HUNG UP THE PHONE, HER PULSES BEATING SO HARD that she trembled.

Why had Hayden called at this black, ungodly hour of the morning? Why had he hung up? *God, God, he's in trouble.*

She'd heard shouts, a woman's screams, the wail of sirens. She felt hollow and frightened. Why screams? Why sirens? *He's in danger. He's in danger.*

She'd understood barely half of what he'd said. She'd heard names—Omega and Edmon and Robert E. Lee. She thought he'd said someone should "get out"—but who? And where and why? She hadn't prayed in years, but now she said a small, fervent prayer for Hayden.

Robotlike, hardly knowing what she did, she went to the kitchen, opened the refrigerator, and poured a glass of cold milk. Standing by the kitchen window, she stared out at the moonlight glittering on the water that covered the ruined garden.

If only Hayden would call back—what trouble was he in, and what did he want her to do? She rubbed the cold glass against her forehead and tried to concentrate. "Oh, hell," she murmured. It was not so much a curse as an expression of infinite weariness. She kept the cold glass pressed against her forehead.

She said another prayer, a longer one, and struggled to center her thoughts. *Call Robert E. Lee Burnside,* she told herself. *Tell him Hayden's in some sort of trouble. That's all you can do.* She put the milk aside, untasted.

She padded silently to the desk and looked up Burnside's home number in the phone book. Moonlight streamed through the window, bright enough to read by. But when she dialed, all she got was his answering maching. She gritted her teeth. She'd always hated answering machines, but never so much as now.

"This is Carrie Blue," she said softly, trying not to wake Lynette. "I just got a call from Hayden. I don't know where he is, but something's wrong. I couldn't understand him, but he said your name and Edmon Welkin's. Please call me. Please." She recited her phone number, hung up, then stood, chewing on her thumbnail.

Knowing she would not sleep again, she went into her bedroom and changed from her nightgown to jeans, her Krazy Kat T-shirt, and her old running shoes. Then she took the gun, still in the book bag, from her bureau drawer and went back to the darkened living room. She did not know why she wanted the gun, only that Hayden had touched it, had put it into her hands.

She sat in the rocking chair beside the sofa bed, rocking softly, the gun heavy in her lap. She stroked the worn LSU book bag as if it had talismanic powers.

Hayden, she kept thinking, *come home. Hurry. Hurry.*

Jon pulled into an all-night Texaco station between Springdale and Fayetteville, Arkansas. He was so close to Carrie Blue now that his skin tingled and his blood danced drunkenly in his veins. He got out of the car to recheck her address in the regional telephone book.

And there it was: **C. Blue 101 Old Spring Road, Fayetteville.** He went inside the station and told the attendant he wanted to buy a local map. The attendant was a gaunt, weathered old man with gray hair and watery blue eyes; he had yokel written all over him, but was friendly.

Jon unfolded the map and searched for Old Spring Road. The name wasn't written on the legend, so he asked the hillbilly. "I'm looking for my uncle's place," he said. "He didn't say it'd be so hard to find."

The old man stared at the map, nodding while his wrinkles did thoughtful things. He seemed to know the answer, but he had to to mull it over, think it out aloud.

"Now, see," he said, "I think it's out east by the lake, I believe, yes, sure is. That lake wasn't always there. Nossir. That there is a manmade lake. They dammed the White River to make that lake. About forty year ago. And there is lots of little unmarked roads what used to go to farms and things.

"Now your Old Spring Road is up here northeast of Fayetteville toward Nob Hill, which is where New Spring Road runs off from Sonora. You don't want that. That is your *New* Spring Road."

He pointed a grease-stained finger at the map.

"Now right here, where the main road forks, you hang left, see? And Old Spring Road was what they called the road where the old Sawyer farm was, but it's burned down and now there's just a little old place there on the lake. Near there once't I caught me a nineteen-pound catfish on a blue Hot'n Tot lure, right to the east. Trolling, if you can believe that."

"That's a big fish," Jon said pleasantly.

"Yeah, but when they get that big, they got a greasy taste," the old man said. "They is not good eatin', but they put up a good fight."

"And Old Spring Road?"

"Well, Old Spring Road, it's off Highway Ninety-five, you take county road five-oh-five. Now that road ain't shown here, but it's there, it'll be on your left, and Old Spring Road's down at the bottom of five-oh-five.

"I know because I used to help grade all these county

roads, and five-oh-five's funny 'cause the last quarter-mile's
in a different county, it jigs into Benton County, but we
done that last quarter-mile as a favor, 'cause Benton County
done the same for us on Sagerfield Road, and you trade these
things off, don't you know."

"I see. Thanks," Jon said.

"Well, you be careful, you drive that five-oh-five slow
because that hill is one steep sumbitch, and we done had a
lot a rain, and it's probably washed out bad."

Jon nodded and smiled.

The old man grinned back, showing bad teeth. "It's
mighty early. You're gonna wake your uncle up."

"It'll be a surprise all right," said Jon.

Hayden's jaw hurt, his knuckles hurt, and although he was
the one pressing the charges, the Rapid City detectives were
playing Good Cop, Bad Cop with him.

Good Cop was a big blond Swede named Anderson. Bad
Cop was a big blond Swede named Hanson. Hayden felt as if
he had been captured by Vikings.

"Why'd you try to make a citizen's arrest?" asked Hanson.

"I had probable cause to believe he'd committed a fel-
ony," Hayden said. "Look, this is a federal matter. I need to
talk to the FBI."

"Right now you're talking to us."

"I have to make some phone calls."

"In good time. You don't need to call a lawyer—yet."

Hayden was worried about Carrie. He thought darkly
that if he smashed Bad Cop in his perfect white teeth, they'd
arrest him for assault, and then they'd give him his phone
call, all right.

But he was saved by a knock on the door. A big, beautiful blond secretary came in. She looked like she should be a
Norwegian princess named Helga. This whole division, Hayden thought, could go around wearing helmets with horns
and riding in longboats.

"He's exactly who he claims he is," said Helga. "P.I.

from Fayetteville, Arkansas. Former ATF. Clean record. Two FBI men are downstairs. They want to talk to him."

Bad Cop gave a snort of derision. "They can have him."

Good Cop clapped Hayden on the shoulder. "How'd you know he was packing unregistered weapons? Good God, he had seven sticks of dynamite, too."

"I had a tip," Hayden said with a sour smile. "Look, I need to make a call. I got clients back in Arkansas I'm worried about. I need to notify someone."

Bad Cop turned his back to Hayden. "This isn't your business office, buddy. You don't bill your shit on our phone."

Once more Hayden thought of hitting the son of a bitch. He said, "There's a woman working for me. I think her cover's blown. If anything happens to her—buddy—the media's going to love hearing what a warmhearted public servant you are."

Bad Cop kept his wide back to Hayden. "Fuck it," he said, voice bored.

"The FBI wants to see him *now*," said Helga pointedly. "I'll send them up." She turned and left.

Good Cop gave Hayden's shoulder another fraternal slap. He sat down on the opposite side of the desk and pushed the phone toward him. "You got time for one call," he said. "Keep it short."

Hayden glanced at his watch. It was almost five in the morning. With luck, Carrie had left her house. Without luck, she hadn't and she'd argue that she didn't need to. There was no time to argue.

The Fayetteville or Arkansas police couldn't help him, no threat had been made to her, and it was too early to get in touch with Robert E. Lee by phone. He dialed Edmon.

After six rings, Edmon answered, his voice so groggy he sounded nearly comatose.

"Edmon, it's Ivanovich. Carrie's cover's been blown on Omega. Maybe yours, too. I don't know how serious it is, but until we find out, I want her away from that lake. Check on her. If she's still there, put her up at the Holiday Inn or any damn place, just get her there and keep it quiet. Understand?"

"Somebody on Omega knows who she is?" Edmon asked. He no longer sounded sleepy. "Who? How?"

"Lacewing. I don't know how. I don't know who she might tell. If it's Quicksilver, we've got trouble, because everybody will know. I called Carrie, but I was interrupted. I don't know if the message got through. You make sure she's out of there as soon as possible. All right?"

"Yessir," Edmon said. "Her and Lynette both."

A surreal jolt chilled Hayden. "Lynette?" he said, gripping the receiver more tightly. "What the hell you mean, Lynette?"

"She's with Carrie. She got in last night. You said it was okay—right? I'll get both of them someplace else. You can t-t-t-trus—depend on me."

Stunned, Hayden thought, *Lynette Pollson's with Carrie? I didn't authorize this. What is this?*

He said, "Lynette's at Carrie's?"

"Yessir. I thought you—"

Hayden spoke through clenched teeth. "Get them out of there. Now. Right now."

"Yessir. But—"

"But what?" Hayden snapped.

"But the sun's not up yet. It's not even five in the morning."

"Do it *now*, Edmon. Don't ask questions. Just goddam do it."

"Yessir. Do you know anything about Brooke?"

"Brooke's fine, get to Carrie." *Good God,* Hayden thought, *why are Lynette Pollson and Carrie together? This is out of control.*

There was another knock at the door. Helga the Norwegian princess was back, with two men who had that cleancut, ice-in-the-veins aura of FBI.

"These gentlemen want to talk to you," Helga said to Hayden.

From the look in the men's eyes, he could tell it would be a long talk.

"Take care of Carrie," Hayden told Edmon, his voice tight. "That's an order." He hung up.

Jon folded up the map and got into his car. The garrulous old man had told him everything he wanted to know. Jon pulled back onto the highway, knowing exactly how to get to Lynette—and that slut Carrie Blue. He thought, *Happy dreams, bitches. I'm on my way.* He switched on the radio and found a golden oldies station.

Bob Dylan sang that now the line was drawn and the curse was cast.

At five-fifteen, the edge of the eastern sky was turning gray, and birds twittered sleepily.

Carrie's phone rang, startling her so badly that she was ashamed of herself. She felt foolish, like a frightened child sensing danger in every sound, every shadow.

Maybe it's Hayden, she told herself. *Maybe he's on his way home.* The phone rang a second time, and Lynette snuggled more deeply into the sheets.

Carrie rose, setting aside the gun, and snatched up the receiver. "Hello?" she said softly. She was disappointed when she heard not Hayden's voice, but Edmon's.

"Carrie? It's Edmon. Don't be alarmed. Hayden just phoned. He told me to get you someplace else as soon as possible."

A fearful catch clutched at her throat. "Where is he? How is he? When's he coming back? Does he have Brooke?"

"He said Brooke's fine. He didn't say anything about himself. He just told me to get you somewhere else. So you'd better wake Lynette and get packed."

"He's all right?" Carrie asked, hope mixed with apprehension.

"He sounded all right. But he wants you in a motel or someplace. I'll be out for you as soon as I can."

"Edmon, I don't need you to help us check into a motel. I can do it myself."

"I feel responsible for both of you," Edmon said. "I'll be there."

Oh, God, Carrie thought tiredly, why had the fates let Edmon be born in *this* century? Why hadn't he been allowed to flourish in days of old when knights were bold and damsels weren't liberated?

"Like I say," Edmon said, his voice solemn, "I don't want to alarm you. But somebody on Omega knows who you really are."

"What?" Carrie said. "That's impossible."

"It's what Hayden said," he insisted. "Lacewing. He said Lacewing."

"Lacewing?" Carrie said, confounded. She had no connection to Lacewing, none. She'd hardly spoken to her. "Edmon, this is ridiculous," she said. "And even if it's true, it doesn't automatically mean somebody's going to cause me trouble. And if anybody tries, I've got a gun."

This silenced Edmon, but only for a moment. "Well," he said, "just don't shoot *me* when I show up. I've got orders to move you. All right?"

Carrie sighed. She told Edmon goodbye and hung up. She stared for a moment at the gun lying on the desk, glad it was still in the book bag so the sight of it wouldn't alarm Lynette.

She switched on a light, then reached down and gently shook the girl's shoulder. "Rise and shine," she said. "We're going to move someplace else, for safety's sake. It's Mr. Ivanovich's orders. Edmon's coming for us."

Lynette's eyelids fluttered open, and Carrie studied the small face, which looked far more vulnerable without makeup. "Where are we going?" Lynette asked. "And why's Edmon coming?"

"He probably doesn't want us to carry our own suitcases," Carrie said.

Lynette sat up and rubbed her eyes. "It's hard to believe he's for real. Such a gentleman. I thought they were a dying breed."

A dying breed indeed, thought Carrie. But she smiled a stiff little smile and said, "Come on. Let's get packing."

• • •

Jon was tired, his eyes bleary, his energy coming from pills and a tense, rising flood of adrenaline. He took a wrong turn when the road forked, didn't realize it for ten minutes, cursed himself when he did.

Light was seeping into the eastern sky, a pearly grayness slowly rising. He wanted to find the women before it was fully light. His plan was to come upon the house as silently as possible and break in while they slept.

He knew now that he had talked to Carrie Blue on Omega many times. She was Greensleeves, the girl from Fayetteville who lived by a lake, and he had been Onfredo. She had told him many details about herself that she supposed were useless. He knew, for instance, that she said she had no dog. That was good.

And she'd laughed that she lived in a small, old rental house that had a leaking roof. An old house meant old locks, weak locks, even broken locks. One way or another, he would get inside. He did not worry. Everything from here on out was ordained.

Lynette would be his, and he would take her away. He could take her back to his grandmother's house in Charleston and keep her prisoner in the basement. Other men had done such things, he had read of it. The house was his now, empty, but it served as his permanent address, and he could go back and live on his father's money.

Lynette was sweet and well-behaved, not scheming, like Kristin. He could keep her for a long time and not kill her until he had to. Maybe he would never have to kill her, and they would live happily ever after, master and slave.

But the other woman, Carrie, had to die as fast as possible. He was surprised that the prospect excited him.

He reached county road 505, which was marked by a blue and white sign. He headed down the road, trees rising thickly on either side. Beneath the canopy of branches, the faint light of dawn seemed to disappear, as if earth had sucked it back down into darkness.

It was like driving through a crooked, leafy tunnel that led down the mountainside. He cut his headlights but kept on his parking lights. He drove slowly, his heart pounding as if it would explode.

The way was as rough as the old man had warned. The car bucked and jounced. Down, down, the road descended, and he sensed he was closing in on the lake and the women were near.

He almost missed seeing a set of tire ruts that led into the woods toward the left, but he always paid attention to such overgrown roads; often they had been of use to him.

Perhaps it had once led to some long-gone building or perhaps it was a hunter's road, used only in season. He pulled off on it, turned off his parking lights and motor. He would approach the house on foot. He would make no noise, and he could scout the territory.

He took a beer from his cooler and drank it down, almost in one long swallow, to calm himself. He tossed the can away and walked back to the main road. From the road, he could not see his car; that was good, he was camouflaged. He made his way downward again, stepping carefully. He did not wish to sprain an ankle or twist a knee in the gouged and rutted dirt.

As he rounded a corner, the tunnel of trees ended, and suddenly, like a revelation, the house was before him, a hundred yards away, lonely and silent. Just beyond it stretched the lake, turning pewter-colored beneath the paling sky.

But something was wrong. The lights were on.

An old white Mercury Lynx that didn't look like it ran sat in the carport. A black jeep was parked in the drive and so was a dark red Honda Civic. Lynette drove a dark red Honda Civic.

His heart beat so hard it hurt him. *She is here,* he thought in exultation. *She is here. She is mine.*

He took a step backward into the shadows and wished he had some bourbon left; another drink would steady him. Instead he reached into his pocket for his knife. He drew it out, unfolded the blade.

Then the porch light went on, spilling its steady illumination over the cement porch, and he blinked at the sudden brilliance. The front door banged open and a small girl with smooth golden hair stepped outside. She carried a suitcase and a portable computer. She unlocked the Civic's back door and put the suitcase and computer inside.

Her hair was like a helmet of gold and framed a pale face he could not clearly see. But he knew. He knew. *Lynette. My love.*

She was loading the car, which meant she must be getting ready to run from him again. His stomach tightened. He must move quickly, decisively. She went back inside, and brushed past another woman coming out the door.

This woman was taller, her build more slender, and she, too, had blond hair, but it was short and curly. She struggled with a large box that she set, with difficulty, in the back of the jeep.

She rubbed her hands on her jeans and went back inside. *Carrie Blue,* he thought, *the dirty, lying spy. Was she moving, too? Or only helping Lynette to move?* He watched as she went back inside. From a distance she looked no older than Lynette, but was that only another one of her deceits?

Lynette came out again, with another suitcase and a backpack that she put inside the car. As soon as she turned to go inside again, he began to slip through the shadows toward the house.

The trees thinned out, but there were enough to give him cover. He thought he could make his way nearly to the porch without being seen. He would seize whichever woman came out next. If he had one, he had them both. Instinctively, he knew this was true.

He stood only a few feet from the edge of the porch, flattening himself against a large mimosa tree with low-hanging boughs. He was perhaps nine feet from the two vehicles, closer to the car than the jeep.

He heard the door open, and it was Carrie Blue, half-dragging a large suitcase. She seemed to have a stupid tendency to try to carry things too heavy for her. All the better, he thought, nerves tightening another notch. She literally had her hands full. And she was so close he could see freckles on her face and arms.

He waited until she was completely caught up in trying

to hoist the heavy suitcase into the back of the jeep, and then he moved.

He seized her from behind in a one-armed choke hold, and with his other hand, held the knife to her throat. The suitcase tumbled from her grasp and fell with a thud. She gasped helplessly, she tried to scream, but only a pained, wheezing sound came out.

But she fought. She drove an elbow into his ribs, she kicked at him, she twisted and flailed.

He could cut her throat from ear to ear right here, but she was exciting him, and after he had secured Lynette, he would take this one deep into the woods. He'd enjoy her useless fighting and then he would kill and rape her.

But for now, he wanted to knock the fight out of her and make her do exactly as he said. He choked her more tightly, and with one swift movement of the knife, he ripped open her T-shirt from top to bottom.

"Hold still," he hissed in her ear, "or I'll cut you open, too." He pressed the knife's point against her bared stomach. He drew it up slowly and pressed it against the underside of her left breast.

"I know where your heart is," he said. "I can dig it out in a minute. Hold still. Behave. Call Lynette. Tell her to come out here, nice and easy. No tricks. Or I dig out your heart and feed it to the fish."

He loosened the choke hold slightly. She had the fucking nerve to drive her elbow into his ribs again, so sharply that he gasped with pain. She also brought her foot down on his instep with astonishing force.

He whirled her around, slapped her hard across the face, so hard that her head snapped backward. Then he put her in the choke hold again, and again pressed the knife underneath her breast. This time he cut her, a nick deep enough to make her flinch in pain. Blood stained her white brassiere, trickled down her stomach.

"No more tricks, bitch," he said. "I can hurt you so bad you beg to die. Call Lynette. Tell her to come out here, her hands up. If she wants to keep you alive, she's got to come with me."

Carrie was breathing hard, but as soon as he loosened his hold, she tried to scream. He cut it off immediately and stuck her with the knife again, twisting it slightly. She groaned, she writhed in his arms, but she didn't stop struggling.

Goddam, he thought. She was making him get hard. She was older than he'd thought, but not too old, she was good-looking, and she had something in her none of his other women had ever had—fire. He liked it.

But it was Lynette he longed for; this one was just icing on the cake. He pressed his mouth against Carrie's ear and bit the lobe hard, until he tasted blood. His erection grew, pressed against her hip.

"Now," he said in her ear, "we wait for Lynette."

But he didn't have to wait. Lynette came out the door with two tote bags, and she saw Jon, she saw Carrie imprisoned in Jon's grasp, and she saw the knife.

Her eyes widened, her crooked mouth fell open, her uneven little chin dropped. The tote bags slipped from her hands and fell to the porch floor, spilling books and notebooks across the cement.

The sight of her filled him with wild elation. He experienced a wave of happiness so strong that it almost brought tears to his eyes. His heart soared, and he felt something he had never felt before in his life. He thought, *I love her. I am in love.*

He said, very quietly, "Hello, Lynette. I've come for you. Do what I say and your friend won't get hurt. I want you to open the trunk of your car. We're going to put her in it."

Lynette looked at him with astonishment and horror. She didn't move.

He'd loosened his hold on Carrie's neck, and she spoke with a calm that unpleasantly surprised him. "Lynette," she said from between clenched teeth, "there's a gun on my desk, in an LSU book bag. Get it. Shoot him, no matter what he says or does. That's an order."

Lynette edged back toward the door.

Jon raised the knife so the tip rested just beneath Carrie's left eye. "You want me to blind her, Lynette? I can gouge her eyes, it's easy. Don't go for the gun. You don't want your friend blind, do you? Of course not."

Lynette stared at Carrie, tears rising.

With the same maddening calm, Carrie said, "Get the gun, Lynette. Kill him. No matter what he does to me."

"Goddam," Jon breathed in Carrie's ear, "you are something, you know that? I am gonna fuck you like you never been fucked."

He bit her earlobe again, tasted her blood. He said to Lynette, "I've got your friend. I'm going to walk into the house and I'm going to take the gun. If you try to stop me, if you try to run, I'll blind her. You understand me, Lynette? Tell me you understand."

Lynette's gaze was fastened on the knife. She nodded. "I understand," she said in a small voice.

"Now," he said to Carrie, "you and I are going inside. I'm going to take the gun. And you're not going to try anything stupid, 'cause I'm tired of that shit. Understand?"

"Yes," Carrie said tonelessly. He half-pushed, half-carried her toward the door. He paused by Lynette and bent. He kissed her full on the lips.

When he raised his mouth from hers, he left a faint smear of Carrie's blood across her lips. "You're beautiful," he said, gazing at her. "So beautiful."

Carrie knew he meant what he had said; he would blind her if she struggled again, and eventually he meant to kill her, and Lynette, too. She also knew their chances were almost zero if he got the gun. They did not dare disobey him if he got the gun.

She wished Lynette would defy him and somehow escape. But the girl stood as if she were rooted to the porch.

The man forced Carrie inside and made Lynette come with them. He was a strong young man, but she could smell liquor on his breath and he was so tense he trembled. *We've got to wait and play for time,* she thought. *It's the only hope.*

Then she thought of Edmon. Good God, Edmon was going to walk straight into this mess. This maniac could kill all three of them.

Stay calm, she told herself. *He'll be distracted when Edmon comes. When Edmon comes, I'll make my move.*

But what move? she wondered in despair. She could feel his erection pressing into her flesh, and his knife's tip was sharp at the corner of her eye.

He reached the desk. He drew the knife away from her eye so he could take the gun from the book bag. Then he turned Carrie to face him. He did it very slowly and deliberately, as if drawing out the moment. He smiled, then slapped her so hard with the back of his hand that she knocked into the wall, struck the bookcase and fell to the floor, too dizzied to rise. She watched him, her jaw throbbing with pain.

He set the knife on the desk, checked the gun's ammunition clip, slid the safety catch off, then turned and pointed the gun at Carrie. But he didn't speak to her. He spoke to Lynette.

"Lynette," he said softly, "come in here. I want you to tie up Carrie."

He reached for his knife, shut it, and thrust it into his pocket. He smiled again at Carrie. It occurred to her, irrelevantly, that he was an extraordinarily handsome young man, but pure evil shone in his dark eyes.

Lynette stepped inside. She looked first at Carrie, then at the young man.

He nodded at Lynette, his expression almost affectionate. "Tie her up, love."

"I haven't got any rope," Lynette said.

He turned his gaze to Carrie. "How about you, bitch? You got rope around here?"

Carrie tried to stretch out the time. "Do you know me from Omega? Did we talk on Omega?"

"All the time, Greensleeves."

"Who were you?" she asked. "Who are you? How did you find us?"

"I was many people. I am many people. I found you because I was meant to. Now—rope. Do you have rope, or do I improvise?"

"Let me think," she said, putting her face in her hands. "You hit me so hard I can't think straight."

"I guess I improvise," he said. He glanced at the sofa bed, still unmade. He turned to Lynette. "Rip the sheets. Into strips about two inches wide."

Get this son of a bitch outside, Carrie thought, *so Edmon sees him as soon as he drives up. He can't take Edmon by surprise, too. Where did this guy come from? I saw no car. I heard no car.*

"Wait," she said, taking her hands from her face and raising her gaze to his. "I've got rope. In the shed."

"Okay," he said. "That's a good girl. We'll go to the shed. All of us together."

Carrie wiped tears of pain from her cheeks. She stood and found she was unsteady on her feet. "I have to get the key," she said. "It's locked."

"All right. You do that," he said.

Carrie made a show of staggering slightly when she went to her desk drawer. God knew she felt shaken and weak, but she would disguise what strength she had. And when the moment was right, she would surprise him with it.

She took the keys from the desk drawer, but that was all; he was watching her too closely. From the corner of her eye, Carrie saw Lynette had inched backward toward the kitchen counter. Her hand slipped behind her.

Get a weapon, Lynette, Carrie thought, as if she could transmit the thought by sheer willpower. *Get any kind of weapon. Don't let him slaughter us like sheep.*

She showed the key to the man. He nodded and gave her his nasty smile. She could see that he still had his erection.

"The shed's outside," she said. "By the dogwood tree. Near the garden."

"Then move," he said. He motioned with the gun to urge her on. "You, too, love," he said to Lynette.

Carrie led the way. Lynette followed, the man came behind, and Carrie was painfully conscious of the gun aimed at her back. If he looked to the west of the house, he would see a clothesline strung between the house and an elm tree, and he would know she didn't have to go to the shed for rope. Would he notice?

She herself had noticed several things. He could handle

the automatic, but did so awkwardly. He was right-handed, but he held the gun with his left thumb wrapped over his wrist, the wrong position. If he fired, the recoiling slide would pinch him, surprising him and slowing him down.

But she wanted the gun before he fired it. Trying to disarm a gunman was an excellent way to get herself shot to death, and she knew it. She had practiced taking a gun away in training classes, years ago. But in classes only. Never in real life.

Slowly she unlocked the padlocked shed, started to swing the door open. She heard the sound of a car coming down the road. Her heart seemed to stall, her lungs freeze. Edmon was coming.

"Who's that?" the man demanded, seizing Carrie by the arm. He put his gun to her temple.

"I don't know," Carrie lied.

Roughly he pulled Carrie behind the shed. "You, too," he ordered Lynette. Wordlessly, the girl obeyed.

He put his left arm around Carrie's neck, imprisoning her. He peered around the edge of the shed, his eyes trained on the road, and slowly he moved the gun's barrel from her temple and aimed it at the path the car must take to reach the house.

That's a bad position, Carrie thought with a surge of hope. If he extended his gun much farther, she could bite him, kick him, give him an elbow strike to the stomach, and grab for his weapon. If she put the right pressure on the right spots of his arm, she could get the gun, she could even force him to the ground if she did it right.

Or, if she could break free from him, she had weapons herself in the shed. A spade, a pitchfork, a rusty ax that stood in the far corner. *My God, could she hit a man with an ax? What choice did she have, if it came to it?*

But at that moment, Edmon's car pulled into the clearing, slowing as it approached the house. It was Lynette who moved. She sprinted from their hiding place and went flying up the road, straight toward the glare of the headlights, her arms out wide, as if in supplication.

"Edmon!" she screamed. "Go back! He has a gun! Edmon, go back!"

"Lynette!" the man roared. He flung Carrie against the side of the shed so hard her breath was knocked away and tiny lights flashed across her vision.

Edmon had to brake in order not to hit Lynette. The man reached the road and was on Lynette, crying out hoarsely in rage, "Lynette!"

He seized her by the arm, yanked her from the roadway, and pistol-whipped her across the side of her skull. She crumpled lifelessly to the ground.

Carrie staggered to the open shed door and clung to it. "Run him down!" she screamed at Edmon. "Do it!"

But Edmon had stopped. His face behind the windshield was a pale blur in the dawning light.

The man raised his gun and aimed it straight toward Edmon. He fired and the windshield shattered into a crystal spiderweb, and across the ruined glass, Carrie saw blood spray, it seemed to her a sea of it—Edmon's bright, young blood.

TWENTY

---⟪⟫---

CARRIE CLUTCHED THE SHED DOOR TO KEEP FROM FALLING TO HER knees. Edmon was dead or dying, and Lynette lay unmoving beneath the dogwood tree.

The man raised his gun and fired into Edmon's car a second time. Another hole punched through the windshield, spinning a new web of cracks among the first set, and the glass shone scarlet in the rising sun.

"No," Carrie whispered. "No."

His back is to me. The realization seared through her like a lightning bolt.

His back still to Carrie, he walked to Lynette. He held the gun one-handed, rather gingerly. The slide must have pinched his flesh, as Carrie had thought.

He touched Lynette with his foot, as if testing a wounded animal to see if it was alive. She stirred slightly. He bent and caressed her face.

"In the car—was that Edmon Welkin?" he demanded. "Was it?"

"Yes," whimpered Lynette.

"Shit," he said, "he made me hurt you, baby."

Galvanized, Carrie moved. Just inside the shed, leaning against the wall, were a rake, a spade, a hoe, and a pruning saw.

She seized the spade, gripped it like a ball bat, and drew it back as she ran toward him.

The man sprang up, turning as he did so, but she was faster. Gritting her teeth, she swung, smashing the back of the spade's iron blade against his gun hand.

Metal clanged against metal, and the automatic sailed into the air like an awkward bird, then plummeted into the grass, bounced, and disappeared into the high weeds beside the road.

He grunted in pained surprise and staggered backward, stumbling slightly. She gripped the handle of the spade more tightly, drew it back and swung again, putting all her muscle into it and aiming for his head.

This time the thick metal blade caught him full in the face with a sickening *thunk,* and his body arced backward from the blow; he staggered, then collapsed, blood streaming from his nose and mouth.

Stunned, he groaned, and she remembered the cardinal rule of struggle: *End it fast.* Panting, she wound up for another swing. He glared up at her, and tried to lunge back to his feet, holding up one arm to ward off her next blow. "Bitch," he snarled.

Carrie swung the spade again as if aiming to knock a low pitch out of the park and into the next county. She put all her might into it and slammed the flat of the blade against the side of his skull, so hard that her teeth rattled and her armbones shivered.

The impact knocked him to the ground in a tumbling heap, and he sank backward, his limbs falling as limply as a rag doll's. His eyes rolled up, showing only white; his jaw sagged. He lay in the grass as still as death, and Carrie thought, *My God, I've killed him.*

She stared at him, her heart pounding. His chest rose and fell, and tiny red bubbles frothed at his nostrils. The edge of the spade had opened a long gash across his forehead. His chest rose and fell, rose and fell.

Her knees suddenly felt watery. She staggered toward the tall grass where the gun had fallen, dragging the spade behind her.

The gun, she thought numbly, when I have the gun, it will be over. And then she must help Lynette, and she must go to Edmon, oh, God—she could not bear to think of Edmon.

She searched for the automatic, but couldn't find it. Then she saw its barrel gleaming deep in a stand of Johnsongrass. She sighed and stepped toward it, wearily throwing the spade aside.

But she had overestimated her own strength, or underestimated the man's.

Suddenly she heard him behind her, she *felt* him behind her, and turned, appalled, to see him hurtling toward her. His face was covered in blood as if by a mask, and his right hand dangled oddly from his wrist. With a cry of rage he sprang at her.

She dodged backward, but he stood, crouched like an animal, between her and the gun. He was close enough to it to turn and pick it up, but did not see it. Blood ran into his eyes. With his left hand he reached toward his back pocket for his knife. The spade lay four feet away from her on the ground, and he would never let her reach it.

His teeth showed in either a snarl or a savage smile, gleaming whitely in his bloodied face. Carrie's heart went hard and cold as rock. *If you kill me, you bastard, you'll have to fight like hell to do it.*

Instead of going for the spade, as he might expect, she lunged at him as he still fumbled, left-handed, in his pocket for his knife. She seized him by his broken wrist, and he screamed with pain and fury.

Like magic, the years melted, and she was twenty years old again, the only woman in her class at the police academy, trained to fight twice as hard to survive. She kept his right wrist in her left hand and slammed her right forearm against the median nerve just above his elbow.

The maneuver was called a front armbar, and she hung on like death; the armbar could inflict excruciating pain and was a subduing hold. His wrist was slippery with sweat and blood, but she ground her teeth, held on, and bore down. He yowled in outraged surprise.

She had wrestled him to the edge of her drowned garden and she knew she was fighting on sheer adrenaline. She thrust down more relentlessly on the nerve, twisted the broken wrist till he shrieked. "Get down," she said. "Get down, you bastard."

With a sound between a scream and a whimper, he dropped, his knees buckling and knelt on the ground. She kept her hold, pressing forward and down at the same time until his body pitched forward, and she had forced him prone.

His face was in the muddy water of the flower bed, and his head thrashed as he tried to twist, gasping for air. Carrie kept the armbar on him and dropped one knee on his spine. She ground her other knee into the back of his neck, forcing his face under water.

She kept him pinned facedown until his choking stopped and his body went limp again. He stopped struggling, and no bubbles rose in the water. He was barely breathing. Then he stopped breathing altogether.

I'm drowning him, the civilized part of her mind said, horrified. *I'm killing him.*

Good, said another, more ancient part. *Make sure he's dead.*

She was crying but didn't realize it until her vision blurred and she had to wipe her eyes against her shoulder.

She could not murder him. She kept her knee on his neck, but released his arm. It sank lifelessly to the damp ground.

She choked back a sob and took off her slashed T-shirt. Her Krazy Kat T-shirt, her favorite. She tied the man's hands behind him. She was good at tying knots. She'd been a Cub Scout den mother for ten years.

She took the belt from her jeans and fastened his ankles together. She reached into his hip pocket and took out his knife. Only then did she roll him over, pulling his head from the water by the hair. The skin of his face was gray, and dirty water dribbled from his nose and mouth.

Deep in his throat there was a tiny, broken gurgling noise, but his chest no longer moved. She felt his pulse. It still beat, irregular and weak.

"Oh, *hell*," she said in bitter disgust. This man had killed Edmon, would have killed them all. But she put one hand under his neck and with the other tilted his head back to open his breathing passages.

She pinched his nostrils shut and pulled his jaw to open his mouth. She willed herself to open her mouth and lower it over his to force air into his lungs again. She shuddered in revulsion when her lips touched his.

He was breathing again, and his right eyelid fluttered. His left eye was swollen shut and the gash in his forehead oozed fresh blood. Carrie took her mouth from his and wiped her lips in disgust.

A shadow fell over her and she looked up to see Lynette standing above her, her face wet with tears. A trail of dried blood snaked from the girl's ear down her neck, staining her golden hair and the shoulder of her blouse. She was trembling almost uncontrollably.

Lynette looked like an exhausted and weeping sleepwalker. She stared down at the bound man as if she didn't see him. "Edmon's hurt bad," she said. "He's hit in the jaw and the shoulder. He's alive, but he's bleeding hard."

Carrie swallowed painfully. "Go to the house. Call 911," Carrie said. "Get some towels to slow the bleeding."

"Yes." The girl set her teeth together and looked at the bound man. "Is *he* dead?"

"No," Carrie said bitterly. "Call 911. And get the towels. Now."

The man's right eye opened; he stared, unfocused, toward the sky. "Lynette?" he said in a slurred voice. "Will you help me, Lynette? I love you."

Lynette turned her tear-streaked face away and walked slowly toward the house, limping.

Carrie rose wearily and walked uphill to retrieve the gun. She was hobbling herself. She bent and picked up the automatic from the Johnson grass.

She stared up the hill to where Edmon's car was parked. She forced herself to walk to it; it seemed an infinite distance away. Dully, expecting the worst, she pulled open the door of his car.

He lay slumped against the passenger door, a neat black hole in his left sleeve. His shirt, which had been white, was now soaked with crimson. Blood covered the left side of his face and head, and it was this wound, not the arm, which had bled profusely. She couldn't tell how bad the injury was.

His breathing was uneven and shallow. She climbed in beside him and tried to examine the wound, but when she moved him, the bleeding increased.

Yet, she thought with a surge of hope, the damage might not be life-threatening. The bullet had entered just below his cheekbone and exited at the base of his ear, grazing the bone, but it did not seem to have entered the skull itself. "Hang in there, Edmon," she said, and because she didn't know what else to do, she sat beside him, holding his cold hand.

Lynette appeared at the car door. She had a stack of towels in her hand. "I called 911. They're coming," she said. "I'll try to help Edmon. But, Carrie, would you take the gun and watch that man—please?"

Lynette looked so terrified that Carrie's heart wrenched in sympathy for her. She said, "I'll watch him, honey. Are you hurt?"

"Some. Carrie—will you please take the gun and watch him? Please?"

Carrie slid out of the car and touched Lynette's face gently. Lynette said nothing, only slipped into the seat beside Edmon. She pressed a towel against his jaw.

Numbly Carrie walked back down the hill. When she reached the bound man, she sat down with a weary thump in the grass beside him. Both her strength and her legs seemed to have given out.

She stared at him with a sensation of unreality. He gazed back at her with his good eye. It was brown and long-lashed, like a fawn's eye, and tears swam in it. He looked at her pleadingly. "I love Lynette," he said thickly. "Can I talk to her? Please. I love her. Please."

"Oh, shut up," Carrie said in contempt, and leveled the gun at his head.

"I love her," he said. "Can I talk to her? Please?"

Carrie sighed and wiped a dirty hand across her face. "I don't think you've ever loved anybody," she said.

He began to cry, hard, as if he were a very young child. "Kill me," he wept. "Please kill me. You don't know how hard it is, being me. Kill me, please."

She shook her head. "I want you to live," she said. "Because I want you to hurt for a long, long time."

"I don't want to go to prison," he said between sobs. "You know what they do to guys like me there? Do you know what you're condemning me to?"

Carrie thought about this for a moment. "Yes," she said, "I think I do."

He lay in the dirt, helpless, crying, bloody mucus running from his nose. "It wasn't supposed to happen like this," he said. "Not this way."

Carrie looked up the hill to where Edmon's gray Mazda was parked. The ruined windshield winked in the sunlight, spattered ruby red.

She could not stand to look at the car or to think of Edmon or Lynette or to wish that Hayden was here. She wanted to feel nothing, think nothing.

She turned her gaze to the sky, which was a flawless blue. The sun shone brightly. It was a pretty, perfect, cloudless day at last.

"I love Lynette," he sobbed. "You don't understand. I love her."

She kept staring at the sky. He was right. She didn't understand.

The doctors agreed Edmon Welkin was a lucky man.

His head wound was serious, but the bullet had not entered his brain. It had fractured his upper left jaw, shattered three teeth, and severed his earlobe, but it had not killed or disabled him.

The arm wound, too, had been lucky. No bone had been broken, no major artery severed. His jaw was wired, his head half-encased in white tape, and his left arm put in a sling, but he would go home within a week.

Lynette had a slight concussion, and the doctors said she was also fortunate, that her injury could have been far worse. She had been sedated and was to stay overnight at the hospital for observation. Carrie's jaw ached and she had a scratchy bandage under her left breast, but that was the worst of it. She, too, was told she was lucky.

We're all lucky, she thought darkly. *We're all so terribly lucky.*

She did not think it lucky to have two innocent young people in the hospital, and she could not stop worrying about where Hayden was. Did no one know? Why wouldn't anyone say?

A doctor named MacKesky wanted Carrie to stay overnight in the hospital for observation, but the thought made her flesh creep. Jon Rosmer was also in the Fayetteville hospital. His room was guarded, and he would be taken by ambulance tomorrow to a prison hospital.

Carrie hadn't known Rosmer's name until police told her, nor had Lynette. Carrie had curiously little feeling about Rosmer or what she had done to him. MacKesky insisted she was suffering from a slight case of shock. She insisted she was not. An odd numbness encased her, that was all, and she was glad. It was like a cocoon. It felt safe inside the numbness.

She was amazed and embarrassed when MacKesky forced a prescription for tranquilizers on her, urging her to use it. "Trust me," he said. "You'll need them."

Carrie had never taken a tranquilizer in her life. If she needed anything, it was one good, stiff drink. And for Hayden to be back home and to be safe, she told herself. She wanted Hayden. What in God's name had happened to him?

She arranged to check into a hotel near the hospital. She told herself she wasn't afraid of returning to the lake house, that she wanted to stay near Lynette and Edmon. It wasn't that she was traumatized, not at all; she just didn't want to go back home yet.

A pair of kindly detectives, the same ones who had taken her statement at the hospital, went out to her house when they got off duty. They brought back Hayden's jeep, her packed bags, and the computer; they even accompanied her to the hotel and wouldn't let her carry anything for herself.

But once they left and she was settled in the hotel room, she started remembering Jon Rosmer, remembering with such terrifying clarity that she shook. She trembled so violently that she frightened herself; it was as if she were spinning out of control, and suddenly, for the first time, she broke down and truly cried.

She sat on the edge of her bed, her face in her hands, and wept so hard she was half-sick from it, her stomach twisting. She stretched out on the unfamiliar bed, buried her face in the pillow and wept until she was exhausted, her eyes aching with the need to cry, but with no tears left.

She lay, limp, spent, and thought that MacKesky had been right. She should have filled the prescription. She glanced at her watch to see if it was too late to go out and get the tranquilizers, and she was dismayed when she saw her watch was gone.

What had happened to her watch? And when? Derreck had given her the watch years ago, on their thirteenth anniversary. It was the most expensive gift he'd ever given her, and she'd always treasured it. Now it was gone because of what that *bastard* Jon Rosmer had done—

She sobbed dryly, remembering what Rosmer had done. She wanted her watch back, she wanted it safely on her wrist again. It did not seem odd or illogical to her to be obsessed by its loss. The watch had somehow assumed an enormous importance that drove all else from her mind.

She sat up and wiped her face. She would go back to the yard and look for it. She had a flashlight at the house. She would go over every inch of the ground where she and Rosmer had struggled, and—

This time the memory of Rosmer flashed so frighteningly clear it was as if she could actually see him, there in the room with her, vivid and bloody, reaching for his knife. She started to shake again. She shut her eyes and hugged herself.

Goddammit, she thought in exasperated fury, *I won't let him do this to me. Goddammit, I will not.*

She made herself rise, go into the bathroom, wash her face, brush her hair. She wore clean clothes, but she had no memory of where they'd come from. That didn't strike her as odd, either, only puzzling. They weren't her clothes. How had she gotten them? When had she put them on?

She thought of her Krazy Kat T-shirt and was wracked by another dry, angry, shuddering sob. *He ruined my favorite T-shirt. The rat. The bastard rat.*

She took a deep breath and tried to put on fresh lipstick. She'd have to learn to do without the shirt, that was all. The style was no longer made, she could probably never get another, but life went on.

She put on her lipstick lopsidedly because her hand was so unsteady. She looked like a white-faced doll with her mouth painted on crooked, but that was all right, it would do, it would just have to do. She went to the bureau and picked up the keys to the jeep. It did not occur to her that she was in no condition to drive.

She would, by God, go back to the house. She would, by God, search that yard. And once she'd found the watch, she'd feel much, much better, and—

The telephone rang, startling her. She approached it warily and picked it up, her hand still unsteady. "Hello?" she said. She believed her tone was businesslike and did not realize it was more tremulous than crisp.

"Carrie, it's Hayden. I'm down in the lobby. Can I come up?"

Her vision dimmed, her head swam. She sat down again on the bed.

"Hayden?" she said almost pleadingly.

"I'm here. In the lobby. Can I come up?"

Her heart did a series of strange, jumping kick-steps in her chest. "Oh, yes," she breathed. "Please. I need you."

"I'll be right there," he said and hung up.

She sat for a long moment, staring at the blue carpet. The cocoon of numbness had closed round her again, tight and protective and painless. What had just happened? Had Hayden spoken to her? No. No. That was impossible.

What was important was the *watch*. To go to the hotel parking lot, get into the jeep, drive back to her house and—

A knock sounded at her door. "Carrie, it's me, Hayden."

She rose from the bed, frowning slightly, thinking, *No, that's wrong. The proper construction is, "Carrie, it is I, Hayden."*

But she went to the door, undid the chain lock, and opened it. Hayden stood there, in tan slacks and a blue shirt. He had a scraped cheekbone and stitches in his chin.

Something seemed to melt slightly in her and give her warmth. The whole world took an odd, unexpected zigzag that put things closer to the way they were supposed to be.

She looked up at him and tried to smile. "Oh, Hayden," she said, "where have you been?"

"Trying to find you," he said, concern in his face. "I started calling about two this afternoon from South Dakota. I couldn't reach you. I couldn't reach anybody who knew anything. So as soon as they released me, I got on the first damn plane I could, but I got stuck in Minneapolis. I phoned from there and found out you were all in the hospital. I went straight there when I got in."

He stared down at her, shook his head, and said, "Oh, screw the logistics, Carrie. I know what happened to you. Are you all right?"

Then she was in his arms. She found out she still had tears left, after all. At his touch, her cocoon of numbness fell away. She felt anguish, fear, exhaustion, confusion, but mostly joy and something like safety.

"I'm fine," she said, winding her arms around his neck and clinging to him. "I'm fine. Oh, Hayden, how are you?"

"I'm here," he said and kissed her. "I never should have left you. If I'd known—"

"You're all right," she said against his lips. "That's all that counts."

They kissed each other crazily, hungrily: lips, eyes, cheeks, chins, noses, lips again.

She meant to have him explain everything, but instead their kisses flowed into lovemaking. They made their way toward the bed, they undressed each other, they touched each other, they could not stop themselves. Carrie forgot her aching jaw, her tired muscles. She lost herself in happy desire and the reality of his flesh against hers.

Afterwards, he held her and they talked, their voices soft. He told her of meeting Brooke and Boyd and what had happened at the motel, of going with the FBI when it besieged the farmhouse and negotiated with Boyd's stepmother. His account was quick, almost brusque, as if he didn't like dwelling on it.

She kept her arms wound around him, fearing if she didn't, he might vanish, this time for good.

"What happens to Brooke and Boyd?" she murmured, holding him more tightly.

Cynicism tinged his voice. "She's going back to the farm with him. He says he needs to stay a while to help his stepmother and brothers."

"His family just let the law come in and take all those guns and explosives?"

He kissed her ear. "The older brother kicked up a fuss at first. But not for long. I think they're glad the old man's locked up. Nobody has to die for his causes now. He sounds like a mean old bastard. The wife was nearly his prisoner, Boyd said. They all were. Authorities in North Dakota got the uncle, too."

She drew back and looked at Hayden's face, caressed his cheekbone. "Brooke and Boyd—do you think they'll last together?"

He smiled dubiously. "Who knows?"

He drew her nearer, laid his cheek against her hair. "I shouldn't have chased after them, Carrie. I shouldn't have left you. Never. I'll never forgive myself."

She kissed his naked throat. "You had a job to do. And I should have told you Lynette would be with me. You couldn't have known."

He took her chin between his fingers and kissed her lips. "You had a job to do, too. You saved her."

"Yes," she whispered unhappily. "But she got hurt. And Edmon, too."

"They're going to be fine," he soothed her. "It wasn't your fault, and they're going to be fine. I talked to the doctors."

She rested her cheek against his chest and thought that Lynette and Edmon might be fine, but none of them, herself included, would ever be the same.

She said nothing.

"Carrie?" Hayden's voice was both puzzled and concerned.

"Yes?" She rubbed her nose against his collarbone.

"Are these my jeep keys in the bed?"

He jingled them near her ear. She felt stupid and embarrassed. She hadn't let go of the keys until she and Hayden had been in bed, both naked, their bodies intertwined. Only at that moment had she remembered she was still clutching them, and then, with a sigh, she'd let them go.

"Honey," he said, "why'd you have the keys in bed?"

She put her hands on his shoulders and nuzzled his collarbone again. "I was going back to the house. I lost my watch in the—the—the struggle."

He stroked his hand over her hair. "You were going back to that house in the dark? To look for your *watch*? Why?"

"To prove to myself I wasn't scared," she said against his chest. "I just wanted the watch. It seemed important."

Suddenly she started to cry again.

He drew her closer. "Carrie," he whispered, "sweetheart, it's okay. You don't have to talk about it."

"I want to," she said, putting her arms around his waist. "If I put it in words, it makes it seem coherent, something that I control, that doesn't control me."

"Yeah," he said softly, "that's how it works sometimes. Tell me then. Tell me all about it."

She started, in a halting way, to describe what had happened, but by the time she reached the part about Edmon, she started to shake again.

"It's okay," Hayden kept saying. "It's okay."

"I never thought I was a coward," she said, burying her face against her shoulder.

"You're not," he said. "You've just got a little post-traumatic stress syndrome here. It's happened to the best of them. I mean that. The best."

She believed him. He held her tightly, and she told him the rest of the story, stopping from time to time to cry. He always dried the tears. He apologized again, saying it was his fault.

"No, no," she answered. "Don't say that. It wasn't."

He kissed her in a way that told her he was going to make love to her again. She was glad, she wanted that, it made her feel whole and happy again. It was a kind of healing.

Hayden took her to breakfast at a little coffee shop on the square. She was still shaky, he could tell, but she was game again and determined to go back to her house after they went to see Edmon and Lynette.

"I don't like your going back to that place to stay," he said. "It always worried me, you out there, isolated like that."

"I have to go back," she said. "It's like getting bucked off a horse. If you don't get right back on, you'll be scared for the rest of your life."

He said, "Carrie, I've got a big house. Too big. Too empty. Come share it."

Her blue eyes looked haunted. "I can't do that. Not yet. I *need* to go back to the other house. To know I can."

God, he thought, shaking his head, *she's impossible.* He said, "Then let me stay with you while you're there. There's nothing wrong with that, is there?"

She stared into her coffee. Maybe she was having second thoughts about how she felt toward him. Maybe she was backing away from him again. Miss Live-Free-or-Die.

But she said, "No. There's nothing wrong with that."

He kept himself from sighing in relief. "But you still want to go back this afternoon? And look for the watch?"

She nodded. "That sounds stupid, too, I suppose."

He reached out and took her hand. It felt tense beneath his own. "No. If it makes you feel better it's not stupid."

She was silent. He looked at the bruise on her jaw and wished they were alone so he could kiss it. He hated Jon Rosmer for hurting her, and if Hayden had been there, he would have killed Rosmer, he knew. Maybe she knew it, too. Her face looked serious, as if she was about to be lost in her own solemn thoughts.

"So you put an armbar on him," he said, trying to sound lighter. "I didn't know you had it in you."

She rewarded him with a weak smile. "I was the best in my class. I had to be. My instructor said because I was a woman, I had to get it perfect. *Perfect.* I thought he was a male chauvinist pig and he was trying to kill me with extra practice. God, I hated him. I wish I knew where he was. I'd send him a dozen roses."

"So would I," said Hayden. "Maybe two dozen."

They fell silent, and he tried to choose the right words to tell her what he had to say.

"Carrie, I have two things to tell you. The first is this. I called the office this morning. We think we've finally traced your Paul Johnson."

Her face went tense and anxiety shone in her eyes.

"There's record of a Paul Johannson having a motorcycle accident in London, Ontario, eighteen months ago with a girl named Heather Smythe. He sounds like the one. An officer heard about our query and phoned. He talked to Robert E. Lee."

Carrie looked more guarded than before, and he could see the guilt in her expression.

He said, "This officer remembered the accident. It'd caused a bit of scandal. Johannson and the woman were married, but not to each other."

Her lips parted and anger sparked in her eyes. "She wasn't his fiancée? He was *lying*?"

"Like a rug. Robert E. got interested, did some phone and computer work. Johannson's spine really was injured, and he really was in a wheelchair—for eight months. But he's almost fully recovered. He's an advertising writer in Detroit. Works out of his house. Thirty-eight years old and married. Two kids."

"The rat," Carrie said indignantly. "The utter SOB—he has a wife? Children? I was turning inside out from the moral dilemma, and he was *cheating on his wife*?"

He smiled and laid his forefinger against her lips. "Look at the bright side. You don't have anything to feel guilty about. He was using you."

"It's disgusting," she fumed. "He's the essence of sleazy. I'm going back to Omega tonight and kill my character. And leave him an e-mail message he won't forget."

"Fine. You've got the right. I'll kill Average Joe. We'll die together and be reborn into the real world."

A wistful expression crossed her face. "The real world. I'm ready to enjoy it for all it's worth."

"So am I." He took a deep breath. Again he searched for words.

He said, "Do you remember what you said to me on the phone last night?"

"No," she said, her gaze falling to his hand on hers.

"You said you needed me. Maybe you do, and maybe you don't. And maybe I need you, and maybe I don't. But I know I want you. I want us to be together. For as long as we can."

"I want to be with you, too," she said, raising her gaze to his. "But there are things I have to do. Things on my own."

"I understand that," he said.

She laced her fingers through his and smiled. "I think maybe you do."

Lynette had spent the morning in Edmon's room. He was groggy, his face was badly bruised, and he couldn't talk with his wired jaw, but he wrote her notes in his precise handwriting.

"You're nice to come see me," he wrote. "I'm not much to look at."

Lynette gave a wry laugh. "Please. You forget who you're dealing with here."

He gazed at her and his face twitched with pain. Then he stared earnestly at his pad as he wrote another message. He showed it to her. It said, "You're a great sight to me. To me, you look beautiful. I mean that."

Lynette read his words and bit the inside of her lip. James Dean had often said that she was beautiful to him. He had often said he meant it. The words should frighten and repulse her. But from Edmon they did not. She sensed Edmon would not lie about such things. He was incapable of it.

She laced her fingers together and clenched her hands tensely in her lap. "You were very brave," she said. "I wanted to tell you that. And that I'm so sorry you got hurt."

He tried to laugh, which obviously hurt him. He wrote, "I wasn't brave. All I did was get shot. I didn't do one other thing."

"That's not true," Lynette said. "He was stalking me. He would have killed me. He was coming for me in Kansas, he said he was. You got me here with Carrie. And when you came for us, it was like a—a diversion. If you hadn't shown up, I don't know what would have happened. You saved me. You saved us. You."

He blushed.

"I mean it," she said earnestly. "You set everything in motion to save me. And probably other women, too."

He blushed more furiously. He seemed unable to think of a reply, and she, too, could think of nothing more to say. Both felt shy and awkward, but she smiled at him and did not leave his side until a nurse came and said it was time for him to rest.

Carrie and Hayden visited Edmon and Lynette at the hospital, ate lunch at Herman's Rib House, then drove to the lake. They searched for the watch until sunset, but there was no sign of it. It had vanished as completely as if it had never existed.

"I think we should go inside," Hayden said at last. He slapped at a mosquito. "We'll look again tomorrow."

Carrie shook her head. "I don't think we'll find it."

He put his arm around her. "Why?"

"It's just a feeling. And maybe it's just as well."

"What's that mean?"

"I don't know," she said. "It's sort of symbolic. Without the watch, maybe somehow time is different now."

He turned her to face him, put his hands on her upper arms. "I want it to be different for you. For both of us. But I still feel rotten, Carrie. I saw your face while we looked for the watch. You were remembering a lot of pain. I wish that I'd been here. That I could have spared you."

She shook her head no, although it was true: she did remember the pain and the fear. She'd seen blood on the grass. Most was Jon Rosmer's. The rest belonged to Edmon and Lynette, and some of it was probably hers. *Our blood has fed the earth,* she brooded. *What seeds will it nourish?*

She pushed the dark thought away.

"If you hadn't gone to South Dakota," she said, "you couldn't have warned us. He probably would have killed us. So no guilt, please. You and I, we had to go our separate ways."

"I hope we don't again," he said.

She laid her finger beside the stitched cut on his chin. She said, "I don't know how our story ends, Hayden. Or where."

He said, "Then you don't know if it ends at all."

"No," she said, and smiled pensively, "I don't."

"Then we'll take it as it comes," he said.

She nodded. "As it comes. Exactly."

He took her face between his hands. "I've been thinking. I'm ready to go back to the War Eagle, to the river. It's time."

"Good," she whispered, "I'm glad."

"I'd like you to come with me," he said.

Her throat tightened. "I'd be proud."

He didn't kiss her, he just put his arms around her and held her. Her arms circled his waist, and she leaned her face against his chest and closed her eyes. She listened to the strong, steady beat of his heart. He rested his chin against her hair.

Then, as if by mutual consent, they drew apart, linked hands, and walked slowly to the house.

Along the shore the frogs began to sing, celebrating the falling night.

Marcia Klemperer was a shy girl, just out of high school and fearful about going to college in the fall.

Plain, insecure, awkward, she had few friends and no admirers. She had never had a beau, had never been on an actual date, and she worshiped handsome boys from afar, knowing they would laugh at her if they knew. High school had been a sojourn in hell for her, and she dreaded that college would be worse.

But over the summer she had found a wonderful new world on her computer, the computer that had been her graduation gift. This new world was called Omega MOON, and it was more satisfying and exciting than any reality she could imagine.

This morning she had been notified by e-mail that her application for a character had been granted. Tonight she was in the Romance Ballroom for the first time as her character, Alison. She had constructed the description with great and loving care. On Omega she left behind her weaknesses and became her dream self.

> You see Alison, a tall, shapely maiden in a diaphanous gown, colored with the soft hues of the sunrise. Alison's eyes are sapphire blue, her nose regal, her lips full and ripe like exotic fruit whose taste you know will be sweet.
>
> Her long red-golden hair cascades in waves almost to her ankles and is more beautiful than any ornament that might adorn it.
>
> The neckline of Alison's gown plunges deeply, revealing the shadowy cleavage between the swell of her perfect white breasts.
>
> Her smile beckons you and invites you to speak.

All of this was utter fabrication, of course. Marcia was short and so thin that she had hardly any breasts at all. Her hair was wiry and dark brown, and she hated it. She had to wear it short because it had cowlicks and an impossible, frizzy texture.

Her eyes were not sapphire blue, but ordinary brown, her nose thin and pointed, and she had a mouth so narrow that it was as if she hadn't any lips.

But on Omega, she was lovely and sensual and inviting. Perhaps, naughtily, *too* sensual and inviting, but what harm was there in that? It was only a game.

And male characters were attracted to her as men in real life had never been. As soon as she went to the Romance Ballroom, the messages began.

> You sense Blue Rider looking for you from the King's Highway. He pages, "My God, you're gorgeous. Want to go to a sex chamber?"
>
> You sense Prince Priapus looking for you from the Garden of Earthly Delights. He pages, "Your description is lovely. Would you join me and let me know you better?"
>
> You sense The Highwayman looking for you in the Bower of Bliss. He pages, "You are ravishing. You bewitch me. Would you join me?"

Marcia's blood danced with excitement, and in happy wonder she said under her breath, "I'm the queen of the Romance Ballroom."

And she chose to go off with The Highwayman.

About the Author

BETHANY CAMPBELL was born and raised in Nebraska.
She has taught at colleges and universities in Nebraska, Illinois, and New Hampshire. She and her
husband make their home in Arkansas with three
cats and a dog passionate about rodents and their
pursuit.

DON'T MISS THESE FABULOUS
BANTAM WOMEN'S FICTION TITLES

On Sale in November

AFTER CAROLINE *by Kay Hooper*
"Kay Hooper is a master storyteller." —Tami Hoag

The doctors told Joanna Flynn that she shouldn't suffer any ill effects from her near-fatal accidents, but then the dreams began. Now she must find an explanation, or she'll lose her mind—perhaps even her life.

___09948-5 $21.95/$26.95

BREAKFAST IN BED
by sizzling New York Times bestseller Sandra Brown

Sandra Brown captures the wrenching dilemma of a woman tempted by an unexpected—and forbidden—love in this classic novel, now available in paperback.

___57158-3 $5.50/$7.50

DON'T TALK TO STRANGERS
by national bestseller Bethany Campbell
"A master storyteller of stunning intensity." —Romantic Times

Young women are disappearing after meeting a mysterious stranger on the Internet, and it's Carrie Blue's job to lure the killer . . . without falling prey to his cunningly seductive mind.

___56973-2 $5.50/$7.50

LORD SAVAGE *by the acclaimed Patricia Coughlin*

Ariel Halliday has eight weeks to turn a darkly handsome savage into a proper gentleman. It will take a miracle . . . or maybe just falling in love.

___57520-1 $5.50/$7.50

LOVE'S A STAGE *by Sharon and Tom Curtis*
"Sharon and Tom's talent is immense." —LaVyrle Spencer

Frances Atherton dares to expose the plot that sent her father to prison, but soon she, too, is held captive—by the charms of London's most scandalous playwright and fascinating rake.

___56811-6 $4.99/$6.99

Ask for these books at your local bookstore or use this page to order.

Please send me the books I have checked above. I am enclosing $____ (add $2.50 to cover postage and handling). Send check or money order, no cash or C.O.D.'s, please.

Name _____

Address _____

City/State/Zip _____

Send order to: Bantam Books, Dept. FN159, 2451 S. Wolf Rd., Des Plaines, IL 60018
Allow four to six weeks for delivery.
Prices and availability subject to change without notice.   FN 159 11/96